SILENT LIGHT

Further copies of this book can be ordered at:

www.silentlight.co.uk

SILENT LIGHT

CHRIS MAY

M𝒫 Mayden Publishing
A DIVISION OF MAYDEN HOUSE LIMITED

This first edition published in Great Britain in 2000 by

Mayden Publishing
Mayden House
Derry Hill, Calne
Wiltshire, SN11 9QZ

Email : mailbox@silentlight.co.uk

A catalogue record for this book is available from the British Library

ISBN : 0 - 9539125 - 0 - 7

Cover photograph of Victoria Tower, Darwen by Fred Hudson
Reproduced with kind permission

Lyrics from Script for a Jester's Tear (Marillion)
Words and Music by Michael Pointer, Derek William Dick, Mark Kelly, Pete
Trewavas and Steve Rothery. © 1983, Reproduced by permission of Charisma
Music Publishing Co Ltd, London WC2H 0EA

Printed and bound by Antony Rowe Ltd, Chippenham, Wiltshire

For my mother

Who gave of her life
To give me life
Until there was no life left

And because, on the day this novel began,
I was not there…

Acknowledgements

The greatest thanks are to my wife, Catherine, for selflessly providing me with the space to write. And to Alison for endless support and encouragement. I am also deeply indebted to Pat White and Emir Kullar for their editing and proofing service, and for teaching me that less is more.

PROLOGUE

So here I am once more in the playground
   of the broken hearts,
one more experience, one more entry
   in a diary, self penned
Yet another emotional suicide
   overdosed on sentiment and pride
Too late to say I love you
   Too late to restage the play
Abandoning the relics in my playground
   of yesterday...

Through the white, frothy clouds overhead, a ray of sunshine suddenly breaks, bathing the churchyard in a mysterious haze of soft, silent light. A battalion of gravestones, in strict military lines, appears to wake from its slumber and stands to attention. Atop the slender spire, a stubby cross, infused with quartz, glitters like the Bethlehem star. Somewhere above, high in the trees, a skylark begins to sing, the only evidence of life in an otherwise tranquil universe. Beyond the immediate boundary of the church grounds the world remains in shadow, gloomy and insignificant.

The first spring morning of the new millennium.

The scene is set.

Sensing he is more exposed under the new light, he shrinks deeper into the rhododendron bush, impatiently counting away the seconds until it is over. He takes a deep breath and swallows hard.

It will not be long now.

What has brought him to this quiet Cheshire village he does not fully understand. Though he is still trying to convince himself that it was a spontaneous decision, the disturbing truth is that he always knew he would come, driven by a compulsion he has never understood and over which he has had no control. Perhaps he is obsessed and only just sane enough to realise it. Perhaps he is insane and therefore unable to realise it. Or perhaps, like the salmon seeking its place of origin, he is simply responding to an instinctive programming to make this predestined journey.

Yet whatever happens he must not be found, not even seen. He has prepared an excuse if he is caught but now it seems weak and implausible. He retreats even further into the rhododendron bush, arranging the foliage around him to provide maximum cover, and then glances at his watch.

It will not be long now.

The unexpected but all too familiar sense of déjà vu catches him off guard. Surrounded by branches and leaves, peering out into daylight, the small disc of his watch face screaming out its silent and indecipherable warning, the acute ache of impatience and frustration : all these have been felt before, in another time, another place. He searches for the event in his memory but without success. He cannot find it because it is not there. He has learnt through painful experience to recognise the hallmark of these intuitions and their sinister, mocking echoes. The sensation passes almost instantly but, in its wake, the reverberations continue on like a great resounding bell.

This has yet to come…

    …Has yet to come…

        …Yet to come.

And he is reminded of the reason he is here. It is because he once saw himself here. All those years before. He has come to fulfil his first premonition. For fifteen years he has seen visions and then chased them into the future like a moth driven compulsively towards the eerie, silent light. He came to this moment not through choice but because it was preordained. And in being here he hopes that fate will accept his co-operation as full payment and will choose finally to find another plaything.

Yet what are fifteen years when memory can replay them all in fifteen seconds? The illusion of time is nature's most elaborate yet simple trick. The past is fact and the future is fiction and neither is real. But that is only from the perspective of the present and it is in the present that everyone lives. Only *now* is real.

But not to him; he has seen further. He now knows that the present is simply the frame of the reel which is passing through the beam and reality the resulting projection. The past is coiled up on the take up spool, the future spins on the feed spool waiting to unfold. The only difference is that one has been committed to memory while the other remains a source of speculation.

But what if nature could be distorted and the reel were allowed to pass through the beam more than once? What would the image be then? The past, present and future all jumbled together? How would it be possible to analyse the confused image while trapped in the present and yet *past*, *present* and *future* have suddenly become meaningless terms?

Over the years he has devoted much time to the debate but only to realise that he will never know the answer as long as his perception of reality is centered on the projected image. For the reel may be never ending; or worse, the first frame might be joined to the last. Perhaps, therefore, it is not the image which defines the truth after all, but that it is in fact the light; the steady, silent light of the projector without which there would be no image and nothing to call reality. And beyond the light, a projectionist, a manipulator, who carefully watches the image and changes the reels...

Before him the current projection is that of a beautiful April morning. It is not particularly hot but neither is it unpleasantly cold. There is a slight breeze in the air but it is hardly enough to bend the grass or rustle the leaves of the rhododendron bush. If anything, this makes his position even more precarious. He would not only have to be out of sight but perfectly still also. He looks at his watch and, as he does so, the sun disappears behind another cloud and the churchyard is plunged into shadow. The skylark halts its cheerful chorus in mid-flow. All around him an abrupt silence descends on the morning and the churchyard takes on the suspenseful atmosphere of a cinema, growing quiet as the lighting is subdued before the main feature commences.

He holds his breath and watches the church door intently. And as it opens, and the dying echoes of the organ float out onto the lawn, the steeple bells come alive, one by one, in a peal of exultant celebration.

She is the first person to come through the doorway. He has not so much as glimpsed her for so long but there is little distinction between this present reality and fond memories. In her wedding gown, fold after fold of pure silky white, she is exactly as he had seen her all those years before. For a few moments they are alone and he realises that the scene is replaying frame by frame – exactly as he had seen it before. She steps onto the lawn, throws back her veil and casts her arms wide to greet the day. Her compelling radiance encourages even the sun to make another appearance and, as she turns back to the door to draw her entourage towards her, the lawn is once more bathed in the light of a spring morning. The remainder of the cast spill out of the church and surround the bride, littering the air above their heads with thousands of specks of confetti.

At first he does not take his eyes off her. This is a film which has been waiting on the spool for more than a decade, and now it is steadily unfolding and passing through the beam. It is a scene in which he had always imagined only two main characters; one on the screen and one in the shadows of the stalls, with a nameless, faceless, superfluous crowd. Yet gradually the crowd takes on its own identity and precocious individuals, with no rights or qualifications, begin to stamp their unwelcome personalities on the proceedings until he can ignore them no longer. They have given themselves speaking parts and are beginning to dominate the scene.

Among the guests are many of his oldest and dearest friends. He has not seen any of them over the years and he had not considered that they would be here. The shock of this discovery is compounded by the realisation that he has become an outsider. For the last decade and a half the world has continued without him. In very little time, the script he has written and rewritten lies in tatters and his dream is turning into a waking nightmare. No longer the protagonist in the grand performance, he finds himself an exile, a prompt without a voice, returning from a life of solitude to face painful anonymity. And to discover that his designated role, the leading male, has been filled by a stand-in without a second thought.

But it was too late now. If anyone had tried to tell her she was making a mistake then she had not listened. And though the prospect of perpetual unhappiness for both of them fills him with a deep sadness, he must live with her decision. Not to have known her at all would have been better than this sense of desolation. But fate had conspired to play this cruel joke on him and he would probably never understand what he was supposed to learn from it.

He watches as the guests mill around, not quite knowing what to do with themselves. The two families are worlds apart; socially opposite and culturally immiscible, and both appear to be equally uncomfortable at being brought together for such an event. The wedding was meant to be an occasion of joy yet there is an air of incongruous misery in the churchyard, hovering over the proceedings as clearly as a smog in paradise. Jollity is acted, smiles are faked and painful pleasantries exchanged. The guests of the bridegroom behave as if they have been thrown into the inhospitable wilderness of a local council estate, trying desperately to retain their southern reserve while forcing gritted smiles for the cameras.

She notices the clash of cultures with apprehension but there is little she can do but pray that it will soon end. She passes from one family to the other, trying to get them to pose for photographs together, but she always finds herself standing between them. And when the photograph has been taken, they at once separate and return to their respective cliques. Across her face appear the unmistakeable signs of uneasiness, an expression he once knew so well and to which he would unhesitatingly run with open arms, filling her void of confidence with a reassuring embrace. But now he can only sympathise in secret as she witnesses this first taste of her future family life and its inherent struggles. With beauty and good fortune she has elevated her family into a world in which they do not belong. Her ambition and determination would allow her no other life. Yet underneath she knows it is a curse - and he knows he has fallen under its spell.

Suddenly, he finds himself staring straight into the photographer's lens as the bride poses for a solo shot. He almost panics, terrified that the blown up print will expose his presence. But the photographer is fast. At the click of the camera shutter he is simply left wondering if he had been about to run or not. He can only smile at the irony of them being photographed together at her wedding, though no one would ever know. For the rest of her days, wherever she may go, he will be watching over her from behind that rhododendron bush.

All too soon the scene is ended. At the church gate, a white Rolls Royce draws up and the bride and bridegroom hurriedly bid their farewells. With sighs of relief, they climb eagerly into the back seat amid clouds of confetti and polite applause. He sees little point in staying there any longer. Without the newly married couple as a focal point the crowd is already beginning to disperse and he is in greater danger of being discovered. In quiet contemplation he watches a few seconds more as the car glides silently to the top of the short rise and disappears down into the valley.

It is over. There was no last minute reprieve and there is no comfort from what he has just witnessed. Whatever he had come here for he has not found. He has seen her again and nothing has changed. Finally, after all this time, the end has arrived and it is as meaningless as the beginning.

He places his hand into his coat pocket and slowly coils his fingers around the stiff passport and the crumpled pages of the transatlantic air ticket. It is the dawn of a new millennium; a time to bury ghosts from the past and to give birth to new hopes, new dreams. But to do that he must first leave this place – with its memories and demons – and move somewhere far away, never to return.

She has gone to begin her new life. And he must do the same.

So I'll hold my peace forever

when you wear your bridal gown

In the silence of my shame

the mute that sang the sirens'

song has gone solo in the game

But the game is over

Can you still say you love me?

1

It was Sunday 7th October, 1984.

The day he lost her. The day time lost its meaning.

The day the premonitions began.

The station clock was approaching 6:52pm as Howard Robinson climbed the last few steps onto platform twelve of Manchester's Victoria railway station and looked around, as though he had reached the top of Mount Everest but was too tired to appreciate the view. The platform was almost deserted and the few people who stood scattered along its length were motionless, their grey forms blending naturally with the dull twilight hue that enveloped the city. As evening fell, the overcast sky merged with the descending darkness and the temperature, which had dropped steadily with the approaching sunset, now hovered just above freezing.

Already, a sombre mist was beginning to develop above the railway tracks and steal across the platform, biting subtly at the ankles of the waiting passengers. Instinctively, they began to pace up and down in a feeble attempt to generate warmth. Apart from the background hum of city traffic, all was quiet.

With cautious steps that betrayed both fatigue and unease, Howard walked slowly over to the nearest timetable and checked the departure time of the next train to Darwen. He knew the train was due imminently but the timetable offered confirmation and this was somehow comforting. The board was smeared with a dark stain and had recently been attacked by vandals. Behind him, a solitary lamp, caked in grime and soot from the city air, offered little light as he struggled to read the information.

After a moment, he moved round the timetable board and began to read the posters plastered on the side of the waiting room which stood at the centre of the platform. A sudden, ice cold draught distracted him and, pulling his collar tightly together, he turned away from the poster board to shelter himself. To his right, the warm waiting room beckoned but, like everyone else on the platform, he ignored it.

Something was wrong.

Howard put the waiting room and timetable behind him and began to walk to the deserted, eastern end of the platform. Repeatedly, he checked behind him to make sure he was not being followed though he still did not know why. There was no one there but as he once more turned to face the direction in which he was walking, the sensation returned with an even greater force and he found that he could not ignore it. It was only through sheer willpower that he prevented himself from rotating in tight paranoid circles in a futile attempt to catch sight of this unseen presence. And though he knew it to be the product of an overactive imagination, the hallucination seemed so real that his head began to spin and beads of cold sweat formed on his brow. But this inexplicable hysteria was not his major concern. He also slowly began to realise that the anxiety he was trying so hard to push to the back of his mind was fighting for release and he would not be able to contain it much longer.

Something was wrong with Melissa.

The words seemed to etch themselves on his conscience. He walked over to another nearby timetable and attempted to read but it was no use. His concentration on the mundane had been a futile effort at avoiding something he knew he must face eventually. Slowly, his stomach started to turn over and his heart began to beat more rapidly. He felt the onset of nausea rising within him and fought to contain it.

On an impulse, uninvited, he turned again. Behind him, nothing had changed. The same cold, grey statues littered the length of the platform. Only a momentary shiver, or the condensation of their exhaling breath, distinguished them from lifeless waxwork models. As he scanned the concrete island on which he was standing, only one thing was different: already the fog had grown noticeably thicker and, through this climbing, billowing cloud, that spread like a cancer all around him, he could no longer see the other end of the platform.

Something was wrong.

Something was wrong with Melissa.

They were two different sensations attacking him from opposite directions yet he knew instinctively they were connected in some way. The sensation of being followed seemed to emanate from all around him while the echoes of Melissa materialised from somewhere within. But the facts refuted both. Melissa was in Alderley Edge where he had left her and he knew he was only being shadowed by the creation of his own mind.

Eyeing the other passengers suspiciously he listened to the rhythm of the city, sensing each dull pulsation as it rippled through his body. Sweeping the air, he could feel the clammy fingers of mist brushing against his hand. He could detect the odours of accumulating traffic fumes and taste the blended flavours of numerous nearby restaurants. Each of his senses told him that everything was as it should be. Finally he gave in to reason and continued his short journey.

At the end of the platform he found himself totally alone. He stared blankly down the tracks, his eyes carefully following them to the point, fifty yards further on, where they disappeared into the thickening blanket of fog. But it was no use.

He was being watched.

2

THIS PARK IS DEDICATED TO THOSE WHO HAVE COME TO THIS CITY SEEKING REFUGE. MAY ALL WHO PASS THROUGH THESE GATES FIND SOLACE, STRENGTH AND TRANQUILLITY IN ITS PASTURES.

L.B. Hozaki, City Mayor, June 2026

Sarjena West pushed the creaking pram through the large, ornate gates of Washington Park. Even after three years exposure to the elements they had weathered well and looked new as the day they were erected. But today she did not notice. She was still listening to the words of the freeholder's agent reverberating inside her head. How on earth could she afford to pay the rent arrears? And in only one week! She did not have anything like that amount of money. Even worse, she did not know of anyone who did. No one who would lend it to her at any rate. She had learned the hard way that the true cost of friendship was to retain certain characteristics: a socially outgoing personality, a home in a posh neighbourhood, a stable relationship, financial security and career prospects - and only a smattering of a range of problems considered to be trendy demonstrating that she was only human and far from perfect.

How could she have ended up in this situation? Two years ago almost to the day she was with Mick, living a comfortable and happy existence with almost no concept of hardship between them. They had bought a new apartment only three blocks from the park. She had a good job with a promising career and Mick had just qualified as a lawyer and was beginning to earn some real money. Any problems which she had claimed to have then were so insignificant she could not even remember them. But then she became pregnant and he had left. And she had not seen it coming...

Now, while she struggled to make a living, the bills continued to pour in and the debts became higher and higher, until she had not only become blacklisted by every credit agency in the city, but they also refused her application for medical insurance on the grounds that she would not be able to keep up with the payments. The bank manager had been sympathetic but unhelpful and the net result of her visit was that she was now down the cost of the bus fare.

Life was a lottery. Perhaps if she had gone through with an abortion, or started up her own business that little bit earlier, or turned left instead of right... But it was too late for such reflections now. She could no longer wait. She needed the money within the week or they would be out on the streets, a helpless mother and her helpless baby. Poor Bobbi. Not yet ten months old and already she was battling for a life with a mother who was so useless she could not even support her own child as far as its first birthday. Sarjena stared beseechingly into the pram as if hoping to find some solution in those innocent eyes. Bobbi smiled back at her and as her lips grinned even wider, she closed her eyes as if in ecstasy. Then, she screwed up her face in that funny little expression she had made her own and let out a long, drawn, happy sigh just for mummy.

It was a beautifully clear afternoon and the park looked all the better for it. The sun was high and beat down with an unusual ferocity. Even though it was late spring, the hot weather did not usually arrive until a couple of months later, when everyone had planned to take their summer breaks. That this sudden heat wave had caught everyone by surprise was obvious since the park, which would normally have been full in such fine weather, was quite empty. Sarjena found that she had the whole place virtually to herself and could wander around at liberty without interruption from stray Frisbees or uncontrolled dogs.

Through the thin soles of her shoes she could feel the heat begin to nibble at her feet as it conducted from the sun-baked tarmac path. Within minutes the sensation had become mildly unpleasant and she turned off the path and pushed the pram up a small, grassy bank onto a large, clean cut lawn. Bobbi appeared to enjoy the sudden change in direction.

Through the springs of her dilapidated pram she could feel the vibration of the slightly rougher terrain and giggled playfully through the entire manoeuvre as if on some kind of amusement park ride. To add to the effect Sarjena made infantile brum-brum noises and laughed openly in response to the delight on Bobbi's face, occasionally reaching into the pram to tickle her under the chin. Once on the lawn, Sarjena abruptly slowed down and became quiet again. Bending carefully over, she pulled back the crocheted blanket and kissed the child softly on the cheek. Poor Bobbi. Always so happy. Always so innocent.

"You know, Bobbi? I had always thought my life would mean something. Until today I had always believed that somebody, somewhere would be thinking about me. But it isn't true, is it? There are seven billion people on this planet yet only a few of them will have lives that really matter. The rest of us just make up the crowd scene and our existence is only registered by computers. I never wanted that for us. I don't want that for you – not a life of survival with no meaning. But I don't know what to do about it."

She sighed and an unwelcome thought entered her head.

Once a refugee, always a refugee.

Dammit! There had to be a way. With one last push, powered by anger and helpless frustration, the pram reached the brow of the small hill and stopped. For a moment it seemed as if it would roll back down and Sarjena held out her arms in anticipation. But the pram remained motionless, waiting for its owner to apply the thrust that would send it careering down the other side of the hill. Any normal pram would have rolled back down, she thought, but this one was so rusty the wheels had practically seized up.

Seconds later, Sarjena joined Bobbi on the hilltop, removed the child from the pram and sat down in the grass. For a moment, she allowed herself to sprawl amongst the cool, green blades, panting slowly, eyes closed, trying to get her breath back. So unfit, she concluded. This was not the right sort of weather for racing round the park with a pram.

As her breathing gradually slowed to a more relaxed level, and her heartbeat gave up the attempt to jump out of her chest and became quiet once more, she became aware that her throat was parched. Abruptly, she sat up and reached into the back of the pram with her left arm, using her right one to support herself in a sitting position. Opening her eyes to survey the scene ahead, at first everything appeared in black and white and it was several seconds before any colour began to seep back into her vision. Without looking, she had reached into the pram and removed a small carton of fruit juice, her eyes fixed solely on the view to the south. Next to her, Bobbi sat silently in the grass, gazing in the same direction with idle curiosity, not really understanding anything she saw.

To her right, on the next hill, the brass band of the Army of God were lethargically packing away their instruments. They weren't very good but they made up for it with sheer enthusiasm. Sarjena had heard them play the week before and was disappointed to have missed them this time. Afterwards, more to have someone to talk to than anything else, she had struck up a conversation with some of the band members. The band played devotedly at the old, wooden bandstand every Thursday but no one came to listen to them any more and they invariably played to an absent audience. Sarjena found in their persistence a source of strength for herself but with it a sense of frustration at the stupidity that they were equally happy to play to no one as to hundreds. They were playing for God, they had said, and if He was displeased then He was more than welcome to strike the bandstand with a thunderbolt and raze it to the ground. There were those, she was sure, who prayed for just that to happen but the old bandstand still stood defiantly on the small hilltop.

Sarjena returned her attention to more local matters and carefully wiped away some dribble from Bobbi's face. Below them, the grassy knoll moved off with a gentle gradient, slightly less steep than the northern rise they had just ascended. Some fifty metres further on, carved out of an otherwise perfectly rounded hillside was a small, circular lake, approximately thirty metres in diameter. Usually the lake would appear to be a dirty grey colour; there was no fresh source flowing in from any direction and the lake relied on natural drainage, evaporation and rainfall to maintain its volume. Today the water was midnight blue, the combination of its usual murkiness and the reflection of the clear azure sky providing an unusually pleasant and relaxing colour.

On the far side of the lake there was a figure squatting at the water's edge. Seemingly a small, ordinary looking middle aged man, he appeared to be playing with some sort of metallic contraption. Sarjena first wondered if one of the band members had wandered down there with his musical instrument but then realised that the man wasn't wearing the Army of God uniform. Sarjena knew that the object was metallic because every so often one of its faces would catch the sun, but beyond this she had no idea what it was. It was much too far to see clearly and she had the compounding disadvantage of having the sun in her eyes.

Beyond the lake the grassy descent continued for a further fifty metres, after which a large oak tree marked the beginning of several acres of woodland. Above the treetops, in the distance, rose the city skyline, a gigantic mass of characterless grey blocks, hazy in the afternoon heat. Scattered liberally across the conurbation were half a dozen or so star-like flares where the sun had caught open windows and made her, alone, the focal point of its reflected rays. For several minutes she watched the scene, diligently monitoring the flares as they slowly dimmed and became extinguished, only to be replaced by an equal number, randomly appearing in other parts of the city. As the sun traced its weary path over the urban landscape, the lights would dim and flare, each pattern uniquely defining the time of day, never again to be repeated.

At the heart of the city the buildings grew taller, towering over the urban sprawl. That was where it all happened, she thought. The whole city controlled from that central square mile, the processor at the core of a giant concrete mainframe. And yet, ironically, the heart of the city was the only place that you could get away from the city. To escape the clutches of the city she, and millions like her, would have to travel at least twenty miles, either to the mountains in the north or the grasslands to the south. But there in the centre, they only had to climb a thousand feet and they were free. There, they could control the city but not be part of it. In a matter of seconds they were able to rise above the concrete, steel and glass and from their huge, luxurious penthouse suites they could watch over their kingdom with nonchalance, and mingle with the stars.

On the east side of the city centre stood the First National Bank, its steel and tinted glass structure glistening pink in the afternoon sunshine.

"Just think, Bobbi. All that money, and we only need the tiniest fraction of it." Her daughter sighed and glanced up at mummy with an expression of perplexity. Then she returned to the horizon as if seeking her answer there, her gaze fixed firmly on the New Century Tower at the very heart of the conurbation.

If the city centre dominated the skyline, the New Century Tower dominated the city centre. Standing thirteen hundred and forty feet high, its ninety nine storeys had housed the American government's economic, social and foreign advisors from the summer of 2015 AD when it was completed. For a while, the New Century Tower had not only been the central core of the city but that of the entire nation. However, since the government's return to the newly built premises near Washington DC two years later, the Tower had housed only the peripheral government departments and had lost much of its former importance. Nevertheless, the building itself remained strikingly beautiful and continued to overshadow the city panorama.

Sarjena turned her attention to Bobbi.

"Come on," she said. "You're going to overheat if you stay out in this sun much longer. Too much of a good thing is bad for you, you know." Wearily, she struggled to her feet and lifted Bobbi back into the pram.

"I'll take you once round the lake and then we'll go home and get some tea."

Before setting off, Sarjena surveyed the scene ahead, mentally planning the route she would be taking. With a brief start she saw that the man who had been on the other side of the lake was no longer there. In fact, he was nowhere in sight.

"Now I wonder where he's got to," she mumbled, half to Bobbi, half to herself. Quickly she scanned the hillside and the borderline of the wood ahead but nobody was around. On the next hill the Army of God band had departed. She was alone again.

"Oh well. Some people must be able to walk faster than I thought," she said and gave the pram a preliminary push to loosen up the wheels.

Suddenly, without warning, she was lying in the grass again, this time on her stomach. She found she had no recollection of what had happened and began to feel a mixture of confusion and terror. A second ago she had been standing up and now she was lying down but she could not remember falling. Her body was burning with an intense heat and she could no longer move her legs or arms. Her chest felt on fire and though she was conscious of breathing heavily, her lungs were not inflating.

What had happened? All she had done was push the pram.

The pram!

Bobbi! What had happened to her baby? With excruciating spasms of pain, she managed to lift her head above the blades of grass. The extreme effort brought her whole forehead out in beads of sweat and obscured her vision. Yet through the blur of her tear-stained eyes she could identify the unmistakeable blue of the pram hood several metres ahead, as it glided inevitably towards the lake.

Bobbi! No! Bobbi! She tried to scream but the words only echoed around her skull and no sound passed from her lips. For what seemed like an eternity the blue shape ahead continued rolling and rolling towards the deeper blue mass of the lake at the bottom of the knoll. There was nothing she could do. She was helpless.

As the pram finally reached the lake's edge and the two blues converged in a whirlpool of sweat and tears, the sound of splashing reverberated around her head, amplified so that she felt as if she were drowning under a huge waterfall of boiling water. Silently, she screamed and screamed and slowly allowed her head to fall back into the grass and her eyes to close. They did not open again.

3

Something was wrong.

Something was wrong with Melissa.

Howard stood at the end of platform twelve at Manchester Victoria wishing he had stayed in Alderley. If he had waited that little bit longer then Melissa would have returned and they would have been able to talk it out. They had been through worse problems before and he was sure that she wanted to talk to him, but he had not been patient enough with her. He took the crumpled note from his pocket and unfolded it.

> *Howard, I really can't go to Darwen with you. I have too much work to do and if I go away for a few days I'll never get it done. I've gone to stay at a friend's house for the night. I'm sorry I haven't waited but I didn't know where you were; you've been ages. It's probably better this way. If I'd stayed I know that you would have talked me into going with you or there would have been a scene. I hope you find the missing jigsaw piece. Melissa.*

He screwed the paper into a tight ball and tossed it onto the railway track before he could change his mind. He heard someone clear his throat behind him as if showing disapproval, but he could not see him and could not therefore be seen. And yet, from somewhere out of the opaque night, a pair of eyes was watching him, burning into him. He could feel it.

That afternoon, something had happened on the Edge. He had sensed it almost immediately but it was a sensation he did not understand; an anxiety with no rational foundation. One moment it had been a calm, clear October afternoon, the next he had been struck by a shock wave, a vague mental echo as if from deep within his subconscious or from another dimension. He had become light-headed and dizzy. And the sky had grown dark. Whenever he tried to put the afternoon into perspective his mind refused to concentrate. Instead it tortured him repeatedly with a single image; his last sight of Melissa as she had paused against the skyline, flowers piled high in her arms, and then, in slow motion, as she sank silently over the threshold of the Edge.

But now the anxiety was caused, not so much by what he had witnessed, but by what he was sensing; a presence whose existence was no less irrational but now more tangible. As each minute passed it seemed even more of a reality. Though directionless, this new sensation emanated from somewhere nearby. He had been haunted by it ever since he had reached the station, as though the two somehow belonged together. This was not something he could ignore. Like a blinding light, or a high pitched screech, it invaded and saturated the sixth sense he never knew he had, determined to be acknowledged.

He was being watched.

At the end of the platform he continued to walk around in circles until he began to feel dizzy again. He immediately stopped but the dizziness would not wane and the nausea soon returned. Further along the platform, he could make out the toneless outlines of the other waiting passengers, their drab, grey, expressionless faces, just visible through the fog, were staring aimlessly in all directions. Whatever was happening to him, he was experiencing alone. No one else was affected.

Suddenly, Howard was distracted by a flare of light behind him. Turning round he saw that the fog had begun to glow where it hung expectantly off the end of the platform. At first Howard was mystified, staring stupidly down the track, searching for some rational explanation for the phenomenon. The light grew brighter by the second; a cruel, ominous, silent light which spread through the fog like a deadly virus permeating through a helpless body.

And then the light was accompanied by sound, a low rhythmical rumbling, growing louder with each second. Howard felt the onset of panic as his mind could find no obvious reason for what was happening. And then he realised. This was it. This was what everything had been leading to. The presence was about to make itself known.

In desperation, Howard turned to the other passengers to assure himself of some help and met with a wall of eyes. Where they stood, they were still motionless, but now they were staring straight at him, gaping like dumb, pathetic animals in startled anticipation. The onset of panic turned to blind panic as Howard realised he was utterly helpless and looked frantically round for some escape. But what was the use of running? There was no escape. The glow continued to expand and soon no patch of mist ahead of the platform had been left untouched. Howard did not know what to do and turned his attention to the direction of Alderley.

Melissa! I love you! What is happening? Why are you doing this?

Suddenly the crescendo reached an ear-splitting climax as the fog exploded and from within burst a multitude of flashing lights which shot out of the darkness and headed straight towards him. Howard was thrown into abject confusion as the lights momentarily blinded him, roaring past. He turned and ran, sprinting as fast as he could down the platform, gasping for breath and trying desperately to remain on his feet. He only just made it. In less than thirty seconds the train had completed its transaction and had disappeared once more into the blanket of fog.

4

In the claustrophobic, overheated confine of the compartment, Howard wrestled against fatigue and aching limbs, his eyes barely able to stay open. As the train pulled away from the station, the usual silence of comatose, world weary passengers was replaced by excited conversation, uncomfortably loud, and dominated entirely by the subject of the fog. Such a 'pea-souper', as one passenger referred to it, was an extremely rare event in the region and those who could remember the last occurrence had delved into their memories of several years past. Very soon a debate had broken out. Strangers who would normally not have passed two words found the bond of common experience too compelling to keep silent and their determination to conquer the elements and make it home was reinforced by sharing the experience verbally. An army of commuters was going into battle. Howard had little patience with it all and remained silent. He looked round at the other passengers disdainfully, wishing that they would all simply be quiet.

The carriage was crowded and there was standing room only. Howard tried to shut off the drone but found himself hustled around a small space like a pinball bouncing between pins. Due to the 'appalling weather conditions', as the news bulletin later described it, many people had decided to abandon their usual buses and cars in preference to the train and it was subsequently recorded that the service had carried, at its peak, twice the usual number of passengers. Even so, nothing was moving around the northern intersect and traffic was reportedly backed up right into the city.

That evening, the whole public transport system seemed to be running behind schedule. It would normally have been able to claim a world record efficiency which averaged over ninety six percent throughout the year and which effectively meant that nothing ever ran late. On the strength of this one night such a claim would never have been believed by anyone who was new to the city. But Howard Robinson was not a stranger and, being accustomed to the precise punctuality with which the network usually ran, even the ten minute delay he had had to put up with proved to be a little more than inconvenient.

Why the fog should affect an automatic railway system, Howard had no idea, but it seemed to have thrown everything into chaos. Of course, they could have been blaming the fog to cover up something else; it would not have been the first time they had done that. Their efficiency statistics were the envy of the world, a trophy that was displayed regularly around the globe, and which they no doubt intended to hang on to, no matter what.

To compound the problem, there were all these extra people. He had been hoping for peace and quiet but the door of the carriage had opened to reveal the opposite. Howard had desperately needed to sit down and it was only through the kindness of one girl that he now found himself able to rest his aching legs. He had even been too exhausted to show his appreciation and above the buzzing conversation he had caught the disapproving murmurs of the girl who was now hanging from a sprung roof strap only feet away. He wanted to thank her but the moment had been lost and he could not even raise a smile.

Removing his gloves, Howard cupped his hands together and blew into them, hoping the warm breath would thaw them out before he hyperventilated. It was about time, he thought, that he stopped all this. He could not take the pace any longer; the hustle and bustle of city life was wearing him out. As each day passed, the simple act of commuting was becoming that much more of an effort. And what was it all for anyway? What was the point of trying to cope with all this hassle just to stay alive? There was more to life than this - more to life than doing the same old meaningless, boring routine day in, day out. In his mind a seed suddenly germinated. He would move away, that is what he would do. He would sell the shop, sell the apartment and move out of the city. For good.

Perhaps he would return home.

As the train sped deeper and deeper into the tunnel, Howard sank deeper into his own thoughts. Around him, the endless sea of unfamiliar faces became nothing more than a blurred mass of colours and the sound of many conversations competing with each other for airspace faded to a low droning noise which his mind was able to ignore…

For some reason he dreamt of Darwen. The magnificent, snow covered moor set against a dark grey, cloud-filled sky; the clear, sparkling spring water flowing down the southern slope alongside the track and luscious, green fields basking in brilliant sunshine, filled with lambs. He could see trees on distant hillsides; forests standing proud and silent in reverence of their surroundings, and below the small, peaceful town bathed in silver moonlight with thousands of stars diligently watching over.

In his mind, he jumped from night to day, from summer to winter. All these images had once been real. He had once been a part of all of them. He must leave the city and find his home, his true home, before it was too late. He must put some meaning back into his life, surround himself with the things he felt at peace with. He must make the images real again.

Then he saw himself standing on a rocky outcrop, overlooking a wide plain. He was standing in the pouring rain; behind him the trees thrashed about violently in the wind. He was in Alderley – standing on the Edge. Even after all this time he still recognised it, the vivid memories surfacing from deep within. He was soaked through to the skin but he did not care. At least the rain was pure. There was no pollution, no acidity. In the distance he could hear church bells echoing up from the town below and along the escarpment. The rain ceased in reply, and fresh sunrays fell on his face. And then he heard a voice, a synthetic monotone, drifting through the trees, the message loud and clear.

"EDEN SQUARE! ALL PASSENGERS FOR EDEN SQUARE!"

Howard woke with a start. Damn it! He was going to miss his stop. Without having time to digest the sense of peace that he had felt while asleep, he was thrown suddenly into a heightened state of stress, the dreams of only seconds before a quickly fading memory coupled with a slightly disturbing echo he felt he somehow recognised. He wanted to stop, to try and remember what he had been dreaming about – somehow it seemed important – but there was no time.

He struggled to his feet and pushed his way through the mass of bodies that lay between him and the exit. He just got there in time. As the doors hissed shut, Howard managed to squeeze through the narrowing gap and almost literally fell out onto the platform. Once there, he paused to gather his wits about him as the other passengers raced by and flooded out of the many exits. Behind, the gliderail slid back into the depths of the underground labyrinth and he soon found himself alone in the dimly lit chamber. Above him, a large signboard creaked as it swung in the draught created by the departing train. In large white letters, on a dark red background, it proclaimed the name of the station.

Eden Square.

From the exit on the platform, it was a five minute walk through The Catacombs before Howard arrived at the bottom of the escalator that led up to the surface. As he made his way through the maze of tunnels, the air had become gradually colder, chilling him to the bone. He gradually dropped further behind the other passengers until eventually, the familiar, rhythmical sound of commuter footsteps faded and he was alone again. In the confines of the tunnel, his own footsteps echoed eerily, reverberating along the tunnel walls and producing the effect of being followed by someone keeping perfect time. A security camera, mounted high in a recess in the wall, whirred round to stare in his direction. Howard stared back, wondering who was so interested in him. Eventually the camera became bored and rotated to face the tunnel ahead.

Once, he heard the roar of an express train passing under Eden Square, the sound resonating back along a tunnel which branched off to his left. For some reason The Catacombs seemed unusually quiet that evening, especially considering the number of excess passengers, and the noise of the train was vaguely reassuring. Shortly after, he heard the sound of passengers stampeding towards the escalator bank and calculated it would be less than a minute before they reached him. At that moment, he knew he preferred the silence.

A small girl startled him. While he had been distracted by the train she had appeared suddenly, silently and now stood a few paces ahead in the corridor, standing by a huge billboard advertisement for Eden Square's burger bar. She was severely malnourished and her taut black skin was stretched like canvas over a near-skeletal body. Her limbs were needle sticks, legs impossibly supporting her frail weight and arms barely able to support the begging bowl she held up in front of her. For all this she was still able to smile beseechingly and her mouth widened to reveal perfect, gleaming white teeth. Gentle tears sucked the remaining moisture from her body and she thrust the bowl towards Howard even more forcefully.

Howard backed off and tried to steer around her but with uncanny accuracy she turned with him, her eyes locked on his. Howard was unnerved and stood frozen to the spot as the passengers from the train erupted into the corridor and turned unhesitatingly towards the escalator bank. Deftly, they swung around Howard and passed through the little beggar girl, trampling her underfoot and breaking her body into fragments. In seconds he was alone in the corridor once more, staring blankly at the space where the hologram had been.

Further along the passageway a poster declared the fortieth anniversary of the continuing Ethiopian famine. Just beyond, another young girl appeared, winked at him and took a bite from a huge, mouth-watering burger. She winked again and pointed to the poster before disappearing into thin air. Howard had to smile at the irony of the mistake and wondered how long it would be before an engineer came to swap the advertising holos over. He turned and covered the last few paces to the end of the passageway. At the escalator, an icy cold breeze was blowing down from the surface, an unsubtle indication of the weather conditions above. Howard paused to brace himself against the cold draught and then stepped onto the moving stairway.

In the entrance foyer of Eden Square station Howard found himself back in the environment he was used to. All around him hundreds of people were pacing about; some randomly, aimlessly, others more purposefully weaving their way through the crowd. Howard decided to join the latter and struggled as positively as he could to the other side of the hall. Although he was already fifteen minutes late, and still had to cross Eden Square in thick fog before he could connect with his bus, Howard could not survive without his evening bulletin. And so he headed in the direction of the nearest news stand, slipped the vendor his personal profile card and waited for a few seconds while the laser printer assembled the latest information according to his pre-programmed specification and threw out a hard copy, neatly creased and folded – and addressed to him.

He paused briefly to glance at the headlines. The front page contained only two items. One of them, as Howard expected, was about the fog, its unusual appearance, its effect on the travel networks and the outlook for tomorrow being much the same. However, the major topic, which dominated most of the page, possessed a headline of three, short words in bright red, souvenir script : "HAPPY NEW CENTURY" At the top of the page was the day's date : October 7th, 2029.

Howard began to read with a mounting cynicism, at the same time walking slowly, subconsciously, across the passenger hall towards the exit.

"January 1st, 2030 will be a day for celebration in more ways than one. At last, The Great Turmoil is over and the new millennium - as it was meant to be - is finally upon us. And that, according to the Standing Committee For Progress And Recovery, is official. In a statement to the United Nations Press, the Committee reported that the developed nations had made significant technological and economic progress over the last year and had surpassed all expectations, achieving two years growth in the last six months alone. The Committee, which has been in session for three days now, was unanimous in its conclusion that the year 2030 AD would also be the year 2000 HTE. In addition, the United Nations Press was also told to expect a complete global recovery before the next five years were out, at which time the Standing Committee For Progress and Recovery would hope to find itself no longer in existence."

Howard was not impressed and he did not believe the governments of half the countries of the world would be either. It would probably take several more decades for their economies to return to their former strength, and that fact alone rendered the conclusions of the Committee farcical. A further two pages inside the bulletin provided a more detailed statistical analysis in addition to the headline paragraph, but the plight of the millions of refugees and displaced, poverty-stricken families was not mentioned. And besides, how could they give him back the last fifteen years of his life? The simple fact was that the people who were well off now were not those that were wealthy then.

The Standing Committee For Progress And Recovery was set up by the UN immediately after The Great Turmoil to monitor the re-evolution of the developed nations, both East and West. At the time, it was estimated that the various civil wars and economic crashes had plunged two thirds of the planet back about thirty years and so, armed with a complete arsenal of historical facts and figures, the Committee created its own time scale.

The scale began in 1984 HTE (Historical Time Equivalent), a purely arbitrary year it seemed, and advanced from there. At first, progress was very slow. The fallout took almost a year to fall out and the re-establishment of basic essentials such as the food supply chain - something which all westerners had previously taken for granted - proved to be frustratingly slow. In that first year, more civil wars commenced around the globe than in the previous decade and this was further complicated by growing civil unrest within Europe and the United States. NATO and UN forces were stretched to the limit, unable to contain the widespread disturbances. During the first two years of recovery, therefore, the HTE scale only moved forward a single year and occasionally would even be teetering on the brink of moving backwards as bouts of famine and disease ripped through the European continent.

From that point on, progress noticeably accelerated and would turn HTE years every couple of months or so until everybody was no longer interested, and the regular reports from the Standing Committee passed by unnoticed. It was the rejuvenation of the world's financial markets – which in economic terms involved careful and complex reconstructive surgery - that had slowed the progress down again, or so they claimed. Either that, or the Standing Committee suddenly realised that they would be out of a job if they did not begin to exercise some control over the advancing years.

Whatever the reason, they had now seen fit to declare the arrival of the year 2000 HTE and the Committee's days were therefore numbered. Howard had always wondered how they had made their calculations since so many factors seemed to have been forgotten. How can a world without Belgrade, Baghdad or Tripoli be the same as it was before war broke out? The picture was such a confusing one.

Many European and Baltic countries were now classed as Second World, feebly attempting to regain their economic position in the world market against the more powerful economies of the East and Middle East. Europe's primary industries had been decimated and there was still much to be rebuilt. Ten years on, vast areas of land, in a band of war torn countries stretching a quarter of the way round the globe, remained infertile, unable either to grow anything of any nutritional or economic value or to support livestock; hundreds of square miles of desolate wasteland.

And then there was Japan. At the turn of the century, the world had seen the Japanese economy grow stronger year by year after a relatively depressed economic period. Eventually, the economy had regained its former strength until it held the largest market share in over fifty per cent of manufactured goods globally, and looked set to increase its footholds in nearly all other commercial markets. It had been the devastation of Tokyo, after three major earthquakes in rapid succession, that had precipitated a global recession.

And then, in the midst of all this chaos, unknown to anyone – and undiscovered for years after – the Russians had played their master card. And the Japanese economy, weakened by the greatest natural disaster in a hundred years, had been the first to be obliterated.

But how anyone could declare that everything was back to normal, Howard could not imagine. Over a decade later, the Japanese economy was still floundering. In all that time, Tokyo had remained a graveyard and no attempt had been made to rebuild it. Today, Tokyo was a shrine, a Mecca for morbid pilgrims all around the world to congregate and witness first hand the death and decimation that had become the focal point of remembrance of The Great Turmoil. Next month would be the fifteenth anniversary of Tokyo's destruction.

As Howard folded his news bulletin and stepped out of the station foyer into the fog ridden street, he wondered if Japan would ever again occupy a position on the global economic stage.

Emerging from the passenger hall, Howard was surprised at exactly how little he could see. Visibility had reached an all time low of one metre. Within seconds, the station behind him had become obscured in the shroud of fog, and its presence could only be detected by the familiar sounds of newspaper vendors and the barrage of typical commuter noises emanating from inside. Closing his eyes, he conjured up a mental picture of the station approach, gained his bearings, and set off in the direction he knew Eden Square to be.

Déjà vu.

It had come from nowhere, like a brick wall suddenly materialising in front of him. Something; he was not sure what.

Already seen. Already felt. A long time ago.

Something to do with the fog. Something to do with the station.

And then a name.

The name.

Melissa.

Something to do with Melissa.

Then he remembered.

He had seen her, three or four weeks ago. He could not remember exactly. At the time he had not been sure, but now he was certain. He *had* seen her. In the shopping arcade. Near to the shop. A ghost from the past. The same Melissa, perhaps slightly older but only by a few years. It was not possible. The same golden blonde hair; the same emerald eyes. Those eyes. It could not have been anyone else. They were unmistakably her eyes.

He had entered the central mall of the arcade and there she had been; right in front of him. Her face. Her hair. Her eyes. Even the same gait, tall and straight, perfectly balanced. Walking towards him. Melissa. Yet it had been so long ago. How could he be so certain? And she just carried on walking. No sign of recognition. No acknowledgement. She saw him but she pretended not to know him. Just ignored him. Walked straight past him and continued down the mall as if nothing had happened. He had tried to follow but she was too quick. Since the angina had set in, his lungs could no longer take that kind of punishment. With each hurried step, he had fallen further behind. More and more people stood in his way. Following the head of golden hair advancing into the distance, weaving through the crowd as if on roller skates. An expert? No. Just young – and agile. Halfway down the mall, at the fountain, he had climbed the steps, risen above the crowd for a better view. Looking down, an endless ocean of faces. Random motion. All the colours of the rainbow.

Except gold.

She was gone.

At the bottom of the station approach he paused and tucked the newspaper under his right armpit to look at his watch. Almost ten minutes to seven. He would have to hurry. His bus was at five minutes to and he still had to cross the square. Above his head he could vaguely see the alternating light of the traffic signal dutifully performing its function of controlling the many cars and taxis in and out of the approach. First red. Then green. Then red again. But today there was very little traffic. Occasionally a solitary car or taxi could be heard crossing the junction and then nothing, just the continuous sound of footsteps all around him. People without faces, without bodies. He waited. Red. Green. Amber. A pale, cold, silent light, diffused by the fog, looking much bigger than it really was.

Déjà vu.

Something to do with the light. A long time ago. Something to do with the light. And the station. And the fog. And Melissa. And the cold. It was so cold. But when was it? Before The Great Turmoil. A long time ago. Too long to remember. But where was it? In England. Had to be. Somewhere in England before the Turmoil. A long time ago.

With the traffic signal back on red and no sound of an engine anywhere near the junction, he stepped onto the road and began to cross. It was not only the feeling of being in the same situation before. There was something else. Something strange. Something different. Usually a déjà vu experience would fade, slowly slip back into the subconscious and remain a mystery for ever. Not even the sensation of the experience could be remembered. It would just precipitate a numbness of having passed through an minor ordeal, like having a nightmare which was quickly overtaken by the events of the following day. And then, in time, the numbness would also fade away and the whole incident would be forgotten. Until it happened again.

But this time there was something different. Halfway across the junction, the déjà vu was joined by a further sensation and his heart skipped another beat. Again, it was familiar. It was another clue. This déjà vu experience was crying out to be remembered. And there was no mistaking this new sensation.

He was being watched.

There was no doubt about it. He could feel a presence. Somewhere near. He had felt this presence before. The same time all this had happened before. Someone or something had been watching him then also. The same presence. Somewhere nearby and yet, at the same time, distant. It was hard to explain. He was confused.

He was still somewhere in the centre of the junction when he realised he should have reached the other pavement by now. The road was far too wide. He knew. He crossed it every evening. At first he thought that in his confusion he had somehow managed to turn full circle and was now headed back the way he had come. However, he convinced himself that this could not have happened and continued across the road in his original direction. Seconds later, when he finally stepped onto the pavement again, he realised his mistake. He had accidentally crossed to the opposite corner of the junction instead of the one side to the square. He recognised the corner by the fire hydrant that had been situated there. It was the only one on the junction.

As quickly as he could manage, he turned to his right and crossed back over. As soon as the familiar flagstones of Eden Square's perimeter were under his feet, he paused for breath and looked at his watch once more. Only three minutes to cross the square or he would miss the bus. He would have to hurry. Ignoring the persisting sensations that were spinning inside his head, he broke into a clumsy trot, electing to let other people avoid him rather than try and avoid them. He would try and remember when all this had happened before when he was in the safety and warmth of his own home. It was not worth missing the bus for. Not in this weather. It would be another hour before the next one and it was much too cold to stand around waiting. If he was lucky, the buses would also be running late. He did not care when it left as long as he could be sat inside it. In the warm.

Yet despite all his intentions, the sensation of being watched persisted, growing stronger by the second, getting closer with each step. He ran faster, trying to convince himself that he was running for something, not away from someone. The presence grew nearer. He ran faster. The presence grew nearer still. He quickened his pace even more, wheezing and panting, the muscles in his legs gradually giving way. Nearer. Faster. Nearer. Faster…

And then it happened. A searing pain in the upper part of his chest. Sudden. Clinical. Deadly.

Heart attack!

He clutched his chest with both hands, his newspaper falling to the floor. All around him he could sense people but he could see no one and he knew they could not see him. Slowly, painfully, he dropped to his knees, still with both hands pressed tightly against his chest. Not yet. He was not ready yet. He still had to find Melissa. Tell her he still loved her. Those few months were the only time he had ever been happy. Really happy. It had been so long ago but his life had been empty ever since. Without her. And now she was in the city. After all this time, she had come back to him. It was too much of a coincidence. He had to find her. He could not bear to lose her again.

Then he remembered…when it had all happened before. A long time ago.

England. Manchester Victoria station. And then Darwen.

The train and the strange lights. The feeling of being watched. It had all happened that evening, the day he lost her.

A long time ago.

5

The pain in his chest appeared from nowhere and was excruciating. Martyn Sorensen sat bolt upright in bed and tried to take another deep breath. Again there was a spasm of agony in the upper left portion of his torso as if his lungs were expanding against a rigid spike in his chest. Each breath, the volume of air was limited by the sudden, yet inevitable, intrusion of pain and he was forced to supply oxygen to his body in short gasps. The intensity of the pain brought him to his senses abruptly. He had been having a nightmare but he could not remember what it was about. Somehow, the burning sensation in his chest had seemed to flow with the dream, a critical part of the plot. Now it was just a poignant reminder of the sinister world he had just left.

Must have been killed again, he thought.

Martyn Sorensen had been in the city police force for almost ten years. In all that time, he had never grown used to the nightmares. If he ever did, he believed they would stop but until then he had no choice other than to live with them. His subconscious fears revealed themselves in his dreams and those dreams fuelled his fears. It was a self perpetuating cycle and he did not see how it could be broken. By day, he would face death and walk away unscathed. At night he would relive the day's events and be forced to watch the alternative conclusions; all the things that might have happened if circumstances had been only slightly different; all the plans that could have gone wrong; all the risks that might not have worked in his favour. By day, he had always managed to survive. At night, he never did.

The occurrence of this particular nightmare was irregular because everything had been relatively quiet for the last few weeks. Usually he only had nightmares after an incident. Even then, it did not happen every time. Martyn did not really like all the deskwork but he tolerated it, and at least it would ensure him a good night's sleep. The Dortman drugs bust had been over a month ago now, a successful conclusion to more than six months of painstaking investigation and patience-stretching stakeouts. He had been catching up on the volumes of paperwork ever since. Fortunately, the start of his secondment to the desk had coincided with the change in the weather. The Dortman raid had been carried out in brilliant sunshine and a temperature of eighty five in the shade. The next day he had begun to write the report staring at an overcast sky speckled with torrential rain and hail. Since then, the climate had been generally and unsociably cold, but at least it seemed to have kept the gangs off the streets and the drop in violent criminal acts had been more than significant.

As the sharp pain in his chest stabbed at him again, Martyn snapped himself awake and concentrated on holding his breath until he felt the pain subside. Slowly, he inhaled and, just as he thought the spasm was going to return again, it suddenly disappeared and he relaxed, taking a few deep breaths to ensure that it did not come back.

Grief, what time was it? Although his mind was now fully alert, his eyelids were stiff as rusty door hinges and an attempt to read the luminous green digits on the clock across the room ended in failure; all he could see was a blurred, shapeless splatter of jade on black. Allowing himself to sink gently back onto the soft down pillow, he concentrated on focussing on the clock as if willing the digits to appear and refusing, out of pure stubbornness, to rub the sleep from his eyes and solve the problem that way. Slowly, the digits materialised. It was 6:52am.

It was only after completing this marvellous demonstration of willpower that he became aware of the fading trill-like noise echoing inside his head. He recognised the sound. The phone. That was what had woken him. The phone had been ringing! Evidently it had stopped now and he began to make a mental list of all the people who could have called at such an early hour, becoming more agitated by the second. He wished he had woken more quickly - it might have been important.

Just then, he heard her voice, a soft, sleepy, soothing voice, whispering in his left ear and melting the frustration from his body.

"It's for you. Chief Lancaster." Martyn took hold of the receiver in one hand and simultaneously switched on the bedside lamp with the other, moving up into a sitting position. His eyes remained closed but he tried to sound awake.

"Hi, Chief. Great to hear from you. It's been so long," he said, half cheerily, half sarcastically. Unfortunately, Chief Lancaster was not in such a pleasant mood.

"Alright, cut the crap; this is serious. I want you to get down here right away. We've got trouble."

"Why? What's the problem?"

"Well, for starters, I've got two government departments breathing down my neck. I don't know; we get a state visit, some guy has a heart attack and the whole world caves in. Did you catch the news last night?"

"How could I?" Martyn said. "I was working late. You sent me down town for the evening, remember? I didn't get back until gone midnight and, in case you've forgotten, this is supposed to be my day off."

"Correction. This was your day off. Get some clothes on and get your ass down here pronto." The Chief's stern voice shot out of the receiver loud and clear and then softened slightly. "Listen, Martyn. I'm sorry. It can't be helped. Brief you when you get in." He hung up.

Martyn let the receiver drop onto the bed and slumped back under the sheets, exhaling a long, drawn sigh. Then, he turned to face Melissa and gently caressed the back of her right ear, letting the long, blonde hair run through his fingers.

"Melly?" She stirred softly and he felt her ear twitch briefly under the touch of his finger.

"I know," she said. "Something's come up."

"Brett sounded pretty desperate. He wants me to go in. There isn't really anything I can do."

He could not think of anything else to say. He had promised to take Melissa to The Great Lakes for a long weekend and had worked every waking hour to take the extra couple of days. Now, on the morning of their departure, his plans had been shattered and the full effect of the Chief's request began to sink in.

"Melissa, I'm sorry. I'll make it up to you," and then, as an afterthought, "if I ever get the chance."

Melissa turned to face him and smiled, a slight trace of disappointment could be seen to cross her lips and then vanish.

"It's okay," she said, bravely. "The weather's lousy anyway."

Martyn reached across and softly kissed her forehead. "I love you," he said, "and I'll make it up to you. I promise."

"I'll hold you to that." She smiled reassuringly, reaching up her arm and brushing his hair back with the tips of her fingers. Then, the smile was replaced with a frown and her forehead became a collection of perplexed creases.

"What's it all about, anyway?"

"Your guess is as good as mine." He shifted into a half sitting position, resting on his forearms and elbows. "Did you watch the news last night?"

"Yes, I saw it."

"Anything interesting?"

"What?" she laughed. "On the news? You've got to be kidding. I only saw it because there wasn't a talk show on."

Having a self-confessed hatred of current affairs, he knew she was teasing him. However, this time he couldn't think of a suitable retort so he chose to ignore it.

"So what's happening in the world, then?"

"Not much," she said, nonchalantly, not wishing to let him get off so easily. Then, realising he was serious, she changed her tone.

"Oh, alright then. Let me see." She thought for a moment. "There really wasn't much at all. Basically, there were only three items. There was all that rubbish about celebrating the new millennium again this New Year. Can you imagine it? Thirty years later and we're going to party as if nothing's ever happened. I don't know of anyone who's got anything to celebrate anyway."

Martyn frowned. "It's all psychological. I suppose they're trying to wipe out the memory once and for all - you know, a fresh start and all that. Try and pretend the Great Turmoil never happened and carry on where we left off. Besides, the feel-good factor is the key to any economic recovery..."

Melissa interrupted. "You don't think anyone is going to fall for that, do you? I mean, people lost their families, their homes, their livelihoods, everything. Their whole lives were completely shattered. They won't ever forget."

"No," he agreed, "but it may give them a chance to try and come to terms with it and move on."

"What do you mean?"

"Well," Martyn ventured. "A few months ago we arrested this down-and-out who's driven himself insane because he couldn't keep his half of a suicide pact. He sat and watched his fiancée bleed to death after slashing her wrist and he couldn't do it. Two weeks later and they would have been married. Now he spends every hour of the day haunted by the expression on her face when she realised he wasn't going to follow her. There's probably only one way he will ever regain his sanity."

He went silent, as he reflected on the arrest, in a seedy east side warehouse, for possession of a desperate concoction of hard drugs. He knew immediately that he was not dealing with someone whose mental faculties were intact. He could not imagine the horror of the thousands of victims who had chosen to take their own lives during and after the Turmoil, but he had witnessed this drug crazed dishevelled wreck relive his own private horror as the police psychiatrist had delved deeper into his pain. And then Martyn realised. He was not reliving the past, he was still there. Every minute of every day he was watching her die and struggling eternally with his own conscience.

"Haven't you just proved my point?" she said.

"What I mean is, he was never even given a chance. He was a down-and-out among a whole city of emotional vagrants – a population who have just given up because every one else has. Maybe you're right; maybe they never will but I think a lot of them really want to try. But it will need a big statement and that's what this new millennium thing is all about. For the first time since the Turmoil, life is almost as they remembered it all that time ago. It's the end of another decade and perhaps this is the chance they need to snap out of it. All some of them want is a good excuse to take hold of themselves and shake it out of their system, and if we're all in it together, the whole thing might just help some of them do it. It won't help everyone but even if it helps a few then it would be worth doing – a new year, a new resolution."

Melissa was not convinced. "Yes, I can just imagine it. I must go jogging three times a week; I must brush my teeth twice a day; I must not stamp on spiders; I must not bite my fingernails; I must pull myself together and ignore the fact that I once lost all my family and everything I owned. How many resolutions have you ever kept? It isn't going to be that easy. This depression has been malignant for more than a decade and I'm not surprised. The whole civilised world nearly broke down. Nothing is going to change that overnight." She paused, during which time Martyn decided that he agreed with her – or else he was too tired to do otherwise. He just hoped she was wrong.

"And I don't think inviting Gremelkov to the party was such a good idea either. It's just asking for trouble."

Martyn's eyes widened. "They did what?"

"That was the second news story. They've asked Gremelkov over for a state visit - a kind of peace mission - and he's accepted. And he's coming here, to the city. I reckon it's an act of martyrdom but somebody obviously sees some sense in it somewhere. It's supposed to be a gesture of goodwill but judging by the public's immediate reaction I wouldn't be surprised if he gets killed."

To the American population who did not know better, which was most of them, Anton Gremelkov was singularly responsible for The Great Turmoil. Consequently, he was widely considered to be the most reviled figure in the living world. But things weren't as simple as that. They never were. In one sense Gremelkov symbolised the typical hard-liner from the New Communist Islamic Alliance. Everything about him was the worst blend of old communist Russian and Middle Eastern religious fanaticism, from his bland taste in clothes to his non-existent sense of humour. He was old, grey and balding - with a thick Ayatollah beard - and keen, piercing eyes. These combined into a natural facial expression of such malevolence that the western media had used it repeatedly to fuel a propaganda war. And this, primarily, had been the main reason why so many people had held him responsible for the global upheaval - and still did.

But Gremelkov was far from innocent, either of causing the Turmoil or of promoting himself as the instigator. Even allowing for media bias, he had undoubtedly portrayed himself, with incomprehensible and dispassionate arrogance, as the prime mover. It was difficult to imagine that he could have caused such a global catastrophe without significant support from other high ranking officials. However, Gremelkov had emerged from the Turmoil as the first Alliance politician actually to crave publicity and the media, giving several high profile interviews to secure his notoriety. To many people, Gremelkov alone was the enemy.

To Martyn, the origins of the Turmoil were far from clear. It seemed to result from a combination of factors but the many rainforests which had been felled to provide written opinion on the matter found little in common. As humanity entered the third millennium the west had become entrenched, for ethical or political reasons, in a number of minor civil wars stretching from the Middle East and the Balkans to the Indo-Chinese islands. In the years that followed, far from reaching resolution, each war persisted, in fits and starts, to become a long term campaign. Inevitably, the strain on public spending, not just on arms but also on economic support, gradually began to show, either in mounting economic deficits or poorly disguised taxation. As the world slipped into a recession, Tokyo was hit by three earthquakes which claimed over 160,000 lives and rocked the world's financial markets. Though the earthquake was quite localised, the impact was global and the recession became a depression – the health of the world economy being deemed to be at its lowest since the second world war. About three weeks after the Tokyo earthquake a series of major computer crashes struck some of the world's key financial institutions.

Over the course of one week, billions upon billions of dollars held in virtual accounts were wiped out. Banks and governments fell and, despite the subsequent panic to acquire cash, the value of most currencies was decimated. Overnight, millions of people found themselves penniless and The Great Turmoil was born.

It was only years later, in a spectacular interview to a European satellite television network, that the reason became clear. It transpired that Gremelkov had headed up an elite unit of Alliance sponsored geeks – technical whiz kids whose sole purpose in life was to hack into the West's corporate computer systems and to devise ways of causing as much damage as possible once access had been gained. For years, at least a part of all the foreign aid received by the former Russia and its allies had been siphoned off to fund this project. It was clear now that in the rush for profit or survival, many institutions had been complacent about security. Some systems were accessed over the internet, some through private channels using seeker and code breaking software routines, some by secretly backing the companies that provided the security systems and others through old fashioned bribery and corruption. Over a period of five years, Gremelkov's team had prepared the ground, planted the virtual bombs and viruses, and then waited patiently for the right time to strike. The aftermath of the Tokyo earthquake provided the perfect opportunity. Already in a state of confusion and panic, it required very little to tip the balance in favour of complete chaos.

When the dust had settled the Alliance emerged as a much stronger economic force on the world stage, sometimes supporting the European countries with financial handouts to build their ailing economies. In an ironic twist of history, relations between East and West had never been closer. And then the truth came out.

Though it was partly surprising that the Alliance had elected to expose their involvement at all, the interview with Gremelkov had been astounding. Rather than a show of remorse for the millions of lost lives and the complete shredding of the very fabric of western society, Gremelkov had appeared smug, even gleeful, at the damage he had inflicted. He came across as both arrogant and defiant but, in some strange way, the enormity of the consequences of his actions did not seem to have fully registered. Yet there was no doubting his intelligence and, for the vast majority, his evil nature.

Recently, in a grossly ill-advised move by the present Alliance administration, Gremelkov had been inducted as a foreign affairs

Ambassador for the Mid-Eastern Alliance. Only half the US population could claim to know the name of the Alliance prime minister, who seemed to change every few weeks, but everyone knew Ambassador Anton Gremelkov.

Martyn said, "I don't believe it. There must be a few thousand people in the city alone who couldn't wait to get their hands round his neck. It's crazy!"

"Oh, I wouldn't worry," Melissa replied. "By the time he gets here, we will have celebrated the new millennium again and everybody will have forgotten about the Turmoil and pulled themselves together. It's all carefully planned really." Melissa's total disinterest in politics was reinforced by an increasingly sharp cynicism which she usually only displayed when she wanted to switch channels, but it was always there. Martyn remembered the Chief's comment about a state visit and shrugged wearily.

"Was there anything else on the news?" he asked.

"Oh, just something about the weather and how untypical the fog is. If they were right, when you finally get up and open the curtains you shouldn't be able to see a thing." Martyn checked the time and realised he'd been lying there longer than he'd thought. He was going to be late but at least the fog would give him a good excuse.

"Well somebody, somewhere has had a heart attack over something," he said. "Probably this thing with Gremelkov."

"Oh yes," she suddenly remembered. "Some old man was found dead in Eden Square. A coronary. That's all it said really. Nobody famous. Didn't even seem worth mentioning. Anyway, how did you know?"

"I didn't. I thought the Chief was talking in riddles again but obviously not. Apparently, that's what all this is about. That *old man* is the reason you and I aren't going up to The Lakes this morning." He sighed. "And for that I really am sorry. I know you needed this break."

Melissa placed her arms around his neck and kissed him. "It's okay," she said. "There will be other times."

Martyn smiled half-heartedly. "I suppose I'd better think about making a move in case it is really serious." Melissa began to stroke the back of his neck, slowly, rhythmically and then spoke in a whisper.

"Make love to me first."

As she climbed on top of him, and he felt the full weight of her breasts pressing against his chest, Martyn gazed into her deep, green eyes and melted instantly.

She was magnetic.

He had no choice.

Minutes later, he was staring up at the ceiling once more, Melissa lying with her head against his gradually slowing heartbeat.

"Relaxed?" she asked. Martyn released a sigh of contentment in reply. Melissa raised her head and propped her chin on the backs of her hands.

"Thank you," she said. "I needed that. I guess you did too." An inflection in the tone of her voice suggested that she was trying to get at something.

"What do you mean?"

"I don't know. You were tossing and turning in your sleep nearly all last night. I didn't think you'd wake up feeling too good, and now you have to go to work which I don't suppose is going to help at all. I just hope you feel a bit better about it now. And, since I've now got the day off, when you get home tonight I'll cook something special."

"Melissa, it's your holiday that's just been ruined. I wish you wouldn't be so nice about it. It will only make me feel even more guilty. Now I'll have to bring home a bottle of wine just to satisfy my conscience." He smiled at her. "I guess I just had a nightmare, that's all."

"Did you get killed again?" Melissa asked, softly.

"Yes, I got killed again." he replied.

"Never mind, you'll win one time."

"The time I win in my nightmare I will probably die in the street. I think I prefer it this way round." He glanced over at the clock, resigned to the fact that he was going to be very late.

"I suppose I'd better hit the road." He kissed her once on the cheek and began to climb out of bed. Suddenly, he stopped and sat staring at the clock.

"I don't know," he said. "This time it seemed different."

"In what way?" asked Melissa.

"Hmm?" he replied absentmindedly. His mind had begun to race frantically, trying to grasp at the fragments of the nightmare that had suddenly revealed themselves.

"How was it different?" she persevered, gently.

"I'm not sure," he said. "This time I wasn't expecting it. All night I had this strange sense that I was looking straight at something but couldn't see it. Then it just came out of the blue. And I haven't a clue what it was."

6

By the time Martyn Sorensen had finally left the apartment, leaving Melissa tucked up in bed, he estimated that he was about an hour later than he should have been - which was about fifty five minutes after he had first received the phone call from Chief Lancaster. If he had left the apartment as soon as he had replaced the receiver, he would have been late. As it was, he was very late. Even so, he had managed to close the front door behind him within five minutes of rising out of bed, and at least looked as if he had made a desperate effort to arrive on time.

After all, he thought, this was supposed to be his holiday. He could at least allow himself the luxury of looking 'casual', as he chose to term it - though he was sure the Chief wouldn't see it that way.

In fact, he had allowed himself enough time for a quick wash and that was all. He had left without a shave, without combing his hair and, more importantly, without breakfast. He looked as if he had not slept for a week and, checking himself in the mirror, his appearance had almost shocked him. Dressed only in a thick sweater, an old pair of jeans and training shoes, he hoped that he was not going to be presented to anybody important but decided that, in the event, he did not really care. In anticipation of his holiday he had sent all his suits off to be cleaned and his wardrobe had presented him with little choice in the matter.

He had gone to bed with his whole body tuned to the prospect of the holiday. Both he and Melissa had spent the week psyching themselves up for their first real break together, and it was only as he had bent down to kiss her before leaving the apartment that the full implication of what had happened began to sink in. Everything had been ready. The hotel was booked, the car had been serviced, the bags were packed, everything. Only two nights before, they had talked about leaving early to avoid the rush hour traffic. In the end they opted for a lie-in. If they had chosen otherwise, the two of them would now be speeding along the highway to freedom; away from the constant drone of traffic and onward towards peace and solitude; away from the urban sprawl and out into fresh air and nature's unspoilt paradise; away from Chief Lancaster and the precinct; away from the city. But they had chosen to leave later, and all their plans had fallen apart with just a single phone call.

As Martyn stepped out of the elevator and into the large glass-fronted lobby of their apartment block, he realised that his vision of racing along the highway had been ill-conceived. Melissa, or the news report, or whichever, had been right. Outside, the fog was still incredibly thick and all he could see through the lobby entrance was the calm, dormant white mist as if the whole building were floating in a cloud. Visibility was down to about three metres. He stepped outside, walked over to the car, climbed in and powered up the Mobile Applications Pack. From the MAP, he selected the traffic report and watched as the monitor displayed row after row of red warning lights. He switched to the rail channel and found the trains were running reasonably well. Immediately he made the decision to walk the half mile to the nearest station and take the underground gliderail into the office. He would get absolutely nowhere if he went by road. Every junction would be a game of Russian roulette and he was doubtful that he would even be able to see the traffic signals in such conditions. At least the weather gave him the perfect excuse for being late and Martyn was even beginning to think that maybe it was a blessing in disguise that their holiday plans had had to be scrapped.

All the same, he could not help thinking about Melissa. He became so preoccupied with her that he somehow managed to take a wrong turning and had to backtrack a block. She had taken the news so well, and had shown the bare minimum of disappointment, but he knew she would be upset. She had been looking forward to this break for weeks. Every evening she would talk about nothing else, dreaming and planning until she had thought of so many things to do that they could not possibly have fitted them all into the short space of time that they had available. Almost had. Martyn felt guilty that he had not protested more on the phone but he had been taken by surprise and only half awake. But perhaps it was not so serious. Maybe if he had pushed the Chief a little bit more, he would still be lying in Melissa's arms waiting for the holiday to start. Surely somebody else could cope with it, whatever *it* was.

The more he thought about it, the more resentful he became. If anyone in the world knew how much he needed this break it was Brett Lancaster. Martyn had made sure that the Chief was aware of his holiday plans and how important they were to both himself and Melissa. However, he recognised that it was untypical of the Chief to overreact. Brett rarely telephoned out of hours unless it was necessary. Given the circumstances, only an emergency would have provoked him into picking up the phone like that. Martyn was tired and fed up but it was too late now. He would just have to make the best of it.

The fog was disconcerting. He was less than half a mile from the apartment yet everything seemed unfamiliar. He had already missed his turning once and had to retrace his steps down a street he rarely used. Eventually, he found himself at the junction he knew to be opposite the station. It was a five way junction and, because he had approached it from an unusual direction, he could not decide whether it was quicker to cross to the left and go clockwise or to do the opposite. Checking his watch he realised that his decision could determine whether he made the train or not. Since there was no traffic to be heard on the road he opted to go straight across the junction and set off at a trot. At the far side, through the fog, he could just make out the faint glow of the traffic signal as it clicked through its sequence. Red. Red amber. Green. Why did that that seem familiar? Mesmerised momentarily by the lights he almost jogged into the fire hydrant on the sidewalk and just managed to swerve and avoid it. He stopped.

Fog. Red. Amber. Green. Fire hydrant. A sense that he was looking at something but could not see it…

Fragments of the dream rushed into his thoughts and almost immediately slipped away. In the station concourse a bell rang – like the sound of a phone ringing…

And then it was gone and he was thinking about the Chief's phone call once more.

Inside the concourse, he briefly broke his train of thought to purchase a ticket and find his way to the correct platform which, as usual, seemed to be another half mile walk from the station entrance. Despite the station being named after his own district, Westlands, he was certain that the line itself could not possibly run underneath it. In the labyrinth that lay between the entrance and the platform on which he was now standing, there had been several sharp turns and he felt sure that the line must actually be under Riverton by two hundred metres or more. An interesting if trivial idea…

Abruptly, Martyn decided that he had more important things to think about. He turned his attention to the very few facts he knew about the Chief's phone call to see if he could try and piece together some sort of logical explanation for why he was now standing on a cold, dimly lit underground platform instead of being half way to The Great Lakes and the great outdoors.

Martyn Sorensen enjoyed solving puzzles. He had made Detective early in his career due to an enviable record in unravelling complex crimes. His success, he believed, was not the result of an excess of ability, but the fact that his mind was constantly ticking over problems and providing shortlists of possible, logical, and sometimes lateral, solutions. His brain was simply a workhorse but inevitably it tired and needed a rest. Usually he enjoyed his work but he sensed in his own cognitive reflexes that he was operating under par and he hoped that the Chief was not about to present him with a complex conundrum.

As he saw it, there were possibly two strands to this problem, whatever it was. First of all, there was the coronary victim. A man - an old man - has a heart attack in Eden Square and the next morning the Chief calls and orders him to cancel his leave and get to the office immediately. He could think of three possible reasons why. One: the man was important in some way, important enough for his death to worry the Chief. Two: there was more to his death than at first met the eye. Perhaps he had not had a heart attack at all, or maybe the attack had been induced in some way. There were several compounds around which could bring on a coronary. Perhaps it was murder. There was also the possibility that he had been scared to death, a heart attack initiated by something he saw, or something that happened to him, and that it was *that* something which was worrying the Chief and not the death itself. Three: maybe the heart attack victim was just the first thing that came into Brett's head when he was trying to find a reason to bring him in. Possibly something else, completely unrelated, was going on.

The announcement that Gremelkov was making a state visit was bound to have serious security repercussions – the second part of the problem. Brett might have been drawing his attention to the previous night's news bulletin just to put him on the scent while, at the same time, letting him know that the matter was confidential. It would not be the first time that he had received subtly disguised messages but they were usually a bit more obvious than that and would normally follow some kind of code phrase such as "Top of the morning" or "Wakey, wakey, rise and shine!". The department had phrases like that for almost every occasion and a few generic ones to cover the rest. It was even possible that the Chief's reference to someone having a heart attack did not relate to the news item at all - or perhaps it was simply a figure of speech.

Martyn was almost ready to bet on the last explanation but for one thing. The heart attack victim, whoever he was, had been featured on the news bulletin and what Melissa had said was true; it was not worth mentioning. People died of heart attacks every day. Across the country there must be hundreds of them. So what was so special about this one? This line of thought brought him right round in a circle. If the problem were not Gremelkov then it must be the old man. If it were a simple murder, it might have featured on the news but it certainly would not have panicked Chief Lancaster. Murders were almost as commonplace as heart attacks these days. However, why had the bulletin run the story as a heart attack if it were a murder? Why had they run the story at all? And, if the victim were important, why had the bulletin not mentioned that? That was the one thing that did not fit. It was a pointless, uninteresting, news item, yet somehow it had managed to gain peak viewing time.

Just then, he was surprised by the train appearing from what he thought was the totally wrong direction and he realised that he had lost his bearings entirely while in the labyrinth. Maybe the platform wasn't under Riverton after all. Since he prided himself on having a good sense of direction, this he took as more evidence that he was suffering from mental fatigue.

Though Westlands station had been quiet, the train was overcrowded and he found it impossible to concentrate on anything. The ten mile commute seemed interminable but otherwise the journey passed by uneventfully - with one exception. Two stops before his own, the gliderail pulled into Eden Square station. As he was staring absently at the illuminated sign on the platform he became vaguely aware of a thought, a slight flicker at the back of the mind, as if some secret inner part of him already knew the truth. He recalled the echo of his dream the night before. It was almost as if a lost memory were fighting to be remembered and an alarm bell had sounded to make him search it out. The sensation remained with him for the long two minutes that the gliderail stood in the station. Then, as the train pulled away once more, sliding silently into the darkness of the tunnel, it was gone.

For a few seconds, he puzzled over the sensation until the constant crushing of bodies in the over-packed carriage distracted him. He had posed a question, heard an answer but had not been listening, and the answer had come only once. Now, he could remember neither the answer nor the question, only that the event had taken place. The memory that had never been a memory was forgotten.

7

The beginning, if such an event exists, occurred just over a year earlier.

Morning broke under an overcast sky. A monotonous drizzle rained down on the campus and the first day of winter term at the university. For Howard the wet weather was a minor inconvenience but he was determined that it should not cause him to alter his plans. He arrived on campus a little before nine, collected and cashed his grant cheque before nine fifteen and had registered his courses and met his new tutor by nine thirty when the bookshop opened. At no stage had he had to queue. As he crossed the university's small shopping plaza to the sound of clicking locks, he noted, with a smug satisfaction, the arrival of the first keen freshers who would create campus-wide chaos by lunchtime. By then, he would be back at the hall of residence with a new stack of books, cross referencing his notes from the summer and gaining a much needed start on his thesis.

Everything went perfectly until he left the bookshop, just in time to take the first bus returning to the halls of residence. As he closed the door behind him and turned up his collar against the rain he was only vaguely aware of the disturbance on the other side of the plaza. A line of traffic had built up on the main internal road and some of the drivers at the back had begun sounding their horns in frustration. At the front of the line stood the first double decker bus bringing students in from the residences, the bus he had been hoping to take back. It had come to a halt while turning left up the short rise to the terminal and was now blocking the road. The windows of the bus were lined with heads, stationary like cardboard cut-outs, and the driver sat motionless with his forearms and chin resting on the steering wheel, seemingly staring into space.

Only slightly intrigued, he set off towards the terminal, head down against the driving rain. At the edge of the plaza he discovered the cause of the hold up. In front of the bus an old, battered Ford Fiesta appeared to have broken down in the centre of the link road, blocking the only route leading on to the main part of the campus. As he watched, a young woman stepped out from behind the raised bonnet, eased into the driver's seat and attempted to start the car. It turned over effortlessly but the engine did not fire. She climbed out of the car, paced back towards the raised bonnet, stared at it for a few seconds and then kicked the front hub cap in frustration. The bus driver shook his head in idle disbelief but otherwise did not move.

Howard witnessed all this as a passive observer and did not remember making any decision to get involved. However, he was suddenly walking by the Fiesta and, as the owner raised her head from under the bonnet, her eyes locked onto his and silently challenged him to walk away. He was trapped.

"Need any help?" he said, stupidly. She stared at him in a way he could not fathom, as though she were both relieved and yet convinced that he was the last person she wanted to see. She brushed a hand through her damp, tousled hair and then across her forehead. A droplet of rain ran down her cheek and fell onto the shoulder strap of her soaked Laura Ashley dress.

"Are you an engineer?"

"History."

"Oh." She sounded disappointed. "Do you know anything about cars?"

"A little," he said, conscious that it was almost a lie. "I think I'd recognise one if it passed me in the street."

She sighed and any attempt at forcing a smile ended in abject failure. She glanced towards the bus and he knew without looking that the glance had been received by over thirty pairs of eyes staring straight back at her. He placed his books on the roof of the car and stepped round to the engine compartment.

"I don't know what's wrong. It just won't start," she said. "Damn it, I hate this car." She kicked it again.

"Try turning it over and I'll see if I can spot the problem," he offered.

She seemed doubtful about this. "Do you know what you're looking for?"

"No," he admitted. "But if you do then I'll turn the engine over while you watch."

She walked round to the side of the car and opened the door. "Say when."

He waited until she was inside. "When."

The engine turned over but not as energetically as before. It did not appear to want to start. "Stop!" He walked round to the door and pulled on the handle. It gave out a painful whine as it opened.

"It sounds like the battery is starting to run low so we'll have to be economical. Do you have any WD-40?"

"No, what's that?"

"It comes in a little blue and yellow can," he said. "You just spray it on the problem area and it loosens everything up and gets it working again. It will also clean your car, drive away any rain water and prevent rust from spreading at the same time. You can even use it to stop your door from squeaking." To emphasise the last point he rocked the door slightly and tensed up at the high pitched noise which resulted.

She looked at him disbelievingly. "Are you making fun of me?" Her frustration was beginning to grow more apparent and she no longer appeared to be trying to hide it.

"Not at all," he said. "I take it you have got some petrol in the tank?"

"Of course I have," she said. "I'm not stupid, you know."

He waited before replying. Then, he just smiled warmly and said, "Yelling at the only person who's stopped to help you seems pretty stupid to me. Now, do you have a dry cloth or a piece of rag?"

Silently, she reached over to the glove compartment and produced a dust cloth.

"I use it to clean the windscreen," she said. "I suppose you are going to get it all dirty now." She handed him the duster. "Do you know what's wrong, then?"

"I think your ignition leads are shorting together but it's impossible to see the spark in daylight. If I can dry the leads, or insulate them, then maybe we'll be able to start it."

He disappeared under the bonnet. Then, about a minute later, he shouted.

"When."

The engine turned over, began to race and then suddenly fired up. From somewhere behind the bonnet he heard a scream of ecstatic triumph and the engine died almost immediately.

"Oh, sugar!"

"It's alright," he reassured her. "This time, when the engine fires, press down on the accelerator slowly and keep the revs high or it will stall again. As soon as it seems to have taken and I've dropped the bonnet, throw it in gear and drive it away. A couple of miles should be enough. You need to recharge the battery and the heat from the engine should remove the rest of the moisture. Are you ready?"

The engine turned and started, the bonnet dropped and the car lurched forward, stalled and then rolled back to its initial position. As Howard stepped aside, he watched the package of books glide silently across the car roof and disappear over the lip of the hatchback.

"Damn. I forgot about them." Howard rushed round to the back of the car and picked up the books. The package had split open and its contents were strewn along the gutter at the side of the road.

"Oh, no. Did they get wet?" She had climbed out of the driver's seat and now stood opposite him. Howard placed the books, one at a time, on the roof of the car. He did it slowly and deliberately, revealing the damage in ascending order of completeness until they were all laid out in a row between them. Across the cover of the last book was the perfect imprint of a rear tyre tread. Screams of laughter sounded behind them as the passengers on the bus suddenly stopped being two dimensional and erupted with life. Howard dared not turn round.

"It wouldn't have been so bad if you hadn't rolled back over them," he said. "They're virtually unreadable."

Even if he had tried he could not have hidden his disappointment at the ruination of his new books but he was not disposed to try. That she looked embarrassed and guilty was small consolation and Howard assumed anyway that the embarrassment was largely due to the tumultuous clapping and cheering which emanated from the audience behind them.

"I don't believe this is happening."

"I am really sorry," she said. "But I did everything you told me and it still stalled."

Something in the way she intoned this last statement stirred and softened him.

"You didn't keep the revs up," he said, calmly. "You let them die off when the clutch bit. Come on, let's try again. Can I drive this time?"

She seemed about to object to this implication that he would naturally succeed where she had failed but instead walked round the car and held out the keys.

"Are you sure you don't just want to abandon me here?"

"If I thought about it, I'm sure that is exactly what I would want to do so don't put ideas in my head." He took the keys. "If anybody on that bus knows me then I'll never live it down if I don't get this heap of junk working."

Fortunately, the engine fired first time and did not stall when he drove the car away. Yet they did not go far before reaching the end of the road and they had still to turn round and drive past the line of traffic before they could escape totally from the humiliation.

"I just hope it doesn't pack up at the first junction or I'm going to crawl under the dashboard and they can laugh at you." It almost happened. As Howard was manoeuvring around the bus, the ignition light came on and the engine began to splutter. Howard slammed his foot down on the accelerator and depressed the clutch. The car jumped forward and almost stalled.

"Move, damn it!" The car lurched again and then suddenly accelerated away. In a matter of seconds they had put the melee behind them and reached the edge of the campus. He turned onto the main road and took a deep breath.

"Thank goodness for that."

"Where are we going?"

"I thought maybe you'd give me a lift back to hall. I need to get changed. It's only a mile away. You can take it from there."

"Where are you staying?"

"Fairchild."

"In that case you can have a lift," she said. "That's where I'm staying too."

"Oh thanks, I'm honoured. But since I'm driving I figured I would go where I liked." He smiled. "Are you a fresher, then?"

"Yes. And no." She said nothing more and he sensed it would be unwise to push it. For the next few minutes there was a semi-uncomfortable silence, semi because he suddenly felt uncomfortable but she did not seem to be so. As they approached the Fairchild Hall of Residence she reached for her bag and drew out a cheque book.

"Do you mind if I post-date it? I haven't managed to cash my grant yet?"

"Sorry?"

"Your books. How much were they?"

"Hey, don't be silly. It was my fault. I shouldn't have left them on the roof. Besides, if I clean them up a bit and dry them out I might still be able to use them. At least they'll look well worn."

"But it's all my fault," she insisted. "If you hadn't stopped to help me they'd still be in one piece. At least let me pay half."

"I won't hear of it. End of subject." He pulled the Ford up in the residence car park and switched off the ignition. An idea suddenly occurred to him and he vocalised it before he had time to realise how it sounded.

"There is one thing you can do. Meet me for dinner later this evening."

She seemed surprised at this, even shocked. He initially thought she was going to turn his offer down flat and he mentally kicked himself for being so direct.

"But I don't even know your name," she said.

He held out his hand. "Howard. Howard Robinson."

She hesitated for a moment and then took it.

"Tonight," she said. "And my name's Melissa."

8

Melissa had still to register her courses and sort out some problem with transferring her bank account so Howard arranged to meet her on campus towards the end of the afternoon. He knew he was taking a chance committing the whole evening to a complete stranger but the alternatives were to stay in alone or attend one of the freshers' balls. He could not contemplate the former since he had spent virtually the whole summer out of touch with the human race. The balls, on the other hand, were tried, tested and loathed. What he needed was a gentle reintroduction to civilisation and perhaps Melissa could provide it. It was a risk but he had not realised the full extent of the risk until it was far too late to undo or regret his decision.

When he arrived at the shopping plaza she was already waiting.

She smiled as he approached and he almost stopped short at the warmth which her whole face conveyed with this new expression.

In defiance of the rain she had simply swapped one summer dress for another and there was no sign of either a raincoat or an umbrella amongst her belongings. Her hair, now dry, was lighter and more voluminous than he had remembered and cascaded natural curls about her face and shoulders, exhibiting both order and chaos in perfect balance. She also appeared to be more relaxed than on their previous, flustered encounter and it was difficult to imagine that this milder, more feminine persona could have been responsible for the foul temper he had witnessed earlier. The combined effect of all these changes caught him off balance and made him decidedly uneasy, so much so he did not even realise that she had begun speaking.

"Hi. Did you manage to fix your books?"

"Sorry?"

"I said did you manage to repair your books?"

"I think so," he said. "I cleaned them up as best I could but I won't know how badly they're damaged until I get them dried. I've left them on a shelf over the radiator. If you put them straight on top the pages might curl."

"Really." Her tone revealed mocked disinterest and Howard mentally kicked himself. He did not want to give her the impression that he was dull and lines like that were not going to help. He just did not know what else to say. She vaguely drew his attention to the many bags around her feet and there was an unspoken hint that he might help her carry them. As she bent down to pick them up, however, a number of papers fell from her arms, some of which were carried off by the breeze.

"Oh no." She stood upright and ran her fingers through her hair in the same way she had that morning - as if she expected to solve her problem by tearing half of it out.

Immediately, she was a helpless, flustered fresher again and Howard relaxed. He set about helping her gather up the papers and shortly returned with a bundle of loose leaves, out of sequence.

He examined the top sheet curiously.

" '...and in these cases, where the subject has claimed to be the reincarnation, or to be possessed by the reincarnated soul, of a former living person much like themselves, it has so far proved impossible to diagnose any form of psychological disorder. And so the question remains...' This sounds interesting. What's it for?"

"Oh, just a bit of light reading for a project. Don't ask me anything because I don't know much about it yet." He began to ask her about it. Surprisingly, she just smiled, provided him with the briefest of explanations and then dried up.

"I'm just going to examine some case evidence and see if I can draw any conclusions. I might not be experienced enough to say whether it's a form of insanity but I should be able to show whether or not their claims are backed up by documentary evidence. Ask me again when I've read a bit more." He shrugged, handed her the papers and took half of her shopping.

Suddenly, conversation was very much easier and they began strolling aimlessly across the campus while Howard pointed out each building of interest and provided her with a short monologue on university life. They eventually reached her car and off-loaded the shopping.

"Are you hungry?" she said.

"I take it you are."

"Starving. I missed lunch."

"Good - because I know just the place."

They ate in a small Italian restaurant close to the campus. Since it was early in the evening, found they had the place to themselves.

"I only discovered this bistro mid-way through last year," Howard explained, "which is a shame because not only is the food good but it's also extremely cheap. It helps the grant go a bit further."

"Is it always so popular? I don't like being outnumbered by the staff. They always flock round you in droves hoping you'll leave an extra big tip."

"Don't worry, it'll get busy later on. If we'd come here after eight you would probably have complained about the poor service. It sometimes gets a bit slow when they're full."

A waiter came and took their order. He hovered round the table, tempting them with wines and a variety of side dishes and then disappeared.

"So," Howard began. "Why don't I start with the traditional fresher's day question: what's your name, where do you come from and why are you here? You'll inevitably be asked the same thing a thousand times tonight so you may as well practise your reply on me."

She smiled. "At my last university the student's union tried to relieve the monotony by selling T-shirts specially printed with the answers." She drew a finger across her chest.

"A: Melissa, B: Cheshire, C: English. I almost bought one but it seemed too crass and I believe they fell to bits after only a week. Anyway, it didn't really change anything. The questions were the same, it was just the format that changed; 'So, your name's Melissa', 'So, you're from

Cheshire. Nice cheese.' I guess it's just something we have to put up with. Besides, it provides the perfect excuse to chat someone up."

"Like who?" Howard said, rather too quickly.

"I don't know. I haven't met anyone yet."

Howard picked up his fork, juggled it around and then placed it back on the table.

"So, you're studying English?"

"Psychology."

"I thought you said English."

"I did. I switched to Psychology. You didn't think I'd be doing a project on reincarnation for an English degree, did you?"

"It's not as stupid as it sounds. I've heard worse. They get up to all kinds of weird stuff in the English faculty."

Howard did not really know whether the idea had been stupid or not. To be honest he had not even made the connection but she was still laughing and he thought it unwise to try and defend himself any further.

"You switched universities and courses? Sounds a bit drastic. What went wrong?" It suddenly occurred to Howard that they had spent almost an hour and a half together during the day and yet he knew absolutely nothing about her. The abruptness of her reply reminded him why.

"I just fancied doing something different," she said and then very unsubtly changed the subject. "What about you? Have you never thought of switching over the last two years?"

"I never thought of switching universities or about packing it all in but I guess I toyed with the idea of changing courses in the first year. Not seriously though. I suppose it must have passed through everybody's mind at some time. The first term was so boring."

"Does it get better then? I hated history at school and I couldn't see how I could ever be excited by it. I think the past is best left dead and buried. There doesn't seem to be much point in digging it all up." Objectively, this seemed a strange thing to say but Howard was caught more by the tone in which she had said it than the words themselves. It was as though she had not been talking about history at all per se but about something else - perhaps herself. He casually reminded her that digging up the past was the only way she was going to complete her own project but did not wait for a reply.

"History isn't like that at this level. It's more interesting when you can do your own thing instead of just learning dates and facts. Most of this year is taken up with a dissertation so it shouldn't be so bad - provided you make the right choice of subject. Besides, I think you can find something of interest in everything if you get into it deeply enough."

"Perhaps, but I would rather be able to study the future. Don't you think it would be fascinating to go forward in time and see what happens?"

"Not really. I think it's more likely to be depressing. If we haven't blown the planet to pieces by the end of our generation then we'll probably have plundered all of its resources and left behind a toxic wasteland in which the human race can slowly decompose. Besides, if you knew what was going to happen you'd have nothing to get excited about."

Melissa suddenly sat up as if about to deliver a philosophical treatise on why he was wrong when the waiter arrived with their order. By the time he had left, the moment had been lost. For a few seconds she examined the contents of her pizza looking for inspiration but it never came.

"What is your dissertation on?"

At first he was disappointed that she had chosen not to challenge him. He hated trivial conversation and had deliberately gone over the top to bait her - to get her to engage in a serious subject. But something told him that he was to have no choice in the matter, at least not on this occasion. Besides, she now had a mouthful of pizza and was incapable of delivering anything but a shower of food.

"I'm studying the American preoccupation with the appropriation of British historical artefacts."

"Oh, you too. My grandmother is always going on about that. Apparently there was a very interesting article in Woman's Own last week."

He smiled. "Basically, I'm exploring and examining the reasons why Americans continually want to obtain bits of our history, specifically larger structures such as buildings and bridges."

"Why should their motives for buying historical artefacts be any different from their motives for buying anything else? They just believe they can purchase anything if the price is right? It's a society which revolves around money. If they can buy war and peace just by waving a big chequebook what is to stop them buying history? It's just another commodity - like pork bellies."

"Don't you like Americans?"

"Not really. They're brash, superficial and uncultured."

She spoke as though she were describing the growing mound of olives at the side of her plate but he was not sure whether she was being serious or not.

"If you feel very strongly about something you shouldn't keep it all bottled up inside. It sometimes helps if you make the odd sweeping generalisation or so."

"Of course it does," she agreed. "I get the same kick out of cramming a quarter of a billion people into a pigeon-hole as I do when I manage to get all my underwear to fit into the washing machine. Except that my underwear always comes out clean."

He suddenly realised she was playing with him – just as he had been trying to bait her a moment before. "You're trying to wind me up, aren't you?"

"No, I am winding you up - just to show you that two can play at starting an argument. It's also revenge for this morning." She grinned victoriously and took another bite of pizza.

"Why? I helped you get your car started, didn't I?"

"Not without patronising me and having a quiet laugh to yourself afterwards you didn't."

"I did no such thing. I had more important things to think about, like rescuing almost a hundred pounds worth of books from an attempted assassination attempt by your car - if you can call it a car."

"What do you mean? What's wrong with my car?"

"It's brash, superficial and uncultured." That was supposed to be the touché reply but he was not to be allowed such a victory so easily. For several seconds she was silent, watching him closely. And as the smile began to cross his lips he felt the full force of her right foot crash into his shin. Above the table her expression remained unaltered but, as her foot made contact with his leg, she simultaneously snapped a breadstick into two clean halves.

"No one likes a cleverdick," she said, simply. Ignoring his pained expression she continued talking as if nothing had happened. "Actually, I do like Americans but we always get the worst kind wandering round my home village. You know the type I mean. The ones who always wear checked trousers and carry golf umbrellas and who seem to have cameras permanently attached and peer from behind the lenses and say things like

'Oh, honey, that cottage is just so cute. Let's take it back to South Carolina.' I once heard somebody say that. I wanted to kick them, too."

"Yeah, I know what you mean. Incidentally, where is home? You said Cheshire."

"That's right, near Alderley Edge." She saw his eyes widen. "Why? Do you know it?"

"Of course. I used to go there all the time as a child. It's hardly a village, though."

"Maybe not," she conceded, "but I like to think of it that way. I haven't lived there long and it's much smaller than the town I came from."

"Where was that?"

"Oh, it was down south."

"Which town?" he persisted.

She hesitated, as though trying to remember. "Bath."

"Bath is a city."

"Is it? That explains why it's bigger."

"Is that where you went to university?"

"Yes," she acknowledged. "But I wasn't really happy there and when we moved house it seemed an appropriate time to switch."

"Why weren't you happy?"

"Oh, nothing dramatic. I just didn't like the course."

She shrugged her shoulders and he took it as a sign that she no longer wished to pursue the conversation.

"Tell me," he said. "That American couple didn't buy the cottage, did they?"

"No, why?"

"Just wondering. As part of my dissertation I'm compiling a catalogue of all American purchases and attempted purchases of historical structures."

"Do you find that interesting?"

"More intriguing. Also there is a possibility of having my dissertation published - but it would have to be complete."

"How many are there?"

"I haven't a clue at present but I don't think there can be that many. I'll just start at London Bridge and work down from there."

As Melissa swallowed the last mouthful of pizza she became restless and seemed keen to leave.

"Shall we get the bill? After all, we don't want to miss all the fun, do we?"

If Howard had responded candidly, he would have been more than thankful to miss 'all the fun'. He had already lived through two successive freshers' balls and he found them tedious in the extreme. In fact, to miss 'all the fun' had originally been his sole intention in asking her to dinner in the first place, though he suddenly realised that his motivation had altered subtly since then. However, he did not want to be branded unsociable and he did not want Melissa to think that he was trying to monopolise her. There was always the possibility that he might enjoy it but the evening looked set to be yet another annual disappointment. He faked a smile, nodded in agreement and called for the bill. However, if he had been honest, he would have preferred to order dessert, to gaze into those soft, mysterious eyes for just an hour or so longer - and to find out why she had lied about her past.

9

Martyn finally crashed into the Chief's office one hour and forty minutes after receiving the phone call - an hour and three quarters late.

"You're late," stated Chief Lancaster. "And you're dead."

"That's twice I've been killed today already." Martyn, only half listening to the Chief, was more aware of the other man in the office; a tall, well-built, officious looking figure, dark skinned, well groomed - the sight of whom immediately made him regret his untidy appearance.

"What did you say?" asked the Chief.

"Eh? Oh, nothing," Martyn replied, absentmindedly. The Chief inspected the pitiful figure that had just walked through the door and took in every minute detail; the sweater, the jeans, the shoes, the hair.

"You haven't shaved." The silent shape in the corner looked across disapprovingly and emitted an air of being very important.

"I left in a rush. By the urgency in your voice I thought my presence was required more than my fashionable dress sense."

"Alright, cut that out!" the Chief snapped. "I don't know why, in that case, you bothered to get dressed at all." The Chief's irritable response took him by surprise. It was completely out of character. Brett Lancaster never lost his temper; he was obviously on edge. But neither was Martyn prepared for a heavy morning and he was determined to disperse the tension that hung in the office. The stranger had witnessed the outburst displaying no visible reaction.

"It's cold outside." The Chief glared at him just like his old headmaster used to, as though Martyn were a child that still had some very big lessons to learn before he could even hope to understand why the world worked the way it did. At that moment, a third voice joined in the conversation.

"Do you think we could get on with it, Chief? What we have to discuss is far more important. You can discipline your man later." He turned his attention to Martyn. "Detective Sorensen, thank you for finally deciding to turn up but, as you can see, your partner has not arrived yet. I trust the two of you manage to get to the scene of the crime with a bit more haste than you have shown this morning."

"Yes, sir," Martyn answered, opting to play safe until he found out who this character was. He decided that his best course of action would be to change the subject as soon as possible.

"Isn't such good news about Gremelkov, is it?" he ventured.

"No! It damn well isn't!" shouted the Chief. "It's a major catastrophe. I don't have anything like the resources to cope with that kind of situation." The tone of Brett's voice betrayed a disturbance he had never before seen in the Chief and Martyn assumed, logically, that the outburst was directed at the stranger as a form of protest. The stranger, however, continued to be unmoved.

So the problem was Gremelkov.

Since he had already hit on a raw nerve, Martyn decided that he may as well go the whole way and get whatever it was out in the open as soon as possible. Brett was acting as if he were about to explode and it seemed like it might not be a bad idea if he were allowed to, though he was evidently trying to show constraint in front of the third party.

"Look!" he said. "Is someone about to tell me what's going on, or do I have to waste the whole of my holiday standing here like a lemon?"

Both the Chief and the stranger appeared about to raise an objection to this abrupt statement when the door flew open and in walked Detective Robert Laurie. He was dressed a little more smartly than Martyn but, all the same, he looked as if he had left his apartment in a hurry. The Chief checked himself and turned his attention to the newcomer, repeating the same phrase that had greeted Martyn just a minute or so before.

"You're very late," he said. "And you're dead." Sergeant Robert Laurie had seemed about to apologise as he entered the office but all such signs suddenly vanished, to be replaced by an expression of curiosity and confusion. Glancing quickly around the room, he presently returned to the Chief.

"I don't get it," he said. Martyn twisted his head round to offer support.

"He said that to me and I didn't get it either." But it still did not appear that anyone was going to offer an explanation.

"Well," said the stranger. "Perhaps now we have all decided to turn up…don't apologise, Detective, we have work to do and we've wasted enough time already."

Whether Detective Laurie had been about to apologise or protest was academic. Martyn was rapidly becoming aware that the stranger was in charge of the day's proceedings. A horrible thought struck him. Maybe it wasn't just today's proceedings! What if it were for a longer term? And what was to going to happen to Brett in the meantime? The department had been under the Chief ever since Martyn had joined it six years before. He had never considered that it might one day be otherwise. At that moment, Chief Lancaster spoke.

"Okay Detective Sorensen, Detective Laurie, please take a seat." He paused while the two pulled up a couple of chairs and sat down.

"First of all, I would like to introduce you both to Commander Colchek of the Special Forces Network." Again, he paused just long enough for the two parties to acknowledge each other and then continued.

"Last night, something happened which could produce serious consequences for both the operation of the police department and the people of this city. If you managed to catch a news bulletin last night, or early this morning, you will know that a man was found dead in Eden Square. Ostensibly, he died of a heart attack. He was not that old but his health was poor and apparently he could have suffered a coronary at any time. Unfortunately for him, and for us, somebody decided that they weren't prepared to wait."

So it wasn't Gremelkov after all. It was the heart attack victim. Detective Laurie interrupted.

"Well? Who was he?"

The question was answered by the Commander.

"His name was Howard Robinson. He was a nobody – apparently the most insignificant individual you could ever hope to meet. We don't know much about him except that he came over from England at the turn of the century. Owns a small shop - a bookshop - down one of the shopping malls in Arcades. Went to church every Sunday. We don't have a file on him and he doesn't show up on any of our computers. The only motive we have for killing him is that someone either doesn't like his books or wants to rid the city of the only decent citizen we've got left."

"How did he die?" asked Martyn. For a moment, it seemed that neither the Chief nor the Commander knew whether, or how, to answer the question. It was the Commander who replied.

"He was killed by a laser beam."

There was a stunned silence and Chief Lancaster shuffled uncomfortably in his chair. Martyn swallowed hard. A slight feeling of nausea began to creep over him but he did not know why. The Commander continued.

"Pierced straight through the heart by a pencil thin beam of coherent infrared radiation. The cleanest, quietest, most efficient way of killing someone I've ever seen."

"How can you tell?" Martyn asked.

"Because it's happened before," said the Commander. The Chief leaned forward and rested his arms on the desk.

"You remember last summer; a Miss Sarjena West was found dead in Washington Park?"

"Yes, I remember; I was living near there at the time," Rob replied. "She was the girl who tried to drown her baby in the lake and then took an overdose or something, wasn't she? Officially it was suicide."

"Which was far from the truth," the Commander said. "She was actually assassinated. No reason, no motive. She owed a lot of money but it wasn't that serious."

"By a laser," Martyn said.

"By a laser," Commander Colchek confirmed. "We spent a week on the autopsy and had to bring in specialists from Europe. In the end, there wasn't any doubt. Last night, Howard Robinson was killed in exactly the same way."

"But I didn't even know such weapons existed. I thought they were still at the development stage," Martyn said.

"In this country they are," replied the Commander. "That's what makes this problem a little more delicate than would normally be the case. In point of fact, according to our intelligence, there is only one place you *might* be able to get a laser gun and that's in the prototype laboratories of the Communist Alliance's headquarters. We are all set to catch up shortly. At present though, if there were a laser weapon available in this country, we would know about it."

Martyn didn't quite follow. "But from what you've just said, there is a laser weapon on the loose in this country and, with all due respect, you don't seem to know much about it."

"Which means that it must have originated from the East. That's the only possible answer."

"So why are they taking pot-shots at seemingly innocent people?" asked Detective Laurie.

"If we knew that, we would probably also know who was behind it," the Commander said. "But I'm convinced that it came from the Alliance countries. If the weapon was developed here than it really wouldn't make sense. There are millions of dollars to be made out of a product like that before you even talk about using it as a weapon. And even then, the military would pay a fortune for it. The laser rifle is not just a new weapon; if it does exist it symbolises the one and only technical imbalance between East and West and I don't need to remind you just how tentative that situation is. They've got one and we haven't. It's as simple as that. It might seem a small thing to you but if this nation developed a working prototype that could be used in the field, then the whole political stability of the world would be a lot less volatile."

"Until they made more than us," muttered Martyn, hearing Melissa's own cynicism of that morning creeping into his voice. There was a brief silence while the full implications of the previous night's murder began to sink in. The political stability of the world? Martyn began to feel ever so slightly out of his depth. Usually, he just tracked down murderers and drug dealers.

"Presumably you made some investigations after the death of the girl last summer. Didn't they reveal anything?"

"Not a thing," said the Commander. "The investigations are still going on and so far we haven't come up with even the slightest clue. We naturally kept the whole thing quiet and hoped it would all be cleared up fairly quickly. I mean, you can't walk round the streets carrying a laser rifle without somebody noticing something. So we kept it low key to avoid the inevitable panic and tried to do it ourselves. But we've found nothing. Absolutely nothing."

"Yet," said Martyn. "Until today there hasn't been another incident. Might that suggest that you may have been sniffing in the right area? It seems to me somebody might have been lying low for a bit."

Detective Laurie looked up. "Maybe it takes that long for the batteries to recharge." The comment was ignored and the Commander continued.

"I don't even know if we're talking about the same murderer. For all I know, there might be several of these things on the streets. We might just be seeing the start of a major epidemic of laser killings by all sorts of insane people. Who knows?"

There was another short silence. Again, Martyn came to the point, echoing the thoughts of both Detective Laurie and himself.

"So where do we come in?"

The Commander shuffled slightly and assumed a position not unlike that of a man just about to play his winning card. Then he spoke, slowly, deliberately.

"The Special Forces Network moves around in different circles to urban police officers such as yourselves. We deal with foreign matters, matters of a delicate diplomatic nature. We are involved with the powerful, the rich, the politically immune, those people whom an ordinary police department cannot touch because the law and all its various loopholes dictate it that way. The Special Forces Network is, if you like, the government arm of the police force or, as some would have it, the police arm of the government. It makes no difference.

"So far, our investigations into the death of Miss West, and our search for the owner of the laser weapon, have been conducted within those circles. I am convinced that the weapon has originated from somewhere in the Communist Alliance and it was not unreasonable, therefore, to assume that it - or they - have been brought into the country under diplomatic cover. However, as I stated before, our investigations have drawn a blank. Though we will continue to follow up our own lines of enquiry, I now recognise that we must open up new avenues and draw part of our attention, at least, to the street, especially in the light of last night's murder. And that, Detectives, is where you come in."

"Why us?" asked Martyn.

"Because we want the best. The department was very impressed with the way you handled the Dortman case. It was a clean, professional operation and we are looking for exactly the same approach here. We need a team who know the streets, have the contacts and can carry out an extensive, painstaking investigation without any cock-ups and without leaving any stone unturned. I want that murderer brought to justice." The Commander paused and then, seemingly as an afterthought, he added, "And we must get hold of that weapon."

At this point, the Chief interjected and proceeded to conclude the briefing.

"Detectives Sorensen, Laurie, you will drop all other cases and devote all your time to this one. I want you to get out there and question everyone you know. Don't miss a trick. If that laser rifle and the person responsible for those murders are out there, I want them found and brought in. Both of them. And I want it done fast. Until we have made some satisfactory headway with this investigation, all leave for both of you is cancelled."

At this last statement, Martyn felt as if salt had been poured onto an open wound and had to push back a small wave of resentment. For whatever reason, probably external pressure, Brett Lancaster was taking a very hard line with this case and, from that point of view, Martyn did not think it was going to be an easy investigation. In Martyn's opinion, each case naturally dictated its own terms in respect of the amount of time that had to be spent on it. There was never any need for the Chief to allocate time to an investigation; it would always happen on its own.

"There are just three further points I would like to make before you go," the Chief said, his tone softening slightly. "First of all I want you to remember that we have not dealt with anything like this before. Lasers are lethal and silent. No clicks, no bangs, nothing. From now on, you have to be twice as careful or you can be taken out as easily as walking into a room. Somewhere out there, in this God-forsaken city, is such a room. Find it, but don't get killed walking into it. Be very, very careful." As he spoke, he gestured towards the door of his office and both men immediately understood the Chief's earlier greeting, but his double emphasis had an almost melodramatic ring to it.

"Second. Focus on motive. If we can find out why West and Robinson were killed then I think we'll crack the case quickly." At this Commander Colchek glared at the Chief as if he had strayed from his brief but the Chief continued undeterred.

"Third. Your investigations are to be thorough but discrete. Don't mention the word 'laser' or we'll have a panic on our hands. I have here a written copy of your brief which contains the autopsy report on Miss West and all other information relevant to the case. There's a copy for each of you. Read it before you do anything else and then find me that laser rifle. You will report directly to me and I will report to Commander Colchek. Any questions?"

There was a brief silence and then Martyn spoke. "Haven't you forgotten something, Chief?"

"What?"

"The news bulletin? It would appear that someone already does know something."

The Chief frowned. "That's my problem," he snapped. "If the news does break, at least I can say that I've got one of my best teams working on it. Now get out of here and *start* working on it."

"Yes, sir."

"Yes, sir." The two men rose, nodded briefly to Commander Colchek, and then left the office, reports in hand. As the door closed the Chief made one final parting comment.

"And for goodness sake tidy yourselves up a bit."

Back in the mêlée of the open plan office which lay outside the Chief's, everything appeared normal and both men could relax a little. Detective Laurie was the first to speak.

"Grief! I've never seen the Chief so crabby and that Commander Colchek was something else. 'Perhaps now we've all decided to turn up...' Who the hell does he think he is?"

"Perhaps," suggested Martyn, "he's even more important than we've both realised. Anybody who can get the Chief worked up like that must have some strings to pull. Listen Rob, I don't know about you but I'm tired, extremely pissed off and very hungry. Let's take these reports down to Angelo's and try and unwind a bit. It's not exactly what the Chief meant when he told us to hit the streets, but I'm going to be useless until I've got some breakfast inside me."

"Well," replied Rob, grinning, "being as conscientious as I normally am, I shouldn't allow it, but as usual you've won me over with that watertight logic of yours. Let's go."

They left the office and made for the elevators which would take them down to the street level, four floors below.

"Say, what's all this stuff about the media already knowing there's a laser assassin on the loose?" asked Rob.

Martyn reached the elevator first, pressed the call button and then turned to answer his partner in his most patronising tone.

"Don't you ever watch the news?"

"Of course I do," defended Rob. "Well, sometimes. Why? What did they say?"

"It's alright, I was only joking. I didn't see it either."

"See what?"

"Well, you know about as much as I do. Think about it. Last night, the network ran a news item on this Robinson guy. When was the last time you ever heard of a heart attack case making the network news? Melissa summed it up in a nut shell. It wasn't worth mentioning. But for some reason they did. And that means that Brett is in a dilemma. If he gets in touch with the network and asks why they ran the story - and they don't know anything - then he is going to make them suspicious. You know what these reporters are like. Once you've aroused their suspicions about something, they won't let go until they've uncovered every last detail. From knowing absolutely nothing, they might suddenly find themselves with the story of the century overnight and start transmitting all sorts of horrific speculations about laser assassinations and the new wave of crime and so on. The number of slants you could run a story like that with is endless but the result will be just the same. Panic.

"On the other hand, suppose they do know something. The last thing we want is for them to tell everybody else. Even if Brett did contact the station and ask them not to run the story, I doubt they'd listen. If anything it would just give them even more fuel for their fire and result in an even bigger panic."

The elevator arrived and they climbed in. Rob hit the ground floor button and leant back against the side panel.

"And you know what they'll say, don't you? That the public had the right to know and that they were only doing their job blah blah blah. Even if all hell is let loose. In this case there is one consolation, though. At least with lasers we're unlikely to get any copycat murders."

"Alright," Rob said. "So you've given me the alternatives. You're usually pretty good with this speculation lark. What do you think they're up to?"

"I don't know but I reckon it could be only be one of two things." As Martyn replied, the digital display above their heads suddenly flashed up a bright orange "G" and the doors opened.

"Either they know everything and they're just playing with us, or they've heard some sort of rumour and are hoping that we'll rise to the bait and give the game away. If I had to choose between the two, I'd naturally go for the latter. Either way, I think the Chief will keep quiet and see what happens. If he tries to stop the story going out he'll just end up in hot water. They can't criticise him for not informing them of police operations. It isn't part of his duty by any means. But if he deliberately goes out of his way to shut them up, they'll most likely drag his name through the gutter. I really don't envy his position."

As they left the police department building and entered the clammy, fog-enveloped street, another thought struck Rob.

"But supposing they ran the story as a heart attack to try and warn us that they would go ahead with the truth if we didn't do anything to try and stop them. Maybe they were giving us the right of veto."

"I already thought of that," Martyn replied. "But I don't think that would make sense on its own – it's too cloak and dagger for a news agency. Firstly, why don't they just telephone the Chief, tell him they know everything and ask him if its okay to run the story? There's really nothing to stop them. Secondly, you are making the assumption that the network reporters and controllers are really quite a decent bunch, deep down inside, and we already know that isn't true. No, I reckon they're on to something but they're not sure what, so they've laid a trap for us. Tonight, they will either run the whole story in whatever exaggerated form they choose, or they will let it drop. I just hope they don't do anything stupid or it will make our position even more uncomfortable. Whatever happens, remember we're now in the middle."

10

Once outside the police department, the chilled air drove both men into silent contemplation, each seeking the introspective solitude of his own thoughts. Martyn had suddenly become concerned. The logical progression of his argument had brought about the creation of a more disturbing idea. Now he was toying mentally with the possible consequences and trying to untangle the permutations that followed. By his partner's apparent quiescence, he assumed that Rob was either digesting the preceding conversation or perhaps drawing the same conclusions as himself. Possibly, he was just echoing Martyn's own quietness, and the stillness of the fog draped around them.

As Martyn had learned, painfully, his tendency towards introspection when trying to work on a problem was not always appreciated by his colleagues. For that reason, Rob had become an ideal partner. Though he was far more comfortable making a noise, Rob had adjusted quickly to this new relationship and always seemed to know when to be quiet. Unlike his other partners, Rob had grown to respect his silence, and to anticipate the period of action that often followed. But that did not prevent him from becoming irritated occasionally, and Martyn would frequently be accused of living in a world of his own, though he was more often endorsed for the results that his long silences generated. For that reason, he could justify it - at least to himself. Even Rob seemed impressed by his assessment of the current situation though, as usual, he chose to hide it in sarcasm.

"If this is what going without breakfast does for you, maybe you ought to miss it everyday."

Brushing the fog aside with one hand, he took two quick steps ahead and turned so that he was walking backwards, facing his partner. "However, if you have anything else to say, would you mind telling me now as I would prefer not to discuss work while I'm eating breakfast; it makes me crabby. Once we get to Angelo's, I would like to give my brain a rest for a few minutes, so speak now or forever…"

They walked in silence for the remainder of the journey and entered Angelo's Bistro about five minutes later. Once inside, they quickly found a table in a quiet corner and sat down. Rob began searching for Angelo.

"There is one other thing."

"Not now, Martyn. Can't it wait? I'm relaxing." Rob slumped back in his chair, stretching his arms wide. "Look, this is me, relaxing."

"They must be getting inside information," Martyn said.

"Oh, come on! You're letting your imagination run away with you. Let's forget all about it for a few minutes, get something to eat and then we'll discuss it. You'll think much more rationally when you've got some food inside you. You'll see."

But Martyn was not about to let the matter drop. "How many people do you think know that Howard Robinson was killed with a laser rifle?" he persisted. "There's the autopsy team, Commander Colchek, maybe a couple more people from Special Forces, the Chief, you and me. That's all."

"I'm not listening to this," Rob replied, and once more began looking round the bistro for Angelo. "Look. This is me not listening to you," he said, and continued to gaze randomly in all directions. Eventually, Angelo appeared from behind a large indoor palm and strolled over to their table, a wide grin monopolising the whole of his face.

"Good morning, Señores. Rough night?"

"What?" Martyn said, absentmindedly.

"The hair, the clothes, the personal hygiene," Angelo gibbered, pointing to each in turn and purposely raising his voice to draw attention to the three of them. "You both look like you fell out the wrong side of bed. You are making my restaurant, my palace of gastronomic delights, look like a shelter for vagrants. You will lose me customers, yes? People do not like to eat with the animals. They want style, cleanliness, class. They will not eat with riffraff. Today, you are looking like riffraff, yes?"

"Palace of gastronomic delights!" laughed Rob. "You're kidding! This is nothing but a souped-up burger bar with plastic trees. And anyway, we are a better class of customer. Like you said, we had a rough night."

"Plastic trees!" shouted Angelo. "Plastic trees! These trees have been specially imported from Jamaica." His voice was now raised so that the whole bistro could hear. "Specially imported from Jamaica," he repeated. "How dare you insult my trees! You, who are nothing but riffraff in my haven of idyllic cuisine."

Sometimes, Angelo could be a real pain in the backside, Martyn thought. For all that, Angelo never changed. No matter what, he was always the same, and it was impossible to tell whether he was being serious or not. He always appeared to wear an earnest frown but his comments ranged from the comic to the ridiculous. Yet he could always depend on Angelo being Angelo. He was one of life's little constants, like sunrise or Mondays. The fact that he was somewhat irritating on occasions depended entirely on the mood of the receiver of his melodramatic remarks. Angelo never changed.

"Angelo?" Rob said. "Do you think you could take our order and get the food? We're very hungry and very tired. I don't even care if the food we get isn't the same as the food we order. Just get us something to eat fast."

Angelo took out a small notepad from his breast pocket and removed a short pencil from behind his ear.

"Two specials," he said, scribbling it down. "And to drink, sirs?"

"Coffee," said Rob.

"Orange juice," said Martyn.

"Will that be fresh orange juice or orange nectar?" asked Angelo, deliberately emphasising the latter.

"Quick orange juice," Martyn replied, gazing aimlessly across the bistro. Angelo evidently managed to interpret this last statement, made a brief note on his pad and then disappeared. Being pressured into silence by Rob, Martyn became quiet and thoughtful for a minute and then picked up his copy of the report and began reading. After a further two minutes and a lot of page turning, he spoke.

"According to this, there should only be ten people who have any inkling whatsoever that Howard Robinson was killed by a laser beam. They've really kept this one under their hats so far."

"I haven't eaten yet."

"Just thinking out loud."

"Well, would you mind keeping your thoughts to yourself. Come on, Martyn. You don't even know if the network has got hold of this story yet and you've already produced a shortlist of possible moles. At this rate you'll be arresting yourself before the food arrives. Listen, you've made an assumption. It sounded pretty logical to me and I'm almost willing to bet that you're right. But for goodness sake don't go jumping the gun. Any progress you make now can only be based on that assumption and it may well turn out to be wrong. And if you are wrong, you'll feel a right idiot when you realise that you could have spent this last ten minutes catching up on some well earned rest instead of driving your brain round and round in circles for nothing."

Martyn smiled. "I thought you didn't want to talk about it." Rob, realising he'd been sucked in, glared at his partner and lapsed into silence. Presently, Martyn spoke again, more quietly.

"Suppose I'm right, no matter how far fetched it may seem or how premature. All of the people in this report are ranks above us. Now don't you think that, under those circumstances, it would be wiser to be one step ahead rather than one behind?"

Whether Rob thought so or not, he did not say, but the frown that developed across his forehead showed that he was contemplating what Martyn had said. Seconds later, Angelo reappeared with two "specials", one coffee and a bright orange drink in crushed ice which Martyn deduced to be the aforementioned nectar. The special turned out to be a savoury pancake with some combination of minced beef and vegetable filling, utterly indefinable by sight but unexpectedly tasty.

"Cheers Angelo," greeted Rob. "Say, won't you sit down for a minute? There's something I'd like to ask you."

Angelo looked wary for a moment and then sat down furtively. "It is not good for me to be seen with riffraff," he said. "It gives a bad impression for the customers."

"Alright Angelo," said Martyn. "We appreciate it and we promise to wear jackets and ties next time. But we did have another reason for coming here. What's the latest word on the grapevine?"

"Preferably not the plastic one," added Rob.

"Ha ha, very funny," said Angelo, and immediately turned his back on Rob and directed his answer to Martyn only. It had been Angelo's talents as a source of information, and not those of his cooking, that had first prompted them to frequent the bistro. They had been eating there regularly ever since. In a perverse act of defiance, the local Mafia had adopted Angelo's as their chosen haunt, specifically because it was frequented by the police. Similarly, Angelo was not a typical informant - he just talked to anyone about anything. Whatever he was told, whatever he overheard. The Mafia almost certainly knew Angelo could not be trusted so they used him either to brag or to pass on false information. Likewise the police. This, though, was not why Martyn came to Angelo's. Using a restaurant as an exchange for lies seemed pretty pointless. What the local underworld did not seem to have figured out, however, was that other informers could use Angelo as a channel of communication while maintaining anonymity. It was this grapevine that he was interested in.

"I am a busy man, Senor Sorensen. This is Angelo's Bistro. Angelo must work very hard to stay in business. He has no time to listen to idle gossip."

"This wouldn't be idle gossip, Angelo. This would be significant. Have you heard anything? Anything at all?"

"I have heard nothing," Angelo replied. "Mamma mia. I must not be seen with you any more. It will ruin my reputation." He stood up to leave. Martyn stood also.

"Keep your ears open, Angelo. You know where to find us." His voice was quiet and deeply sincere.

"Okay," Angelo agreed, and returned to the kitchens.

"Mamma mia?" said Rob. "He isn't Italian, is he?"

"Hell knows."

"Do you think he knew anything?"

"I don't think so. I think he genuinely does believe that we are going to scare his customers away if we don't shave in the morning. You never know, he might be right."

Walking back to the department, Rob finally returned to the subject in question.

"Any more great thoughts?" he asked. "I think I could handle them now."

"No more thoughts."

"So what do you want to do with the rest of the day? We seem to be in no man's land at the minute. I mean, how the hell can we look for a laser rifle without being able to mention the word 'laser' to anyone? It's crazy. I almost hope the story does break. It'll make our job a lot easier and at least everyone will know what we're talking about."

"That's probably the first constructive thing you've said all morning. And I think you're right. We should play for time today. Read the reports this morning, which probably won't tell us anything, and then check out Robinson's place this afternoon, which I don't think is going to tell us anything either. We need something else to happen."

"Sounds great," said Rob. "Especially coming from someone who wants to keep one step ahead." Martyn smiled. His partner liked to play the fool but he could sometimes be very sharp. He'd left himself wide open for that one, he thought.

They walked back to the office in silence, almost repeating the contemplative journey down to the bistro but in reverse. As they reached the end of the street on which the police department stood, Rob stopped and turned towards him.

"So what do you really think this is all about?" he asked. "I mean, really."

Martyn also stopped but continued to stare into the fog ahead of him as if searching for his answer in the opaque air. Presently, he spoke.

"I don't know. But I've got a bad feeling about this."

11

Martyn had been right about the usefulness of the report and it seemed he was equally correct about the amount of valid information to be obtained at Howard Robinson's apartment. Not that there was no information; the whole place was crammed with a wide variety of books and magazines, stacked on bright red aluminium shelving from floor to ceiling. In the room in which he and Rob were standing, the shelving extended around all four of the walls, with the exception of the doorway, a pair of French windows leading to the third storey balcony, an ornamental stone fire place and one corner occupied by a giant rubber plant. About half a dozen other plants were scattered liberally between the rows of books. At random, Martyn pulled out a paperback from one of the shelves.

"Stranger In A Strange Land", he read aloud.

"Seems like that's what he was," Rob said, without looking round. "Nobody has this many books. Hardly any of my friends have books, period. He must have been living in the middle ages. This is more well stocked than the city library."

"Yeah," Martyn replied, thoughtfully Blowing the dust from the top of the paperback, he placed it back on the shelf.

On their return from Angelo's, they had been intercepted in the lobby of the department by two Special Forces officers, in plain clothes, and escorted to their office suite on the fourth floor. In their absence, the office opposite the Chief's had been vacated and re-furnished with their own desks and stacks of files. The evicted Captain was standing in the resulting space in the open plan area, his desk and files thoughtlessly scattered about him. While he tried to appear composed, as if mentally organising his new territory into some semblance of order, he was visibly shocked at being thrown out of his office.

A silent wall of eyes watched their reappearance with interest and the geographically deposed Captain gazed intently at them in search of an explanation, to which Martyn could only shrug his shoulders. The two SFN officers hastily ushered them through the open plan area to their new domain, allowing them to speak to nobody. Immediately, the Chief appeared.

"Until this investigation has reached a satisfactory conclusion, or until such time as it makes no difference, I want you both in here where I can keep an eye on you and where you won't be disturbed. I don't want any of the others to know what is going on until it becomes necessary." He indicated the piles of case notes around the room. "You will no longer be responsible for any of these so they don't belong in here. Find alternative homes for them by lunchtime." He left, taking the two SFN men with him.

Under his breath, Martyn said, "And I love you too."

Rob examined his own mountain of documents. Seemingly at random, he picked up a single sheet of paper, screwed it up into a small ball and tossed it into the waste paper basket.

"Well, that's a start." He began to drag his desk into the far corner of the room. "I don't get it. Does this mean we've been promoted?"

The remainder of the morning was spent fruitlessly sorting through the reams of files and passing on existing cases to colleagues. They, in turn, insisted on knowing what was going on and would not accept the silence of confidentiality as an answer, which only made the whole process even more laborious and time consuming than it should have been.

Throughout the morning Chief Lancaster's office was inundated with so many visitors that Martyn began to think he only knew fractionally more than anybody else. All of the visitors were unfamiliar and most had walked straight into the office without knocking and without exchanging a word with anyone. At no time did the Chief appear. With each new arrival, Martyn would stop what he was doing, sometimes in mid sentence, and scrutinise the figure from across the open plan area, hoping for some clue to their identity or some indication of the significance, seriousness or consequence of their visit.

After two hours, and with only one case left to dispose of, he was still none the wiser and was beginning to feel uneasy. The steady stream of people in and out of the Chief's office continued, spaced at intervals of approximately ten minutes, and Brett Lancaster himself had yet to make an appearance. To make matters worse, apprehension was beginning to permeate the department, infecting all around him, and the atmosphere had soon become distinctly tense and uncomfortable. Forcing his eyes away from the Chief's office, he picked up the last file and looked around for someone to delegate to, just as Rob returned, empty handed.

"Well, that's the lot. How many have you got left?"

"Only the one, and that shouldn't be too much of a problem. Now where's my old partner disappeared to? I can't let him get away with this."

"He's on the next floor but I wouldn't..."

Martyn did not catch the end of the sentence; he was already on his way to the stairwell. He did not see much of Andy Holland anymore. Since their partnership had been dissolved over a year before, when Rob had first joined the department, he rarely crossed paths with his old partner. Martyn and Rob worked mainly on drugs while Andy had been assigned to homicide. It was not always possible to separate the two, since the majority of homicides were drug- or syndicate-related, but when they did not bump into each other, they would occasionally touch base over dinner.

Andy believed very strongly in the philosophy that a partnership in homicide was a bond for life; the many horrors of death would eventually take their toll on the most robust sanity if not diluted by sharing them with a partner. They had worked together for almost two years and in that time had formed an emotional union that neither of them would admit to openly but which, for Martyn, would make it all the more difficult to keep the confidentiality of this new case. He did not expect his old partner to take a simple 'no' for an answer, especially if he was expected, in turn, to take the last case file off his hands.

On the next floor, in the homicide open plan office, a duplicate of the layout below, Martyn was surprised to find the atmosphere equally tense. By coincidence, Andy Holland's desk occupied the space directly above his own, or where his own had been until breakfast time. Though he was sensitive to the tension, he did not give it any other thought and strode over to the desk where his old partner was sitting, deeply engrossed in his own thoughts. With a brief explanation, now well rehearsed, he placed the file in the only tray in the department that was not already full.

"I've saved you the best one for old time's sake. Give you a chance to keep your hand in since we don't see you around narcotics much these days. It's pretty straightforward. The drop's being made at seven on Monday and I want to make sure that it's the last deal the scumbag ever makes. Come Tuesday morning, he'll be off the streets for good and it'll be one less dealer we have to worry about."

"Oh, great!" the sergeant replied, almost hysterically. "Come Tuesday morning, I'll probably be off the streets for good too. What are you trying to do to me? You want me dockside at seven to break up a drugs ring, your partner wants me downtown at eight to expose a prostitution racket and the next morning I'm supposed to be handing in a fully detailed report on why a simple, straightforward supermarket robbery turned into a multiple homicide bloodbath."

Martyn stopped short.

"I don't get it. When was that?"

"Hell, Martyn, where have you been? It'll be all over the papers this evening."

Martyn could only return a blank stare.

"I've had a few problems and I'm also not allowed to talk to anybody. I haven't heard anything about a bloodbath. What happened?"

"Early this morning; down in the Wilson district. They opened up with everything they had. As soon as we arrived. No warning. Nothing."

Martyn lowered his voice to a near whisper.

"How many casualties?"

"Seven," he replied. "All women and children. Three dead, two serious."

"Shit! And they got away?"

Andy looked at him and, as an agonised look of despair crossed his partner's face, Martyn realised he had touched the raw nerve.

"Martyn, I learned a hard lesson this morning. In fog like this, everyone gets away." He swallowed hard. "And if they accidentally stumble across someone in the process they don't ask questions. They just shoot."

"Hey Andy, I'm sorry. I didn't know. Damn! I've been in this place for over two hours now and I didn't know. Nobody has said a thing." He pulled up a chair and sat down.

"It would have happened to any of us, you know that. We've never had fog like this before. I never even gave it a thought."

"Yeah, well learn from me. It's the only damn productive thing that's going to come out of all this. Martyn, tell me, how do you tell someone that his wife and kids are dead because the police have never seen fog before?"

"Hey, you're not being fair on yourself. None of us would have acted any differently. How could you do anything else?"

Andy appeared not to hear him.

"And to make matters worse, I have to sit here as all those people go in and out of the Chief's office downstairs and I haven't a clue what they're saying about me. For all I know I could have been suspended twenty times in the last two hours but I'm made to sit out here and wait like the goddamn condemned man without a blindfold. That's what's really getting to me. I just wish they would get it over with."

Martyn had not known what to say. He wanted to tell his ex-partner that all the visitors to the Chief's office downstairs were nothing to do with him but all of a sudden he was not so sure. Instead he decided that he would be wise to beat a hasty retreat. He hesitated, in deliberation, and then went off in search of his current partner, leaving the last of his case files in the tray. Later he would carve out time to support his old partner but right now he had been given another agenda which wouldn't wait.

He found Rob on the other side of the office, head buried in a filing cabinet.

"I think we're making ourselves unpopular," he said. "Right now, I'm all for getting out of here."

"Got the feeling that we're not exactly flavour of the month myself," Rob replied. "Managed to successfully get rid of all your cases, then?"

"Yes and no."

"What's that supposed to mean?"

"Well, I got rid of them all but I'd hardly say I did it successfully. It's taken me two hours and I really screwed up with Andy. I didn't know about this morning's bloodbath in Wilson."

"Well I tried to warn you but you shot off before I could get the words out. I almost made the same mistake. Everyone seems to be keeping pretty quiet about it, and with the Chief's sore head beginning to show signs of contagion, it's beginning to get oppressive in here."

"So let's go somewhere else. I don't feel as if I'm achieving much while my desk and filing cabinet are both standing empty. I need to collect more paper from somewhere."

"That's rich coming from the crusader for less paperwork, more results." Rob began searching through a drawer. "I'll be right behind you, partner. Give me another couple of minutes to get sorted."

"Yeah sure." Martyn plonked himself down on the floor beside the filing cabinet. "You manage to read the report?" he asked.

"Waste of time," Rob replied. "I mean, I read it but it was a waste of time. You?"

"Same."

"And this afternoon we're going over to Robinson's place to waste even more time."

"Can't think of anything better to do. It's either that or staying here and watching thousands of people going in and out of the Chief's office all afternoon."

"Yeah," said Rob. "I noticed. Do you think they've got anything to do with us?"

"I did, but in the light of more recent information I'm not so sure. Andy thinks they're all out to get him. And they just might be."

"Maybe. Apparently there's a preliminary inquest on Tuesday. Long time to have to wait to find out. I gave him the prostitution bust on Monday evening to take his mind off it."

"You are kind."

"Well it's better than having him sitting at home worrying and if he doesn't do something really stupid, it'll give him more points on Tuesday."

"Oh I agree, I agree."

When Rob had finally finished clearing out the desk drawer, some minutes later, they left the building as quickly as possible. Martyn decided he could really use a shower so they took the underground to his apartment. By the time the gliderail had reached Eden Square, Rob had brought the conversation back round to his stomach, as he invariably did.

"....and a bit of Melissa's home cooking would certainly not go amiss," he concluded.

"What?" Martyn replied, absently. Already, the day had seemed so long that the events of the early morning had long since been forgotten. But then, directly under Eden Square, the same eerie sensation returned, quite unexpectedly, as though he was suddenly seeing everything through someone else's eyes. Again, he felt that he already held all the answers, that they were hidden away in the depths of his subconscious and all he had to do was find the key that would unleash them. He strained to grasp at some of the abstract thoughts floating around his head but the train soon left the station and the sensation was gone.

"I said a bit of Melissa's cooking would be very welcome," Rob repeated.

"Oh, right. Actually, I'm not sure if she'll be there. She said something about using the opportunity to do some shopping."

"Well I suppose I'll have to put up with your cooking instead then."

"Correction. You'll have to put up with my *cooker* instead. I'll be in the shower. You'll be making lunch."

"In that case, I hope Melissa's there or we won't be eating anything very appetising."

"Don't tell me you still haven't bought a cooker. Are you still eating nothing but take-outs? I thought you would at least have learned to prepare a simple meal by now. Anyway, even if she is there, I don't think she'll relish the thought of cooking anything special this lunchtime. She's doing a meal tonight. Which reminds me, I need to pick up a bottle of wine sometime."

Martyn had been right. When they arrived at the apartment it was empty. Martyn took a shower and shaved while Rob was left to conjure up a meal from what remained in the freezer. Melissa had deliberately let stocks run low in anticipation of their holiday. They had only been going away for a few days but it seemed like a good opportunity to have a good clear out and start again with fresh stocks on their return. Martyn took one look at the meal his partner had prepared.

"Oh well, best laid plans…"

They arrived at Howard Robinson's apartment at two o'clock. Luckily, from the bus stop, it was only two minutes walk and they had found it with ease. They were also fortunate in catching the concierge before his afternoon stroll and thereby obtaining the keys without too much trouble. Once inside, they briefly explored the whole apartment once and then begun a more detailed search. After only fifteen minutes it became obvious that if they were to find anything at all it would be in the study or library or whatever it was. The kitchen, bedrooms and bathroom were scarcely lived in at all, being only partly furnished and poorly decorated. Only the last room showed any signs of being cared for; not only was it relatively cleaner, it was obvious that more than a minute's thought had gone into its decor and furnishings. Howard Robinson's whole life appeared to evolve around this one room.

"I don't want to sound pessimistic but I don't think we're going to find anything here and we could spend hours doing it," Rob said. He walked over to the bureau in the centre of his side of the room and sat down.

"Doing what?" asked Martyn, not quite comprehending.

"Not finding anything."

"Oh."

Martyn had picked up another book and was deeply engrossed in one of its pages. Abruptly, he pulled himself away from it and turned to face his partner.

"All the same, we've got to keep looking. It's the only source of information we've got. Anyway, I'm enjoying myself. There's some very interesting stuff here."

"You've got to be kidding. I hate books. Reading this lot is going to drive me round the bend."

"We don't have to read them all - just make sure there isn't anything obvious - like a name in the front cover, that sort of thing. Tell you what. I'll cover the books, you go through the drawers of that desk. There might be something in there."

Martyn went back to the door by which they had entered the room, took a deep breath and began on the top shelf of the first rack, systematically going along each row to the end of the rack and then dropping down to the next row, then the next until he was down on his hands and knees on the floor.

"Nice room this," he said, half to himself.

"What do you mean?" Rob's voice came from somewhere behind, followed closely by the sound of a large wad of paper being thumped down on the desk top.

"I don't know. It's hard to say. It's very relaxing, atmospheric. Doesn't really belong here, in the city. You know what I mean?"

"No," said Rob, reaching back into the top drawer. "I think it's horrible. Too many books. Too arty. Too pretentious. No one has a room like this."

"That's what I mean. No one else has a room like this. That makes it special."

"No it doesn't. That makes it weird. And that makes the owner weird too."

"I'd like a room like this."

"And that makes you weird as well," Rob said. He slammed another file onto the desk as though to add strength to his conclusion.

"You're not enjoying this, are you?"

"No."

"I can tell. Found anything?"

"No."

The two continued their search in silence. As Martyn reached the first corner of the room, he heard Rob close a drawer and move onto the other side of the desk. He opened the book he was holding; first the front cover, then the back cover followed by a quick flick through the pages. He hung the book by its spine to make sure nothing fell out and then placed it back on the shelf. While still on the first shelf, he had questioned the logic of meticulously replacing the books - normally he would not have bothered - but there were so many that to leave them all on the floor would have resulted in such a colossal mess by the time they had finished that he would not have been able to complete the search.

Besides, it would have utterly destroyed the character of the room. For some reason he could not explain he was behaving as if the owner were still alive and about to return home. Something familiar about the room was difficult to define. Somehow it reflected the personality of its owner. As each minute passed, Martyn felt that Howard Robinson, a man he had never met, was becoming more real to him.

And yet there was more to it than that. He also felt at home. Howard Robinson was not only beginning to take on a form but, for the first time in his career, Martyn felt he was beginning to relate to the victim. He did not only like the room, he loved it. He imagined it on a hot summer's day with bright sunshine streaming through the French windows, or on a quiet winter's evening, candlelit, the plants casting long, flickering shadows across the endless shelves of books. And with each imagined scene, he felt even more empathic. This room did not reflect only its owner, Martyn thought. It also mirrored himself more than any other room he had ever been in.

Just then, a clatter of hollow metal on wood directed his attention back to Rob.

"What's that?" he asked.

"Don't know yet. I found it under the desk."

The object in question was a large metallic case, resembling a small trunk, similar to the storybook image of a pirate's treasure chest. Rob began fumbling with the catch and had soon worked it open.

"Ah, this is more like it," he said. "Seems to contain a load of personal effects from old England. Historic stuff, this. I'll let you know if there's anything of interest."

"Okay." Martyn continued to stare at the trunk. In time, Rob glanced up at him once more.

"Well? What are you waiting for? Back to your books."

Martyn reluctantly turned back to the shelf he was working on. Rob knew that he would be more than interested in the contents of the chest. Being born and raised in England up to the age of eight Martyn was continually on the look out for anything that could help him piece those lost years back together. The traumatic experience of his exodus during the Great Turmoil had left him with few memories and all the English reading material he possessed from that time had omitted the finer details that would bring those memories flooding back. Patience was not one of his greatest virtues. Though he continued to scan shelf after shelf, he suddenly became totally uninterested in the books and waited silently for Rob to announce his findings.

By the time he had reached the second corner, with two walls still to go, Rob still had not said anything. Whether he had genuinely not found anything or was keeping quiet on purpose, Martyn did not know, but he had begun to reach saturation point with the book collection and was not at all eager to start on the third wall.

"It's no good," he said, placing the last book on the shelf and leaning back against the wall. "There's nothing here."

"I wouldn't say that," Rob replied. The tone of his voice was a mixture of confusion, concern and amusement. Martyn looked on expectantly.

In his hand, Rob was holding a single sheet of paper, about twenty or thirty centimetres square. The expression on his face was difficult to define. He half looked as if he had read a very funny joke. At the same time, his expression was that of somebody who had seen a ghost. As the light caught the piece of paper, Martyn saw that one side of it was glossy - a photograph. Rob leant over the desk and passed the sheet to him.

"Who does that remind you of?"

The photograph was of a young woman, perhaps nineteen or twenty years old. She had long, golden blonde hair which radiated in waves from the centre of her crown. Her twinkling green eyes had so much depth that the picture took on a new dimension, eyes which held both a childlike simplicity and a mysterious intelligence. Her skin was pure and smooth as the silk scarf around her neck and her smile was one of both admiration and acute happiness. Beyond all doubt, she was beautiful.

Martyn looked up at Rob, knowing that his expression was the same as Rob's had been a moment before, only more so. He stared back at the photo and then at Rob again but could say nothing.

"Look at the other side," said Rob.

He turned it over. On the back was a short message - even the handwriting was familiar. In the top right hand corner was the date: "June 1984".

The message was simple.

"Howard. Love you always. Melissa."

12

Life with Melissa had never been simple. Their meeting on the first day of term had created a bond which allowed them neither to spend too much time together nor to break contact completely. Melissa had set out with determined vigour to forge an independence for herself, wary of making any strong ties before she was ready and making a point of distancing herself from anyone who attempted to develop any kind of relationship with her.

But she was not a loner, far from it. Howard had watched her curiously during the fresher's ball as she mingled with the other students, never spending more than five minutes with anyone before disappearing off into the crowd again. She did not directly approach one person, she simply waited for someone to talk to her - and someone always did, usually within seconds. All her drinks were bought for her and, by the end of the evening, she had probably given her name to everyone in the residence.

"After all," she had later said, innocently. "It's unlikely that the first person you meet will be your closest friend."

But Melissa was not the first person Howard had met. He had already been at the university for two years and he had never known anyone like her. She was undeniably attractive but the university was not short of beautiful women. There was something inherently wonderful about her to which he was magnetically drawn. Her personality was intrinsic to her features and enhanced her beauty far beyond the mere physical. It fired her eyes, echoed in her laughter and flowed with her tears. Melissa radiated a charisma that was essentially enigmatic - it was the only constant trait she possessed.

Day to day she was highly unpredictable. She would undergo catastrophic mood changes that no one could keep up with. Outwardly she was almost unstable, a catalogue of contradictions, but there was always an underlying tone to her behaviour that left the impression she knew exactly what she was doing. Everything was done to extremes. She was both self-assured and insecure, affectionate and cold, generous and mean. She combined the poise of a mature and sophisticated woman with the childish playfulness of a little girl in a way that seemed so natural. Each front was equally attractive but the strange confusion of their juxtapositions was captivating.

As the term progressed Howard began to piece together Melissa's erratic behaviour and, gradually, to make some sense of it. She never ceased to surprise him and he became no less intrigued, but out of the apparent disorder a pattern did start to emerge. Slowly, he became aware of her deep and unappeasable dissatisfaction with her own life.

No matter where she was, or what she was doing, she was never entirely happy and rarely did not wish she were somewhere else. When they were together she would talk incessantly about her friends in far away places as though she were trapped in a prison and they were free. Alone in her room, he soon discovered, she would read volumes of glossy magazines and exotic holiday brochures. Her desire for a fairy tale life was an obsession and the magazines her addiction. Her prison was of her own making. Wherever she went, it went with her. Always, she longed to be somewhere else and when she arrived she wanted to return to where she had just been. She was a restless spirit, yearning to exist in a time and place that she could never reach because it did not exist.

For Melissa, the university was a stepping stone, a passing existence which she was forced to undergo on the way to her final destination. Her university friends she treated in the same way - just temporary. Without even realising it she moved among people like a queen on walkabout, always polite, extraordinarily pleasant and instantly magnetic - but only passing through. In those who tried to get close to her she instilled a sense of inferiority. Those who did not seem to care she ignored.

Often, Howard felt he was no exception. Every time she spoke she implied, or he inferred, that she would willingly end their friendship for even the merest improvement in her own circumstances. Though frequently hurt by this, he was captured by her sadness and driven by a deep desire to make her happy and contented - but that was part of the trap.

Yet Howard knew instinctively that it would be naive to assume that this self-obsessiveness was simply the outward display of her inner prime motivation. She did not seem capable of such gross callousness and common sense would constantly warn him of his own frustration-born prejudice. To attribute to Melissa all of these characteristics without redress would have been unfair. In one clear respect Melissa was like any other human being. She needed other people, perhaps even more than most. And she did care, deeply, but she did not know how to show it. Either that or she was unable to break down the barriers she had erected around her.

She hated to be alone. Even when she was it was usually to test how long it would be before someone cared enough to come looking for her. Though she was not an extrovert she did like to be the centre of attention. Basically, Howard concluded, Melissa was insecure and confused. She was beautiful and intelligent and knew it but she needed also to be loved and recognised its value. Yet she could not accept the gifts that were bestowed upon her or that the present held her ultimate destination. The mystery of Melissa was to understand where she belonged and then become that place. But that was easier said than done.

To add to the enigma Melissa also had a strange habit of disappearing, sometimes for days on end, without prior or post explanation. When she returned she did not like to be questioned about it but equally she hated it when her friends behaved as if nothing had happened. Over the course of the first term she had disappeared four times, usually for two or three days. Howard had innocently queried her the first time and subsequently thought better of it. Instead he decided to pretend that he did not even know that she had been missing.

Following her second disappearance he waited a whole day before she finally stormed into his room and demanded that he remove the 'biggest spider in the world' from her sink. He naturally obliged, or tried to, but after almost an hour the spider was still nowhere to be seen. Melissa concluded that it must have escaped down the plug hole, though this would have been impossible for its purported size, and subsequently ran the cold water at full blast until Howard turned off the tap.

"Do you think it has drowned?" she asked, timidly. Howard contemplated the bowl, confused at feeling protective towards both Melissa and the spider.

"If it's down there I think it will have dissolved."

On the third occasion of Melissa's absence Howard put the same plan into operation with virtually identical consequences. Twenty fours hours after her return the door of his room abruptly caved in and Melissa was standing there.

"Oh hi, I didn't know you were back," he lied.

"I need a hug." She looked unhappy but made no movement towards him. Howard relented, rose from his chair and gently embraced her. As he did so she took a deep breath and he felt the minor disturbance of her quiver ripple along his body. In that moment he wanted to kiss her but she left no opportunity. Instead she thanked him and left the room. He knew he was expected to chase after her but he waited until she was sure he wouldn't before doing so.

It was following her fourth disappearance that the pattern was broken. The last week of the autumn term had seen a flurry of Christmas parties and social events which Melissa had seemed reluctant to be committed to. When she subsequently vanished over the penultimate weekend Howard was disappointed but not altogether surprised. She had been away for four days but this time on her return he had become so swamped with deadlines and invitations he genuinely did not notice.

The weather was awful. It was one of those evenings when he was actually glad to remain inside. Daylight seemed to have disappeared unusually early and out of the night came the constant sound of drizzle on the window. Howard had decided to shut himself away for the evening to try and finish an essay when suddenly, without warning, the door flew open and Melissa breezed into the room in her own inimitable style.

"Hi," she announced. "I got bored so I decided to come and see you."

Howard put down his pen and sat back in his chair, amused.

"I'm not sure whether that's a compliment or not."

Melissa smiled, half cheekily. "Well, perhaps you'll never know. Maybe it's destined to be one of life's great mysteries."

"I'm sure I won't lose too much sleep over it. Did you have any specific reason for coming to see me or could you not think of anything better to do?"

She smiled again. "That's for me to know and you to find out." With that, she threw herself down on the bed and, after removing a few hair slides and grips, tossed back her head and shook loose her crowning glory, grinning defiantly. Howard was not really in the mood for twenty questions so he did not venture a reply. He knew from experience that this was the best way to find out what she wanted anyway. If he had opted to play games it would have taken a little longer, that was all. This time he was right. After a brief silence Melissa suddenly changed the subject.

"A little bird told me you've been seeing Jenny Whatsername," she said, cheerfully, though not so cheerfully that Howard could not detect the note of tension in her voice.

"Who's the little bird?" he asked.

"Oh, just someone."

"Oh."

There was another silence and again Melissa broke it.

"Well, have you?" she asked.

"Have I what?"

"Have you been seeing this Jenny person?" she persisted.

Howard could see little point in going round in circles so he decided to play it straight.

"Put it this way. I sort of got paired off with her at the weekend, and we had a good time, so I asked her to the film at the union on Monday night - but it's nothing to write home about."

"Film good?" she whispered, meaning something completely different.

"It was okay."

"When are you seeing her again?"

"I asked her out for a drink on Friday."

"Oh." Melissa lapsed back into silence. All this time Howard had been watching her closely, wondering where the conversation was leading and being deliberately evasive until he knew. Melissa, for her part, had been asking all the questions while sitting on the bed and staring at the floor, never once looking up. Abruptly, she rose to her feet, pulled a chair across the room to the desk and sat down again meeting him squarely in the eyes.

"Howard, I don't want you to start going out with Jenny. If you do then you won't have as much time to see me and I couldn't bear that. You won't come round to my room anymore and I won't be able to come and talk to you because she'll be here and then I won't have anyone else to turn to and when she isn't here you won't be able to see me because you'll have work to do and...and..." The words came out in a mad breathless torrent and then faded suddenly. Tears welled up in her eyes as she paused for breath.

"Howard. I love you."

Howard was stunned. He knew deep down that he had waited months to hear those words and when they finally came he was totally unprepared. Melissa paused and waited for a reply but Howard was speechless. Instead he stood, leaned across the desk and pulled her gently towards him, oblivious to the sound of his books as they crashed onto the floor. Hugging her tightly, he lowered his head until it became buried in the beautiful mane of golden blonde hair. Melissa began sobbing her heart out, repeating the words "I love you" over and over again. Howard could only hold her and kiss away the tears from her cheeks. Eventually, she collapsed in his arms, as though suffering from nervous exhaustion, and fell into a deep sleep.

All too soon it was morning and the warm, silent light of a new day cast comforting shadows around the room. The essay deadline he had been trying so hard to meet the previous evening had been forgotten, blown away as quickly and as easily as the clouds that had carried yesterday's rain. Paying little regard to the lecture timetable pinned to his notice board, Howard rose briefly to place his wastepaper basket outside the door, indicating he did not want to be disturbed, and then returned to bed until midday.

All that morning Melissa was silent, clinging to him like a Koala. He had never known her like this and the intensity of her emotions was both rewarding and disturbing. He wanted to believe that it was all for him but instinctively he knew that was not the case. Last night she told him she loved him, words he had come to believe he would never hear. But that was last night.

He was brimming with questions and Melissa was bottling all the answers up inside her. In him she had found release but from what he did not know. She had unburdened herself of a mountain of pent-up emotions but, in the final analysis, the cause was still a mystery. And he did not have any sense of comfort that this would last.

13

On a warm Saturday morning two weeks before Easter, Howard had woken to find himself in an otherwise empty bed, though he was sure it had not been so when he was last conscious. The previous night he had gone with Melissa, and almost everyone else in the hall, to celebrate the long awaited demise of term. The weeks before had been devoted entirely to dissertations and projects in an all-out concerted effort to meet the Easter deadline. Socialising, sex and sleep had all disappeared into a vague memory that would be cherished and maintained until it was all over.

While Melissa had become engrossed in the psychological stability of the reincarnated soul, sometimes to the detriment of her own sanity, or that was how it seemed, Howard had been busy unravelling the psyche of the American obsessive historian. More recently, however, he had spent most of his time compiling the catalogue which, as it transpired, included everything from bridges and barns to castles and cottages. A publisher had already shown an interest in publishing the work and, to that end, he had been awarded travel scholarships to finance one trip to Amsterdam and to spend the summer in the States interviewing some of the people he was writing about. However, though the catalogue was still far from finished, the submission of his dissertation to the university had seemed like an appropriate juncture at which to take a break and join in with the celebrations.

Since Howard was rarely given to drunken sprees, the effects of the binge began to be evident early on. His last memory was one of another memory as he realised he had not eaten for hours and there was nothing to prevent the alcohol from going straight to his brain and flooding it. Which, he assumed, was exactly what must have happened.

He did not notice the hangover until he stretched out his right arm and pulled on the curtain. For a brief instant, the light came pouring in and he snapped his eyes shut in reaction to the sharp pain across his forehead. In the semi-darkness he attempted to lift his head from the pillow but, as he suspected, it was far too heavy. There was nothing else for it; he would have to stay in bed all day.

Melissa had other ideas. She had such a unique way of entering a room, like a tree load of autumn leaves on the crest of a gale, that even with his eyes closed he could not have mistaken her for anyone else. This particular morning, she acted out the part of a hospital matron who had entered a ward containing an awkward patient.

"Well, how are we this morning?" The first word came from the door, the last from somewhere near the window.

"Not the curtains."

"I see. That bad, is it." It was not a question. Even without looking he could tell she was smiling gleefully at his fragile state. The curtains remained closed and he felt the mattress tilt slightly under her weight as she sat on the edge of the bed.

"Where did you sleep last night?"

"Oh, here and there."

"Here." This was not a question either. It was a statement of confirmation that required further confirmation.

He did not want to rise to the bait of her tease but he found it incredible that he could have possibly spent the night with her and not know, for sure, that he had.

"And there," she repeated. "I systematically seduced and made passionate love to all the men in C block."

"Oh, was it fun?"

There was silence but he could sense her smiling inwardly.

"Wait a minute. C block is a girls' block."

She laughed out loud. "And, as far as I know, you were the only man in it; the only one not otherwise occupied that is."

"This is C block? I thought I was in my room." Their rooms were virtually identical. There were only two different layouts in the whole residence and one was the mirror image of the other. With eyes closed, it was a simple mistake to make.

"And you seduced me?"

"That's right. It was wonderful. You should have been there. I think you might have enjoyed it."

"I don't believe you."

"Well, that's the best part. You'll never know whether I did or not, will you? It will be my little secret."

"Some secret," he said. "I don't think I could have done. Not in this state."

Melissa gently pulled back the quilt and, as the chilled air made contact with his skin, he realised he was naked. She giggled like a little girl.

"We'll put it to the test. Let's see if you can rise to the occasion. If I'm right, you buy lunch." She began caressing his body, moving her fingers from his navel to the inside of his right thigh in slow, deliberate strokes. His first inkling that he was going to lose the bet came when he no longer felt cold.

"Oh dear, look what I've done," she said, triumphantly.

"Well now that you've proved your point, what are you going to do about it?"

She climbed onto the bed and straddled his body, balancing on her knees and toes. With melodramatic flair, she removed her T-shirt. She was not wearing a bra.

"There is only one thing to do."

"Melissa, I have a vicious hangover. I can't."

This was a lie and she knew it. Nothing had ever dampened his desire to make love with her and he was sure it was not about to be extinguished now. Without words, she would naturally know how he was feeling. Sexual telepathy would override anything he said and their natural rapport would dictate her actions. In that respect Melissa was so very special.

"Sex is good for headaches. I don't see that a simple hangover should cause too much of a problem. Besides, Melissa is having a little present for looking after you last night." She lifted her skirt to her waist. She was not wearing panties.

"What about Howard? Does he not get a say in this?"

She leant forward so that the tips of her breasts brushed against his face and the morning scent of her unperfumed body overwhelmed him. With surprising precision, she lowered herself onto him and he was inside her, their lovemaking hidden beneath the hundred folds of her skirt.

"Screw Howard."

Afterwards, they lay in silence, he with his arms wrapped around her, one softly tracing the ripples of her backbone, the other hand buried deep in her hair, massaging the nape of her neck. His hangover was cured.

"Lunch is on you, then."

"I'm not sure I can eat anything. It may work wonders on headaches but it does nothing for unsettled stomachs. I think I might stay in bed and write the day off. What time is it, anyway?"

"It's almost midday. Oh no, I almost forgot. You have to get up. You got a parcel and the post room shuts at twelve. If you don't get it now, you'll have to wait until Monday. I tried to take it for you but they wouldn't give it to me. You have to sign for it."

"Let it wait until Monday."

"No," she said, suddenly bursting back into life as his hangover immediately returned. "You have to get it now. Don't you even want to know what it is? It looks really strange."

"I can wait."

"Well I can't." She threw some clothes at him. "Come on, I want to know what's in it even if you don't."

"It's my parcel. If I want to leave it there until Monday then I can." But Melissa was adamant.

"No you can't. Just go and get it." She lifted one side of the mattress and he fell into a crumpled heap on the floor, a confused mixture of human flesh and striped duvet.

Five minutes later, he returned with the parcel, a rectangular box wrapped in plain brown paper. He did not recognise the handwriting but the address, including postcode, was perfect.

"I thought you said it looked really strange. It's the most boring looking parcel I've ever seen." He removed the paper to reveal a grey cardboard box, one inch deep. There were no external markings to indicate what might be inside but the box had a distinctive rattle which he thought he knew.

"It sounds like a jigsaw," Melissa said.

He opened the box. It was a jigsaw. At first glance he guessed there were about five hundred pieces, half of which appeared to be grass, the other half sky.

"Well this looks exciting."

"Who is it from?"

"I don't know. It doesn't say. Wait a minute, there's a card underneath." He pushed the pieces to one side of the box and removed a plain white piece of paper, about the size of a playing card. Hand-written, in black italic capitals, was a single word.

LANDMARK.

"What does that mean?" Melissa asked.

"Haven't a clue." He inspected all the packaging again and then waited while Melissa checked it over herself. There was nothing more, not even a postmark, to suggest where the parcel might have originated.

"Maybe it's an anagram." Melissa studied the card, turning over the letters in her mind. "Do you know anyone called 'Mark'?" He shrugged, indicating that he did not.

"Perhaps you have to do the jigsaw to find out who sent it."

"Thrilling."

Melissa unexpectedly changed the subject.

"What about lunch? Do you feel up to it yet or are you going to worm your way out of having to buy me a meal?"

"How about tomorrow?" he said. "We could go to a country pub somewhere. My treat."

"Okay, it's a deal. And I've got an idea. I'm hungry even if you're not. So, while I go and get a snack from the dining hall, why don't you see if you can complete the jigsaw before I get back. I need to go to the shops as well so I guess I'll be about an hour or so. That should give you enough time."

Though quite unenthusiastic, he accepted the challenge. It was a mindless thing to do and that was exactly what he needed. Clearing all the text books from her desk, he tipped the contents of the box onto the stained, wooden surface.

"Off you go then."

An hour and a half later she returned.

"How did you get on?"

"There's a piece missing. Right in the middle." She came beside him and looked over the almost complete puzzle. The bottom half of the picture was a monotonous green, rising up to meet an equally monotonous and washed out sky. At the summit of the hill, or where the summit would have been, there was a hole through which the surface of the desk shone with humourless incongruity. In the bottom right hand corner of the picture were two more words, in tiny block print.

Darwen Moor.

"Wow, that's interesting. How many thousands of these do you think they've sold?"

Howard indicated the hole in the centre.

"There's something there - at the summit. Look, you can see the edge of it on the next piece. It appears that the only bit that's of any interest at all is the one we haven't got. It must be a monument or something." Melissa examined the adjoining pieces but could add no further comment.

"Where is Darwen?"

"In Lancashire, I think. Somewhere north of Manchester. I'm not really sure. Have a look in your atlas." Melissa fetched her road atlas from a shelf, checked the index and found the page.

"Here it is," she said. "You were right. It's about as far north of the city as Alderley Edge is south. It's kind of stuck in the middle of nowhere." She laughed. "Hey, this is spooky. Darwen is on the A666. You've been sent a jigsaw by the devil."

"Actually, it's the beast, not the devil." Howard examined the map thoughtfully. "The road to hell," he said, half to himself. "Curious. I've never been near the place and I don't think I know anyone who has."

"Well it looks as though you're going to have to rectify that if you want to find out what the missing piece shows. Maybe we could drive up there when we next stay in Alderley," she suggested. "It's the only way you're going to find out."

Howard picked up the card that had arrived in the jigsaw box. He turned it around in his hand as if it might make more sense read upside down or vertically.

"I guess so."

14

When Martyn returned to the apartment, some three hours later, Melissa was already there. Entering the lounge, he could hear her in the adjoining kitchen, singing blithely to a song on the cable music channel. Swept along with the sound was the distinct aroma of Hawaiian pork and honeyed barbecue sauce, one of his favourite dishes. Evidently, she had not heard him come in.

He stepped over to the Venetian pine serving hatch which separated the two rooms. Through the grille he watched as she fervently tossed a prawn salad in a bowl, occasionally stopping to eat a bit. Though the grille hid him well, she was too engrossed in tossing-eating the salad to notice him. Displaying a talent he had never before seen, she also seemed to have perfected the art of eating and singing at the same time without spitting food everywhere.

From the wad of papers he was carrying, he removed the photograph and held it up against the grille so he could see both Melissas together. Involuntarily, he shivered. It was uncanny. He felt sure that, at any distance over twenty metres, they could quite easily be mistaken for each other. There was really only one distinct difference. Martyn Sorensen was in love with the girl in the kitchen. For the girl in the photograph he only felt fascination - and unease.

In a way he could not begin to fathom, he somehow knew that the photograph was the central piece of the jigsaw – and it scared him. For that reason, he had already decided not to show the photograph to Melissa. He could not explain why but instinct told him to keep it under wraps until he could find out more about the other Melissa – if that was possible. After finding the picture in Howard Robinson's apartment, Rob had soon become bored and they had decided to call it a day, agreeing to meet early next morning at the precinct. To Martyn, however, it was as if the discovery of the photograph were the clue they had been looking for and the only one they would find. Motivated purely by this instinct, he had opted to spend the rest of the afternoon there. As expected, he had found nothing more.

He took one last look at the picture and felt his heart stab in the same way it had when Rob had first shown it to him. Then he placed it back in the loose file and went into the bedroom where he packed it carefully into the bottom drawer in which he kept his personal effects. Though they lived together, they each respected the other's privacy and he knew Melissa would only go into the drawer in an emergency. Likewise, he would never intrude on her personal belongings which she kept in a similar drawer above his.

In a sudden, forced change of mood, he abandoned all thoughts of the photograph, threw his coat onto the bed and went back to the kitchen.

"Smells good," he said.

Melissa turned to see him leaning against the kitchen door frame. She smiled, delightedly.

"Oh, hi. I didn't know you were here. In fact, I was beginning to wonder whether you'd make it back at all. I was worried you'd be working all night." She came across the kitchen, threw her arms wide and kissed him.

"Sticky fingers," she said. "I've been busy."

"You mean you've been picking at the tossed salad"

"I haven't touched it!"

"Well you haven't made very much, then." The bowl now had only half the contents he had first seen. Melissa looked perplexed.

"Well I haven't eaten any. Anyway, I've made a large casserole so you won't want a lot of salad. Please don't say I haven't done enough; I've been really careful to try and get everything right." She smiled coyly.

There was something about that smile that made him melt, that made him want to grab her and hold her very tightly, but this time he stood his ground.

"What's wrong? Are you feeling guilty because you've eaten half of it?"

"I have not eaten half of it!" she protested, adamantly. "I haven't touched it."

"So why have you got a piece of lettuce leaf hanging off your lower lip?"

"Oh, aren't we the clever little detective today, then? Martyn, you know how messy I am. I get stuff everywhere." There was another guilt edged pause. "Okay, maybe I had a teensy weenie nibble." She stopped to brush the non-existent leaf from her lip.

"Oh, you swine!" she screamed and flung the sticky fingers into his hair, covering it in a mixture of salad, honey and vinaigrette dressing. Then she stepped back, her smug expression one of avenged self satisfaction. "Serves you right."

Minutes later, for the second time that day, Martyn was in the shower. It was not until he was standing under the steaming jet spray that he realised how tired he was. After a few seconds, he was content to close his eyes and let the water fall over him. Shortly, he heard Melissa enter the bathroom and throw the clothes he had worn that morning into the wash basket.

"I wish you wouldn't leave your clothes lying around in great untidy piles. It makes the place look a mess."

Even behind the shower curtain, he could picture the sarcastic smirk across her face and the devastation that he had not dared to notice in the kitchen.

"Yes ma'am. Sorry ma'am. Won't happen again ma'am."

"Good. Did you got all that stuff out of your hair yet?" she asked - then, without waiting for an answer, "I've left the casserole simmering. It will be ready in about twenty minutes - "

Suddenly, the curtain flew open and there was Melissa, standing in her bathrobe. In one deft movement the bathrobe had dropped to the floor and she was naked.

" - which just about gives me enough time to take a shower too."

She stepped in and stood facing him. If Martyn had been half asleep half a second before he immediately snapped awake and felt the rising warmth within him. Without saying anything he pulled her gently towards him and kissed her forehead as she entered blindly into the spray. They kissed.

"It seems a long time since this morning," she said. "I missed you."

He remained silent and responded by kissing her again. Slowly, he brushed his right hand against her hip and let it rise, almost glide, around the curve of her waist to her left breast, gently squeezing it in his palm.

She moved closer to him, lifting her long hair with both hands and draping it lovingly across his shoulders. They kissed once more. He relaxed the hand on her breast and left one finger orbiting silently around the perimeter of the curved flesh, subtly spiralling, inching its way towards the centre where, with the co-operation of one of natures minor miracles, the flesh became hard and erect under his touch.

Melissa lifted her right leg and pressed her body even closer to him, raising herself onto tiptoe. As her body moved against his, he felt his erection creeping between her thighs until, with a catastrophic suddenness, destiny and choice, if they had ever existed, were no longer tangible concepts. There was no way he could escape from this even if he wanted to.

The room was in darkness except for one solitary candle in the centre of the table, flickering, almost undetectable, in time to the soft panpipe melody from the invisible cable hi-fi system. Martyn scooped the last piece of cheesecake onto his spoon, examined it and then placed it in his mouth, allowing it to melt slowly on his tongue before swallowing.

"That was delicious," he said. "Thank you."

"You mean the meal."

"I meant the cheesecake."

"What about the Hawaiian pork?"

"That was delicious too."

"And the hors d'oeuvre?"

"Simply phenomenal. What was left of it."

"And what about the aperitif?"

"Hot and wet."

Melissa smiled and appeared to blush ever so slightly. "Don't be rude," she said.

He bent forward grinning. "I wasn't. That just shows the way your mind works. I was referring to the shower."

"Of course you were, darling." Her tone carried the cynicism of the defeated. She brushed the bottom of her lip with a napkin, leant forward and blew out the candle so that the smoke wafted into his eyes. "Take that, you rat."

With that, she stacked a number of plates and carried them off into the kitchen, returning almost immediately. She quickly re-lit the candle and moved it to a more prominent position on a coffee table, in the centre of the lounge.

"Let's cuddle up on the sofa," she suggested. "You can do the dishes later."

Martyn left the table and moved across the room to join her. "Oh thanks," he said. "I don't want to sound chauvinistic or anything but some of us have to work tomorrow and I have no intention of doing the washing up tonight."

Settling cosily into the corner of the sofa, he pulled her towards him.

"Well that is chauvinistic. Why should I spend the hard earned holiday I don't even want doing all the housework?"

"Well, for a start, I think it's fair to say that you make most of the mess that creates the housework. I know you really excelled yourself with that meal but I hate to imagine the state of the kitchen now."

"It's not that bad," she said.

"Everything's subjective. You would have described the devastation of Tokyo as 'a bit of a mess.' "

"Alright, I'll agree to do the washing up - even though I'm also working tomorrow."

"You're working?"

"Yes. I went in and explained what had happened about our holiday and everything and they said I could cancel my leave if I wanted to and take it some other time. So I did. Better than lounging around the house all day."

He leaned forward and kissed the crown of her head.

"Listen, Melissa, we will go away soon, I promise. I'm working on a new case but it shouldn't take too long. I might have to work some funny hours again, though."

"That's okay. I'll bide my time making a mess and clearing it up again - starting with the washing up tomorrow."

"I do love you, you know," he said. "I feel very blessed."

"I love you too. And you deserve far more than this. Maybe when you've finished this case we can book some more leave and go somewhere even more romantic than the Great Lakes. Somewhere hot, perhaps, like the Caribbean or… Martyn? How long do you think this will take?"

"Hard to say right now. Could be we're barking up the wrong tree entirely, in which case it might take months of pointless investigation, or it could all be over in a couple of days. Depends. We just need to get started."

"Don't you have any clues?" she asked.

"Yes." He hesitated. "Well no, not really."

"What's that supposed to mean?"

And so began the relentless questioning. One thing about Melissa that both attracted and frustrated him was her insatiable curiosity. She simply hated to be kept in the dark about anything. Though she knew he was not supposed to talk about his work, she attempted to get round this by asking vague questions. At the end of this indirect interrogation, she would have formulated in her own mind some kind of picture as to what was going on. It may be a complete distortion of the truth but, whatever version she kept locked inside her head, it seemed to satisfy her. His hesitation in answering her last question would inevitably have set some cogs in motion and only added fuel to her curiosity.

He still thought, intuitively knew, that the discovery of the photograph was a clue but at the same time he did not see how it could be. Anybody could have been given the task of turning over Howard Robinson's apartment and, to anyone else, the photo would have meant nothing. Rationally, it could only be his personal connection, or his own subconscious insecurity, that had sparked his uneasiness. After all, Rob knew Melissa but the photo had appeared to amuse, rather than disturb, him. It could only be an unfortunate coincidence which, if he were not careful, could become an obsessive red herring. But there were two personal rules he could never ignore; firstly, his intuition pressed him to keep digging behind the photograph; secondly, he never believed in coincidences.

He decided that the best way to answer her question was with the truth, or, at least, a vague version of it.

"Let's just say that I found something unusual while searching somebody's apartment but I don't see how it can be a clue."

"But you suspect it is."

"I don't know," he said. "But if it is, I'll be damned if I know why."

There was a moment's silence, in which he found himself staring thoughtfully at the candle, and suspected Melissa was doing the same. Like Melissa, he was also a naturally curious person. Even if he could not answer all her questions, he could sympathise with her situation. Right now, he wondered what macabre incident she had concocted out of the information she had so far gleaned from his answers. He knew he had not told her anything but he could almost hear her brain tick over as she read between the lines. After a minute or so, she broke the silence.

"Martyn? Who is Howard Robinson?"

At first it seemed like a normal curiosity-provoked question, perhaps a little more direct than usual. But then he realised what she had said and his heart skipped a beat. It was the first time Howard Robinson's name had entered the conversation and his mind was suddenly filled with all kinds of thoughts as to the source of the question. His first thought was sparked by the fear that she had seen the photo but then he remembered that only the name Howard had appeared on the back. He mentally kicked himself for thinking irrationally and then remembered their conversation of that morning. As Melissa had said, morning had seemed so long ago he had almost forgotten but he was suddenly aware that she might be more in tune with him than he first thought.

"Sorry?" he said.

"You know. What's so special about him? Why is he so important? I've never heard of him."

"I didn't know he was important."

"But he must be. Or else why would anybody want to assassinate him?"

"What?"

"And with a laser rifle too. I mean, he must have done something, mustn't he?"

"Melissa! What are you talking about?" He pushed her away slightly and turned to face her, visibly shocked. She, too, appeared shocked, seemingly because he was.

"Well that is what all this is about, isn't it? Your new case?"

"Yes, but how the hell did you know?"

"Know what, darling?"

"How did you know that Howard Robinson had been killed by a laser rifle?"

Her expression turned from shock to sudden comprehension and she smiled.

"Easy. It was on the six o'clock news."

Martyn immediately disappeared into the bedroom and made a telephone call. Minutes later, he returned to the lounge and rejoined Melissa on the sofa.

"You don't have to go in, do you?" she asked.

"No, luckily. Apparently our number one ace reporter is out of town tonight. Won't be back until tomorrow morning. He obviously knew when to make a quick exit and nobody seems to know where he's gone. Therefore, according to the Chief, I can relax for the rest of the evening."

"Meaning you can't," said Melissa, matter of factly.

He smiled and pulled her closer towards him.

"Meaning that I'm the one who's supposed to be on top of this case and so far I seem to have been the only person who hasn't had a clue what's going on. And I don't like it."

"But if the Chief says it's okay to take the rest of the evening off then surely he can't be too worried about it. You'll probably have the whole thing wrapped up by tomorrow night and…"

"That's what's really worrying me. This morning the Chief was acting as if he were at the end of his tether when really there was relatively little to worry about. Just then, on the phone, he seemed perfectly calm, yet I could hear all hell breaking loose in the background. There were phones ringing and people shouting right through the conversation."

"Well isn't that what it's always like down there. I can never get through to you when I call. And on the rare occasions that I've actually gone down to see you it's been like a madhouse every time. Besides, what about that awful tragedy in Wilson? What a horrible thing to happen! And in case you hadn't heard, the death toll went up to five this afternoon. Surely that must account for some, if not most, of the activity."

He knew that Melissa was trying to introduce some rationality into the conversation but he found her arguments patronising, even though she evidently had more facts at her fingertips. That, in itself, only made him more irritable. However, it suddenly occurred to him that she might be driving at something else. There was an inflexion in her voice which suggested a logical progression which was not yet complete.

"Melissa, what exactly are you trying to say?"

Melissa lay down with her head across his thighs and stared up at him.

"Martyn, you never call him 'the Chief'; you always call him 'Brett' when you're with me. He's one of your best friends and you're suddenly talking about him as if you hardly know him. All I'm trying to say is that I know you too well and I wish you wouldn't try and hide it. Something's worrying you, isn't it? And it's more than being irritated at missing the six o'clock news."

15

Martyn awoke next morning to find Melissa cosily snuggled against his body, her head lying on his chest and her hair cascaded untidily about his neck. She was breathing steadily and against his lower ribs he could feel the soft protrusion of her breast and the pulsing of her heartbeat. Slowly, he lifted his left forearm, resisting the temptation to run his fingers along the smooth skin of her back. He gently eased her head onto the pillow and crawled out of bed. He dressed quickly and quietly, grabbed a muesli bar and a glass of fresh orange and left the apartment. Melissa slept on.

Outside, the fog had cleared and it was a beautiful, crisp autumn morning. He was thankful that he was able to use the car again and even more thankful that he had risen in time to avoid the rush-hour traffic. He powered up the MAP and confirmed that the roads were clear – a row of green lights appearing from top to bottom of the small screen.

For the early part of the morning he was on his own. Owing to a shortage of manpower and an overflow of work, the Chief had decided to divide teams on information-gathering assignments. As a result Rob had gone off to investigate a phone tip off in which the caller had claimed he could reveal the location of a cache of laser weapons. For reasons unknown to Martyn, the Chief had suspected the call of being a hoax but it had to be investigated anyway. Before he reached Richmond, he tried to raise Rob on the radio link but there was no answer. Rob, as usual, was still in bed.

The house, located in a select part of the suburb, was only a few kilometres away and he arrived within a quarter of an hour of leaving home. From a pocket, he pulled out a scrap of paper on which he had scribbled down the details : "Greg Miller, 232 Halcyon Gardens, works for City Network News as a reporter, occasionally presents breakfast show." This last piece of information was evidently intended to replace a full description but Martyn had never watched breakfast television and he had never heard of a Greg Miller.

Halcyon Gardens turned out to be a small cluster of twelve houses built round a peaceful, Y-shaped cul de sac, landscaped with trees, ornamental gardens and clean, well-kept lawns. Martyn pulled the car up underneath a willow tree and walked towards the house. Even without looking he could imagine the garden behind with its summer house, barbecue patio and swimming pool – all furnished with an array of tropical plants.

The house itself was comfortably large, Swiss in style and predominantly white with intentional splashes of green ivy. At first, it appeared to be lifeless and he was concerned that he may have missed Miller for the second time. But as he approached, he could hear the faint sound of radio chit-chat from somewhere round the back of the house. Through force of habit he chose not to ring the doorbell and instead carefully opened the wooden doorway which led into the back garden.

Immediately behind the garden wall was the patio, with large pine, parasol covered tables and an ornate brick barbecue. Beyond the patio stretched a large, richly green lawn surrounded by rockeries and flowerbeds : the flowers had largely disappeared by this time of year, leaving a collection of green nests waiting patiently for the next spring. At the end of the lawn stood the wicker summer house, enrobed in honeysuckle vine. In the summer months the vine would have been in full flower, scenting the whole garden, but now it had clearly surrendered to the cold climate. Separating the patio from the lawn was a crystal clear swimming pool reflecting the blue sky above.

Correct on every count, he thought.

The source of the radio appeared to be a kitchen, which extended into the patio area. At the end of the extension, access was gained between the two via a patio doorway in French window style. Both doors were wide open. Martyn walked stealthily across the patio towards the kitchen extension, knocked lightly on the glass and stepped casually through the doorway.

"Good morning," he said, cheerfully.

On the opposite side of the kitchen, a raven-haired woman had placed a bowl of fresh fruit on the table and was about to re-arrange a vase of flowers. He guessed she was in her early thirties yet she carried an air of sophistication and intelligence that he usually associated with older women.

"He's not here," came the reply. The woman turned to face him and he was sure at once that he recognised her from somewhere but he could not quite place the memory. "So if you don't mind, I'd rather I didn't have to answer all those silly questions over again. I'm very busy and I don't like repeating myself."

Martyn moved further into the kitchen and took a seat at the table. Then, deliberately, he helped himself to an orange from the fruit bowl and began peeling it.

"Had to skip breakfast this morning," he said. "Just to see you. You don't mind, I hope."

He expected her to react. It was not his preferred style of questioning but she had already set out her position and this approach would help him achieve a result sooner. Instead she smiled calmly and sat down on the opposite side of the table.

"Well, now you've made yourself at home, I suppose that means I'm going to be forced to answer all these questions again anyway."

"Afraid so. If they'd been satisfied by your first attempt, I wouldn't have had to drag myself out of bed at such a ridiculous hour to come here and ask them all again."

"Okay, but can we make it snappy, I've got a busy day ahead." She snatched the orange from him. "I can't stand to watch any longer. Here, let me peel it for you." In an instant the rind lay in a single coil on the table and he was holding the orange once more.

"You've got longer finger nails," he said.

There was silence.

"Well, aren't you going to ask me anything?"

He took a slice of orange and placed it slowly in his mouth.

"Mrs Miller..."

"Jacqui." The tone of her answer held an acknowledgement that she was, in fact, Greg Miller's wife. While she seemed to assume that he knew that, he had not been certain. Even before she spoke her Christian name, he was sure that he had already known it but could not remember where from.

"Jacqui, as you're in a rush, or so you claim..."

"I do have a …"

"…and as you already know what the questions are, you could save us both a lot of time if you just answered them and I'll prompt you when you miss something out. Okay?"

"Okay."

"Off you go then."

There was a pause and then she answered. "No, no, no, no, yes, no, yes, no, no."

He ate another slice of orange. "Alright, we'll do it the hard way. Your husband, I take it, is not at home?"

"No."

"Are you expecting him back this morning?"

"No."

"Do you know where he is?"

"No. Listen, young man, the answers are still going to be the same even if you do insist on asking the questions all over again."

He guessed they were about the same age, he perhaps a little older but in one sentence she had suddenly turned the conversation round, demonstrating her quick wit and adding an element of patronisation in one go. Martyn admired her for it but displayed no outward visible reaction. Instead he needed to get back the initiative quickly. Not being able to think of anything immediately he fell back on his original ruse. Standing up, he walked over to the fridge, took out a slice of cheese and a carton of pineapple juice and returned to the table. He handed the carton to her.

"Could you open this for me? I'll only spill it all over the table. I'll need a glass too."

"Anything else?" she asked calmly.

"Well, I suppose if it's going to take you all this long to answer a few simple questions, you might like to start thinking about lunch as well."

"I already have done." She walked across to a cupboard, removed a glass and placed it on the table next to the opened carton. "But then I realised you wouldn't fit in the microwave."

It suddenly occurred to him that she might actually be prepared to play this game all morning, despite claiming that she was in a rush. He decided to adopt a second, more brutal approach.

"Right, I've had enough of this, and even if your time isn't precious, mine is. Mrs Miller, your husband is in serious trouble, you know that. He might also be in serious danger so let's cut the crap and do some straight talking for a few minutes, can we?"

The response was instantaneous. Although she remained calm, she could not hide the tears which suddenly appeared at the corners of her eyes. Everything before had been a front.

"Alright, that's fine by me. But firstly, my name is Jacqui and secondly, I don't know that my husband is in trouble. In fact I don't know anything. I would be very pleased if someone would actually tell me because I don't know what the hell is going on and I'm worried sick." Her voice was beginning to sound edgy, almost quietly hysterical.

"All I know is that Greg came home last night enthusing about some exclusive story he'd got hold of. He'd been on a high all day about it. Then he tells me he's got to go away for the night, maybe two. He packs an overnight bag and leaves. I didn't worry, he sometimes has to do that. So do I occasionally. It goes with the job. Anyway, the next thing I knew was the phone ringing at two in the morning and all these questions about Greg being fired at me. I thought I was having a nightmare."

"Two in the morning? How come they didn't call you before that?" The question was meant to be rhetorical but she answered it anyway.

"They may have done but I wasn't here. I didn't get back until about one."

"Where were you?"

"Working." The answer was clearly evasive.

"Where?"

"All over the place. I'm a reporter, for pity's sake."

"Which story?"

She went silent, inwardly debating the form, and perhaps the content, of her answer. If she lied, he would spot it.

"You won't like it," she said.

"Right now, there are a lot of things I don't like but I have to put up with them anyway. One more won't make any difference."

Once more she paused to reflect on her answer.

"I was interviewing the families of the victims of that supermarket massacre. The full report will be in this morning's newspaper."

"And I won't like it."

"It doesn't reflect well on the police department," she said, half apologetically. "You know someone else died in the night, a six year old girl. Did you know that?"

He did not know but neither did he show it.

"You make it sound as if they were all shot by policemen. In fact I wouldn't be surprised if this report of yours doesn't even mention the bastards who actually did all the shooting. If it's anything like normal press coverage it'll be a catalogue of police mistakes and naive criticism. Do you know something, Jacqui? If we'd waited an extra ten minutes before bothering to turn up, you wouldn't even have anything worth printing because it would have all been said before."

She poured herself a glass of orange juice.

"Were you there?" she asked.

"No. And I'm damn lucky that I wasn't because I don't believe it would have made any difference. Except this way I get to keep my job a bit longer. How would you feel if your article resulted in a rise in unemployment?"

Thoughtfully she raised her glass and took a sip.

"You don't like reporters, do you?"

"I have many reasons not to. I've met too many parasites who earn their living by sensationalising other people's misery. Which reminds me, who was your husband interviewing yesterday?"

"I don't know."

"And you don't know where he is now."

"No. Look, I've already told you everything I know. Now please tell me what's going on."

She locked his eyes with hers; another tear ran down her cheek. She was genuinely worried and she was telling the truth. If he levelled with her, there was always the chance that he might spark off some new information that she had not thought relevant, or that she had simply forgotten about.

"What do you think will be the main story in the papers this morning?" he asked.

"Mine," she said, emphatically.

He looked at her quizzically, to see if there was any doubt. She looked at her watch.

"Well, we'll soon see. I have all the papers delivered every morning. They should be here by now. Please excuse me a second."

She left the table and disappeared through a door leading to the front of the house. In less than a minute she had returned carrying half a dozen newspapers which she carefully placed on the table before re-seating herself. The headline on the top copy was self-explanatory : "Massacre."

"That's mine," she said. Martyn got the impression that, under normal circumstances, she would have been proud to reveal her efforts but now it was more of an admission of guilt than a boast. He picked up the paper and placed it to one side. The headline on the second paper told a similar story : "Fog Raid Leaves Eight Dead." Again, he placed it to one side so that it lay immediately next to the top copy. He spread the remaining four copies across the table and read out loud their respective headlines.

"Assassin - New Threat To City" He glanced up at Jacqui but her face remained passive.

" 'On The Loose.' That's your husband's contribution to the morning's news."

"He's purely a television reporter. He doesn't write for papers."

"He does now. Look, it's over three pages long. He's obviously put a lot of thought into this."

Without going into any more detail, he put the paper down and held up the last two copies. The first headline read: "Police Make Double Blunder."

"Half and half," he said. The second headline was more specific; "Laser Assassin Strikes In City - Alleged Police Cover Up."

"I think you lose, three and a half to two and a half," he said. "Beaten to the post by your own husband, a television reporter."

She said nothing. With the evidence before her, there was not a lot she could say. He could tell by her expression that she had little idea that the story was to steal her headlines, let alone that her husband was the source behind it.

"So why exactly are you looking for Greg?"

"Because, until yesterday, we didn't even know there was a laser assassin 'on the loose.' In fact, your husband knew before we did and I need to know where he got his story from because he may have put himself in danger."

"From whom? The police department?"

Martyn paused for a second before answering.

"Well they're not very happy with him. I'm not sure that he realises how serious this situation is. Someone has been murdered with a weapon that isn't even supposed to exist and our police department is now crawling with government officials and the phones are ringing more regularly than in your news room. And - I'll be honest with you - we don't know anything. The only person that seems to is your husband and that means he's potentially in danger. Perhaps he even knows who the assassin is, which makes his position even more precarious. It simply becomes a question of who gets to him first."

"I don't know where he is."

"Where has he gone in the past?"

"I don't know. He never tells me and I never tell him. It's best that way. My husband is an intelligent man, detective. If he is in danger, he will be the first to know it and he won't have left any trace as to his whereabouts."

"That may be true but he's left you as a sitting target all the same."

"What do you mean?"

"I mean, if you can't find a way of getting to him then the next step is to find a way of bringing him to you. All you need is the right bait. It would be a lot easier if we got to him first."

Jacqui Miller went quiet for a moment.

"How do I know I can trust you?"

"You don't. But you don't have any choice either - unless you want to hire your own private detective. And he'd have to be a bloody good one because he'd be starting out way over his head."

"So is that your brief, then? To find my husband?"

"No, it's to find the laser assassin but finding your husband seems like a good place to start. So where would I start looking him?"

She thought about this and then shrugged her shoulders.

"Okay, let's see."

They talked for over an hour, bouncing ideas off each other until they had enough possible lines of enquiry to keep an investigator busy for a whole year. Jacqui listed all his relatives, all his friends, at home and abroad, all of the hotels she knew he had stayed in over the last few years, all of the colleagues at work who might know his secret hideaways but, when they had finished, nothing had struck home as being the obvious lead and they were still no nearer to deducing his whereabouts.

If Jacqui Miller had been 'very busy' she showed no sign of wanting to leave in a hurry and, for the present, seemed to have become totally absorbed in the affairs of her husband. It was after nine when Martyn finally made to leave. But before he went back out through the French windows and onto the patio, he turned to her and spoke.

"Haven't I seen you before somewhere?"

Jacqui smiled. "I thought policemen had good memories when it came to faces."

"Only when they're criminal faces or in connection with an investigation. If I have met you before it must have been in pleasant circumstances, otherwise I would have remembered."

"I'll take that as a compliment," she said. "We have met before but I'm not going to tell you when or where it was. You'll have to ask Melissa."

He was slightly surprised. "How do…?"

She had already moved to the doorway opposite the patio and opened it.

"My husband will be alright, won't he?"

"I can only guarantee that when I know where he is."

16

Howard had returned from the travel agents just after midday and went straight round to Melissa's block. Already her room had become a hollowed shell, all its contents crammed into a small pile of cardboard boxes in one corner and only the wispy trails of dust to lay testament to the year they had passed together. He paused there, reminiscing, and then left as the first pangs of nostalgia began to bite.

He arrived at his own room out of breath. Melissa was there. She was seated on the window ledge, arms clasped around her knees, staring out across the deserted courtyard and deep in thought. Howard collapsed onto the bed and drew a long sigh.

"I've been really efficient," he said, evidently pleased with himself. "I got everything I needed and it's barely lunchtime. Game for a picnic?" Melissa did not respond. "Oh, and I just remembered. I got a first."

She stirred and looked up, smiling weakly. In fact it seemed hardly a smile at all and Howard wanted to ignore it. He repeated slowly, in a whisper, "I got a first."

Melissa turned round and he saw that her face was tear stained. In the same instant she reached out and grasped a magazine from the desk and tossed it towards him. Even before it had hit the floor his heart had sunk. He had rehearsed this scene in his mind over and over but now he was left speechless. He gazed into her eyes, silently pleading with her to make this easy for him, but he met only an ice-cold, impassive stare. She spoke in a low voice, chilled and accusing.

"How long have you known?"

Howard did not know what to say. He suddenly saw the whole year pass before him and wondered at the coincidence that everything, including his relationship with Melissa, should be divided into academic terms, three neat packages of mystery, happiness and mystery again. And now, the final scene, the day before year end.

Despite Melissa's impromptu declaration following her fourth disappearance they had not been able to see each other over the Christmas vacation and Howard had paced his way impatiently through the prolonged break until he could return to the university. But it had been worth the wait.

Melissa entered the second term a new woman. It was as though a great weight had been lifted from her shoulders. She was more relaxed and cheerful than he had ever seen her and all her forced inhibitions had simply disappeared. The lent term realised Howard's vision of heaven on earth and he could not spend enough time with her. There were no more strange absences and she seemed to have lost her obsessive determination to escape into the future. For ten weeks Melissa radiated happiness and Howard gradually began to believe that she had inadvertently found the future she had been trying to escape to - and that he was a part of it.

Perhaps he had become too complacent, or maybe it was another inevitable turn of the tide. Whichever, it transpired that their starry eyes were not to shine for long. The change was subtle and inexplicable. On the surface nothing had altered but Howard detected undercurrents he could neither define nor clarify. At the time he had attributed the change wholly to Melissa and that it had something to do with the mysterious jigsaw that had been delivered at the end of the second term. For some reason she had suddenly become nervous and edgy. But the jigsaw had turned out to be an incidental omen and it was not until he embarked on the first of his two study trips, shortly after, that the real truth was revealed.

Now Howard sat on the bed and stared down at the floor, silently cursing himself. Over the course of the year she had slowly moved into his room, putting up silly posters, surrounding his pillow with stuffed toys, filling a drawer full of lingerie and toiletries. Melissa had accumulated so much junk that her own room could not contain it all and some had inevitably spilled over into her 'second home'. He soon had a shelf full of her books and more of her records than his own. That morning he had left her to pack it all away and did not even stop to consider the possible consequences - but it was too late for regrets.

"How long have you known?" she repeated. Howard picked up the magazine and studied the two cover photographs set side by side. The first, labelled '1922', appeared to have been taken around that time. It pictured a young woman, her lithe, naked, sepia-toned body in mid-Charleston, exuding sexuality, captured and frozen for generations of eyes to lust over. Whether it was art or pornography was academic - the intention was clear. Yet her smile was so bright, so naive as to give the picture a subtle and mysterious eroticism. The second photograph, labelled '1982', repeated the pose and the mood. The resemblance was precise and uncanny. Beneath the two pictures was a short caption suggesting an enigma: "La Princesse Perdue?"

"How long!"

"Melissa, your picture was plastered all over Amsterdam. What was I supposed to do? Ignore it?"

"You knew all this term and you never said anything?"

"I didn't know what to say. I still don't. It doesn't change anything."

Melissa appeared to be on the verge of hysteria, tears were streaming down her face and her eyes were filled with anger.

"How can you sit there and say that? It changes everything. Everything!" She attempted to compose herself. "Who else knows?"

"I don't know. I haven't told anybody if that's what you mean. Melissa, listen to me. If we have to go through this then let's get it over with and forget about it. I made a decision long ago that I wasn't going to ask you and I don't require an explanation now. I've learned to live with it and I can continue to live with it."

"But you never threw it away," she said, accusingly.

"This isn't fair, Melissa. You're acting as if I'm the one who's on trial here. I don't want to defend myself and I don't want you to feel you have to defend yourself. I don't want to know."

"Why?"

"It's your business."

"That's not the real reason, is it? Why don't you want to know really? Are you scared of what you might find if you look too closely?"

"Melissa, I was in a shop in Amsterdam. It was a normal shop. It sold newspapers and magazines of all kinds. Then suddenly, there you were, staring down at me from the shelf. What was I supposed to do? I had to buy it. Surely you understand that. Of course I'm scared. Every time I go into a bookshop I wonder if I'm going to see you on another cover. Every time you disappear for even a few hours I can't help thinking where you might be. Have you any idea what it's like?"

Melissa was quiet. The bitterness was still there but she was trying to subdue it. He reached out to touch her but she recoiled and moved out of arm's reach.

"No one was supposed to find out - not ever."

"Melissa, was that very realistic? I knew the first day I met you that you hadn't been to university before. You made such an effort to pretend you knew all about it but you didn't even know where Bath was. Curiosity is engrained into everyone, especially in a place like this, and you went out of your way to encourage it. Nobody knows any more about you now than they did at the beginning of the year and they're all aware of it. But you can't expect to be able to vanish for days on end without people who care about you asking questions, even if it's only to themselves."

Melissa sighed. "How much do you know?"

"Hardly anything, and I'm happy for it to stay that way if that's what you want."

She thought about this, but it seemed she had already reached a conclusion long before he had even entered the room.

"Howard, if we don't talk then you'll never be able to trust me, and I'll never be able to trust you because I know you haven't ignored this. You can't have done. It's not in your nature. I think we should talk and I think we should both be totally honest with each other."

Melissa's suggestion would have been warmly approved if Howard had not suspected her motives to run in contradiction. What she wanted, Howard believed, was for him to be totally honest with her so that she could be selective about what she told him subsequently - and that was never going to work. In addition, Howard did not want to hold such a conversation in the room they had spent so many happy times together. He suddenly felt a strong desire to be completely severed from his present surroundings so they drove out of town and picked up a local river path on foot. It would have been a perfect day for a picnic, as Howard had suggested, but neither of them could eat anything. Melissa had warmed slightly but could still not bring herself to hold his hand and walked beside him maintaining a steady gap. In time she began to speak.

"It all started three years ago - after O-levels. I wanted to stay on at college and go on to higher education but my parents wanted me to leave and get a job."

"This is when you were in London," he added. Melissa frowned and he realised she had hoped she would not have to go into such detail.

"We were living in Campden and struggling to make ends meet," she continued. "It was so hard on my parents. They had both been brought up to expect better things but nothing had ever gone right for them. I remember when I was a child we used to live in a large house near Chester but then my father lost his business and we had to move into this poky little terrace in the city. Ever since, they'd been trying to get out and only sinking deeper and deeper. When I finished my exams my parents were so far in debt that they needed another income just to pay off the bills. They never learned to adapt to their new lifestyle. It wasn't that they stubbornly refused to make cuts, they just didn't know how to. They really did believe they were getting by on the minimum necessary to survive.

"I don't think they really wanted me to sacrifice my education but they had no choice. We had so many arguments. I ended up with good grades and refused to leave but I also felt guilty. I didn't know what to do. I began looking for jobs but only half-heartedly and I secretly signed up for college. I spent the whole summer pretending to go for interviews and forging rejection letters to myself.

"Then a friend of mine got a modelling assignment and suggested I try and get in on the act. It was only a short contract for beach and swimwear. I hated every minute of it but it paid well. Everything roller-coastered from there. I signed up with an agency where I could dictate my own terms. That way I could work evenings and weekends and still have time to attend college during the week. I had to take the occasional day off but it didn't really interfere with my studies. At first it seemed I had the best of both worlds."

As Melissa continued to talk it appeared she became less reticent and allowed the words to come out. She went into all of her modelling assignments in great detail and they were two miles further downstream before she reached the part that was not to come so easily. In all this time she had kept a rigid gap between them and Howard had not dared to try and cross it.

"Around Christmas the agency had a call from a publishing company in France - if you can call them a publishing company." She went quiet and Howard waited patiently for her to resume. "They said they had seen my photograph in a fashion magazine and noticed how similar I looked to Princesse Marie, the celebrated Moulin Rouge stripper from the Twenties."

"Never heard of her," Howard said.

"Nor had I. Nor has anyone as it turned out. But they told me they thought it would make an interesting article. There was no mention of nude modelling; just a few photos, a bit of background and a quick sale to some seedy French gossip magazine. It all seemed so innocent."

She went quiet again but this time Howard did not believe she was going to continue. Inside he was beginning to grow angry and frustrated, not at Melissa but at the situation he had no control over, as if it were happening in the present and he could do nothing about it but provide a shoulder to lean on.

"So what happened?"

"I went to Paris over the New Year. They told me they could get ten times more for the story if I took my clothes off. If I didn't they weren't even sure they could sell it at all and I wouldn't get my fee. They told me they had a magazine waiting to buy and that it did not have a circulation in England so no one would see it. They were very nice about it. I had nothing to lose and everything to gain. You know the rest."

Howard realised immediately he knew no such thing. This had all happened two years before and had only concluded at the start of their relationship. He did not want to know anymore but he could not help himself. Yet before he could say a word Melissa began crying.

"I couldn't help it," she said. "They ran the story in some tacky magazine and said I was the reincarnation of Princesse Marie. You don't know what it was like. They almost managed to convince me that it was true. Several other magazines bought the story and the money came rolling in - all from one photo session. I didn't even appear nude in most of them.

"My parents never really knew where the money came from but almost overnight they had managed to settle all their debts. And then they began talking about moving back up north. They set their hearts on it and I couldn't disappoint them. We got carried away, all of us. But I was in a different ball game. Before I could think about the consequences I was trapped in a contract for twelve more photo sessions. When the story died they wanted more from me. They began selling to soft porn magazines on the Continent and there was nothing I could do about it. We had moved to Alderley Edge and taken out a mortgage on the new house. If I'd broken the contract it would have cost me a fortune and we would have been back in the slums. I couldn't do that to my parents. My father got a much better job and now he's taken on the whole mortgage himself. Things worked out so well for us after we moved and I guessed it was a small price to pay at the time."

"And was it?"

"It was horrible. They treated me like a piece of meat and they wanted more and more from me. But I could have coped if I thought..." She took a deep breath.

"Go on."

"I hoped that no one would ever find out. I don't want to keep paying for this for the rest of my life. I thought it was all over and then, within six months..." She stopped walking and sat down on the riverbank staring at the shimmering reflections in the water. "Oh why the hell did you ever have to buy that magazine?"

"I didn't do it on purpose and it doesn't make any difference." She gave him a sidelong glance, that same accusing stare he had received earlier.

"Melissa, it was in a normal newsagents. I don't buy soft porn magazines, I don't read them and I don't condemn anyone who poses for them. I've been through all this already and I don't care. So why should you?"

"Does it boost your ego going out with a porn queen?"

"Will you quit this! It hasn't exactly been easy for me either, you know. Listen, I'm only going to say this once. You can't run away from this for the rest of your life. Wherever you go there will always be a chance that it will catch up with you. So make a stand now, while it's easy. Melissa, I love you and I want to support you but I can't if you shut me out."

"Do you love me or my body?"

"Oh, don't be stupid. How can you say that?"

"I can't help it. I have to be absolutely sure and I'm not. If you knew some of the men I knew then you'd understand. Before I came here wherever I went everybody assumed that I was a dumb blonde without an ounce of brain. Sometimes I didn't even feel like a human being. I thought I'd be able to escape all of that by coming here. I thought you were different, a friend who was interested in me as a friend. But even you sometimes treat me like a sex object and I wonder if you're all really just the same."

Howard's initial reaction was to defend himself vehemently. After a moment's thought he chose not to, not because he believed she was right, or because he suspected she was letting off steam, or because she was being totally unfair, but for a combination of all those reasons. Whether fair or not she was being honest with him and he knew that nothing short of complete honesty would suffice as a response.

"Melissa, I do love your body. Sometimes I think I could spend hours just playing with your hair and staring into those beautiful eyes. Sometimes when I'm with you all I want to do is touch you, undress you, make love to you. If that is what you mean and I've hurt you then I'm sorry, I really am, but I never understood, never even suspected, that you felt that way. If we were to stop sleeping together I admit I would find it difficult. I'm not sure if I could cope but I know I'd try. Right now I'm confused. It feels like I don't really know you at all but I do know one thing. Tomorrow I'm leaving for the States. I'm not going to see you or hear your voice for three months and I'm going to miss you like hell. And if you don't want to see me when I come back it's going to hurt, really hurt. Melissa, I love you and I don't want to lose you."

For what seemed like an eternity she did not move. He watched as she systematically tore off every blade of grass within reach and tossed them into the river. He waited in silence, patiently counting away the minutes, not daring to push her for a response. He witnessed the turmoil that was going on inside her but he could do nothing. He did not know her exact thoughts but he watched her struggle with each of her nightmares in turn, trying to do what he had failed to do, to face the problem head on and to purge herself of her shame. Piece by piece she was attempting to bury the past and embrace a new future. He realised she had never really faced this before, she had just trusted to fate that it would never happen. But it had.

They sat in silence until the last blades of grass had disappeared from sight, carried away on the river tide with each of her memories on board; one blade of grass for every photograph they had ever taken. And when it was over, still she said nothing. She simply burst into tears and fell sobbing into his arms.

17

By the time Martyn got back to the department it was almost nine thirty and both Rob and Brett were seated in the Chief's office, in all appearances waiting for his arrival before beginning the day's business.

"Find anything?" he said to Rob as he entered.

"Nothing," Rob replied. "Turned out to be a small warehouse selling laser guns as part of their range of club and stage equipment. Some weirdo has launched a one man campaign against the place. Having had me called out at sunrise to investigate this so called 'arms store', I find him pacing up and down outside the front reception with a placard saying 'Ban Lasers'. According to witnesses he'd been there all night. Apparently, he's the local religious nut."

"Sunrise?"

"Well, maybe not sunrise, but it was damned early."

The Chief broke in. "How about Miller?"

"Dead end, at least for the present. Went missing without trace yesterday. His wife doesn't know where he is. Didn't even know he was behind the story. Apparently he has lots of secret hidey holes for occasions such as this. Doesn't share them with anybody, not even her."

"You believe her?" the Chief asked. Martyn paused, knowing he was expected to make a subjective decision which would form the basis of their next steps.

"Yes, I believe her. If she's lying, she's a damn good actress."

"Alright. Bearing in mind that Miller is our only lead, where do you suggest we go from here?"

"That isn't easy. We could assume that she was lying and have her tailed. Probably pointless. If she's as good an actress as that she certainly won't be stupid enough to let herself be followed or inadvertently to reveal her husband's whereabouts. For completeness though we should keep the APB out on his car and also monitor his card transactions. I left her in no doubt about the danger he might be in. If she does know where he is, I think she might bring him to us. We could, on the other hand, start questioning all of Miller's colleagues, acquaintances and friends. Probably worth trying but I have a hunch that will be another dead end."

"We have already started, first thing this morning, beginning with the TV network."

"And?"

"So far its another dead end."

Martyn frowned as the implication of what the Chief had said dawned on him.

"Wait a minute. You knew I wasn't going to find Miller there this morning, didn't you?"

The Chief sat back, always pleased at any demonstration of his being one step ahead in an investigation.

"I guessed you wouldn't find him there. After all, he wasn't there all yesterday evening, he wasn't there all last night, and if he had turned up, you still wouldn't have found him there because I would have had him arrested and brought down here straight away."

"You had the house watched?"

"Only until you - or he - arrived, after which the ball was planted firmly in your court."

Martyn, and by this time Rob also, was beginning to feel slightly confused. Evidently a lot had happened during the night that they did not know about and he guessed there was still more to come.

"If Miller had turned up in the middle of the night, I expect you would have told me. I mean, I would have looked pretty stupid turning up at the crack of dawn and demanding of Mrs Miller that she tell me where her husband was, only to be told that he was down here."

"Of course you would have been told but the question is academic since I did not expect him to turn up and so far I have been proved right."

"I still don't understand. I thought this was supposed to be our case and yet I feel like I'm the last person to know what's going on."

"Me too," echoed Rob.

"Of course it's your case. I'm just having some of the unlikely leads and the routine groundwork covered for you, that's all. If it wasn't your case I wouldn't have waited for you to show up this morning before having Mrs Miller interviewed. I would have had her dragged down here last night when all hell was breaking loose."

"So why didn't you?"

"Because I wanted you to interview her. You're better with women."

Martyn laughed. "What! So why didn't you have us both dragged down here last night?"

Brett Lancaster sat back in his chair and folded his arms, radiating his most paternalistic expression.

"I was going to but when you phoned in I guessed you wouldn't have been very pleased at the interruption to your evening and I didn't have the heart to do it. I am human after all. And besides, you've both been working too hard recently. You both need a holiday but I can't let you go. Not yet. But I'm damned if I'm going to kill you with work now - not if it isn't necessary. And last night wasn't important. On the other hand, today is important. We have got to find that laser rifle as soon as possible. We've got public pressure to contend with now and the only way we're going to get rid of that is to tie up the case as soon as we can. So Martyn, you hadn't finished. Where do you suggest we go from here?"

"Well, besides the two options I've already mentioned, and which we seem to have already dealt with or discounted, I reckon we have three more. Firstly, we can do nothing and wait for Miller to turn up on his own. Secondly, we can try and lure him out into the open, though I haven't a clue how, and thirdly, we can turn our attention on ourselves and try and find out who gave Miller all his information because he sure as hell didn't make it all up out of thin air."

The Chief redirected his attention to Martyn's partner.

"Rob?"

"Seems to have covered everything. Just two points, though. We still haven't been to the scene of the crime. There wasn't any point yesterday, because of the fog, but I think maybe one of us ought to go this morning. You never know. Secondly, how do we know Miller hasn't got his information from the killer?"

The Chief looked to Martyn. "Well?"

"We don't for certain," he said. "Theoretically, they could be in cahoots or the killer might be using Miller to hold the city to ransom." He removed a small cardboard file from under his arm and placed it on the desk. "However, Miller has a perfectly clean record. A bit ruthless in business but never a lawbreaker. In fact, he speaks out against the criminal sector more than any other journalist and he's provided a lot of useful information to this department. Also, I read all the papers this morning and there wasn't anything in any of them that we didn't know already. If the story had originated from anywhere but inside the police department there would have been at least some minor discrepancy between our facts and his. As it stands, I could have written the article myself and there wouldn't have been any difference between the two."

"Except for a few spelling mistakes," Rob said. "Okay, I accept that, if only because you're a natural cleverdick. So where do we go from here?"

"Like you said, the scene of the crime. This case seems to progress fastest when we don't do anything. I bet if we go down to Eden Square and waffle about, something will happen before lunchtime."

"How do you figure that?" Rob said.

"Well, look at it this way. Assume somebody in the department has been passing information about this case to the media. I don't like being one step behind anybody in my own case, but at the moment we don't know who is doing it or why. However, since it is now our case, and since we have to take it personally, then we have to accept that someone is playing games with us and they haven't stopped yet. We only have two reasonable courses of action. Either we try and find Miller, who is our only lead, and whom I think will prove to be very elusive, or we appear to go off looking in the totally wrong direction and wait for our mystery man, Miller or otherwise, to make the next move to bring us back into line. And hopefully, when he does, he will also make a mistake. Chief?"

"I don't like your idea of wasting time but, for now, I'm prepared to go along with you. Logically, it makes sense and Rob is right; you might turn something over at Eden Square. The immediate area has been cordoned off for a couple of days but no one has had chance to go over it with a fine tooth comb since the fog lifted. Forensics are going down later. This isn't a school picnic. If there is anything left in that square I want it found, is that understood?"

They both nodded.

"Right, before you go, there are a couple more things we have to discuss." Brett glanced at his watch. "For a start, I don't like the idea that we have a mole in the department. But if it is true then the sooner we face the fact the better. Off the record, have you any idea who it might be?"

"We discussed this yesterday morning," Rob said. "If we assume that the same person was responsible for both the heart attack and the laser stories then we have a very short list of suspects, limited to the three of us and the handful of people mentioned in Robinson's autopsy report."

Brett nodded. "Can I assume that the three of us are discounted? Rob?"

"Well, out of everybody, I think I've evidently got the least idea what's going on, so it can't be me." He indicated towards his partner. "On the other hand, he's far too much of a smart ass to be above suspicion."

Martyn laughed. It could not be Rob. In the one year that they had been partners, Martyn had grown to trust him like a brother. There was no way he could be involved. He was a good cop, always making himself out to be more stupid than he really was, but he certainly was not capable of being behind all this. He was far too lazy for one thing. Similarly with Brett. He often forced himself to remain aloof to emphasise his position as their Chief but the three of them had learned to rely on each other. To even consider not trusting one another, when they had each put their lives on the line on numerous occasions, was not something Martyn could easily imagine. But he did not say that.

"I think we can discount everyone in this room, if only because the first news bulletin appeared before the existence of the laser rifle was disclosed to this department. And I would tend to support my partner's view that we are talking about the same person."

"Thank you," Rob said. "I'm glad that, even under the present circumstances, when you come into this office complaining that you don't know what's going on and then give the impression that you are the only person alive that does, that you still have confidence in your partner, because I would like to declare here and now that I haven't a bloody clue what's going on and I don't understand how you do."

"He just never gives his brain a rest," Brett said. "I thought you'd have got used to it by now. Right, so who does that leave us with?"

Martyn fished a copy of the autopsy report from the Chief's desk.

"What about this Commander Colchek character? He left a nasty taste in my mouth."

Brett Lancaster shook his head.

"If you two are prepared to trust me, then I will have to trust him for the same reasons. I've known him ever since I've known both of you. He's a bit abrasive but he's straight down the line. If you want my opinion I'd have to say 'no'. Besides, there is even less reason for him being behind it than the rest of us. He's suffered most of the embarrassment for the whole thing. It was because he was concerned that the story might leak that he brought us in on the case in the first place. That's why there was so much secrecy yesterday. The investigation wasn't supposed to have been brought down to this level. If he's playing both the devil and the saint in the same breath then I reckon that he, also, is a very good actor. Not only that but I think he's genuinely desperate to get hold of the laser weapon. There are a lot of people breathing down his neck too."

"Okay," Rob said. "I'm prepared to accept that. So who's left?"

Martyn turned the pages of the autopsy report.

"Three people, led by a Professor Harper, conducted the autopsy. The same four who were present at the autopsy on Sarjena West last June. In addition, the two investigators who were handling the case were George Manciani and John Reynolds. Never heard of them."

"They wouldn't be very useful investigators if you had. They work almost entirely under cover." Brett Lancaster frowned. "It isn't going to be very easy to pin anything on any of them. They all have top grade security clearance."

Martyn shrugged his shoulders. "We don't really have any choice, do we?"

Chief Lancaster looked at him as if wishing there were still two answers to his question.

"I'll talk to Colchek," he said.

Just then, the intercom buzzer sounded on the Chief's desk. He flicked a switch and a female voice came over the small speaker,

"Everything is ready, sir, if you would like to proceed." Brett glanced at his watch, rose from his chair and reached for the reply switch.

"Excellent," he said. "We're on our way." He returned his attention to Martyn and Rob.

"Before you dash off to the scene of the crime, I've gathered everyone together for a little unarmed combat session in the firing range. And I've arranged a little demonstration for you. I'll think you'll find it interesting. Please follow me."

Without another word, the Chief walked over towards the door and left the office. Martyn glanced at Rob, who was evidently as puzzled as he was, shrugged his shoulders a second time and followed Brett Lancaster out of the office.

"Curiouser and curiouser."

In the elevator the Chief selected the basement level and then relaxed against the interior wall of the cabin.

"Either of you two remember the name Raspov, big in the news about a year ago?"

"Russian," Rob said.

"Very good," the Chief replied, sarcastically. "Do any better?" He turned his attention to Martyn, who was already deep in thought. Raspov. He remembered the name. A defector from the Communist Alliance, he had fled to Britain over twelve months before. An expert in laser weapon technology, Raspov had been a prize catch for the West and a serious, and embarrassing, loss for the Alliance. Following rumours of death squads despatched to Europe, Raspov was secretly transferred over to the American government in fear of his life. The last thing anybody had heard was that he was safely hidden somewhere in an American controlled state. Then his name vanished from the papers and news bulletins as if it had never existed. At the time, Martyn remembered thinking that, despite everything, the Alliance death squad had ultimately been successful and Raspov had become no more an embarrassment to the Russians than he was to the American government who had tried so hard to protect him. He was surprised to hear the name again and the logical connection between Raspov and laser weapons took only the slightest spark of lateral thought.

"I thought he was dead," he said to Brett as they stepped out of the elevator into a dimly lit basement corridor. The Chief turned to the right and headed towards the shooting range.

"So did I," he confessed. "But they obviously thought this was serious enough to drag him out of the woodwork. They wouldn't go to all that trouble over one man if we were never going to get anything back out of him, would they?"

"Who is 'they'?" Martyn said, rhetorically.

Brett stared up at the ceiling, only inches above his head, as if gazing into the heavens.

"Who knows?" he said. "'Them.'"

As they entered the ante room of the shooting range, a short man, middle aged with a neat, short cut of dark hair and old fashioned round spectacles hurried over to meet them. He gave an instant impression of being an academic, slightly eccentric, who could only be at home in a laboratory, quietly secluded, away from the rest of society.

"Mr Lancaster, sir. Please come in. We are all ready for you."

He shook hands with the Chief and then shot a beaming smile, strangely disturbing, towards Martyn and Rob. His accent, though predominantly the result of exposure to the West Coast, held an unmistakeable hint of Russian intonation. Martyn offered his hand to him.

"Mr Raspov, I presume."

"Very good," Raspov said, and then, turning to the Chief, "Did you tell him?"

"I hinted at it," Brett confessed, "but I'm not sure he wouldn't have guessed anyway. You never know with him. Mr Raspov, I'd like you to meet Detectives Sorensen and Laurie who will be heading up the investigation. I am sure they will find what you have to say very interesting."

Raspov took both their hands in turn.

"Welcome, gentlemen. We will talk later. But first I must ask you to take your positions. We are all waiting for you."

Raspov led them onto the range, a large bunker completely enclosed in concrete, about the length of a tennis court. Martyn suddenly realised why the office had seemed so deserted. At the far end of the range their colleagues were standing, shoulder to shoulder, in a single line, directly in front of the target area. They were in unarmed combat gear and all were stripped to the waist. Their female colleagues were stood to one side, some silent, others whistling and joking at the expense of their male colleagues.

In the centre of the range stood a solitary camera, mounted on a tripod, surrounded by lighting equipment and mirrors. The combined effects of the two highlighted the line of men in such a way that it reminded Martyn of an identity parade. They all showed signs of nervousness or self consciousness; he could not tell which.

"What's going on?" he asked.

Brett Lancaster stepped forward.

"Mr Raspov," he explained, "is not just an expert on laser light; he is an expert on all light, an optical genius so to speak, and a very keen photographer. For the last few months he has been working as a professional photographer in the city, doing work for magazines mainly. It's been an excellent cover. No one knows who he really is. Anyway, before he answers all our questions I thought it was about time we had a team photo, so get your shirts off and join the rest."

"Why the bare chests?" Rob asked.

"Good question," Martyn muttered and wandered off towards the line. Behind him, he heard the Chief's answer. "So all the girls can have a good giggle." And then, since this was evidently not a satisfactory reply, he turned to see Brett ushering Rob towards him.

"Everything will become clear," he said.

As Martyn walked past the camera he stopped momentarily to examine the equipment. It appeared authentic enough. Raspov caught his gaze.

"You are a suspicious man, Mr Sorensen? It is not always a good thing to be so."

"Never done me any harm yet."

Just then, one of the younger female cadets came over and a general clamour went up at their arrival.

"Come on, Martyn, Rob. Don't be shy. Get your clothes off."

Martyn unbuttoned and removed his shirt and then handed it to the girl.

"Don't know what you're laughing at. He's doing a topless one of you lot next." He walked over to the line and took his place, Rob following closely behind.

Raspov took his position behind the camera and began making a few minor adjustments while looking through the lens. After a few seconds he raised his head, smiling, and held the shutter release chord up in the air.

"That is perfect," he said. "Is everybody ready? There is no need for you to smile. And..."

Everything happened in a fraction of a second. Martyn had been staring forward at the camera and the surrounding lights. He was wondering what the mirrors were for and had thrown a questioning glance towards Raspov and the Chief, who was standing directly behind him. The glance was met by a boyish, knowing grin and an excited gleam in Raspov's eyes as he depressed the shutter release.

There was a blinding flash from the bank of lights, immediately followed by the sound of shattering glass as one of the mirrors cracked and fell in shards at Raspov's feet. As the photograph was taken, Martyn saw the girl's smiling faces turn to gasps of horror and incomprehension. Somewhere further along the line somebody fell backwards and crashed noisily against a wooden target. Without knowing why, Martyn also felt as if he wanted to fall backwards and he was forced to take a step to regain his balance. To his left, he sensed Rob's body jerk slightly to one side as though he had been slapped across the face. Then came the pain, sharp and searing, first in the upper right arm, then the left, then across his torso. He looked down at his own chest to see a red weal, like a perfectly straight whip lash, carved neatly out of his flesh. He quickly noted that everyone in the line bore the same mark, in each case at an identical height. Then he realised.

When the explanation had been made and the protests lodged, Chief Lancaster led Martyn and Rob towards the camera, where Raspov was busily packing away the equipment. Soon the four of them were left alone in the range.

"Sorry about the mirror," said Raspov. "Slight miscalculation on my part. Could you get someone to clear up the glass?"

Raspov's mannerisms, the way he spoke absentmindedly, the feverish activity with which he went about his task, all projected such an eccentric personality that it was difficult to retain a solemn attitude to what had happened. To Raspov the whole thing had evidently been a huge joke.

"Wasn't that dangerous?" Martyn asked, still rubbing moisturising cream into his chest.

"Not at all, not at all," Raspov protested. "It was necessary."

"Can't see why," said Rob, nursing his left arm.

"But you must!" insisted Raspov. "If someone is trying to stab you then you know about it. If somebody throws a spear, or a rock, or a firebomb, or fires an arrow at you then you can see it. If someone shoots at you then you can hear the bang. But if somebody fires a laser beam in your direction you won't know about it until you feel it and then you must have learned to recognise it for what it is. If you are hit by a stationary beam directly, the chances are you will not feel any pain, you will not survive. But the advantage of the laser is that it can be fired in an arc, like a sub-machine gun, but its effects are very much weakened. Then, if you react quickly enough, you may have a second chance. But you could be sliced three times in the time it takes you to realise you have been hit once. Remember these burns, my friends. Remember the pain. In a few days these wounds will be healed. You must remember the pain and learn to recognise it."

Martyn looked at Brett for verification. The Chief nodded.

"The laser panned you all in four tenths of a second. The camera and the beam were synchronised so we should have an interesting photograph of the demonstration. I only wish I could have photographs of the looks on your girlfriends' faces when you go to bed tonight."

"Oh, that reminds me," Raspov said. "You may find it stings in the shower." He laughed.

"Very funny," Rob mumbled.

Martyn decided to change the subject. His mind had been ticking over once more and there were still several questions which Raspov had to answer. He picked up one of the shards of broken glass and began examining it.

"Mr Raspov, can you bounce lasers off mirrors generally or are these special?"

"The mirrors are special but, in any case, the answer to your question is 'not for long'. When a powerful infrared laser beam strikes a normal mirror, most of the heat is absorbed and only a fraction is reflected. The glass becomes hot, expands and shatters in a very short time, usually within a second. In theory, the mirror should not have shattered because it was reflecting the beam for less than half a second, well within the specification. Also, since the beam achieved its full sweep before the mirror shattered, there must have been a problem in heat loss. Fascinating. Now let me see…"

What began as an explanation had soon sent Raspov onto another mental plain and he became lost in a world of his own. Martyn quickly dragged him back into the present ; there were still a few more questions they needed to ask him.

"Are you sure the beam switched itself off when it had finished carving holes in us?"

"Of course, of course. It was timed to go off when the camera flashed. And since it did flash..." He picked up a piece of the broken mirror, "...but this is very interesting..."

"Mr Raspov, we don't have time for that now. Perhaps you wouldn't mind thinking about it later. We still need to know what exactly it is we are looking for."

But it was too late. Raspov was already heading across the range towards the laser transmitter which he had so effectively hidden behind a stack of crates and boxes, right next to where the last man in the line had been standing. The laser itself was about the size and shape of an old English post box, Martyn thought, about human height and mounted on a short pedestal. Attached to the pedestal was a small control box, presumably to supervise the timing and the laser's rotation during the demonstration. Raspov made a quick check of the equipment and then ambled back towards them.

"Not exactly portable, is it?" he said.

Everyone got the message.

"I still can't believe the laser rifle is here, in the United States," he continued. "It is too soon. They could not have developed it in time."

"Who couldn't?" asked Rob.

"The Alliance," Raspov answered. "The rifle must have originated in the Communist military; no other nation is advanced enough. But so soon? It does not seem possible."

"Were you anywhere near to producing the laser rifle when you left?" Martyn said.

"Sure we were, but there is near and near. As I explained to your Commander Colchek, we had been given a target, a plan. The prototype was to be produced by the end of this year and we would go into full scale manufacture beginning in January. The project was my - how you say – 'baby'? Yes, the project was my baby but, in my heart, I never believed it would be completed in so short a time. I did not know if it would be completed in my own lifetime. We had problems with the power supply, you see. To do what has been done to those two people requires a vast amount of energy and that energy cannot be carried around in your pocket. I could produce a laser rifle tomorrow; that is not the problem. But it would hardly burn a hole in a sheet of ice. Power is the problem."

Martyn listened to Raspov very carefully. Although he had first appeared reluctant to talk, it seemed now that he could not provide enough information. Rob was already beginning to switch off and had begun pacing round in circles. Brett Lancaster had evidently heard it all before, at an earlier meeting which he had not disclosed to them. If anything had come out of that meeting, they had not been briefed, so it was unlikely that any useful information had been gleaned. Martyn was determined to get something more out of Raspov than his predecessors had. Something Raspov had said gave him an idea.

"Mr Raspov, why did you defect?"

He replied without shame, without hesitation.

"Mr Sorensen. I can see in your eyes that you have already guessed the reason for my, shall we say, sudden departure. I was scared. I did not want to be a failure and I knew the project was doomed. In my country, to fail in such a task is unforgivable. There is no second chance. What is the point in carrying on for one more year when you know you are wasting your time? I did not see it. I was left without a choice."

"And fourteen months later, are you still sure you could not have done it?"

Raspov smiled, spotting the hidden question with ease.

"I believe you would make rather a fine chess player, Detective Sorensen. Do you play?"

"Sometimes."

"Good. We must have a game in the near future. You would like that?"

Martyn accepted. "Sure," he said. "Now supposing you answer the question."

Raspov continued without argument.

"The laser you see behind you is a modified version of the latest American Airforce anti-aircraft weapon. For the purposes of this demonstration, it was an ideal design, not least because I designed it myself. Of course, the government of your country would not pay me all the attention that they did simply to let me loose as a freelance photographer. Your country is no better than mine, Mr Sorensen. They speak grand words of freedom and democracy but they would not have rescued me to let me be free. They wanted to know what I knew. They wanted me to build them a laser rifle. I had come out of prison and entered a jail. It was no better, no worse. But it was too late for me, I had made my choice."

"So?"

"So I told them everything I knew about lasers. I initiated the research into the hand held laser rifle. I advanced the project as far as it could go, as far as I had gone in Communist Russia, then I explained to them why it could not be done and they let me go. I have been a photographer ever since, until yesterday."

"What happened yesterday?" Martyn asked.

"He was an obvious suspect," the Chief interjected.

"I was an obvious suspect," Raspov repeated.

Rob nodded towards Martyn. "He was an obvious suspect," he said. Martyn ignored him.

"You say you did not believe a laser rifle could have been developed in such a short time. What is your opinion now?"

Raspov's reply was solemn, allowing a faint trace of defeat to pass his lips.

"I have examined the reports. I have seen the bodies. There can be no doubt. I was wrong."

18

Rob and Martyn decided to take the train from the department and arrived in Eden Square around midday. Picking up a kebab steak from a wagon parked outside the station they wandered down the station ramp and across to the plaza. In seconds they had disappeared from view, hidden among the hoards of people and multi-coloured paving stones.

Almost as soon as the train had shot out of the mouth of the tunnel, and the first blurred image proclaiming 'Eden Square' had had time to register on the retina, Martyn had been overcome by that same uneasy sensation he had first experienced the morning before, on his way to the department. Now, the tension was so great that he found himself chewing the same piece of kebab steak for over five minutes, unable to swallow it. His stomach had formed a tight knot and he had lost his appetite. He folded the mass of spiced lamb, salad and pitta bread into the paper and stuck it in the nearest litter basket.

"Not hungry?" Rob asked.

Martyn answered with a grunt, indicating that he had still not swallowed the last mouthful. For a moment, he looked about him, scrutinising the paving stones under his feet, and then made for one of the many ornamental gardens that were dotted around the square. Contrary to the Chief's information, it did not appear that an area had been cordoned off. He found a bench under a miniature palm and sat down. Rob joined him, kebab in one hand, rubbing his chest in the other.

"Hell! It's still painful."

"You should have put moisturiser on it like everyone else," Martyn replied. "Serves you right for wanting to preserve your macho image."

"But it smells awful," Rob protested. "You reek like a perfumery. Haven't you noticed how many strange looks you've been getting?"

"Me? I would have thought it was more to do with the fact that you haven't stopped scratching your chest since we left the department."

Rob popped the last piece of the kebab into his mouth, screwed up the paper and tossed it into a nearby bin. Then he quickly changed the subject.

"I didn't realise how hungry I was. I could easily eat another one of those. In fact, I could have eaten yours."

Martyn pointed across the square. "Well if you want it, help yourself. It's only over there."

Eden Square, built at the very heart of the city, was one of the few aesthetically pleasing sights in the conurbation. Being the focal point of the city's transportation networks, it was originally built as a pedestrian thoroughfare between the rail and bus terminals which lay on opposite sides of the plaza. However, the square also acted as a natural barrier between the business and commercial sectors. As time went by, the area to the east of Eden Square continued to grow, an expanding jungle of large stores, shopping arcades, restaurants, clubs, extending the full two kilometres to the docklands and then spreading south along the coast. Immediately to the west of the plaza the business sector also continued to grow, but in a vertical direction. Confined to a relatively smaller area, office block after office block joined the tightly packed cluster, sprouting unexpectedly from the ground and rising into the air with breathtaking speed. And, one block from the plaza, towering so far above the city that most of the cluster was dwarfed in its presence, the New Century Tower dominated the skyline.

In stark contrast to the tall skyscrapers which surrounded it, the plaza was entirely flat, exactly three hundred metres square and paved with almost ninety thousand flagstones of various pastel colours. From above, it appeared as a large psychedelic kaleidoscope without rhyme or reason. The arrangement of the flagstones had been selected randomly by computer and the results had been published in a thirty page booklet, circulated prior to construction.

More thought, however, had gone into the positioning of the ornamental gardens and the various works of abstract modern art which adorned its surface, each occupying just enough space to stand independently among its distinguished neighbours. By far the most spectacular of these, and the main attraction for the hundreds of thousands of tourists which passed through the square each year, were the three Aquashow fountains, built in consecutive years from 2025 onwards. The first had been the simplest of the three, a giant multiple fountain with the central jet rising to a height of twenty metres. The fountain was impressive enough during the day but, in the evening, when dusk once more fell on the city, casting its familiar grey shadows, the banks of lights placed at the base of each jet provided one of the most spectacular light shows that the new century had seen.

One year later, in 2026, the Aquashow clock fountain had been constructed; three concentric rings of coloured water jets displaying the time in hours, minutes and seconds. The most recent fountain was undoubtedly the most impressive. Four stainless steel tubes, each standing in one corner of a square pool, fired high pressure jets of water horizontally across the water surface so that all four collided in mid air over the centre. By varying the water pressure at each nozzle the point of collision could be made to shift position. Using sophisticated controls, the spray appeared to dance in the air, jumping from corner to corner, sometimes spinning in circles over the pool.

"I thought we came here to examine the scene of the crime," said Rob, after a few minutes. Martyn raised his arm once more and pointed in the direction of the waste paper bin in which he had thrown his kebab steak.

"We have," he said. "We just passed it. Over there, near that circle of yellow paving stones. There wasn't anything to see."

"How do you know it was there exactly?" Rob asked.

"Because we know from the plan that it was around here somewhere and I recognised the pattern of slabs from the photographs in the autopsy report."

Rob looked at him disbelievingly.

"But that pattern can't be unique. There were about sixteen paving stones in the photo and there are close on a tenth of a million in the whole square."

Martyn leaned back and folded his arms, his expression blank. "Yes, but they haven't all got little black crosses marked in the corners."

Rob slumped back in the seat, showing positive signs of frustration with his partner's sudden change of attitude.

"And there wasn't anything to see?" he repeated, trying to sound less irritated than he really was. But it was Martyn who broke the tension.

"What did you expect? Great big footprints and a murder weapon? Unless you expect me to get down on my hands and knees and dig around in the cracks between the paving stones which, incidentally, should have already been done, I don't intend to move from this very comfortable seat. We may as well try and figure out what might have happened. After all, we're only killing time."

"Is that all this means to you? Just killing time. I thought we might find something useful here."

"Like what, for heaven's sake! This is Eden Square, the biggest pedestrian thoroughfare in the city. Whatever clues turn up in the lab from the other night could have belonged to any one of twenty thousand people. And since yesterday several thousand more people could have trampled over anything they left behind. There's no point to this whatsoever."

"Hey," Rob protested. "This is your partner here. What are you mouthing off at me for? All I did was to give us the perfect excuse to leave the department, get some fresh air and relax a bit, and you take the opportunity with both hands and go all irritable on me. What the hell did I do?"

Martyn let out a long sigh.

"I'm sorry," he said. "I feel a bit tense. I got this knot in my stomach the second we arrived here. I don't know why."

"Do you think you may have seen something?" Rob suggested. "Maybe subconsciously…"

"No, I don't think so. I'm not sure what it is. Just something about this place that isn't quite right. I don't know what. I feel I'm supposed to make some kind of connection every time I come here but it's all very vague."

"Alright," said Rob. "Let's do what you suggested a moment ago and try and figure some sense out of all this, starting with what happened the night before last." He waited for an acknowledgement and then continued. "Okay, Howard Robinson leaves his book shop in Arcades just after six. He paused and indicated a direction to their right. Through the gaps in the tenement buildings, which lined the eastern side of the plaza, they could see, less than four kilometres away, the distinctive glass domes which characterised the Arcades shopping area. Martyn nodded and Rob continued.

"He walks from the shop to the Arcades gliderail station and takes the Richmond line to Eden Square, arriving here at around six forty. We have an eyewitness who says she saw Robinson closing the shop at around six and several people confirm that he took the train from Arcades station to here not long after that. So far, no one has confirmed seeing him en route to Arcades station or after he left the train here. We know from computer records that he bought a newspaper in the station hall even though no one remembers serving him. From there, he comes down the station driveway, crosses the road onto the plaza, walks about fifty metres towards the bus terminal on the other side when suddenly somebody steps out of the fog and blows him away with a laser rifle at point blank range. His body is discovered at five minutes to seven by another pedestrian dashing from the bus terminal to the station. From the moment he left the shop to the discovery of the body, all the timings are perfect. There isn't even a minute unaccounted for. With me so far?"

"You mean there's more?" Martyn spoke almost absentmindedly. Usually he would have plenty to add but for now he said nothing and seemed strangely preoccupied.

"Sure," Rob continued. "The next news bulletin on the network, less than two hours later, reports the incident as a heart attack, something they normally wouldn't have bothered with, certainly not within such a short space of time. The next day, Miller reveals the full truth on the network and in a number of world exclusives, and then disappears into thin air as the fog lifts. What we're left with is a murder without a motive, using a weapon that isn't even supposed to exist, and the only person with any answers has gone into hiding. The whole thing is as clear as mud. Make any sense to you?"

Martyn remained silent, staring directly toward to the station ramp, his eyes carefully searching for something. Rob spoke again.

"And then, to cap it all, my partner suddenly gets the heebie-jeebies about the only nice place within a fifty mile radius and doesn't listen to a word I'm saying."

"I'm listening," Martyn said. "It seemed a pretty fair summary and, for what it's worth, I agree with the conclusion. It doesn't make sense."

"So?"

Martyn shrugged his shoulders.

"I don't know," he said. "I really don't know."

Inside, Martyn was battling to control the muscles which had involuntarily tightened over his whole body. It seemed the longer he remained in the square, the more tense he became. With his sudden loss of appetite had come an overpowering thirst and a parched throat. He could sense the flow of adrenaline around his body and the throbbing inside his head as his heart began to beat faster. While listening to Rob, he had been trying, in vain, to come to terms with the emotion, pretending that it was his imagination and that the sensations would go away. The symptoms he recognised as those of extreme stage fright but that did not make sense either. In the end he gave in, deciding that a problem shared was probably the only release, and exposed his innermost thoughts to his partner.

"I think we're being watched."

Rob's reaction, as it should be, was not a reaction at all. He relaxed back in the seat and crossed his right leg over the left, leaving the ankle balancing on the edge of the knee. He projected a false grin out into the square. His gaze followed his partners. Towards the station.

"Where?" he said.

"I don't know."

The grin disappeared.

"What do you mean you don't know?"

"I mean I *feel* as if we're being watched. There is no evidence to back it up. It's pure intuition."

"Oh, great," Rob said. "And I thought you were the rational one." He began to look round the square. Hundreds of people passed before his eyes. "I don't suppose this psychic antenna of yours is up to homing in on the general direction of this peeping tom, is it?"

Martyn could not decide whether his partner was taking him seriously or being flippant. In the end he decided it must be the latter.

"I know it sounds crazy but the only vibes I'm getting from this place are that we're being watched. I'm sorry if that doesn't provide us with a motive or a murder weapon but it's all I've got. Take it or leave it."

"If it's all the same to you I think I'll reserve judgement. It's probably the after effects of that moisturiser. Come on, let's take a walk and see if we can fathom all this out. You're making me feel nervous."

They began walking across the plaza, away from the station, towards the bus terminal.

"I have a theory," said Rob. "So far we haven't found even a slight trace of a motive for either the murder of Howard Robinson or of Sarjena West. In fact, so close have we not come to finding a motive that I'm beginning to favour the idea that there wasn't a motive at all, at least not one that was personal. Now supposing they happened to be in the wrong place at the wrong time and that's all it is. Supposing Howard Robinson is crossing the square when he suddenly, accidentally, comes across, say for example, two people making a transaction. One million dollars for one laser rifle. He sees them, they see him, and he pays with his life."

"You don't think he was followed and assassinated?"

"No. If he was followed from his shop in Arcades then whoever it was had plenty of opportunity to bump him off then. It doesn't make sense that somebody would have waited for him here. He may not have turned up. Besides, no motive."

"And Sarjena West?"

"Same. The park was practically empty that day. There were no witnesses. She pushes the pram over the crest of the hill, sees something she shouldn't have done, gets shot at point blank range and the pram rolls down the hill into the lake. Fortunately it floated. What do you think?"

"Plenty," said Martyn. "First of all, I think you're right. There is no motive for either killing and I don't think we'll find one. However, there is still the possibility that Howard Robinson was mistaken for someone else, though that isn't as easy to believe in the case of Sarjena West. I don't, however, think that they could have just happened to see something they shouldn't. Who would arrange to make a transaction in the middle of Washington Park or Eden Square when the city is full of dark corners and alleyways which were made for them?"

"But Washington Park was empty and the Square was covered in thick fog. Both were ideal."

"Yes, but how would you know that Washington Park was going to be empty tomorrow? And look where these transactions were supposed to have taken place; Washington Park is full of trees and little nooks and crannies away from the beaten track but Sarjena West was killed in one of the most exposed parts of the whole park. The same with Howard Robinson. If you were going to be audacious enough to meet in Eden Square, at rush hour, albeit in thick fog, you would have to agree to meet by some recognisable object like a statue or one of the ornamental gardens. But look where Robinson was killed. Not only was it right away from any such object but it was right in the middle of the pedestrian route between the bus terminal and the station, give or take a few yards. Making a transaction there would have been stupid. They were bound to have been spotted by somebody. And besides, if Robinson and West were killed purely because they stumbled on some kind of transaction then that more or less implies that laser rifles could be changing hands at an alarming rate, and yet no one is using them except when they're forced to. And that doesn't make sense."

Rob looked back to where Howard Robinson had been found and frowned.

"So where does that leave us?" he said.

"Depends whether you believe in coincidences or not."

"What do you mean?"

"Well, during that conversation we have discovered a common link between the two murders. Both were committed in a wide open public place."

"But we always knew that."

"Yes, but did we always realise or appreciate the significance?"

"Obviously not," said Rob, "because I still don't. You'll have to explain."

"I can't," Martyn replied. "But I don't believe in coincidences."

They arrived at the clock fountain. The tallest jet indicated that the day was still in its thirteenth hour. As each second passed a smaller jet of water on an inner ring would rise and then fall, only to be replaced by another slightly further around the circle. The fountain looked like a giant clock face without hands, the numerals being represented by shaped flower beds cut out of the paving stones which surrounded it. They watched as the second jets ticked their way round the ring. As they lapped the hour jet at twelve, the minute jet disappeared very briefly and then reappeared slightly closer towards them.

"Twenty three minutes past twelve and all is well," said Rob. "I could watch this for hours."

"Unfortunately, you won't have time." The voice came from behind them, pleasant but authoritative. They turned to face the stranger.

"Allow me to introduce myself. My name is John Reynolds, Special Forces Network. And this is my partner, George Manciani."

"Good afternoon, gentlemen." The second voice also came from behind. Rob turned to face Manciani, Martyn did not bother. Reynolds spoke a second time.

"It seems that you're wanted back at the department," he said. "Miller has turned up. He's being held for questioning but, on instructions from his wife, he refuses to talk to anyone but you."

"Have you been following us all the time?" Rob asked.

"Oh, come now," Manciani said. "Do you think we've got nothing better to do than chase you two around? We had to come out here when Miller wouldn't tell us anything."

Martyn glanced back at the Aquashow clock.

"Just a minute," he said. "How long have you been trying to question Miller?"

"He turned up about two hours ago," Reynolds said.

"Two hours!" Martyn exclaimed. "Why the hell weren't we told then? We were still back at the department two hours ago."

"There were a few questions we needed to ask him," Manciani said, "and I think you'll find we had priority over you."

"Priority! This is our case! Miller is our witness! What the hell gives you priority?"

"We do," said Reynolds. "But since he refuses to speak to us at all unless you're present, it's something we'll just have to live with. Next time, we'll remember to pay a social visit to the suspect's wife before we interview him. Martyn decided this last comment did not merit a reply but, in the event, Reynolds did not allow him time for one. "Your car is waiting over there, at the bottom of the station driveway. Shall we go?"

Reynolds and Manciani began walking back across the square, leaving Rob and Martyn by the fountain. Rob was visibly seething.

"Two hours ago," he muttered. "The bastards."

"I'll be damned if I'm going to let them get away with that," Martyn said, "but while we have the upper hand we may as well make the most of it. Come on." He turned and led the way behind the two SFN men.

To be honest, Martyn had been surprised to hear that Jacqui Miller had instructed her husband not to speak to anyone else. He did not think he had made that strong an impression and now the connection with Melissa and Jacqui Miller's parting shot sprang up in his mind. With the events of the morning, he had forgotten about it. *You'll have to ask Melissa.* He still could not remember where he had seen her before. If Jacqui Miller did not explain it to him this afternoon, assuming she was still with her husband, he must remember to ask Melissa when he returned home. His thoughts were still with Jacqui Miller and the morning's encounter when Rob interjected.

"That psychic stunt of yours is pretty amazing."

"Sorry?" Martyn said, surfacing back into the present.

"I've just realised something," he continued. "For Reynolds and Manciani to have turned up at the clock fountain when they did, they must have been watching us from the moment you first said we were being watched, probably before. I'll never question your intuition again."

With his mind still on the events of six hours before, he had forgotten about his earlier suspicion. But it was true. Since the arrival of Manciani and Reynolds, he had not felt he was being watched any more. However, towards Manciani and Reynolds he felt nothing while the sense of menace surrounding the square had continued to grow stronger. While he was in conversation or mentally distracted it was possible to ignore the sensation. It seemed to be both within him and yet be intrinsic to the square at the same time. Now, Rob's observation had suddenly made him aware of how dry his throat was.

"I really need a drink."

"What? At this time of day?"

"Not that kind of drink. Just a drink. Water, anything. I'm parched."

"Must be that laser etched chest. Making a demand on your bodily fluids. It's a good sign."

Naturally, Martyn was not convinced. "Maybe," he said.

When they were halfway across the plaza, still several metres behind Manciani and Reynolds, Martyn's attention was suddenly caught by something on the eastern side of the square and he stopped.

"There's Melissa."

He was not sure where she had come from or how he had come to spot her among so many people but, even at such a distance, certainly out of earshot, her gait and her long golden hair were unmistakeable.

Rob said, "Long way to come on her lunch hour, isn't it? I thought she was working on the other side of Arcades, hospital rehabilitationation or something." He looked in the direction Martyn had indicated. "I can't see her."

"Over there," said Martyn. "Up the side street, walking away from us. Wearing a black dress and carrying a bunch of flowers. You can't miss her."

Rob followed his gaze but remained unsuccessful.

"Which street?" he asked. "I think I must have the wrong one."

"The one next to the Australian embassy block. Where that juggler is. Too late, she's gone now."

He watched as Melissa reached the end of the short side street. Briefly, she glanced back across the square in their general direction and then disappeared down the flight of steps leading to the street below.

"That's the street I was looking at," said Rob and continued walking across the plaza. Martyn threw one more glance at the side street, which was now empty.

Two things puzzled him.

He had never seen the dress before.

The flowers had not been wrapped.

19

Three weeks after his return from America, Melissa finally conceded an invitation to Alderley for the weekend. At least that was how it had seemed. Though she must have had his return date etched on her mind - he had written so many postcards reminding her - he had telephoned from Heathrow to discover she had gone to Spain for a short holiday. She arrived back in England the following week but had already arranged to stay at a friend's house for a couple of days. The reason, as given, was that she wanted to make some headway on a series of essays which she had to write before her second year at university and she needed to be somewhere she couldn't be distracted.

In the meantime, Howard set about finding somewhere to live in London. It did not take very long. He visited one letting agent, organised two viewings and took the first – a sparsely furnished flat in Islington - simply because it was already vacant. The next day he moved in with two large boxes, a rucksack and a suitcase, together containing the sum total of his worldly possessions. Without unpacking, he set about translating his thesis into a book and, by the end of the week, he had cobbled together a reasonable draft of a manuscript ready for proofing.

That left exactly one week before he had to begin work and before Melissa started her new term. He had wanted to spend all of it with her but she had been reticent to give him any more than the weekend on account of her essays. Eventually he had persuaded her to go with him to Darwen for a couple of days and at last solve the mystery of the missing jigsaw piece. It was an excuse but it was the only way Howard could be sure they would be alone.

Finally, after three weeks of impatient frustration, the weekend arrived. He had come up from London amid the mass exodus that always accompanied Friday evenings, taking an hour and a half to get out of the city, and only a further two hours to travel halfway across the country. Melissa was not at the station to meet him, as planned, and he had fought his way along the high street against driving rain, reaching the house soaked, tired and miserable. At the same time, he was relieved that only two inches of wood now separated him from what seemed an earthbound paradise. He rang the bell and then leaned back against one of the two white pillars that straddled the porch.

When more than a minute had passed he concluded that the doorbell was not working. Though he was already saturated, he took shelter from the rain by pressing himself against the door to take full advantage of the cover which the narrow porch provided. He pounded the brass knocker and the hollow echo of the resounding mahogany gave the impression that the house was empty. Certainly the front rooms were unoccupied but they were also back-lit, indicating that there was, perhaps, some life at the rear of the house. He knocked again. No answer.

Ten minutes later, he was blinded by glaring headlights as a car pulled into the driveway. Howard felt his stomach churn and he tensed as Melissa clambered out of the car and slammed the door. In truth, after all the delays, he had not expected this to be easy but already their reconciliation did not bode well. Surprisingly, Melissa had also been caught by the rain and it was immediately evident that she was not in a pleasant mood. But whatever was on her mind, it dissipated as soon as she saw him. Sitting on the doorstep, soaked to the skin, he looked so pitiful that she could not help but feel sorry for him. Which was exactly what he wanted.

"Howard, I'm really sorry," she said, fumbling for her door key, "I must have just missed you. Got caught in traffic." As the door opened, they almost fell into the hallway.

"How did you manage to get wet? Did you have the sunroof open again?" It would not have been the first time.

"No I did not. I had to leave the car to look for you. I couldn't believe you would walk in this."

"I didn't have any choice. My train got in almost three quarters of an hour ago. It was even on time. I didn't think you were coming."

Melissa removed her jacket and began to prise off her boots. "I thought you said it was due in at twenty to."

"Twenty past," he corrected. "How many times have you taken that train? It always comes in at twenty past, you know that."

"But when you called, you said 'twenty to' ", she insisted.

"No, I didn't. I never even mentioned the time. I assumed…oh, what the hell are we arguing for? I'm dripping all over your parents' carpet here. I need a shower and a change of clothes."

Melissa was already at the bottom of the stairs.

"Likewise," she responded. "Grab yourself a towel. I'll be very quick." She smiled cheekily but he felt he could still detect a slight hint of annoyance. Before he could object, she had already climbed to the landing and grabbed at a bath robe draped over the banister. With her back turned towards him, she unfastened her damp dress and allowed it to slide the length of her body to the floor. Her bra and panties quickly followed. Briefly, he glimpsed her nakedness before she threw the robe around her shoulders.

"Put the kettle on if you want." The bathroom door closed behind her.

Howard stood gaping at the pile of crumpled clothes at the top of the stairs but he saw only the after-image of Melissa's body, a frozen figure of smooth, perfect skin moulded into sensuous curves. He no longer felt the cold and damp or the droplets of water falling from his face and hands to the floor – just those forming in his eyes.

I love you.

He had hoped that she would invite him to share her shower and the cold finality of the door closing had left him dejected and frustrated. Melissa had always been uninhibited about her body and often went without underwear around the house, but with that inhibition there seemed to be a total lack of awareness of the effect her slender figure had on him. This was not the reunion he had hoped for.

Yet he was not surprised. He had expected it. Melissa had not been caught in traffic and he knew she had deliberately missed him at the station. It had taken him a long time to come to terms with her unusual behaviour but he had learned to recognise it for what it was. By being offhand with him, she was trying to draw attention to herself. At least that was what he hoped – the alternative was unthinkable. Something was upsetting her and he was expected to gently break down the barriers until she succumbed, usually in a flood of tears, and poured out her heart. Then he would hold her in his arms and run his fingers soothingly through her hair until she fell asleep. At some point during the night they would make love and all the worries of the week would be forgotten in a tidal wave of emotion. Howard lived for those moments. He prayed that this time was no different.

He knew she had left the bathroom door unlocked but he did not know whether it had been intentional. Had she purposely removed her clothes in full view to tease him or to entice him to join her under the shower? Or had she been totally oblivious to his libidinous stare? Perhaps he was trying so hard to look for signs that he was plucking them out of thin air. Though they were close, and though he probably knew her better than anyone before him, he could not read her mind and he often wondered if she could ever be capable of such deviousness. Her feminine charm was so powerful, it seemed, partly because she was naïve and innocent. Yet how could she be – after all that had happened? It had been three months since that day by the river. Three months too long.

His train of thought was broken when the bathroom door suddenly opened and she emerged, enveloped in the towel and a cloud of steam.

"It's all yours."

Howard loved Alderley Edge. Lying about twenty five kilometres south of Manchester in rural Cheshire, it was a small, picturesque town that could easily have been uprooted from an area of rolling, Cotswold countryside and transported two hundred kilometres north to form an oasis in the bleak, harsh landscape of the North West.

The Edge itself, from which the town derived its full name, was the popular title of a densely wooded scarp slope which suddenly ended the monotonously flat plain that stretched, to the north, as far as the Mancunian conurbation. It was in fact the Edge that Howard was most fond of. Steeped in folklore and legends of wizards, witches, druids, goblins and all sorts of funny goings on, the Edge held a magical fascination for him. Being a Mancunian by birth, Howard had visited Alderley many times as a child. Through all those visits, despite giving the appearance that Alderley's outlandish history was only kept alive by the National Trust and the local tourist trade, Howard constantly perceived something in the air, an unnatural stillness. It told him that all had not yet ended there and it was to experience this sensation that he was addictively drawn back to the Edge. So when Melissa had first told him she lived in Alderley, it simply provided him with one more reason to fall in love with her.

He knew Melissa did not really understand why he always wanted to go up to the Edge but she would always accompany him and practically considered the woodlands to be her back garden. There, she always seemed so relaxed, as if she were an intrinsic part of the environment. For some reason, the woods helped her to forget the worries of the world and she was visibly more carefree, almost as if the world outside no longer existed. On the Edge they would escape together – to be alone, uninhibited, happy.

That Sunday, for the first time since Howard had been coming to Alderley, Melissa had not seemed very enthusiastic to go and had even suggested that she would prefer to stay behind and get some things ready for university. By this time her response was not so surprising. She had been in a strangely introverted mood all weekend but, try as he might, he could not get her to reveal whatever was preying on her mind. She was evidently preoccupied with something but was not willing to discuss it. Yet it was a reflex, almost peripheral reaction which had most caught his attention. Although she must have been expecting it, his suggestion that they went for a walk along the Edge had first met with a glance of shocked surprise. Though he only caught her in profile, he was sure that another emotion had manifested itself during that brief instant. Fear. The next second, it had gone.

"Besides," she concluded, "the weather is going to turn lousy and I don't want to get soaked again. And if the fog comes down, it won't be safe to be up on the Edge. Last month, someone almost got killed falling off Castle Rock because they couldn't see where they were going."

"Melissa, the weather is perfect. There isn't a cloud up there. And who said anything about fog?"

The sky had been an unusual deep blue so that it was impossible to tell whether it was, in fact, a cold summer's day or a warm wintry one. It was early October so either was possible. Whichever it was, the outdoors had certainly been inviting. Their departure had seen bright sunshine and a very light breeze. Whatever had caused Melissa to change her mind he did not know, but it was with a positive degree of reluctance that she finally went off to find her sheepskin coat. Usually they would have taken the car but, since they often could not find anywhere to park, today they had decided to walk. From Alderley, the Edge was approximately two kilometres up the Macclesfield road which began a short distance from Melissa's house.

While some measure of confidence had been restored to him in persuading Melissa to go up to the Edge, he found that his frustration with her general demeanour over the weekend had been joined by an attack of nerves. Provoked by her unusual reaction to the suggestion of a walk, Howard's own thought processes had suddenly become erratic, imagining all kinds of reasons why she might be behaving the way she was. The one thing he would not do would be to bring up the subject of her sordid past. He had promised her - and himself - that it would be forgotten and he intended to stick by his promise. He did not want to admit to himself that he knew the real reason she had been behaving strangely - that she had still not forgiven him for discovering her secret - though he was also sure that she never would if he kept returning to the subject. As a result he was even more determined never to mention it. While he had attempted to continue their relationship where it had left off, and although they had made love on both nights since his arrival, he preferred to find some other excuse for the lack of enthusiasm and her distance. He began to suspect that something had happened on the Edge while he had been away; something she did not want to reveal but which had fuelled her reluctance to go there. As Howard's mind raced with the endless possibilities, they walked through the town in silence, never together, never too far apart.

And that is when it happened.

Not far from the Macclesfield road they rounded a corner and came upon the local Anglican church, set back some distance from the road and fronted by neat lawns. A narrow gravel path meandered its way down to the crooked, iron-mongered gateway which provided the only entrance in the shoulder-high stone wall encircling the entire perimeter. His view of the churchyard was obscured by a line of mature trees and bushes behind the interior of the wall. They crossed the street and followed the wall as it began to climb towards the woodland above.

Melissa's family were not great churchgoers; rather they belonged to that great congregation who attended weddings, funerals and the occasional midnight mass at Christmas. At least, they gave that impression but Howard was not sure, when he thought about it, if they had ever been. Yet he was sure that Melissa would choose to be married in a church and he suspected that this was the building in which the marriage would take place if it became her decision. Involuntarily, he paused in contemplation and suddenly became aware of a peel of bells coming, not from the church, but from somewhere in the distance, up towards the Edge. He glanced at his watch.

It will not be long now.

Suddenly, he felt displaced - that was the only way he could describe it. He had not even time to focus on his watch face when the sensation struck him. He felt dizzy and became aware that he had reached out to the stone wall to steady himself. The peel of bells had grown louder and now seemed to be all around him. In retrospect, it was as though he had been catapulted into a dream. The street, the church, everything was exactly the same as it always had been but they no longer seemed authentic - their images enveloped by a soft haze which gave them a slight edge of unreality.

He reached up and pulled at one of the branches which overhung the stone wall. The branch leaned under his weight, parting the foliage and opening up a view into the churchyard. Immediately, the bells stopped.

The bride stood alone at the entrance to the church, dressed all in white and cradling a large bouquet of flowers. In profile, her face was obscured by her veil and he only caught a glimpse as she turned to go back into the church. But it was enough. No less beautiful, no less youthful, no less graceful in her movement, his recognition was instant. He turned to Melissa in surprise and incomprehension and was surprised to find her smiling at him, visibly more relaxed – and still wearing the sheepskin.

"Are you okay?" The words seemed faint, distant. He returned his attention to the church. There was no one there. The church door was closed, forbidding, its form renewed with a flat, cold, sharpness. There never had been anyone there. He was back in reality. When she received no answer, Melissa shrugged and continued walking up towards the Macclesfield road. With only the briefest hesitation, he turned his back on the church and followed her. From somewhere ahead the peel of bells struck up once more, driving him forward. Towards the Edge.

20

At the top of the hill above Alderley town, they passed by the path that led to Castle Rock and continued along the road, choosing to begin their hike into the woods at the entrance by Beacon Lodge. The adjoining car park was empty.

"Look at that," Melissa said. "We could have driven. Strange though; I thought it would have been busy today."

Howard detected a slight moan on Melissa's part but was equally mystified at the lack of other visitors. He embraced the clear sky with a sweeping gesture of his arms.

"Maybe they're all trying to avoid getting caught in the force ten gales and freezing fog." Melissa cocked her head on one side, pulled her sheepskin coat tightly around her and smiled weakly.

"You'll see," she said.

Almost immediately he did. As they left the road and entered the woodland, Howard was on the point of retort when he was struck by a strange sense of foreboding, as though he had stumbled into a new atmosphere. The boundary was as well defined as a brick wall. Without warning, the air had become strangely menacing and alien to him and his heart seemed to freeze from the shock. He almost lost his balance.

"What's wrong?" Melissa asked.

"Nothing. I went dizzy for a second, that's all. I'm okay now."

For a moment she appeared concerned and then seemed to think better of it. She stepped off the path and ambled into an area more dense with trees. Howard paused for breath until his head stopped spinning, wished she had chosen to stick to the path, and then followed her. It was only after recovering from this initial turn that he noticed something else: where there had been clear blue sky only minutes before there was now dull, grey cloud. A strong wind had suddenly flared up, tearing through the trees and whipping their branches violently through the air with wild, clawing swoops.

"Ow, that hurt." Melissa ignored him. Ducking to avoid colliding with another branch, which seemed suddenly to appear from nowhere, Howard returned his attention to the sky, not quite believing the weather could have changed so quickly.

"I think we're going to get wet," he said, half to himself. He expected an 'I told you so' reply - Melissa loved to be proved correct. However, it was with a positive if slight tone of annoyance that she chose to answer him. In the strong wind her voice seemed strangely distant.

"Well if we do, it will serve you right for making me come here. I told you the weather was going to turn bad but you wouldn't listen, would you?"

"What do you mean? I didn't force you to come!" Howard shouted, defensively.

"Yes you did. You gave me one of those looks."

"What looks?"

"One of those looks that says you'll be offended and upset if I don't do what you want. You always look at me like that when I don't want to do something and you do."

"Melissa! What are you talking about? You've never objected to anything I've wanted to do. Ever!"

"I don't get the chance because you always give me one of those looks," she said, conclusively, and turned to continue walking through the trees. Howard was thrown into confusion by the sudden eruption of the conversation and his first reaction was to try and get to the bottom of it. Melissa was obviously upset about something and the sooner she got it out of her system, the better it would be for both of them. As he turned to chase after her, a branch whistled out of nowhere and caught him squarely across the forehead. He yelled in pain but Melissa either did not hear or chose not to. He screamed at her.

"What the hell is wrong with you this weekend?"

She did not stop. "Nothing's wrong."

"Sure it isn't. You've been acting like this since I arrived. I've been looking forward to seeing you for three months. I missed you like crazy and this is all I get. It's as if I don't exist. You're in a world of your own and you only come out of it to bite my head off."

"It's not me who's in a world of my own. I can't even have my own thoughts without you intruding on them. I've told you, nothing's wrong. What else do you want me to say?"

"You could tell me you love me. For once."

At this, she appeared guilty, or embarrassed, but did not soften. "It's no good. You've annoyed me now. I can't turn it on and off like a light switch. And even if I did tell you, it wouldn't make any difference because you would know, and I would know, that I had been forced to say it and it would sound insincere."

Howard was about to react angrily. Instead, he checked himself and took a deep breath.

"Melissa, I feel very alone here."

She did not look at him but turned towards the direction of the Edge and stared into the trees. For an instant – before she turned her back on him - he thought he saw a tear form – or perhaps it was just the wind.

"Ultimately, we're all alone."

She set off again, this time at a fair pace. Initially, Howard was stunned and did not attempt to go after her. But he was not prepared to leave things there. He had to know what was troubling her and make her believe that he only wanted to be there if she needed someone to talk to. However, despite all the best intentions, he found he could not feasibly hold a conversation and fend off the attacking branches at the same time. So he decided, for the present at least, to abandon the conversation. As it was he did not have any choice. In no time at all, Melissa had forged so far ahead that she was soon out of earshot and subsequently out of sight.

It was at that precise moment that the wind suddenly dropped and a shaft of late afternoon sunshine, a solitary beam of pure, silent light, burst through the cloud and illuminated a clearing about twenty metres ahead. Melissa was standing there. She turned and smiled coyly at him, her eyes deeply saddened. While Howard was still trying to come to terms with her sudden outburst, she appeared to have already forgotten all about it.

Howard stared at her. The realisation of what he was seeing, coupled with the strange smile on Melissa's face, unnerved him and he stood rooted to the spot.

Something was wrong.

While the wind had been blowing at near gale force, Melissa had not been bothered by it. While he had been struggling to stay on his feet, Melissa's hair had remained perfectly undisturbed, not one strand succumbing to the power of the storm. He stood dumbfounded, trying to tell himself that he was imagining everything. He didn't feel well and his mind could not think rationally.

Melissa smiled weakly at him again and then turned away to walk further into the wood. Howard found his feet once more and began to follow her as she moved off in the direction of the Edge. Occasionally, she would stop to collect some flowers and had soon amassed quite a number. What she intended to do with them Howard had no idea and, for the present, he did not really care to know. As they progressed towards the Edge, the sun, like a large supertrouper, continued to illuminate her path while he remained in shadow.

Drifting back through the trees, Howard could hear the strains of a soft, haunting melody. It sounded like a solitary horn, strangely distant but from no particular direction and he began to feel as if he were stumbling through a waking nightmare. Never had he heard anything so eerily beautiful.

As Melissa wandered off through the bracken she seemed to be lost in a world of her own, oblivious to Howard and everything about her, completely absorbed in her own thoughts. Howard began to feel even more uncomfortable. His head ached and his limbs felt weak as he grappled with the uneven terrain. And though he did not perceive that he was moving slowly Melissa continued to gain ground ahead of him. She did not even appear to be walking quickly and that did not make sense. His head was spinning with an imagination out of control and he could not contain his thoughts in a rational sequence.

Something was wrong.

He turned his attention back to Melissa who was now some fifty metres in front and still heading towards the Edge. He was still able to hear the disturbing melody and, though the sound was now much fainter, his brain seemed to amplify the notes so that they echoed painfully among his thoughts.

This continued for what was perhaps a further five minutes, though to Howard it seemed an eternity. While Melissa forged on ahead through the woodland, Howard trudged unsteadily behind and the distance between them gradually widened. He did not understand. The Melissa he had left behind at university was not the Melissa he had returned to. Over the summer something had changed but she would not talk to him about it. The widening distance between them was not just physical. As Melissa grew further and further away Howard sensed the creeping realisation that the girl he thought he knew so well was becoming more and more a stranger to him. And as he tried to grasp hold of this sinking reality he became even less sure of his surroundings. He was losing her.

Something was wrong with Melissa.

On and on he stumbled. He sensed a presence all around him that he could not explain. His mind became a mass of swirling images and he tried desperately to gather his thoughts together. He could still hear the haunting tune echoing around his head and he became plagued by visions of sunlit flowers and violent branches; of dull, grey, ominous cloud and lone sunbeams; of howling gales and quiet, peaceful lovemaking.

His head began to ache with the onslaught of this vague information. He stumbled forward with his eyes half closed, unsure where he was going. Suddenly the clouds parted and he was struck by the full force of the sun's rays on his face, conducting warmth throughout his whole body. He opened his eyes fully and found that he was standing in the druid's stone circle. To his right, some way off, he could see Melissa trekking on, still cradling the flowers she had gathered. In that instant he decided to abandon the chase and sat down, exhausted, on one of the druid stones.

And then he realised what it was. Melissa was wearing a dress, dark, with a muted floral design around the hem. It was not the dress she had been wearing when they left the house. There was no sign of the sheepskin. For confirmation, he panned the wood, his eyes sweeping full circle through the trees and the bracken. And his fear was confirmed. It was October, and there was not a single flower in sight.

He turned his attention once more to Melissa. For a moment, the full form of her body appeared against the skyline as she paused by the Devil's Grave. She quickly glanced behind, the skirt of her dress sweeping the air, her arms filled with flowers, her face with sadness. And then, just as quickly, she vanished over the Edge and was gone.

21

They arrived back at the department soon after three o'clock. Rob was still visibly seething about Miller, Martyn was still wondering why Melissa had been down in the Square, and both Manciani and Reynolds were clinging to the two of them as if they were prisoners about to make an escape bid. Under the present circumstances, such an attempt would have been impossible and impractical. Both Martyn and Rob would have preferred to interview Miller without the presence of the two SFN agents but they had no choice. As it turned out, the Chief had been obliged to leave the precinct on another assignment so they were not even able to raise a complaint about the matter. By the time they had passed through the Special Forces bureaucracy and allowed Miller a cooling off period between interrogations, another hour had passed.

"I don't know anything. I've already told you."

As the door opened, it was the first thing he said. He had said it a hundred times already but his words had fallen on deaf ears. Now he was drained; there was no emotion in the voice, no thought behind the sentence. By this time, he was repeating the words robotically. He did not look up. His eyes were locked on the bare surface of the far wall and they remained there. He was leaning forward in the chair, forearms resting on the table before him, his fingers clasped tightly together. Martyn and Rob entered the room behind the two SFN agents. In addition to Miller, a uniformed officer was also seated on the opposite side of the table, equally emotionless. Apart from the table and two chairs, the room was empty.

"Where's Mrs Miller?" Martyn asked.

"Down the hallway drinking the coffee machine dry," Manciani said. "She refuses to leave but we couldn't allow her to stay in here. We also have the sub-editor of the National and one very expensive lawyer out there."

"How did you manage to keep him out?"

"Special circumstances. Section thirteen paragraph two point twelve, 'If a suspect is likely....'"

"... alright, don't quote the whole thing. Leave this to us." Rob walked into the room and signalled for the uniformed officer to leave. Manciani and Reynolds adopted a relaxed position against the back wall, directly facing Miller. Martyn sat down in the chair which the officer had vacated and introduced himself.

"Are you ready to talk?" he added, gently.

"I've already told you. I don't know anything," he repeated. "And even if I did, I would not reveal my sources. I'm sorry I can't be more helpful. You'd better send the next one in."

"This is not a game, Mr Miller. I spoke to your wife this morning and I trust that the reason you are down here is a direct result of that conversation."

Miller was silent.

"Mr Miller?"

Nothing. His expression was one of blank obstinacy. He had chosen to be silent. Martyn turned to Manciani and Reynolds.

"What has he told us so far?"

"Nothing," said Reynolds. "We already told you. That was twice as much as he'd previously spoken up to now. You just got it all, straight from the horse's mouth."

Ignoring this remark, he turned his attention back to Miller.

"Do you realise how much danger you might be in?" There was no reply. Manciani and Reynolds smirked condescendingly.

"Rob, could you fetch Mrs Miller in here?"

"Sure," replied Rob, and began making for the door. He was interrupted by Reynolds.

"I hope I don't need to remind you that suspects should not be interviewed in the presence of..."

"Shut up, Reynolds," shot Martyn, abruptly. "I thought we had an agreement that you would act as silent witnesses, not walking regulation books." He rose from the chair.

"Rules are rules," said Manciani.

"Thank you for reminding me," Martyn said. "But I wasn't aware we were holding him as a suspect. Now if you don't mind, gentlemen, I don't believe I'll be breaking any rules if I go and talk to Mrs Miller without your presence. And when you've finished interviewing your *suspect*, I would like to talk to my *witness*. In the meantime, I'll leave him in your very capable hands. Good luck."

With that, he casually left the room. Rob paused, gave the two agents a beaming smile, and then followed.

"Was that wise?" he said, as soon as the door closed behind them. Martyn turned on him, visibly fuming.

"If Miller knows anything at all he isn't going to tell us with those two idiots hanging around. The only way they are going to get a word out of him is if they torture him, and if that happens, I'll be the first person to start throwing a few of those rules back in their faces. In fact, I'll throw the bloody book at them." He checked himself and took a deep breath.

"We're much better off out here. There's a good chance that Jacqui Miller knows quite a lot already, especially if she was the one who persuaded her husband to turn himself in. While Miller refuses to speak to those two paper pushers, we might get the chance to forge ahead. Come on."

Rob followed him down to the annex where Miller's wife, lawyer and oracle were waiting in the lounge. As they approached, they could hear a succession of voices arguing within. Opening the door, a young policewoman was trying frantically to fend off the demands of the three parties.

"I'm sorry, sir, but I'm afraid it is out of the question to..."

"Now listen to me, young lady. I know the law and under section seven of the custody statute, I am perfectly within my rights to demand an audience with…"

As Martyn and Rob entered the room there was a sudden silence.

"Excuse me, sirs, but the Chief will see you now. Lieutenant, would you escort the two gentlemen to briefing room one?"

"Certainly, it would be a pleasure," she replied, anxious to see the back of the 'two gentlemen' once and for all. Jacqui Miller also made to leave but Martyn prevented her.

"I'm sorry, Mrs Miller, but I'm afraid you won't be able to attend this meeting. I'm sure your two colleagues will be more than pleased to explain the relevant law prohibiting your presence in due course."

Both men threw her a puzzled expression and followed the lieutenant out of the lounge. As soon as they had gone, Martyn ushered Jacqui Miller out of the door on the opposite side of the reception area and took an elevator to the top of the building, putting as much distance between briefing room one and themselves as possible.

"Why is it that they get to see the Chief and I only get to see you two?"

"Simple," said Rob. "They don't get to see the Chief."

"What?"

"No Chief," he continued. "They've been escorted to another empty room which, it pleases me to say, is even more uncomfortable than the one they've just left. Unfortunately, I don't see them staying there very long. I think they'll quickly run out of patience."

"They'll be absolutely furious," Jacqui Miller said. "And I don't see them letting you get away with it."

"That's okay," Martyn replied. "We've got a perfect pair of scapegoats."

At the top of the building they found an empty conference room. Jacqui and Rob pulled up a couple of chairs and sat down around the table. Martyn walked over to the far side of the room and stood by the window with his back to them. Situated on the west side of the police department, the transparent wall offered a panoramic view of the city. Already, the autumn sun lay low in the sky and cast glitter strewn shadows across the rooftops. Layer upon layer of urban sprawl had gradually filled the space between his feet and the horizon. In the vast jungle below there was only one place where it was possible to escape the claustrophobic existence in which life was spent crawling up and down the narrow fissures between tall, oppressive tower blocks. A mile away, where the rooftops and penthouses appeared to drop through a hole in the ground, he could see the space that had been created by Eden Square. And beyond that, silhouetted against the late afternoon sun, the New Century Tower and the clique of copycat skyscrapers defied it to advance any further.

"Your husband isn't being very co-operative," he said. He did not turn round.

"Well what do you expect?" Jacqui Miller exclaimed. "I spent the best part of the morning persuading him to turn himself in and those two Neanderthals pounced on him as if he were Jack the Ripper, Charles Manson and Anton Gremelkov rolled into one. I thought you said he would be safer in your hands. The last time I saw him he looked like death. You lied to me."

Overhead, an air liner appeared and began tracing a thin white line across the sky, toward the setting sun. Martyn moved away from the window and sat down opposite Jacqui Miller.

"I didn't lie to you," he said. "He just turned himself in to the wrong people. And the worst part is, there isn't a lot we can do about it - not at present, anyway."

"You mean he has to stay with them? In custody? I thought he was your witness."

"I wish he were," Martyn said, then repeated the phrase, half to himself. "I wish he were."

Jacqui Miller was becoming more aggravated and the controlled frustration began to expose itself in her voice.

"How long?" she demanded.

Martyn looked her squarely in the eyes. "Hours?"

"Days." Rob was now sitting on top of the table, facing the window.

"Weeks."

Jacqui turned from Rob to Martyn in turn and then returned her attention to Rob expecting the logical progression to continue.

"It depends," Rob said, without turning from the window.

"On what?"

"On how long it takes them to get the information they want…"

"…but what if they never get it?"

"…or how long it takes us to find the laser assassin."

Something in Jacqui Miller's eyes shifted and they suddenly grew wider as if some revelation had manifested itself within her.

"What are you getting at?" she said. "I'm not stupid, you know. This little rapport that you two seem to have has been too well rehearsed. Now perhaps you wouldn't mind cutting the charade and telling me what on earth is going on here!"

Martyn shrugged his shoulders, rose from the table and wandered over to the window again. By now, the jet stream above had broken up into small wispy clouds. The jet itself was closing in on the horizon, still etching a trail over the city where gradually the stream had turned to a dark grey, slicing the setting sun in two, thoughtlessly ploughing through the air and a perfect blue sky.

"This isn't a simple case of murder," he said. "They are taking this very seriously. They have to." He glanced round at Jacqui Miller and uttered three words that were supposed to explain everything.

"Politics. National security." He turned back to face the sunset. "Given the present circumstances and the sensitivity of the situation, they could keep your husband indefinitely. And they will if they think he knows something. Those two men in the interview room are SFN agents, working directly for the government. We can't even tell them to wipe their feet on the mat before they come in. In police matters they outrank us twice over. But that doesn't mean they outsmart us. At present, they're lost, way out of their depth. For reasons which we're not even sure about ourselves, this investigation has been brought down to department level and we've become involved out of necessity. Among the streets and ghettos, Reynolds and Manciani have one great disadvantage; they don't have a clue what they're doing. They wouldn't know how to catch a common thief any more than we would know how to expose an undercover Alliance agent. And that's where we come into our own. While the investigation stays in this city, we have the advantage. If you want to get your husband released you have to help us."

"How?"

"By telling us what your husband knows," said Rob.

"I see." The voice was cold, an impenetrable monotone. "Why are you telling me all this?"

"Your husband gave me the impression that he wasn't going to say anything and I wasn't prepared to spend all afternoon with Reynolds and Manciani waiting for it. But eventually he will crack. And it will be unpleasant. They are professionals and they've had tougher cases than your husband to deal with. Now you can do two things. You can tell me what your husband knows so that we can go away and wrap up the case. Without a case they won't need your husband."

"Just like that."

"Just like that," Martyn said, trying to speak with conviction.

"And?"

"You're a journalist, Jacqui. Thanks to your husband, the city is in a panic over this laser assassin. It's the major story and you are holding all the strings. They are holding your husband, possibly even torturing him to get their information..."

"Torturing him?" she exclaimed.

"Jacqui, you are a distraught wife. No one is going to sue you for slander. You have a city-wide audience to air your grievances to. You can create so much bad press around this that they'll have to release your husband to get everyone off their backs." He paused. "Or charge him."

"Charge him? But he hasn't done anything, he doesn't know anything. What can they charge him with?"

"If they were desperate they could try murder."

"Murder! My husband? The laser assassin? The scourge of the city. You must be joking!"

"Then where did he get his information?"

There was silence. On the surface there was no emotion but the fine creases which appeared on her forehead revealed the mental battle that was being fought within. Her husband was saying nothing and she wanted to support him with her silence. But she was trapped, emotionally and logically. They had played a card she could not better, and her husband's freedom was at stake.

"Greg is one of the top reporters in the city," she said. "There is only one thing that makes a journalist a successful journalist. Information. And to get information you have to have sources. Greg has good sources, important people in top positions. Including one high ranking police officer."

They did not ask. They waited.

"I don't know who it is, nor does Greg. Even if he did he wouldn't tell me who it was. I wouldn't tell him either. Even journalists have a code of ethics. Anyway, over the years this source has given Greg some of his biggest stories, always anonymously, always accurate. The information is always given voluntarily, seemingly without reason. I know Greg has tried to find out who his benefactor is but he has never got anywhere near. However, considering some of the information he's been given, he must be high up."

"How does your husband receive the information?" Rob asked.

"By post, mainly. Special delivery. Sometimes he has had to collect packages from Eden Square station or even the airport. There is never any hand-written material or accompanying note. There is no way of proving that all the material came from the same person. Apparently, it usually comes in the form of Photostats of secret documents and confidential internal memos but I've never seen one."

"And you say your husband has never repaid the favour?"

"Never. One day, about three years ago, Greg says he received an incident report of a murder down in Arcades. He didn't know what to do with it, didn't know whether it was authentic or some practical joke. Anyway, he hung on to it and waited to see what happened. The same evening, the opposite channel featured the story on their nine o'clock bulletin and the next day there was a furore in the press about a leak in the police organisation. Greg decided to keep his copy of the report under his hat. Since then, he has received several more anonymous packages and obtained some scoop stories from them. But as far as I know - and I'm bound to believe my husband - no money has ever changed hands. For some reason, and there could be several, this anonymous benefactor wants certain confidential incidents to become public property. But I don't know why."

"What about the other evening? What happened then?"

"Not much. Greg was at the studio when he received an email telling him his parcel had arrived at the hotel. I saw the message myself and that's all it said: 'Package arrived at hotel.' Anyway, once before he had been told to pick up something from the Cavendish, so he went down there. It is only a couple of hundred metres from the studio. At the Cavendish someone had left a small letter for him and inside there was the key to a safety deposit box on Eden Square station. As you know, it was very foggy so Greg decided to take the underground and went straight from the hotel to Eden Square. Greg said it didn't seem worth going back to the studio first and he was probably more curious about this one anyway because this was the only time he had been sent to collect a key and then directed somewhere else."

"And what did he find?" Martyn asked, wishing she would get to the point.

"Hardly anything. Inside the box was a transcode message, apparently used between precincts where there is a danger of interception. Whoever sent it, and the person to whom it was sent, had been torn off the top. And all it said was that some guy had been found dead in Eden Square, a suspected victim of a heart attack."

"But what kind of story is that?"

"It isn't," agreed Jacqui. "But someone had gone to a lot of trouble to get this information to Greg without being exposed. Not only that but the information had to have been sent by the same person as before because of the hotel, and he or she had always been reliable in the past. So Greg decided to take a small risk and run the story anyway, hoping that an explanation would follow. He carried out a check on the alleged victim but came up with nothing. You know the rest. The story was quickly sneaked in at the end of the bulletin. Next day Greg received a copy of an internal report detailing everything, including the murder of Sarjena West last summer. Your names were down on the circulation list, along with those two goons downstairs."

"Sounds like the one we got. You saw it?"

"No. I haven't seen anything. This is all from Greg. He wouldn't show me any of the evidence and I haven't a clue where he hides it all. Certainly not at home."

She took a deep breath as if she had come to the end of a long confession. "So what are you going to do now?"

22

Martyn left Rob to escort Jacqui Miller to her car. There seemed little value in continuing their conversation to the point of mental and emotional fatigue. They had made their point and there was no profit in repeating it over and over again. By her reaction it was clear she understood and now it was up to her. It had been a long day and he wanted to get home to Melissa. He thought once more about their aborted holiday. His mind and body were both crying out for a break from routine but, as yet, there was none in sight. The case intrigued - even worried - him in a way he had not experienced before, but his desire to find the assassin was slowly being dampened by the perpetual drain on his physical and psychological resources.

Although it was rush hour, the evening was unusually quiet and hollow. Driving west towards Richmond along the Arcades Boulevard, a golden crest on the horizon was all that remained of a glorious sunset. The sky overhead was now a deep blue and the first stars were beginning to appear above the grey rooftops. The Boulevard was very Parisian in style. Along each side of the carriageway the equi-spaced elm trees were cluttered with sparrows delivering a tuneless, yet relaxing, evensong.

At ground floor level, behind the trees, the whole avenue was decorated with brightly coloured neon signs, advertising everything from expensive perfumes to cheap burger joints, some tracing out complex patterns in the air, flashing, rippling, all out of synchronisation, confusing the brain and unbalancing the natural pulse of the body. Along the sidewalk dark shadows, human shaped with no faces, lurked suspiciously and mindlessly in shop doorways, having nowhere else to go. This was the life he used to know; the cheap vice and cheap violence, living to survive and surviving to live, a life with no purpose and no direction; existence at its most basic level.

Three years sweating blood on the street and there was still no sign of change. The fight against crime was in equilibrium; for every criminal locked away a new one would be born. And when the crime rate became too high, there was only one way to bring down the figures and that was to relax the laws. When he had first arrived in the city, even a few ounces of marijuana could fetch five years. But soon, half the population would have had to be locked away. To be caught in possession of soft drugs could no longer be considered a crime. Now they were selling "grow your own" kits in the department stores and the dealers were all released to peddle harder drugs.

He was glad to be no longer working narcotics; it was a mindless job and he was now well out of it. In a society where morale and morality were low, the streets were like a gaping black hole with a hunger that would eventually consume all the love, faith and hope of the entire population. One day, the city would wake up to find itself lawless and soulless, the victim of its own mindless greed. And when it happened, he would be well out of that too.

Passing a supermarket on the left, he thought of Andy Holland, his old partner, a classic victim of the 'wrong place, wrong time' syndrome. What he had said to Jacqui Miller earlier that morning had been true. More effort and publicity would be put into bringing down the police force than to catching the hoodlums who raided the supermarket in the first place. He wondered if the robbery had been planned in advance or if the fog had suddenly provided them with the perfect opportunity to carry out a spontaneous raid, knowing that it would keep the police away longer and throw a blanket of confusion over their getaway. Whichever was true, he predicted that he was not the only person to realise that thick fog provided the perfect setting for an armed robbery. Next time the fog made a rare appearance, so would a number of armed gangs, and history would inevitably repeat itself.

The strange stillness of the evening pleasantly disturbed him. It was not menacing or brimming with electric suspense. Nor was it the stillness of death, as would have been the case if a great plague had swept the city streets and wiped out the population. It was more like the aftermath of some great event, like a street carnival or a riot. People were moving around but it seemed they moved in slow motion, dragging themselves through the streets while in deep thought or some narcotic, moronic state. The street was littered with all kinds of rubbish; bottles, cans, small and large cardboard boxes, suggesting great activity. There was no breeze to waft it about and it lay on the ground, motionless and untidy, like a work of abstract still life usually found at the city art gallery. All at once, high in the sky over the road ahead, another star appeared and twinkled nervously as if making its very first appearance on the world's stage.

As the commercial seediness of the neon plastered avenue gradually transformed into the tranquillity of suburbia, his heart soared with a sense of freedom and longing he had not felt in a long time, and he ached for the open road, heading west to the Great Lakes with a cool breeze and starlight rippling through his hair, and Melissa by his side. On the way back to Richmond he passed the freeway exit and he was almost tempted to throw the car into the slip road and fly from the city towards the open countryside. But Melissa was not with him and the time was not yet right.

In less than a mile, a road sign indicated the direction to Richmond, along the main rat race, the same road he drove down almost every day of his life. More than ever, the road was both oppressive and magnetic, drawing him towards it like a journalist to a grisly accident. He indicated and turned off automatically, his mind resenting these natural instincts with a slight bitterness. Twice he almost turned round and went back to the freeway but the car never changed direction and soon it was sitting in front of the apartment once more. For a few minutes he sat motionless, gazing at the night sky and drinking in the beautiful autumn evening. Then he stored the memory away in a private corner of his mind and went into the building.

23

Something was wrong.

That was the last he had seen of her. By the time he had returned to the house Melissa had been and gone. Even now he could not believe she had deserted him on the Edge and disappeared into thin air - but it was true. She had left him a key to enter the house and inside he found a quickly scribbled note which effectively asked him to leave again. The sheepskin coat had been thrown over the back of a chair. There was no sign of the flowers.

Something was wrong with Melissa.

He did not want to go. He was tired. His body ached and his head would not stop thumping. All he really wanted was to go to bed, to sleep, and hope that when he woke up it would all have been a silly nightmare. But he packed, slowly, lethargically, and in a daze. He could hardly remember anything that happened afterwards but somehow he made his way to the station to take the train out of Alderley.

And so he found himself on the platform of Manchester's Victoria station, waiting for a train which would carry him on to Darwen. All he knew was that he felt lousy, that he could not make sense of anything that had happened and that he was going to Darwen alone to find a missing jigsaw piece he no longer had the remotest interest in.

All he knew was that his life was about to change - and he was being watched.

24

Martyn's thoughts were still racing west along the freeway as he turned the key and opened the door on the darkness of the apartment. He was about to switch on the light, abruptly abandoning all thoughts of the open road to wonder why it was switched off, when he was grabbed from behind in a bear hug. With silent efficiency and lightning speed the arms had wrapped themselves around his lower torso and locked together, squeezing tightly. His initial reaction was one of blind panic as he realised the intruder must have already encountered Melissa, who should have been home hours ago. Instinctively, he raised both arms in the air and was about to drive his right elbow into the intruder's stomach when a voice spoke from out of the dark.

"Boo," it said.

He froze. What the hell did she think she was doing!

"For crying out loud!" he screamed. "That was a really stupid thing to do. Don't you realise I could have killed you!"

He switched on the light and spun round, anger blazing in his eyes. Melissa stood there looking very sheepish, like a small child who knew she had done wrong but was not quite sure what.

"Sorry," she whispered. "I meant it to be a joke. I think it backfired."

She looked up at him, her eyes wide as saucers, and took a deep breath, lifting her breasts tight against the white cotton T-shirt she was wearing. He was overcome by a confused mixture of emotions; anger at her blind stupidity, dread at the thought of what might have happened if she had spoken an instant later and passion, an overwhelming desire to rip her clothes from her body and make love to her there and then. But he did not move. Melissa seemed to read all of these thoughts from his face and slowly raised her right hand and brushed her fingertips against his cheek as if smudging over an invisible tear.

"I'm sorry," she repeated. "I didn't think. I was stupid."

Gradually, the anger began to subside under Melissa's gentle massage. However, he was still tense and in one quick movement he placed both his hands under her armpits, lifted her off the floor and pulled her towards him until their lips met and the tension flowed away in that brief moment of reconciliation.

"Don't ever do that again."

He began kissing her more fervently, his lips moving indiscriminately around the contours of her face and neck. Then he carried her across the lounge, through the open doorway leading into the bedroom and set her down gently on the bed. He dived onto the bed next to her, rolled over and found himself staring into a panoramic landscape of the city, illuminated from the side by a solitary lamp. It had not been there that morning.

"What the…"

He stopped short, speechless for the second time in only a few minutes and lay back, trying to absorb the finer details of the painting. Melissa was lying beside him, holding her breath expectantly as she waited for further comment.

"Like it?" she said, eventually.

The scene depicted the city skyline as viewed, he deduced, from the north west. Somewhere to the right of the picture a setting sun threw evening shadows and a pale, reddened, silent light onto the skyscrapers of the commercial sector which rose like a bell-shaped curve in the centre of the painting. The sunset was emphasised by the lamp, set deliberately a few centimetres from the bottom right hand corner of the picture and pointed directly at the subject's primary focus; the New Century Tower. In the painting the city was alive, vibrant, moody - and beautiful.

"It's good," he said, knowing that it was a totally inadequate appraisal. "You did this?"

He turned his head towards her and his question was answered for him. Across her brow was a faint trace of smudged paint. He had not noticed it earlier.

"It was supposed to be a surprise," she said, gleefully. "Do you really like it?"

"Melissa, it's brilliant," he exclaimed. "How long have you been working on this?"

"A couple of months. I had to have something to do all those nights you were away. I haven't painted for a while, not since I was at school in fact, but I felt inspired. I'm actually quite pleased with it."

Martyn was looking puzzled.

"Where was it painted from?" he asked.

Melissa got up and walked over to the picture, using her arms to help him visualise the perspective.

"I did the sketch in Washington Park," she said. "On the hill near that bandstand. It was only rough but I also took some photographs and then finished it back here. It's been hiding in the back of my half of the wardrobe." She performed a small curtsy and then switched the lamp off. "Come on. As long as you don't mind it being there you'll have plenty of time to look at it later. Dinner's ready."

In the semi darkness of the bedroom he continued to stare at the painting. A thought crossed his mind, too quickly to be remembered, too vague to be reassembled. He shrugged, shook his head slowly, rose and left the room.

All the anger at Melissa's 'surprise' had now left him, extinguished by a combination of wonder, respect and surprise at his own state of inner tension. Now he was more relaxed he felt the same way he always felt in Melissa's company. He could have quoted every cliché from the dawn of history and they would have all been equally true. She did make him feel alive. He could not imagine life without her and he wondered how he could possibly have deluded himself that he was living happily before they had met. Of one thing he was certain: he was in love with her.

Suddenly, he remembered the events that had taken place earlier that day and began looking around the room.

"Where did you put those flowers?" he asked.

Between a mouthful of chicken pasta he could just make out her reply. "What flowers?"

"I saw you in Eden Square at lunchtime," he replied. "Or at least, I saw you walking down that cobbled road towards the old town. I couldn't stop to talk; I was in the middle of something."

"Well, you would have made a real fool of yourself if you had because it wasn't me. I wasn't there."

"I see," he said. "You're determined to get one surprise right tonight, aren't you? Okay then, you're right. My mistake. I didn't see you. I saw someone who looks like you and who walks like you. Yes, I know, nobody else could possibly walk like that but there you go, it couldn't have been you because you weren't there. And if I happened to have seen you coming out of a florists with a big bunch of flowers then maybe I ought to make an appointment with a psychiatrist. Or maybe," he added, taking another forkful of pasta, "maybe you've been putting something in the food to make me go mad."

Melissa ignored this last comment and went back to the one preceding it.

"*Nobody walks like that.* Like what? What's wrong with the way I walk?" she exclaimed. Then, without waiting for a reply, she suddenly veered back to the subject in question.

"Martyn, I was working until three at the hospital."

"Lunchtime."

"If I could get to Eden Square and back in my lunch hour, and still have time to buy a bouquet of flowers, I'd be breaking the world land speed record. It's alright for you lot to spend your days leering after girls in the street but I don't get those kind of breaks. Anyway, I don't need to go to Eden Square to buy flowers; there are plenty at the hospital. There's even a florist there. Furthermore, I don't know of any florist in Eden Square. What did you mean 'nobody walks like that'?"

Martyn did not answer. Even as she spoke, he simultaneously realised that he did not know of any florist in Eden Square either and what she had said made sense. That left only two possibilities. Either Melissa had been en route from the hospital to some unknown destination or it had not been her at all and he was mistaken. But if she was leading him on she was making a very good job of it. Over the course of his career he had become very adept at spotting lies, especially with people he knew well. There was no indication that Melissa was trying to hide something but he decided to stare her out before proceeding.

"Were there any other witnesses?" she said, mockingly.

"Rob was with me."

"Well he must be as blind as you are, then."

A chill went down his spine. There was still no indication that she was lying but there was more to it than that. When he was near Melissa he felt something stir inside him, a kindred flame. It was a sensation he had never experienced with anyone else but it was there. It was real and he had felt it when he had seen her in Eden Square earlier that day. If the girl he had seen had not been Melissa then that special bond he had come to believe in could be no more than a figment of his imagination, and that would be hard to accept. But there was no point in pressing her. He decided to drop the subject and admit he had been wrong.

"Who's Jacqui Miller?" he asked.

"Why?"

"I met her today and she seemed to know who I was, and who you were, but I don't remember ever seeing her before."

Melissa rose from the table and began clearing the plates away.

"How come you met her today?" she asked.

"She's married to some guy called Greg Miller, who happens to be the most wanted journalist in the city right now, and not just by the media moguls."

Melissa raised her eyebrows, clearly not comprehending.

"He wrote the articles on the laser assassin and was responsible for all that TV news coverage the last few nights. He is being held incommunicado at the precinct."

"Oh, I see," she said. "Sorry, I don't ever read the journalist's name, I just read the articles. He isn't the assassin, is he?"

"I doubt it. Hopefully, they'll let him go soon, if they haven't done so already. The whole incident seems to be upsetting Mrs Miller more than anyone else."

"Poor Jacqui," said Melissa. "She used to be my school teacher back in the third grade. Taught me everything I know about history, which isn't a lot, but we got on very well anyway. I think she liked me because I was fascinated by England. Because I was English and had never been there, and because that was her favourite topic. She used to talk for hours about London and the English countryside. She made it sound so lovely. I wish I could have seen it too. She left when I was in the fifth grade; in fact she went off to become a journalist too, didn't she? I remember now."

"How does she know me?" Martyn asked.

"Because I introduced the two of you at that Christmas party we went to last year, the one at the hospital. Remember?"

"I remember the party but I don't remember her."

"Well, see if you can remember a time when I was gone for a long period and you got jealous and thought I might have eloped with one of the doctors."

"It never happened," he said. "But come to think of it, there was a time when I remember being relieved to get rid of you so I could chat up some of the nurses."

While Melissa was piling the crockery into the dishwasher Martyn decided spontaneously to make one final check. He went into the bedroom and opened the wardrobe. On the left hand side hung all his own coats and jackets - some of them had not been worn in ages. In theory, the right half was Melissa's; in practice it was more like two thirds. Almost a complete fashion catalogue, covering all four seasons, had been crammed into those few cubic metres and nearly everything, Melissa claimed, was 'too small' and a serious diet would be required if they were ever to be worn again. Most of her wardrobe consisted of dresses, which was unusual because few women wore them any more. On Melissa, all clothes were modelled at their best, reflecting her natural beauty. She was the sort of woman who could wear almost anything and make it look stylish or sophisticated. Her dresses were mostly old fashioned, floral or lacy, and gave her an aura of femininity which could rarely be seen in the city, where sweatshirts and skin-tight pants reigned supreme. Melissa often looked as if she had just stepped off a plane from Oklahoma and even on a Saturday afternoon in Arcades, when the streets were crammed with weekend shoppers, she would rarely fail to stand out in the crowd.

At first sight, the dress he was looking for did not appear to be there. The one he thought he had seen Melissa wearing in Eden Square that lunchtime had been a distinctive deep charcoal, decorated with subtle pale flowers around the base of the skirt. Part of his training and subsequent experience and, he believed, a significant amount of inherent natural ability had, over the years, cultivated a memory and an attention to detail that was almost photographic. On this occasion, however, it was hardly a remarkable feat of human recall. The girl, whoever she was, had drawn his attention immediately and the dress she had been wearing had held it. If he had seen Melissa, and he still could not believe it had not been her, then the dress would have been distinctive if only for the reason that he had never seen it before. Having known Melissa for so long now, it was only on very rare occasions, and becoming rarer still as the weeks went by, that she wore something he did not recognise.

He slowly fingered his way through the rack, pausing only twice as he came across, first, a lilac dress with a wallpaper pattern of pastel flowers and then a light blue dress splattered with small white diamonds. If he had been able to combine the two styles and dye the result black then the combination would not have been too far from the one he had seen. Which only served to fuel his conviction that it must have been her. But by the time he had finished searching along the rack he was left with two conclusions. The dress he had spotted earlier that day was not in the wardrobe and he was grudgingly prepared to admit to himself that he had made a silly mistake and was acting even more stupidly by following up his conviction in this ridiculous manner. However, in a city where such dresses were the exception rather than the rule, the dress he had seen in Eden Square was so similar to one Melissa might have worn, and was actually worn by someone whose outward appearance and mannerisms were so close to those of Melissa herself that the coincidence was almost too unnatural. And Martyn, by instinct, did not believe in coincidences. That lunchtime he could have sworn he had seen Melissa.

He had also not forgotten the photograph, now hidden, for reasons which he could not explain, in the bottom draw only feet from where he was standing. In some ways the photograph made his mistake easier to accept. If somebody could resemble Melissa so closely that it scared him enough to hide her photograph then surely it did not take a great mental leap to accept that someone else, at a distance close to a hundred metres, might also resemble her. However, the discovery of the picture made the coincidences of the past two days even harder to deal with. In fact, all the events leading up to this present confrontation of rationality over gut feeling made him uneasy.

And that, fundamentally, was the problem. He was uneasy. He should be able to shrug all this off as a random sequence of coincidences which he normally would not have even connected. But he could not. The case made him uneasy, Eden Square made him uneasy, the photograph made him uneasy and the fact that the woman he had thought to be Melissa turned out not to be Melissa also made him uneasy. Something was wrong.

Just then, Melissa called from the lounge. Closing the wardrobe door, he left the bedroom and all thoughts of unrest behind him. He found Melissa kneeling on a chair, gazing out of the window at the night sky, her chin resting on her hands. She was rocking back and forth, slowly and rhythmically, humming a thoughtful tune. Suddenly, she seemed to sense that he was there and turned to face him.

"You know what I'd like to do right now?" she said. The question was obviously rhetorical but he encouraged her anyway.

"Go on."

"I'd like to get in the car and drive right out past the city limits," she continued. "I want to get away from all this neon and concrete and just be alone under the stars. I want to race down the freeway and then turn off and find somewhere really quiet and peaceful, to get away from this place for a while. It's such a beautiful evening."

She climbed to her feet and stepped across the room to put her arms around him.

"Won't you take me?" she asked, her eyes silently pleading with him to say "Yes".

"I'd love to," he said.

Melissa flung her arms round his neck and kissed him on the cheek.

"Oh, thank you. It will be like spending a night of our holiday together." She pulled back slightly to look into his eyes. "And if we find somewhere really isolated we could make love under the stars. What do you think?"

"I think I know just the spot," he said. Holding her more closely he kissed her softly on the lips. On a night like this, in an isolated part of the country, with all that fresh air to use up and someone like Melissa to share it with, he knew that making love was an inevitable conclusion.

Martyn picked up the car keys from a jacket pocket, found a suitable disc to play during the journey and turned towards the door. At that moment the bell rang. Melissa looked up with a pained, anxious expression on her face. She sat down on a nearby chair.

"Oh, no. Who can that be?"

"Don't worry," Martyn said. "Can't think it's anything important. Probably one of the neighbours come to borrow something. I'll get it."

Martyn opened the door and found himself staring straight into the face of Brett Lancaster. The Chief's expression was serious, worried, displaying the battle scars that result from a great deal of pressure.

Martyn could not guess the exact reason for his visit but of one thing he was sure; if it were not important he would not be here. Brett Lancaster believed in the sanctity of the home. He did not only respect social privacy; he maintained that it was vital for his officers to have a second life totally unconnected with the police department.

Unfortunately, he did not have control over the amount of work and, with limited resources at his disposal, this unwritten rule largely remained an ideal to which he could never aspire. At first, Martyn did not know what to say. He always liked to anticipate things before they happened and his mind was racing to find the obvious connection between the Chief's presence and the day's events. It was also on other things and his heart sank as he realised that the rapidly fading images of the open freeway, of making love with Melissa under the stars, were to remain just dreams.

"Brett?" he said, after a short pause.

"Good evening, Martyn. Can I come in?"

"Oh, sure. Sorry."

He ushered the Chief into the lounge and they sat down. Melissa appeared from the bedroom carrying her coat. When she saw who it was she was not quite able to hide the slight trace of disappointment which crossed her face. The Chief turned towards her.

"I'm sorry to disturb you," he said. "Were you about to go out?"

"We were going for a drive out of town," Martyn said. "Thought we'd head out west and get some fresh air. It's a nice evening; we wanted to make the most of it."

"In that case I'll try and make this as short as I can." He turned once more to Melissa. "But before I continue I think you are owed an apology and at least some kind of explanation, though I realise it will be little compensation." If Melissa had been about to protest, the Chief did not wait.

"I know how much that holiday meant to you, to both of you, and I really wouldn't have asked you to cancel it if it wasn't important. Melissa, the fact is Martyn is someone I can't do without. He's one of the best officers in the city - the whole country even - and to me he is indispensable. I don't know why, but everybody is terrified of being struck down by some science fiction heat ray while they're hanging out the washing or shopping in the market. While we've had two deaths from this laser rifle in the last four months, hundreds of people have been shot dead by all kinds of maniacs for all kinds of reasons. It isn't rational - in fact it's all out of proportion. But right now the whole city is in a panic over this laser freak and I need Martyn to help me find him.

"To be honest, I would have let you take your holiday but I was overruled by one of the bureaucrats above. They thought it was important to be seen to put our best man on the job, and Martyn received so much media attention earlier this year that he was the ideal candidate. Ironically, I think that having Martyn on the case has only increased the panic. In the short term I probably would have been better off fronting some anonymous rookie so we wouldn't be seen to be overreacting. But in the end it wasn't my decision and all I can do is say I'm genuinely sorry it turned out like this."

Melissa looked at the Chief oddly and then offered him a warm, sympathetic smile.

"Don't worry, Chief, I suppose it goes with the territory. I've got used to it by now. Anyway, if Martyn finds the laser killer as quickly as you believe he will then it won't be that long before we can go on holiday, will it? Hopefully we'll get some time in a few weeks or so. I just hope it's before the winter sets in. Would you like a drink?"

At the mention of a holiday in the near future Brett Lancaster had smiled weakly and then nodded appreciatively at the offer of a drink. As Martyn saw it, the Chief was relieved he had not had to answer Melissa's question. But she had made her point. When Melissa had disappeared into the kitchen Martyn spoke.

"That was some speech, Chief. A bit over the top though. You don't think Melissa would fall for all that, do you?"

Brett Lancaster remained impassive. As Melissa returned from the kitchen, with a beer for the Chief and an ice cold lime sling, he turned to Martyn and replied, sternly and sincerely.

"I meant it."

Melissa handed the lime sling to Martyn and gave him a light peck on the cheek.

"I expect you two have some things to talk about, so if you don't mind, I'll go and make myself busy. Don't worry, I've got plenty to do. Call me if you need anything. Oh, and Martyn, don't hurry, we can do the drive some other time. This won't be the only clear evening we have." With that, she went into the bedroom and closed the door behind her.

In the emptiness she left in her wake, a brief silence descended on the room. Both the Chief and Martyn were left staring at the doorway where Melissa had been standing, Martyn partly regretting the cancellation of their nocturnal jaunt and partly wondering what was on the Chief's mind. He appeared to be deep in contemplation as though he had noticed something amiss or had been surprised by some action or words he had not expected. Then, whatever it was, Martyn watched as he committed it to memory for future reference and turned to face him once more.

"Sorry," he said. "I didn't mean to break up your evening."

"That's okay. What's the problem?"

"I came round to see how the investigation was going. I didn't get back until late and I got the impression that things had been happening while I was away. From what I hear there were more sparks flying round the precinct this afternoon than there were on the shooting range this morning."

Martyn laughed. He had forgotten about the Chief's laser demonstration and he realised that the soreness must have eased off during the course of the afternoon for he no longer felt any pain. He wondered what the Chief had really come to see him about. It had to be more than for a status report on the afternoon's events. He undid the top button of his shirt and peered down at his chest.

"Nice one," he said. "Now then, about this afternoon. Presumably you knew that Miller had turned up while we were still scratching round trying to figure out where he might be."

"Couldn't help it," the Chief said. "I was informed, naturally, but I was under orders to keep the lid on it. Besides, if you had been told, there would have been nothing you could have done and I thought it was better you got on with something useful than spend your time complaining about Miller."

"Well, in any event they couldn't get him to say anything so they sent out the goon squad to fetch us and see if we could do any better."

"And?"

"Miller was turning himself in to me. If that had happened we might have got some information out of him. As it turned out, Reynolds and Manciani had done their Gestapo double act and he was practically a vegetable when we arrived. And he certainly wasn't in the mood to talk to anyone anymore. We didn't stick around very long. However, we did interview Mrs Miller and I believe she told us everything that Miller himself could have done."

"Which was?"

"That Miller gets a lot of information from a mole within the police force, including everything he published on the laser assassin, allowing for a bit of journalistic license."

"Any idea who it might be?"

"None. All his info arrives at some neutral ground anonymously and, from what Mrs Miller was saying, he usually has to go on a treasure hunt before he gets it. Whoever it is, he knows how to cover his tracks. He even sends untraceable emails. However, even if we find out who it is, that simply gets us back to square one because it's unlikely to bring us any nearer to the killer, is it? Not unless they turn out to be one and the same. Apparently, he or she has been supplying information for years. I think we could waste a lot of time looking for the mole. It's a red herring."

"Okay," the Chief said. "If I agreed to that, and I have to say it would be with some reluctance, what else do we do?"

"I don't know," Martyn replied.

Chief Lancaster looked at him in astonishment, or was it dismay? He was not sure. Then he took a deep breath and fell back in the chair.

"Great."

For the next few seconds there was silence. From the bedroom they could hear the faint sound of a tune being hummed as Melissa pottered around the bedroom, occasionally entering a percussion solo as cupboard doors were snapped open and closed and drawers slid back and forth.

"You must have some idea," said the Chief at last.

Martyn hesitated. He had literally reached a dead end, at least for the present. But that did not mean he had nothing to say. He just was not sure that he wanted to tell the Chief at this time. However, there was nothing else he could say and the Chief was evidently expecting an answer.

"Brett, occasionally I get brainstorms and go off on a tangent to the way an investigation seems to be going. And when it turns up trumps and brings in results you can never understand how I figured it out."

"You keep telling me it's intuition."

"Yes, but you never believe me. You always think I'm holding something back. You think I've had access to information that no one else knows about. But it isn't true. You can call it what you want but intuition is as good a word as any. Brett, I know when someone is lying to me. I know when something doesn't make sense even before I've figured out why. I get these alarm bells in my head every time something steps out of sequence. It's hard to explain but it happens. And whatever I feel about someone, I trust that feeling and I keep trusting it until it goes away."

"And what is your intuition telling you now?"

"Nothing. Well, it's telling me I don't like this case very much. There is something about it that is very wrong, something which is staring me right in the face and I can't see it. But as far as I can tell, no one is lying to me. Nothing makes sense but nothing is out of place. It's as though we're barking up the wrong tree entirely, completely missing the point."

"Have you not had any bad vibes about anything a little more specific?" Brett asked. On the face of it, the Chief seemed to be taking him very seriously as if he had known all along that his claims of unexpected revelation were substantiated.

"Three times," he replied. "Yesterday I got a bad feeling about the fog...and then we had the supermarket massacre."

"That isn't intuition, that's psychic," Brett challenged. Martyn smiled wryly and looked relieved.

"Just testing," he said. "I didn't know whether you were taking me seriously or not. But I am sure there's something significant about the fact that the second murder was committed in the fog. If someone wanted to murder Howard Robinson they could have gone round to his apartment and done it much more neatly. He hardly spoke to the neighbours and, as far as we can tell, he had no friends. Whoever has this laser rifle, there is no way they could have murdered anyone in Eden Square if it hadn't been foggy. It was rush hour. There were too many people around."

"'They'?"

"Pardon."

"You said 'they'. Meaning that you suspect more than one person?"

"Only because, according to Raspov, there would have to have been at least twelve of them; one to fire the rifle and eleven to carry the power pack. I don't know, that doesn't make sense either, does it? And that leads me nicely on to my second bad vibe. I had alarm bells when I first met Raspov and look what happened. I posed for a photograph and ended up with a stripe across my chest."

The Chief interrupted. "Presumably, the third is going to be a bit more helpful."

"Not really. It's just that every time I go to Eden Square I get alarm bells again. Last week I was passing through there regularly as if it were my own back garden. Now I can't go near the place without it raising my hackles. But I don't know why. There's something I've missed down there, something I can't quite put my finger on. Maybe something's changed and I haven't consciously spotted it yet. I don't know."

"That isn't very helpful," the Chief observed. "Let me put my original question to you another way. What are you going to do tomorrow morning? I'm prepared to be open minded up to a point but even if I'm prepared to accept it, I don't think I could tell Commander Colchek that my best man was wandering up and down Eden Square waiting to see the light. I need something more positive than that."

Martyn indicated the drinks cabinet and the Chief nodded patiently. He walked over and fixed them both a whisky and soda.

"Let me answer that by asking you a question to save time," he said. "Suppose you tell me why you came out here tonight and then I'll adapt my answer to suit because right now I'm not sure what I plan to do. I was banking on another brainwave before I woke up tomorrow morning."

He handed the drink over to the Chief.

"Alright, I'll spell it out for you. I wasn't around this afternoon because I was called to two meetings at the last minute. The first lasted two hours and only two things were discussed. One, the city is in panic mode over the laser assassin and everyone is going mad for information we don't have. It's a vicious circle. The more they ask the less we can tell them and the more they panic. It's totally irrational but there you go. Two, the gang who robbed the supermarket have got to be caught as soon as is humanly possible.

"But it's crazy. No one seems to be that concerned about them even though they killed four times as many people as the laser assassin and only took minutes, not months, to do it. Everyone has learned to live with armed violence and they accept it. It's a blood hunt now. They have to be caught because the law requires vengeance for what they did. You know something? I sat in that meeting for two hours and no one mentioned the fact that they had to be caught to prevent another robbery or another bloodbath. With the laser assassin it was an hour of 'who's going to be next?' or 'when will he strike again?' With the punks who massacred those innocent people they only wanted to bring them to justice. It was almost as if they wanted them to strike again so that the prize would be even greater. They are not afraid of hoodlums because they understand their mentality. But the laser assassin is different. They fear him — or them - because they don't understand, because he is an unknown."

"I know how they feel," Martyn said, a little too flippantly. "If I had the choice I think I would rate my chances with a whole gang of hoodlums a lot higher than I do with the assassin. Maybe I'm being influenced by the panic in the press but I feel this is more a battle of intellect than a straightforward murder case. At least with hoodlums you know where you stand and you know how to deal with them effectively. They'll find that gang in a couple of days. They've got too much to go on not to catch them. Eight dead people in a robbery is a lot but the crime is no more difficult to solve. It's like you said. The body count makes it more of a blood hunt."

The Chief looked concerned.

"Martyn, whatever you do, don't get carried away with the media legend of the dark stranger with the deadly secret weapon. Whoever it is, he's human. He's like you and me, and this is just like all those other cases you've solved. And when he's behind bars he won't look different from any other prisoner. Anyway, there's an even more important reason why you have to crack this case quickly."

"The second meeting?" Martyn guessed.

"Correct. It was about this crazy idea to allow Gremelkov to come on a visit. I knew there would be trouble but I didn't expect it to be so much so soon."

"Why? What's happened?"

"What's happened is that the total combined law enforcement network in the city has received a total of over fifty death threats against Gremelkov in the last twenty four hours. And that's not all. We have received clear and precise instructions from the government to investigate every single one."

"What!"

"It's true. Some of them will be hoaxes but they can't all be. In short, we are expected to keep Gremelkov alive for the duration of his visit. And if fifty people a day are that determined I don't see how we've got a cat in hell's chance. I only hope he gets himself killed in Washington or New York, long before he arrives here."

"So why is he coming here at all? There are so many refugees residing in the city the government must know that there are likely to be attempts on his life. He's obviously very unpopular. Surely they can't be so stupid."

Chief Lancaster shrugged his shoulders and emptied his glass. "Ours is not to reason why. East and West are walking together on a very precarious tightrope and the choice between pushing the opposition off or clinging on to them for dear life is very finely balanced. Gremelkov is on a critical diplomatic mission. If he succeeds perhaps we can begin making positive steps towards the international peace we have never known."

"And what if he gets killed?" Martyn said.

"I don't know," the Chief replied, shrugging his shoulders once more. "The Alliance must equally know the risk they are taking. They must realise that Gremelkov might end up dead. I don't think they'll start a war over it so long as we appear to have done everything in our power to prevent it. And that is why we have to investigate all these threats. And that is why you have to find this laser assassin quickly. It's an investigation we can't afford to waste time on. But neither can we forget about it."

When Melissa eventually materialised from the bedroom, she found him sitting alone in the dark, deep in contemplation. The sound of the door opening disturbed his train of thought and whatever he had been thinking about was quickly forgotten. The bright light from the bedroom doorway hurt his eyes and he squinted as though he had just woken up. Through the darkness he smiled weakly and, though he could see little, he sensed the gesture was returned.

"Brett gone?" came the voice.

"A few minutes ago," he replied. Melissa closed the door quietly, crossed the lounge and knelt at his feet, resting her head against his chest.

"Serious?" she whispered.

"Nothing I can't handle, and nothing for you to worry about. It appears Gremelkov is as unpopular as you predicted he was going to be. Fifty people have already threatened to kill him if he comes to the city. It's going to be a tough winter."

"Well why don't we forget all about it for this evening and get an early night?" Melissa suggested. Her voice was soft and inviting. There was no sign of disappointment at the disruption to their planned evening, nor of any resentment at the Chief's sudden appearance.

"Sure," he said. "Sounds like a great idea. I'll take a shower and then I'll join you."

Melissa picked herself up and made her way back across the lounge towards the bedroom. At the doorway she paused, lifted the sweatshirt over her head and let it drop to the floor. She stood, half naked, silhouetted by the bedroom light.

"No you won't," she said, "Because I'll be in the shower too."

Martyn dragged himself out of the lounge and into the bathroom only to find that Melissa was already under the spray.

"Come on, slowcoach," she called, from behind the curtain. "If you take any longer I'll dissolve."

He undressed slowly, sleepily, and pulled back the curtain. Melissa stood there, her eyes closed, allowing the water to cascade from the top of her head all around her face and the meandering curves of her body. He stepped into the jet and almost immediately let out a cry of anguish. Melissa opened her eyes in alarm and screamed without thinking. Clenching fists and gritting teeth, he tried to control the searing pain that ran through his body. Across his chest, in a perfect line, the weal began to glow bright red.

"Damn! I forgot about that."

25

The next morning, Martyn woke early and decided instantly that he could not be bothered getting out of bed. Instead, he turned onto his back, propped himself up against the pillow and lay motionless, staring at Melissa's painting on the wall. After a while he became uncomfortable and slid back under the duvet to stare at the ceiling. The bedroom was filled with dull, grey shadows and he deduced that the clear sky of the night before had given way to rain clouds and the day would be overcast. Beside him, Melissa lay sound asleep, breathing steadily. Without realising it, his own breathing adopted the same rhythm.

He still had not figured out how he was going to proceed with the case. Without that motivation, there seemed no point in going down to the precinct. What he needed was peace and quiet, time to think.

He had already discounted Greg Miller as a suspect but if his wife, Jacqui, had been telling the truth, that did not necessarily mean he could tell them nothing more - nor did it mean that his informer knew any more than he did about the identity of the assassin. It was an avenue that would have to be investigated but it would not be easy and it was unlikely to be fruitful. Whoever had access to the information that Greg Miller had received must be high up in the force. Within his own precinct he suspected that only Brett Lancaster himself would have much of a chance of uncovering anything.

The alternative that would inevitably have to be considered at some point was that the syndicate lay behind it all. Up to now, this possibility had been discarded - or temporarily put aside - by all concerned, partly because no one wanted it to be a syndicate killing and partly because it did not seem to be one. Yet the majority of crime in the city was syndicate-based and the weight of such statistical evidence was always on his mind.

Though the syndicate was generally referred to in the singular it was actually made up of twelve smaller factions, all competing against each other. Without in depth knowledge of what was going on behind the scenes, it was impossible to define clearly the areas in which one group's interests began and another's ended. In effect, the movements and concerns of the twelve factions were so complex and out of control that the police department itself was effectively another faction, fighting to protect the interests of those people who had not already been sucked into the sophisticated and confusing web of corruption.

Usually, if a crime had been committed by the syndicate then it would reek of the syndicate. Mob killings, drug rings, corporate fraud all bore recognisable hallmarks or manifested coincidences which were too unlikely to be credible. They were never admissible as evidence. If the key witness in a syndicate murder trial was discovered floating head down in the dock, no one would comb the quayside looking for a banana skin. But coincidences did not constitute evidence; they were merely circumstantial events. From the mob's point of view, another murder was as easy a way to solve a problem as any. The accused could not be held for killing the star witness since they were in police custody at the time; the perfect alibi.

What the written law could not account for was the possibility that a network of people could think and act as one, that anyone connected with the syndicate could be held jointly responsible for all crimes connected with the syndicate. Such a law would be both irrational and unworkable but it was no more farcical than the present system. Presently, very few key witnesses survived trials and consequently they found very few key witnesses. The whole pathetic syndrome was scandalously perpetuated; death, trial, freedom, death, trial, freedom.

These days he very rarely worked on syndicate cases. It was so routine and soul destroying that even the police force had lost interest, and barely put any effort into solving them.

Over the coming weeks almost the entire force would set about chasing their tails in a vain attempt to keep Gremelkov alive. In the same period the syndicate would take the lives of perhaps another twenty people and introduce a further two hundred to hard drugs or bankruptcy. Sometimes there seemed little point in doing this job.

The murders of Howard Robinson and Sarjena West fitted no pattern that the syndicate had previously demonstrated. Usually, it was possible to name the victim and figure out the motive and a shortlist of suspects in a couple of hours. Then there was the evidence to collect. If they found enough then the case would go to trial. If not, the file remained technically open, but nobody ever looked at it again. Occasionally, the suspect would himself turn up dead a few weeks later, in a revenge killing by a rival faction, and that would justify the absence of a trial. Sometimes, they would press ahead with a trial they could not hope to win simply to create bad publicity for the accused in the expectation that this would severely damage their operations once they were acquitted and freed. The system would even justify the expense of a futile trial if the accused were then found murdered in the street a few days later. After all, if a member of the public was dissatisfied with the course of justice, no one would worry too much if they decided to serve out their own.

The first problem here was motive. Neither Howard Robinson nor Sarjena West had any known connection with the syndicate. On the contrary, both were quite independent and led relatively solitary existences. Of the few people that claimed to be friends of Sarjena West, none seemed to have appreciated her financial position at the time of her murder and all stated that they had not seen her for several weeks before. Putting together those few weeks had not been easy but she had not disappeared completely. Both the hospital and the bank had records of at least two visits to each over the fortnight. Her parents, who lived out of state, had not been in contact with her for five years.

The whereabouts of Howard Robinson was more difficult to establish. He had no friends at all that they had come across. On the face of it, he seemed to be a creature of habit, spending six days a week in the book store in Arcades and returning home in the evenings. Neighbours said he spent most of his spare time alone in the apartment, sometimes reading quietly, sometimes playing music, though never so loud that they were disturbed by it. They had never known him have any visitors and the telephone, which the people next door could hear clearly, had rarely sounded. He did not keep an email address or a cable connection so there was nothing to trace there.

The natural conclusion to draw from all this was that both Sarjena West and Howard Robinson had been killed simply because they were in the wrong place at the wrong time, as Rob had suggested earlier. But Martyn could not accept that. There was a piece of the puzzle that did not fit and that piece was Howard Robinson. For some reason the man and his mysterious, solitary life disturbed him. And it was not just because of the photograph. Even before Rob had found it, hidden away in the large chest, the experience had already begun. He had been through Eden Square and sensed something he could not explain, something he now had confirmed each time he returned there. He had been over to Washington Park and felt nothing, seen nothing. Even Sarjena West's apartment, which was now occupied by someone else, had proved to be a fruitless visit. At first, he had even thought the same about Howard Robinson's apartment, but now he felt sure he had missed something, something very significant that could turn the tide of this investigation. He just did not know what it could be.

He also had to consider the possibility that his obsession with the murder victim was only on a personal level, far removed from the investigation, and that he was now allowing it to cloud what was basically a simple, routine issue. Perhaps all this was really one long series of strange coincidences after all, with the rest being the product of an over-stretched brain and an overactive imagination. Perhaps he was wasting his time even thinking about it. His concentration span was low and it was more likely that the answer would come to him in a flash of inspiration than with hours of intense, irrational thought.

Lying in bed, his attention suddenly focused outwardly, towards the bedroom itself, as the light from the window gradually grew brighter with the new dawn. When they had first moved into the apartment, Melissa had taken on the responsibility of decorating the bedroom almost immediately. Martyn was only too happy to let her do so. He had trusted her taste more than his own and had more than enough work with the lounge, bathroom and kitchen. Of course, he had helped her with the actual decorating but Melissa had chosen the colour scheme and bought all the fixtures and fittings which gave the room its character. The result was what he had hoped for. He had wanted the bedroom to be feminine and peaceful and it was Melissa's artistic touches that had made it just that.

Decorated primarily in soft beige, the door, curtains, carpet and skirting were a complementary combination of various shades of sand. The rest of the furniture was made of antique pine and a number of bushy green pot plants gave the room a distinct natural feel. The single window in the room faced south; in the summer, when the sun poured through it, the room radiated with a soothing golden glow. On a clear night, with the curtains open and the bamboo venetian blind parted, the full moonlight would flood the room with soft, eerie shadows. It was a lovely room in which to make love.

But it was not him. He had not fully realised that before. He loved the room because it was a reflection of Melissa but he could not have created it in the same way she had. In Howard Robinson's apartment, in that room full of books and antiquated furniture, he had felt at home. Few people read books anymore; it was easier to download dramatisations from the network, or to load the latest best-seller into an electronic organiser. Martyn rarely read books either but he was not sure why. He could easily claim that he did not have the time but the truth of the matter was that he had never been in an environment in which he was encouraged to study literature and his fascination with books was more romantic than practised. In Howard Robinson's room he could see himself, sense his own presence as if, under different circumstances, and with time, money and loving care, his own room would have evolved in much the same way.

At that moment, the early morning sun broke from behind the ceaseless mass of grey cloud and a single ray of pure, silent light found the small gap between the curtains and spilled into the room. Beside him Melissa stirred, muttered something unintelligible and turned over, burying her head under the pillow. He wanted to wake her, to hold her, but he thought better of it. In a surge of spontaneity, he jumped out of bed and wandered into the bathroom.

He did not bother to hurry to the precinct. There was no point. A slight detour took him via Eden Square where he parked the car and strolled around for ten minutes hoping for inspiration. His prediction about the weather had been accurate and above him the sky was filled with dull grey cloud, hovering ominously. Strangely, his apprehension at being back at the square was very slight and he soon realised that he was wasting his time. There would be no revelation here.

There was none at the precinct either. As he strolled into the office, he was met only by the sound of a phone ringing out on the opposite side of the floor and the low hum of a nearby computer terminal. The whole area was empty except for one solitary figure, sitting behind a desk only metres away.

"I don't suppose this is a national holiday that no one told us about, is it?" he asked. "Where is everyone?"

Rob took in a deep breath as if preparing to make a long speech he had been going over, then wafted a sheet of paper in the air.

"In the last twelve hours a total of seventy two death threats against Gremelkov have been noted. These have been divided up equally among the whole department who are now out on the streets and in the Hall of Records investigating them all."

"And you've been left holding the fort."

"I've been left because I, like you, have to find some other idiot who's going around murdering people with laser beams for no apparent reason. However, all I've actually done is to take receipt of a further nine death threats against Gremelkov. This is all completely stupid. If anyone really wanted to kill him then surely they wouldn't go to so much trouble trying to stop his visit taking place. And even if he does come, the result of all these poison pen letters can only be an increase in security on the day, which would make any assassination attempt next to impossible."

Martyn pulled up his chair, sat down and rested his chin on the palms of his hands.

"I wonder how many people here would be willing to take a bullet that was meant for Gremelkov," he said.

"Well, I damn well wouldn't," Rob replied instantly. "If any of these death threats turn out to be genuine and I ended up saving Gremelkov's life then at best I'd be hated by almost everyone in the country and, at worst, I'd be totally paralysed and hated by almost everyone in the country. I may not be the smartest detective on the force but neither am I a complete idiot."

"Don't you think any of them are genuine?"

"Martyn, the whole situation is ridiculous. The entire department is out there chasing rainbows and harmless lunatics. And while they're doing it, there's a file full of real, actual bona fide cases which have been shelved - including the supermarket killings." He held up a piece of paper. "Look at this one. It was sent to the City Radio offices a few days ago. 'If Gremmlekov wants to be a yunok, let him come. Ballcrusher.' The spelling isn't even correct and the handwriting is almost illegible. You can't take that seriously. Whoever sent that is subnormal. If we were to follow it up based on that we'd be questioning half the city's population." Rob put down the sheet of paper and then picked up another.

"Then take this one. It was sent by the Aftermath League from their HQ in Richmond, signed, sealed, dated and everything. It's quite a long letter but the gist of it goes like this; '...if Gremelkov's visit is allowed to go ahead as planned, it would be a sad day for our city and an insult to those who have suffered at his hands...' and then further down '...you must, of course, have realised that you would be taking on the responsibility for keeping our visitor alive during his stay and that there would almost certainly be several attempts on his life within that period...' and so on. Now that, to me, sounds like the most intelligent thing anybody has had to say on the subject so far and it has arrived here in a file with all the others."

"Why?" asked Martyn, believing he had somehow missed the point.

Rob shrugged his shoulders and his expression indicated that he knew the answer but still didn't understand it.

"The two sections I read out have been high lighted. Apparently we have to find out why the Aftermath League believe someone is going to try and kill Gremelkov..."

"...But everyone thinks that Gremelkov is going to be killed. It was the first thing I thought of when I heard he was coming..."

"...I know, but get this. Apparently the expression 'sad day' can be construed to mean that someone is going to be murdered or something is about to be destroyed. The League used to borrow the expression during their more rebellious days last decade when they chose to take more direct action to achieve their aims. How's that for tenuity?"

Martyn, half frowning, half smiling, replied, "Well, it's very poetic."

At this, Rob appeared to remember something and dived back into the pile of paperwork on his desk.

"Poetry? You want poetry! We've had loads. Look at this one. It was attached to a photograph of Gremelkov and sent to the City Hall yesterday." He passed over what seemed to be a small business card, still attached to a newspaper photograph of the Alliance Ambassador.

How silently, how silently,
The wondrous gift of death is given.

Lazarus

Martyn tossed the card back on the desk and watched as Rob collected up the mass of paperwork in one sweep of the arms. He hesitated and Martyn thought he was going to throw the whole lot into the waste paper basket. Instead he deposited the pile on the desk next door.

"They let him go."

"Who?" said Martyn, failing to make the leap.

"Miller. They released him last night. He's been told to stick around in case he's required for further questioning but they finally let him go."

"I don't suppose he'd be too receptive to more questioning, anyway. Not after what they put him through."

"Maybe when he's cooled down a bit," Rob suggested. "Apparently, when he left last night he was yelling promises that a damning report would be in the paper's first edition this morning but it never appeared. I expect he got home and collapsed with nervous exhaustion. If he's anything close to human he'll be fast asleep right now so we shouldn't have any worries until tomorrow morning."

"I don't think I'll be worrying about it at all," Martyn replied. "He has every right to make a noise about it. I just hope Jacqui Miller has the sense to realise, and convince her husband, that it wasn't our fault."

Rob seemed satisfied with this. For the first time since Martyn had arrived at the office, Rob appeared to relax and eased back into his chair.

"So what do we need to worry about?"

For the following eleven days the investigation began to draw up to a dead end. There was nothing else to do but go through all the tedious routine procedures in an effort to look busy and in the hope that someone, or something, would suddenly bite and be hauled in. As each day passed, more of their time was spent wading through files and reports, compiling computer database information in a vain search for some common ground, interviewing suspects with the most tenuous connections, reading yet more files. Was there a link between the death of Sarjena West and murders previously committed in and around Washington Park? Did Howard Robinson's death have anything in common with other killings around Eden Square? Did Greg Miller have any dealings with the syndicate? Did either Sarjena West or Howard Robinson resemble anyone who might have had good cause to be murdered? Were there any suspect terrorists or known spies from the Alliance nations entering or leaving the country around the time of the two murders?

There were so many vague possibilities, so many straws to be grasped, and each new idea had to be covered meticulously before it could finally be discounted. And yet, throughout all of this tedium, Martyn continued to hold the belief that he knew the answer. He knew why Howard Robinson had been killed almost as if he had dreamt it the night before but could not remember anything in the dream. All he needed was a catalyst, a trigger sparked by some simple everyday act, and the floodgates would open and all would become clear.

If it had been a normal week, in which the department had ticked over under the average crime rate, then both Martyn and Rob would have been placed under a great deal of pressure to produce results. As it turned out, despite the general increase in departmental stress, the level of pressure on the two of them was surprisingly small. For the most part, they were left to deal with the investigation as they saw fit.

After a few days the media outcry and subsequent panic had dropped to barely a murmur, as it always did. News was only news while it was new. Then it became a lead weight around the neck of the sales figures. If news did not occur then it had to be invented. Martyn had often wondered how the papers would stay in business if there were no murders, rapes or robberies to report - and how far might they go to ensure the crime rate did not drop if their business was threatened?

In that late week in October, for the media at least, it must have seemed that Christmas had arrived early. Greg Miller had done a first class report on police brutality and how the force had wasted twenty four crucial hours torturing him. Meanwhile, somewhere in the city, there was still a lunatic with a laser on the loose. On top of that, each of the funerals held for the victims of the supermarket raid took place within four consecutive days. As each day passed, the police department could only lament the lack of progress achieved in bringing the criminals to justice.

The gang had appeared and disappeared as quickly and as silently as the fog bank they had so effectively used as a cover.

The plethora of death threats against Gremelkov provided, in themselves, enough material to keep the papers going for a whole year. This was partly because many of the letters arrived at their own offices and were never passed on to the police department until they had been printed, reprinted, plagiarised and fully analysed by experts who had suddenly found themselves on the newspaper staff following a state of non-existence. The time the police allotted to the investigation of these so called death threats was naturally criticised, especially against the backdrop of the more serious crimes. However, this criticism was something that both Rob and Martyn found themselves agreeing with, and despite the media's repeated demands, an explanation for this flagrant waste of resource was not provided.

By the end of the first week, for Martyn and Rob there seemed to be no choice but to sound out the known syndicate bosses. They could not approach them yelling accusations with no foundation, but neither did they want to appear to be begging for information. In the end they decided on a more subtle approach and began paying visits under the vague pretext of 'making general enquiries' about the death threats against Gremelkov. This was not so implausible since the whole city had by now caught the fever and sacks full of colourful, anonymous letters were being delivered with every post. The Gremelkov situation had quickly become a bureaucratic can of worms and therefore it was generally understood - by the syndicate at least - that surprise visits and 'general enquiries' were going to be a standard feature of life for a while.

Martyn and Rob did have one major advantage. Their handling of the Dortman bust had earned them a modicum of respect within the syndicate. Since then, they had not been the object of any derision or criticism, something they had previously been used to. During the second week, they made 'general enquiries' in over twenty known syndicate establishments and uncovered nothing unusual. In the present unsteady climate, following the death threats against Gremelkov and the two assassinations, it seemed that everyone was anxious to lie low and stay out of trouble. The casinos were playing straight, without exception, and there was no evidence of drug pushing in any of the clubs or bars which usually provided the necessary front. For two weeks there were no murders, no armed robberies, no successful drug busts and not even the slightest suspicion of fraud anywhere in the city. As the level of police activity reached a maximum, crime seemed to come to a standstill.

Martyn found this situation very hard to deal with. Any major crimes which had occurred in those two weeks would have placed the department under a level of stress it probably could not have coped with - but to have no crime at all was unnatural and in some ways even more unnerving. It seemed that everyone he spoke to was trying to hide something, not in the usual sense, where each party fought off accusations in a mad flurry of unrehearsed words, but with a strange, placid, refined manner. As if all had received instructions to keep quiet. A common bond of fear and expectation ran through everybody. For the first time in his career, Martyn was convinced that the syndicate - as a single, collective organisation - actually did exist.

26

Manuel Cassida stood at the very edge of the luxury pool, lit a cigar and smiled. He was wearing an expensive, white linen suit and gold-rimmed sun glasses. His podgy frame teetered above the water as he turned on the balls of his feet so that his heels were projecting over the edge. He relaxed. Manuel Cassida liked living dangerously. Even more, he loved to project an air of confidence which he knew unnerved people. It was a game he played.

"You know something," he said, to no one in particular. "To me it is always summer." He removed his sunglasses briefly, held them up to the sun that was not there, wiped them with his handkerchief and put them back on. Against the dull, cloudy sky his white suit stood out in stark contrast. This time he spoke directly to Rob.

"I swim every morning at dawn - even in deepest, darkest January. It's good for the soul. You should try it."

Martyn had allowed his partner to conduct the interview because Rob had requested it. Manuel Cassida was a notoriously difficult interviewee and Rob felt the experience would be good for him. He had been tempted by the sheer challenge but so far he was not getting any further than any of his predecessors. After fifteen minutes of wordplay he had made very little progress. For his part, Martyn was dividing his time between trying to gauge Cassida's reaction to the questions - which was difficult with the sunglasses - and keeping an eye on Cassida's bodyguard, who was six feet six and made of iron and did not appear to have been blessed with a warm personality.

"I call him Goliath," Cassida had said, as if talking about a pet. "Strength of an ox but very little upstairs, if you know what I mean. Just the right combination of power and loyalty."

The bodyguard had turned into a pillar of stone at the entrance to the pool patio, his arms folded across his chest. Martyn had nonchalantly taken a seat at a poolside table leaving Rob to tackle Cassida. Up to now, Cassida had directed most of the conversation and seemed happy to continue to do so. As usual, he was confident, arrogant and smelled of evil intent. It was always the same. He tolerated the questioning but it was obvious that two cops meant nothing to him.

"Actually, I was expecting you two lads days ago," he said. "You took your time getting around to me, didn't you?" Before Rob could reply, Cassida continued. "As it happens, I could have saved you a lot of time. Now let me see, you want to know if I've got a laser rifle stashed away somewhere, am I right?"

"Well it wouldn't have been my first question but since you brought the subject up, would you care to answer it?"

"Yes." He did not elaborate further.

"Yes, what? You would care to answer the question or you have got the laser?"

"Both." He shrugged his shoulders and winked at Goliath. His bodyguard attempted a smile but only managed a grimace.

"It is not illegal to own a laser," Cassida said. "I've checked."

"And you used it, or allowed its use, to murder two individuals?"

"A shot in the dark," Cassida retorted. "A ray of hope but totally off target." He laughed at his own joke. "How many times have I told you? Crime doesn't pay. I'm a businessman and currently lasers are big business - or haven't you been keeping up. Even the police are after one." He laughed again. "I'm going to make a fortune out of them. At least, they'll compensate me for the loss I seem destined to make on my *I Love Gremelkov* sweat shirts. I don't think they're are going to be too popular."

He threw his head back and guffawed uncontrollably. Rob turned to Martyn, shrugged his shoulders and threw his arms wide, deliberately slamming his forearm across Cassida's chest with just enough force to ensure that he lost his balance.

"Whoops."

As Cassida crashed into the pool, Martyn jumped to his feet, expecting Goliath to come to the aid of his employer. Ironically, the bodyguard remained motionless and emanated an air of smug satisfaction. Cassida came up coughing and spluttering and swam to the edge of the pool. He remained in the water and continued laughing for almost a minute. Martyn shook his head and sat down again waiting for Cassida to finish his act.

"Temper, temper," Cassida said, eventually. "I thought you'd hold out longer than that." Instead of climbing out of the pool, he began treading water.

"You know what's wrong with you two lads?" he continued. "You really don't know whose side you're on. You think everything is simply black and white, good versus evil. Let me give you a piece of advice - for free. Life is never that simple. If you keep looking in the wrong places then you'll never find what you're looking for. But because I like you, I'll help you out. If I do come across a laser at a reasonable price, I'll let you two have first refusal. Can't say fairer than that now, can I?"

He laughed again and kicked off from the side of the pool.

"Goliath, please show our guests to the door."

The bodyguard led them back through the house in silence, their footsteps echoing loudly around the marble interior, a huge crystal chandelier tinkling lightly in the breeze as the main door was opened. Goliath grimaced again and Martyn tried his best to reflect the expression.

"Thanks, Golly."

Outside, Rob climbed into the car and slammed his fist against the dashboard in frustration.

"I really screwed that up, didn't I?"

"Hmm, well if you mean you didn't get any information at all, risked retribution by the city's most dangerous criminal and played right into his hands then I suppose the answer must be 'yes'. I think you were lucky he was in such a good mood."

Rob sighed and looked hopefully across at Martyn.

"Did we really not learn anything at all? Have we wasted almost two weeks touring the mansions of the rich and corrupt for nothing? I can't believe that. Something is going on - I can feel it."

He looked back at the huge house trying to grasp onto that something, knowing, as all his predecessors had known before him, that such wealth could not have been generated legally but never being able to prove it.

"What was it Cassida said at the end? What did he mean by that?"

Martyn turned the ignition and put the car into gear.

"He didn't mean anything," he said. "He never does." He swung the car round and started down the long drive which would take them back to the real world.

"But that's not to say it wasn't good advice."

27

The train journey from Manchester Victoria to Darwen took only twenty minutes but it had seemed more like twenty hours. The ten second sprint from the end of the station platform to the train had left him panting for breath and he had almost collapsed into his seat. He was vaguely aware of having pulled two muscles in his right leg but his head was spinning with so many confused thoughts that this seemed relatively trivial.

By the time the train reached Darwen, his mind was so fogged that, ironically, he began to think more rationally. There was more to this than mere hallucination. This was a sensation he had not felt for a long time but it was undoubtedly familiar. He was ill. He knew that now. His body was weak, he was shivering and his head was spinning. All the symptoms of flu, he was certain; the termination of the clean bill of health that had lasted for over ten years.

The station at Darwen stood on the top of a hill and for some reason this was immediately apparent even though the fog had reduced visibility to less than ten feet. The station itself was silent. Nobody else had alighted from the train and there was no one to collect his ticket. Deserted. Outside the station, he found a cobbled forecourt, bathed dimly in the soft, silent light of a neon street lamp. For a moment the world ahead appeared to consist solely of that single street lamp and the cobbled path, with nothing but emptiness beyond. Then the fog swirled slightly to reveal a road leading from the forecourt. There seemed to be only one direction to go in and that was down. Since the map indicated that Darwen the town lay in the valley of Darwen the river, this seemed the logical way to proceed. Picking up his hold-all, he set off down the hill, switching the weight of the bag from arm to arm every twenty paces or so.

He could not remember how far down the hill he had travelled. His mind held a vague recollection of having walked down the middle of the road between an endless succession of street lamps, parked cars and the faint outlines of terraced buildings which lay beyond. About five minutes after leaving the station, the sound of music had drifted back through the night from somewhere ahead, further down the road - the low rhythmical thud of a rock bass line. For some reason, he began humming the haunting melody from the solitary horn as he had heard it that afternoon on the Edge. He was startled to find that it fitted the bass line perfectly, making an altogether more eerie combination. As he grew nearer, he began to hear the real melody and the strain of distinctive and raucous male vocals. Immediately, he recognised it as a recent chart hit and the melody of the distant horn no longer matched or held any meaning.

By this time he could see lights ahead and was able to make out the dim outline of a large three storey building. Nearer still, the fog thinned and it became apparent that the light was coming from a row of ground floor windows. The building became more solid and it was possible to distinguish between brickwork and the black holes that indicated the positions of windows on the upper floors. Then, suddenly, a row of lights came on along the first floor, illuminating the sign that ran along the side of the building underneath the windows.

The Millstone Hotel

Below this, at the end of the wall, another sign:

Fine Beer   Good food   Residential

From then on his memory only contained vague images of a number of events strung together in no particular order. He had found the door to the hotel on a corner of the building. There was a single lamp above. Once inside, he had wandered through a small porch which was neither inside nor out. In front of him were two glass doors which led into a bar. He suddenly felt very conspicuous and paused before entering.

The bar was busy but not overcrowded. Just inside the door, on the left, was a fruit machine surrounded by three youths. Luckily, they were so absorbed in the machine they had not noticed him. To the right was a staircase which he presumed led up to the guest rooms. Beyond the fruit machine was the bar itself, stretching almost the full length of the lounge area. Two people were serving, a man and a woman, roughly his own age. A further ten people, nearer middle age, were engaged in various conversations along its length. Mounted on the wall opposite the glass doors was a large, curved video screen showing a BBC documentary. Opposite the bar a dozen or so older people were sat around a row of tables, pints and shorts in hand, their eyes fixed on the programme. The immediate impression it gave was that of a local, rarely visited by strangers, and it was this that made him apprehensive. Whatever reception he received, he was sure not to pass through unnoticed and he was in no fit state to be the centre of attention.

With sudden determination, he switched the weight of his hold-all from right to left hand, pushed open the glass door and entered the bar. The onrush of warm air caught him completely by surprise and sent his head spinning. As soon as he stepped inside, he lost all control of his balance. His last realisation was that he was about to make even more a fool of himself than he had guessed. He had not collapsed straight away, though. Somehow he had managed to get to the bar and ask for a room. Then he had collapsed.

28

He had been trapped on the side of the cliff for what seemed like hours now; slowly struggling upward, both arms and legs weak with exhaustion. Yet as each hour passed, it appeared he had not made any progress at all. From out of the darkness, the rain pummelled unceasingly against his back and the gusts of wind, rising and falling with increasing ferociousness, threatened to rip him away from the rock face and send him hurtling into the depths below. After each pause, the wind would renew its attack and he would press himself hard against the rock, trying helplessly to melt into its unyielding form, clinging onto the jagged stones and finger-tight crevices for dear life.

Miles above, in another time, another place, he could see the line of the cliff top, its gnarled edge appearing to fall away into a vertical plane. And though he could clearly see the extent of the face to which he was clinging, stretching away to infinity in both directions, the cliff top above arced in a complete circle, like the mouth of a vast creature snarling at the world outside. And in that world there was clear blue sky. It appeared yellow but common sense told him that it must be blue and that somewhere, presently out of view, the sun was shining brightly.

He did not know how he came to be on the cliff face or what lay below. He did not dare to look. Instead his eyes were fixed firmly on the moon-like disc of daylight which hung over him; a warm, silent light and the promise of peace and security to come; something to strive for.

Melissa suddenly appeared, leaning over the edge of the hole. She was wearing the dress he had bought for her the previous year, and her long blonde hair fell loosely over her head and cascaded down the side of the rock face so that he almost believed he could reach out and touch it. But the risk was too great. If he could grasp hold of the golden vine the nightmare would end and he would be safe. If he failed, he would fall. It was teasing him. Was it a safety rope or a trap? For the first time, he doubted.

He looked at Melissa for some sign; something in her eyes that would tell him it would be alright, but it only raised more doubts. Her expression alternated between a concerned frown and an encouraging smile. But was she concerned that he would fall, or that he would not? Was she encouraging him to climb, to be with her again, or was her encouragement for the wind, cheering each attempt to dislodge him from the rock? Her eyes told him nothing. And again, he doubted.

At that moment, he was engulfed in water. A huge wave swelled up from somewhere beneath him and swept him from the cliff, a dandelion seed plucked from its stem in a light summer breeze. He had not expected it and had heard nothing, seen nothing. He found himself floating in a vast sea rising ever upward towards the light above - and Melissa. A number of times he felt he would be dashed against the cliff face but the water steered him skilfully away from the rocks, rising, rising, faster and faster, speeding towards the champagne explosion that would fanfare his return to the world. The light grew brighter until his eyes could no longer bear the intensity. He closed them. The last thing he saw was Melissa holding out her arms to receive him. Everything was going to be alright…

Howard Robinson woke with a start.

He was staring at the white paper globe lantern which hung over his bed. The lamp was on but at the edge of his vision, he could sense daylight streaming through a crack in the curtains. It must be late. He lay still, not daring to move until he had fully recollected his situation. He was conscious of his heart beating rapidly, his metabolism racing with the dream which was now fading into obscurity. Gradually, his heartbeat slowed and reality returned.

With eyes fixed on the plain white ceiling, he lay motionless. He could not determine the time but he guessed at late morning. From somewhere outside he could hear the steady tick-tock of the old Grandfather clock he had passed several times on the landing, the sound amplified ten-fold by the silence. He also knew that his watch must be somewhere around, probably on the bedside cabinet, but he made no attempt to look.

It was Wednesday. He knew that. The combined effects of the influenza and being confined in a strange room for two days had given him a sense of reality which was slightly off-centre, but the days and nights still passed and he remembered the two copies of The Times which he had last seen lying on the floor next to his bed the previous evening. Those alone had been his contact with the outside world. As yet, there had been no word from Melissa and she was the only person who knew where he was.

The first thing he had to do was to check the post.

He could only guess what had happened after he had collapsed in the bar. He vaguely remembered being helped up the stairs by a man whom the girl behind the bar had unsuccessfully tried to introduce as the landlord. Howard had not seen his face. He had been visited by a doctor sometime that night or the next morning, it was impossible to judge. His temperature had been taken, as had his pulse. Instructions for his recovery had been left with a warm, matronly woman who had evidently been allotted the task of nursing him. The same woman had returned at regular intervals, with hot drinks and offers of food, but he had never felt hungry. The last time he had seen her was the previous evening when she had popped in with the two copies of The Times.

Already, it was Wednesday morning and it seemed the worst was over. He still felt weak but no longer feverish. His head was heavy and he was reluctant to move it. When the knock came at the door, the sheer noise made him wince and he called for the person to enter without taking his eyes off the ceiling.

The door opened slowly and someone stepped inside.

"Good morning. How are you feeling today?"

The voice was soft, young, female with only the slight trace of a Lancashire accent. He rolled his eyes as low as he could without moving his head, but she was still standing by the door and he could not see her.

"Fine," he replied. "On top of the world."

The sound of his own speech also made him wince and the phrase dropped to a whisper before the end. She must have noticed this for she dropped the volume of her own voice.

"Good. That was a nasty flu you had there. For a while we all thought you were going to die. I'm glad you didn't. Nobody would want to stay here if they thought we killed off our guests." He heard her take a couple of steps into the room. "I've brought you something to drink," she said. "Where would you like me to put it?"

Without waiting for an answer, she walked over towards him and placed it on the bedside cabinet. "There, that will do."

She picked up the watch from the cabinet, glanced casually at the time and replaced it.

"Quarter to twelve," she said. "What are you planning to do with the rest of the morning?"

Carefully, she sat down on the side of the bed. He vaguely recognised her as the girl who had been serving behind the bar on the night of his arrival. She was tall, slim, with long, auburn hair and cheeky brown eyes. She had a distinctive button nose and her face was pixie-like, not unattractive. Her dry sense of humour amused him, but he knew that to smile would result in severe pain, and to laugh would be certain death.

"I think I'll spend the rest of the morning sorting through my mail," he replied. "I'll drink this while you go and get the sack."

She shook her head. "No sack," she said. "Just another of your hallucinations."

"What? No post?" His voice was half disbelieving, half disappointed, but still hopeful. "I was expecting a letter."

"No post," she insisted. "So you'll have to talk to me instead." She passed him the cup from the bedside cabinet.

"My name's Susannah but you can call me Sue."

He took the cup thankfully.

"Pleased to meet you. I hope I haven't been too much trouble."

He was sincere but he didn't know whether it came out like that. Susannah smiled.

"I don't see how anyone who has spent the best part of three days sleeping can be any trouble at all. The only trouble we get round here is occasional rowdiness and we can hardly accuse you of that, can we?"

This time he did smile and it did hurt.

"Where's the other lady who's been looking after me?"

"That's my mum. She got bored with you. Said it was like looking after a doormat. She's gone out for the day. Left the tedious work for me to do instead. Would you like something to eat?"

"Not yet. Mind if I wait a bit?"

"Not at all," she said. "But I think you ought to loosen up a little. If you stay in that position much longer rigor mortis will set in."

He was forced to smile again but this time the pain was not so bad. Slowly, with seemingly great effort, he raised himself into a sitting position, examined her more closely, and then collapsed back onto the pillow again.

"Well done," she said. "You deserve a medal for that. And at least you're not hallucinating now. In fact, you're beginning to act fairly normally. Tell me, why is it that when a man is first introduced to a woman, he always looks at her breasts?"

He was taken aback by this last question. At the same time, he admired her directness and he did not try to deny it. Something about her openness told him he could dispense with conventional etiquette and just be honest.

"Sometimes it's the only way of verifying that it is a woman."

"And other times?"

"It's a source of inspiration," he said. "When you're in the state I'm in, it acts like a tonic, gives you the will to live. I can't explain it; it's instinctive."

"Oh, I see. Well maybe I ought to have got you The Sun instead of The Times then." She rose to leave. "I'll come back in a short while."

"Are you sure I haven't got any post?" he tried, one last time. "Not even one letter?"

"Quite sure," she replied, and then smiled, knowingly. "But you are going to have a visitor this afternoon."

He suddenly became very alert. Melissa! It had to be. She was the only one who knew.

"Oh good. What time will she be arriving?"

She smiled again. "Well, either Dr Lake has had a sex change since I last saw him or you must have been pretty desperate for that source of inspiration when he last came round." She laughed as his faced dropped. "I'll come back in half an hour or so. Alright?"

"Just a minute," he said. "Don't you even want to know my name?"

She stopped at the door.

"I already know it. While you were ill, you were babbling away like one of the brooks on the moor. We couldn't shut you up at one point. You were imagining all sorts of things; something about being followed through the fog by someone carrying a bunch of flowers. It was really weird. Anyway, your name is Howard Robinson. You came up from Alderley Edge on Sunday, by train, and you're here to look for the missing piece of a jigsaw puzzle. Really weird."

She left the room.

29

It was on a cold Thursday morning, late in October and three weeks after the assassination of Howard Robinson, that Angelo was killed.

Martyn came in late following an extended solo investigation the previous evening and he immediately made for the briefing with his partner. To avoid interruptions Martyn insisted they go somewhere quiet, so they took themselves up to one of the committee rooms on the top floor of the building. Every so often he would begin to feel cooped up in the office and somehow the panoramic view of the city allowed his mind to untangle itself from the knots of day to day problems. As he reflected on the open sea of rooftops and narrow streets below, and the clear winter sky above, he felt immediately better - but no more inspired.

"I agree with you," Rob said. "I think something is about to happen, something big enough that everyone has been stunned into silence, but I'll be damned if I know what it is. Also, though we've sought out everyone we know with a syndicate connection and asked a lot of questions, I wouldn't even hazard a guess as to which one of them was behind it - and I can't think of anyone else to approach."

For a moment Martyn was silent. With his back to Rob, he continued to gaze out over the city.

"I don't know any more than you do but there's one thing that's bothering me. Think about it. What could be so big that everyone is scared to talk? That's one question. Yet if this thing is so important then why does everyone know about it? If you've got a big deal coming up then you would try and keep it quiet, right? You don't tell everybody and then force them into silence. So what kind of event would everyone know about and yet keep to themselves?"

"Or who would you say people were most scared of?" Rob interjected. "Even if we don't know what it is, we may be able to hazard a guess as to who is behind it. It can only be Cassida or Smiley Richards; no one else has enough muscle. But why would they have had to tell anybody anything? Word could have got round through the grapevine. Gossip spreads through the syndicate like wild fire, we both know that.

Martyn turned to face him, his expression revealing uncertainty. "True, but then why didn't we get to hear about it. We've got enough informants in that organisation to print a daily newspaper. Gossip spreads information and mis-information; it doesn't spread fear, not on that scale, not in a city this size."

Rob considered this. "It depends on who spreads the gossip," he concluded. "In my book that still leaves us with Cassida and Richards. They are the only two factions powerful enough. I can tell you they both give me the creeps."

"Who scares you the most?" asked Martyn, pointedly.

Rob appeared to give the question some thought but his answer was positive.

"Cassida," he said. "But that might only be because he's a better actor than the others."

"True, but Richards did appear nervous yesterday. He was more uptight than I've seen him in years and I don't think it was us he was concerned about."

"So who scares *you* the most?"

Martyn's answer was not immediate. First he frowned, then stood up and walked slowly and deliberately back over to the window, as if the answer were outside. At the window he paused, and then turned his back on the city to face the question.

"Whoever has the laser weapon," he said.

Just then the door opened and Chief Lancaster stepped into the room.

"So there you are. What are you doing? Looking for rooftop snipers?"

He joined Martyn by the window and quickly scanned the buildings below.

"Seems pretty quiet," he said, wryly.

"It's nice to be able to hear a pin drop instead of the phone ringing," Martyn replied. "Chief, if you were worried that someone in the syndicate had a laser rifle, who would you be most concerned about?"

"I'd be equally concerned whoever had it," the Chief replied, almost mechanically.

"No you wouldn't," he argued. "If it fell into the hands of one of those sleazy pornshop owners in the docklands you'd be almost relieved. They don't have the intelligence to hang on to it for very long and they're not likely to do anything really drastic with it anyway. They don't have the imagination. But who would?"

The Chief shrugged his shoulders. "Alright then, Cassida or Richards. Probably more Cassida."

"That's what I said," Rob agreed. "I wouldn't trust either of them an inch but somehow Richards seems more wary of Cassida than Cassida of Richards."

"So why don't we play a hunch and bring in Cassida," suggested Martyn. "We don't have anything better to do."

"On what charge?" Rob said.

"Who cares? Possession, traffic offences. It doesn't matter so long as we find an excuse to get him out of his home territory. Something is going on out there. Whatever it is, I think Cassida knows about it, even if he isn't involved. He isn't likely to talk openly but there's a chance he'll let something slip if we push him hard enough. We need to get him here and scare him enough."

"Seems a bit drastic," Rob said. "Cassida is the least likely person to crack. Why don't we pick someone a bit more talkative? The first thing Cassida will do is refuse to speak to anyone until that pain of a lawyer of his is present and then we'll have gone through all that hassle for nothing."

"No, it has to be Cassida. For one thing, he is likely to know more than anyone else but I get the impression he is the least likely person to be scared of talking. He's too cocky for that. If he isn't behind whatever is going on then he may be persuaded to help us if only to preserve his own power base. If he is behind something then bringing him in for questioning can only buy us more time since he is liable to be more cautious if he suspects we're onto him."

Up until this point Chief Lancaster had remained silent but he suddenly entered the conversation with a question.

"What makes you think the syndicate is behind anything? Why couldn't it be an outsider?"

Rob replied. "You can just tell, Chief. You know what it's like. When you've spent all your life on the streets you can almost smell it. It's a sixth sense."

The Chief turned to Martyn for agreement and he found it. Martyn knew that what Rob had said was true and he was also aware that his eyes showed it. Brett Lancaster would have accepted his silence as a satisfactory answer but there was something else, a faint echo in the way the Chief had intoned the question, that had left a curious resonance in the air.

"What outsider?" he asked.

"You're very quick to jump at things like that," he said. It was almost a criticism. "I just wanted to make sure you had checked out all the possibilities before you went out on a wild goose chase. If you had asked my opinion before, I would not have said that the laser assassinations were the work of the syndicate. There are no hallmarks there. But, in deference to your sixth sense, I give way to your greater experience on the street and admit that I was probably wrong."

"Why?" asked Martyn.

The Chief produced a small piece of scrap paper from a side pocket and waved it in the air.

"Phone message for you," he said. "That's why I came up here. It seems that your friend Angelo has come up trumps again. He'd like to see you urgently."

30

As soon as they had entered the restaurant, it was immediately apparent that something was wrong. Usually, Angelo's was a fun palace, never full but always buzzing with that familiar and characteristic party atmosphere that lay behind its reputation. Outside, the pink neon sign above the window flickered continually, three hundred and sixty five days a year, twenty four hours a day:

Angelo's - it's so pretentious, it isn't.

Whether it attracted customers or turned them away was questionable, but Angelo liked it.

That morning, there was an unexpected and perturbing air of impatience inside the bistro. A low murmur of dissatisfaction ricocheted back and forth across the dining area; customers drumming fingers on the table, some playing thoughtlessly with the palm displays or shuffling restlessly in their seats. And all those customers facing the bar were staring straight ahead, eyes fixed intently on the doorway through to the kitchen, willing it to open. For no apparent reason Martyn sensed the hairs on the back of his neck rise and he instinctively reached for his gun, which was nestled reassuringly against his lower left back.

During the day Angelo, obstinately and unrealistically, chose to run the bistro alone, only opting to employ a couple of waitresses in the evening when it became too busy for one man, even Angelo, to cope. Rarely did he let the service slip. Even when it was unavoidable, he would always be on hand, fluttering round the tables like a demented butterfly. He would try desperately to reassure his clientele, as he liked to call them, that normal service would soon be restored and begged them not to leave. He never really understood that normal service was exactly what most of his customers had come to the bistro to avoid. Then he would disappear back into the kitchen to make headway with whatever problem was on the menu that day until he decided that it was time to make another appearance in the restaurant.

This elaborate and entertaining system had evidently broken down. There was no food on the tables and it appeared that there was no intermittent floor show either. As two of the customers brushed past them and out of the door, muttering "Wouldn't bother, mate." as a parting piece of advice, Rob, without hesitation, started off towards the kitchen.

"Looks like Angelo has got problems. Maybe we can help him out."

With only slight hesitation, Martyn removed his hand from the grip of his handgun and stepped in line behind his partner, following faithfully but with a little more caution.

As Rob reached the kitchen doorway, Martyn noticed that he twitched nervously as if suddenly aware of a danger. Once more, Martyn found himself reaching for the handgun.

"Hold it," Rob said, raising his right hand. With his left he reached out and slid the tips of his fingers down the edge of the door frame. Gently, he rubbed them together and held them up to his nose. Then he too reached for his gun.

"Well, it sure isn't tomato relish."

Whether it was the sight of blood, the sudden appearance of the two handguns or some other disturbance elsewhere, neither of them were sure but there was suddenly a piercing scream behind them followed by the sound of tables and chairs being frantically pushed to one side.

"Mine," yelled Martyn. He spun round with lightning efficiency, raising his gun to eye level, both hands clasped tightly on the grip. As instructed, Rob remained absolutely still, all his concentration trained expectantly on the kitchen doorway. Almost before the echo of the scream had finished resounding in his ears, Martyn found himself staring down the barrel of his handgun straight into the wide, terror-stricken eyes of a young woman. Whatever the reason, she had stood bolt upright, sending the table and two chairs crashing down about her. In a reflex action the customers on both sides suddenly moved away, not having time to assess the reason for her behaviour. Now she stood motionless, her hands covering her mouth. About her, like falling dominoes, people were successively turning their attention to the fracas.

She was staring right at him so there could be no other reason. She had simply seen the blood and the guns and reacted. Realising she must be thinking he was about to shoot her, Martyn turned once more to support his partner.

"It's okay. Just a nervous diner."

Rob nodded in acknowledgement. "No point in hanging about. Are you ready?"

"Right behind you."

Without hesitation, Rob flew through the kitchen doorway. Before it had even begun to swing back towards him, Martyn had dived in behind. Both had handguns raised.

No amount of training could have prepared them for what they saw. The kitchen was a mess and appeared to have been ransacked. Yet none of the furniture had been disturbed. The tables, chairs and work surfaces were all intact and in their normal places. All the cupboards were mounted on the wall as they had always been and the frosted windows remained in one piece. Yet every cupboard door had been opened and the contents spilled out and scattered around the room. The two upright fridge freezer units, which stood in the corner, had been emptied and the food stocks slopped pointlessly on the floor, thawing in a pool of water as the ice melted rapidly in the heat of the kitchen. Jars had been smashed, bottles broken and pans turned over, spilling their contents down the side of the industrial gas hob unit. Bags of sugar and flour had been burst and thrown around the room. Much of the flour dust had still not settled. It was suspended in the air, like a cheap theatrical imitation of mist or the aftermath of a small explosion.

Even in death there was no sign of compassion to spare Angelo any indignity. No attempt had been made to hide his body or cover up the cause of death. The tableau which stood before them had been created with them in mind. They both felt it, deeply and personally. And instantly. Angelo lay face upward on the large table which dominated the centre of the kitchen. Both his arms and his legs had been staked out and pinned down with a number of kitchen knives and a large pronged spatula. His naked torso had been sliced open from the neck to the waist, almost as if he were being prepared for cuisine by a professional butcher. There seemed to be little possibility of any blood remaining inside his body. Much of it had been liberally splattered across the walls and ceiling. All his clothes were soaked and the pool which lay over and around his defiled body had left none of the table's surface uncovered. Angelo's head lay motionless, wrenched violently backwards, and his eyes stared lifelessly up towards the ceiling. A single apple, pale green, had been stuffed into his mouth.

Martyn sat at the small bistro style table in the darkest corner of the restaurant trying, and slowly, slowly succeeding to fight back the tears and the nausea, the imminent onslaught of the one checking the advance of the other, each sensation flowing in waves through his body. In the kitchen he had almost vomited, not so much because of what he had seen, which seemed almost too sick and contrived to be real, but because the sweet aroma of Angelo's fresh home cooking had turned suddenly and cruelly into the vile stench of death. A death so horrible that its scent was unique, the product of a mind that was warped beyond imagination. The sight of Angelo had turned his stomach but it was the immediate realisation that he had mistaken the stench for Angelo's cooking that had almost caused him to be sick. In one second, Martyn had recollected all those meals he had eaten in the restaurant behind him.

As Rob turned away, groaning incoherently, Martyn had gagged violently and only just managed to control it. Then, the stench itself began to turn his stomach. As his head began to spin, he was in danger of losing his balance. He made a quick exit from the kitchen and made for the only place he knew could be free of the smell. Despite his churning stomach, he managed to keep his head, aware that the killer might still be around and conscious that he had to carry out certain routine actions immediately. As he emerged from the kitchen, gun still in hand, the crowd backed off two or three steps in confusion and he hissed at them.

"Nobody goes anywhere. Sit down."

They sat. Before retreating into the corner he ordered one of them to call the police. Then, when he was satisfied that his command would be obeyed, he became silent. He still had not spoken a word when Rob came over to him five minutes later and the sound of patrol car sirens could be heard in the distance, speeding towards them.

At first, neither of them spoke. Nothing Martyn could think of seemed an appropriate thing to say. Silence, on the other hand, was appropriate and, as it continued, it seemed even less fitting that it should be broken. Finally, Rob said, "This is a little too close to home. We're going to get the bastard that did this."

Martyn still said nothing. Slowly, he was beginning to realise that Angelo's death was not in itself an ending, not for them anyway. He felt as if he had emerged from a heavy battle, bruised and tired, defeated but still alive. Only now was he beginning to put the battle in its own context, that of a small event in a much bigger war - a war which had neither been won nor lost but one in which they were undoubtedly on the losing side.

He and Rob had still to carry on fighting that war long after they had left this particular battlefield.

If Angelo had not been able to pass on the information he had intended for them, he had still given them one thing which was equally important. He could sense the anger in Rob that he too was beginning to feel. Slowly it climbed above the numbness and shock. Now the conflict was more personal and he knew that neither of them would shy away but would rise to battle with even more determination. Angelo had given them the will to win, and they would win.

"We'll get the bastard alright," he said. "But first we've got to get our own act together."

31

Neither Martyn nor Rob stayed behind at the restaurant any longer than they had to. No sooner had the patrol cars pulled up on the forecourt outside than they beat a hasty retreat and headed back to the precinct on foot, abandoning their own car where they had left it, down a nearby side street. Martyn needed time to think, time to adjust himself to facing the shock of Angelo's death. Though Rob had initially headed off towards the car, he had raised no objection to walking.

Martyn also needed the fresh air. Despite his perpetual claims that the city atmosphere was as polluted as a chimney flue, on the walk back to the precinct the air tasted so clean that his lungs seemed to be drawing in pure oxygen. But everything was relative. After the sickly sweet stench of death in the restaurant, even the stale air of a derelict mineshaft would have been an improvement. In the bistro, before the patrols had arrived, he had been praying for the emptiness of deep space. He could not imagine that a vacuum could be worse than that stench. In the street, the fresher air could only have been produced in heaven and the effect on his turbulent stomach was almost instantaneous. Even so, the smell of freshly baked bread and pastries, which occasionally floated out of the cafes would immediately make him feel nauseous again, and he found that he was subconsciously holding his breath as he passed each one.

Of course, there had been lots of questions to answer but they could wait. There was also a strong possibility that the kitchen was riddled with clues leading to the identity of Angelo's killer but there was no way either Rob or Martyn was going to look for them - it would not have been physically or emotionally possible. They had not sought approval before leaving; just announced their departure and left. Only the boys from Forensics, with their cast iron stomachs and cold, calculating rationality would have the nerve to sift through the mess.

No matter how hard he tried, Martyn could not shake the image of Angelo's lifeless and mutilated body from his mind. He tried thinking about the case, thinking about the previous evening, imagining he was driving along the freeway under a cloudless sky, laughing and joking with Melissa and making love under the stars. But nothing worked. Time after time his mind was filled with images of Angelo and food, both met with equal repulsion, until he began to wonder if he would ever be able to eat again.

It was not until they had arrived back at the precinct, and he had found the letter on his desk, that his mind found something else to chew over Within seconds, all those horrific images that had haunted him for the previous half hour had suddenly been replaced by curiosity, vague apprehension and the hope that they could perhaps solve the case and avenge Angelo's death in one fell swoop.

Even had it not been signed Martyn would have recognised the scrawled handwriting, and the tacky paper with a pastel Hawaiian sunset melted onto it. It was from Angelo.

652 Atlantic Blvd

There is a much talk in the jungle. Next shipment of light metal arrives Tuesday at the north docks. Not sure which one. You will need many men. Armed.

Angelo

Martyn passed the letter over to Rob and picked up the phone, quickly dialling the internal number of the think-tank, the police information department.

"Hello, Cassie? It's Martyn. Listen, I need a full list of ships coming in on Tuesday, midnight to midnight. I know it's a lot but I can't pin it down any tighter. And I need it yesterday."

He did not wait for a reply and put the phone straight down.

"So what does it mean?" asked Rob.

"Don't really know," Martyn said. "But we could hazard a guess, an educated one."

"We could?" Rob picked up the note again and studied it more carefully. "Well the 'jungle' is the syndicate, we know that, and 'metal' means arms, that's straightforward, but what does he mean when he says the shipment is light. What do we want to know that for?"

"We don't," said Martyn. "It doesn't say the shipment is light, it says the metal is light. As in bright light, which I guess is about to dawn on your brain any second now."

The immediate expression on Rob's face suggested that was exactly what happened.

"Lasers!" he exclaimed. "Light metal equals laser rifles. Clever. He obviously wasn't as stupid as he made out." He thought for a moment. "So all we have to do is stake out the north docks and we'll catch our man red handed."

"Nail on the head," Martyn said. "All we have to do is spend a day on stakeout, backed up with whatever additional information we obtain between now and then, and it'll all be over." He shrugged his shoulders and sighed. "So why do I get the feeling it won't be as simple as that. It all sounds too easy."

"Why shouldn't it be?" asked Rob. "If it wasn't for Angelo, we wouldn't know anything about it. He got himself killed trying to get this information to us."

"Maybe. But up to now we have always been one step behind and I don't intend to go to the docks with my eyes blinkered. Angelo wasn't killed, he was turned into an exhibition piece. That disgusting scene was for our benefit and I could feel someone laughing at us all the way down to the dock on Tuesday, where we could be conveniently set up again. And again and again until we become the laughing stock of the whole city. Right now there are lots of things we don't know, most of which we've already taken for granted.

"For a start, we don't really know whether the call we got this morning was from Angelo or not. We need to find out who took the call and see if we can confirm that either way. Next, we don't know whether Angelo's killer knows he sent this note to us or not. If Angelo confessed before he was killed then it's highly probable that the north dock is going to be a lonely place on Tuesday and we could spend all day staking out a non-event."

He picked up the piece of paper and wafted it in front of Rob's eyes as if trying to wake him up.

"He may even have been forced to write it. We don't know. It's Angelo's handwriting but he isn't usually so subtle."

When he had first seen Angelo's body earlier that morning, staked out like a lab specimen, he had not only felt sick with horror at such a grotesque scene but there had also been a deep sense of personal insult in the nature of Angelo's death. He had felt as if he were being provoked. And with that provocation came the birth of an even stronger inner force; an insatiable anger, a driving determination to find Angelo's killer, to gain control of a situation in which he was rapidly losing ground.

His initial reaction had been a burning desire to take up arms and fight, one all out confrontation in the streets of the city, to hunt down Angelo's killers like rats in a maze of sewers and then wipe them out in a final pitched battle. But that was not normally his style. There was nothing intelligent about a show of strength or the use of brute force. It would reduce the city to a war zone, a place where the population lived in constant fear of reprisal and counter reprisal. Soon, the rage would pass and then he would be left with the same situation he had before; a battle of wits with an unknown adversary. But now, more than ever, he did not intend to lose.

When he discovered Angelo's note he had immediately seen the one foothold he needed to get back in the race. They, whoever 'they' were, had got to Angelo but they had been too late to prevent him passing on the information and that one mistake was going to be their downfall. Then, as he considered the alternatives, he began to lose confidence again. How did he know whether Angelo's note was genuine or not? It could be another set up or diversion. He was confused again and that confusion was gradually leading to despondency. One way or another they would have to stake out the docks on Tuesday. Whatever the truth, they could not afford to miss the chance, however slim.

In any investigation it was better to have too much information than too little, even if a substantial proportion of that information at first appeared to be conflicting or misleading. When the forensic team returned, in the early part of the afternoon, with the second note from Angelo, events seemed at first to have taken another turn for the worse and the picture became even more bewildering.

They had not found anything significant. "No fingerprints or alien fibres; nothing appears to be missing, no signs of a struggle, no curious objects of any significance, just a hell of a lot of blood and this."

A hand thrust the plain brown envelope at him. His name had been scrawled on the front. Again, he recognised the handwriting as Angelo's. Underneath his name was the address of the police department.

"Found it at the bottom of a drawer under the cash desk. It's several days old, judging by a brief analysis of the ink, and we even found the pen it was written with. Looks like he meant to post it to you but for some reason never got round to it. We haven't established the exact cause of death yet but we'll get on with the post mortem straight away. He's on the slab now. Hopefully we'll have something before you go home tonight."

Martyn picked up the first note and passed it over.

"See if the ink on this matches the same pen, will you? If it doesn't, see if you can locate the pen that did write it."

Only when he had been left alone once more did he open the note. Rob had already disappeared to witness the post mortem. It was something that he could not have faced. He had never been able to separate the body from the person, to draw the line between his own emotional state of mind and the cold, clinical attitude that was needed to do this job. He could be rational but not detached.

The note read :

Tuesday

I have been trying to call you all day but you are not there. The man you are looking for is known as Lazarus. I don't know where he came from but he is somehow mixed up with the jungle and everyone is scared. He is trying to kill me. Last night my apartment was ransacked and Blackie was dead. I dare not go back

*again. You must catch this man before he gets me. You
know where you can find me. I have still to earn a living.*

Angelo

Martyn placed the note back on his desk, picked it up, read it a second
time and then put it down once more. Like the first, it had been written
on the pastel coloured bistro notepaper with the tropical design. Unlike
the first, it had been placed in a plain brown envelope. Furthermore,
forensic had been right, the letter was apparently two days old. So why
had he not posted it? Who the hell was Lazarus? And why had he been
after Angelo? He wondered if this letter would mark the turning point in
this investigation.

Or was he being set up again?

He did not feel like sitting around, waiting on the post mortem results.
He could not concentrate in the office. Instead he decided to go back to
the apartment early, download some thoughtful instrumental tracks from
the music channel and do some serious logical reasoning. On the way out
he had called by the forensic labs and retrieved the first letter. It had not
been written with the same pen as the second. Although they had made a
thorough search of the restaurant, and found a number of other pens, the
one which had been used to write the second letter had not turned up.

About an hour later, Melissa came home to find him sprawled out on the
sofa, his head propped up with a great pile of cushions so that he could
see the notice board he had erected before him. On the board were two
sheets of paper. Somehow, she knew that they were not meant for her
eyes. Without giving the board a second glance, she came and knelt down
on the floor next to him.

"Albinoni. Adagio for organ and strings in, let me see, G minor, I think.
Must be serious."

He lifted his hand to her face, gently running his fingertips along her
cheek and then through her hair.

"Angelo's dead," he said.

"Angelo? Dead?" she repeated. "How? What happened?"

"He was killed this morning."

"Killed? By who?"

He shrugged his shoulders.

"I don't know," he answered. "Yet."

She threw her arms round his neck and hugged him tightly. "Oh, Martyn. I'm really sorry. That's awful. I know how close you two were. What can I say?"

He knew from experience how very difficult it was to sound sincere when sympathising with the death of a stranger in the presence of a long standing acquaintance. One of the worst aspects of his job was the breaking of bad news. As Martyn held Melissa in his arms, he reflected on how silly her words sounded. He had never been close to Angelo; he could not even contemplate the prospect. He had known him a long time and he could even, in some strange way, mourn his death without knowing for whom he was mourning, but close they were not. And yet, right now, it would not have mattered what she had said. He needed her and she was there; that was all he cared about.

He wanted to make love to her but, for a reason he could not put into words, it did not seem appropriate. It was almost as if the desire to make love had been born out of his grief at Angelo's death or, even worse, that he wanted to make love despite Angelo's death. It would be like laughing at his funeral. But it was also a panacea. It would make him feel better. It was a celebration of life. He wanted the intensity and the release. He felt like a tightened coil, waiting to explode. He needed to perform an act of passion, of violence, to satisfy his own frustration and helplessness. He wanted Melissa and he wanted her now…

Later, as he sat, naked, on the sofa, cradling her, the ever changing picture on the television screen casting flickering shadows across their bodies, he was filled with an inner peace he had not felt for a while. It was a sense of satisfaction, a purging of the spirit and a belief that, in life, he lacked nothing because he wanted nothing more from it.

Yet this must necessarily be the calm before the storm. With any thoughts on life there were always counter thoughts on death. They were like the two poles of a magnet; one could not exist without the other. As he began to think about Angelo again, life immediately became a luxury to feel guilty about. Not until he had found Angelo's killers would he be able to rest easy. And then, inevitably, there would be something else to do.

It was only when the news programme came on that he was forced into action. As the opening credits flashed onto the screen, Angelo's bistro provided the background pictures to the evening's lead story. He remained motionless. There was no way he could have switched the programme off without Melissa knowing he was trying to protect her from something he did not want her to see. But that was half the reason why he found himself wishing that the transmitter would suddenly trip out, or the programme be replaced by some bland music and a still photo of a winter sunrise over the Atlantic. More and more, the sordid and violent events that made up his days were finding ways of following him into the haven he shared with Melissa. He resented their presence in his home and the corruption of the innocence he wanted so hard to preserve. But also, he was scared that the real life events of that morning were all too clear in his mind and too recent for such a vivid reminder. Yet that same fear transfixed him and he could not tear himself away.

"This morning, the relaxed party atmosphere of this small restaurant in downtown Arcades was shattered when the owner, known simply and affectionately as Angelo, was found murdered in his own kitchen and in what can only be described as a bizarre and sickening bloodbath. Our reporter on the scene was Jacqui Miller. Some viewers may find the following item disturbing."

Martyn's concentration was focused not so much on the screen as on Melissa's fingernails as she tightened her fists and dug them into his shoulder. When it was over she had said nothing but, in the subdued light, he could see her breasts quivering and feel the tension running through the rest of her naked body. He lightly kissed her bare shoulder.

"Darling," he whispered. "I have to go out for a short time. There's something I need to do."

32

It took him a long time to locate the place because there was no record of an address and the information had been so sketchy. When he finally arrived he discovered the door unlocked and already ajar. He pushed it open further. As the stench of emptiness and desertion flooded out into the hallway, it caught him by surprise and he almost gagged for the second time that day. The odour was not so dissimilar to the sickly sweet stench at the restaurant and he deduced that Angelo's domestic culinary repertoire had been much the same as that provided for his clientele.

The whole apartment block was unnaturally quiet. From the outside it appeared derelict, nestling inconspicuously along a quiet wooded road close to the western edge of Washington Park. He had seen no one, heard nothing. The only sounds which broke the eerie silence were those of a church bell chiming midnight, some way off - away from the city - and that of the door creaking as it swung slowly open.

It seemed to have been vacant for months. The whole building did. He was surprised not to find a thin layer of dust and smatterings of cobwebs over everything. It was probably damp that gave the apartment its characteristic staleness but he felt that it, too, was in mourning for its departed owner. In the darkness which accompanied the beginning of each new day it was barely possible to see anything. From the shadows and silhouettes before him he concluded that he was in a large reception lounge containing very little furniture.

The layout of the apartment was fairly standard. To his right was a small and basic kitchen area and behind it an open doorway leading into a compact bathroom. He fumbled for a light switch and found one. There was no response. It was impossible to tell whether the fault was due to the bulb or caused by the absence of electricity. So far, there had been no evidence of power anywhere in or near the building.

The floorboards did not feel sound but he was determined not to have gone to all this trouble for nothing. If the floor were to swallow him up, or send him crashing down into the room below, then so be it. It was too late to turn back. He walked over to the only window in the room and looked out over the district of Washington Park. He noticed first that the window was broken near the top and lower down the glass was cracked from one side of the frame to the other. Beyond the fragmented glass there was a small stretch of derelict wasteland which extended as far as the small track road which ran up to Atlantic Boulevard. There, a single line of sleek poplars swayed silently in the night breeze.

He turned to face inwards. The twinkling star-bright light of the distant neons, shining softly through the poplar branches, illuminated the room as best it could. The apartment had been ransacked, but there was so little in it that, in near darkness, the vandalism had gone unnoticed until now. In one corner of the room a table and several chairs, it was not possible to say how many, lay piled in pieces on the floor. Bits of broken pottery were strewn across the bare floorboards and glittered vaguely in the dim light. A cupboard door had been wrenched off and its contents – mainly packets of dog food – had been scattered liberally around. Two ferns, of several years growth, had been pulled from their pots and thrown across the room where their foliage had already begun to decay. Great chunks of plaster were missing from several parts of the wall as if someone had indiscriminately taken a sledgehammer to it. On the other side of the room, to the left of the window and opposite the entrance from which he had come in, there was a single wooden door, drawing his attention immediately in exactly the same way the kitchen door in the bistro had done that morning. It was closed.

In the darkness his mind conjured up irrational fears. With one of the senses temporarily out of commission the others became more acute. In the near silence he could hear his own heartbeat, he could detect the faint odour of the decaying fern leaves and he could taste in the air the very last meal that had been eaten in the room. He could also feel the rising hairs on the back of his neck. Whatever it was he had come here to find, in his heart he knew it lay beyond that door.

In the bedroom, as spartan as the other rooms, and dominated by a single bed which he could just make out in the centre, the window faced south. Through it the pale, silent light of a waxing moon streamed into the corner, illuminating a small section of floor and wall. Like an empty stage in an abandoned theatre, where there were plays but never any players, this play was one short scene. A single line scrawled across the silver wall; a single word, glistening menacingly in the ghostly light. Powerful and devastating as that left by the hand of God yet embodying the childish futility of the most mindless graffiti artist.

LAZARUS.

He walked slowly towards the window and wiped his hand over the surface of one of the letters. It was still sticky and he realised with horror that it was not paint. He was not nauseated by the sight or smell of blood, he had grown used to that a long time ago. It was the source of the blood that concerned him. Walking towards the lighted window he had passed through a shroud of darkness. But, like the room next door, it was probable it would reveal its ugly secrets only when the light was behind him.

He did not hesitate before turning round, and though he was none the less shocked, he was not surprised. The whole of the room seemed to have been daubed with the same meticulous frenzy as the restaurant kitchen. The walls were covered in dried blood, swept over its surface in wide crazy circles, spreading from high up near the ceiling to the floor where large splashes had left inkblot patterns over its surface. The bed, more clearly seen in the new light, had been deeply stained and it was immediately apparent that it had been pulled into the centre of the room to fulfil a purpose. Not only did it remind him of the large table in the centre of the kitchen, it was the same scene, the same sickened mind, the same personal insult. This was also meant for him to see, to demonstrate that it had all been planned days earlier, down to the last detail.

This had been the dummy run.

Above the bed, hanging grotesquely from the severed lamp flex, Angelo's one and only faithful companion had paved the way.

33

Martyn arrived at the precinct next morning a little later than planned. He had called by Angelo's apartment on the way in to see if the fresh light of day could throw up any more information. As he quickly discovered, the forensic team were at work stripping the apartment bare in their search for any microscopic clue which would provide the vital lead. Following the previous night's discovery nothing seemed real anymore and the team completed their task thoroughly and efficiently, methodically photographing and itemising each specimen as nonchalantly as if they were dismantling an exhibition stand. It did not take a considerable time before he became irritated by this and decided to leave.

He walked into an unusually quiet office to learn that his presence was immediately required on the top floor in the conference room he had used the previous morning. He checked his desk for messages, picked up a few sheets of paper, retrieved a file from Rob's cabinet and then made his way towards the elevator. He entered the room one minute later in what appeared to be a heated discussion.

To the right of the doorway, seated around the end of the table, were the three familiar faces he half expected to see; Commander Colchek, Reynolds and Manciani. Further round the table he recognised the head of the Special Forces Network pathology lab, who had personally conducted the autopsies on Sarjena West and Howard Robinson. Chief Lancaster was standing by the window with his back to them while Rob, evidently at the centre of the argument, was pacing up and down the far wall of the room, gesticulating madly.

"…and arresting the guy wouldn't make any sense at all. It doesn't even add up that he's responsible. Besides, what is the point in blowing everything now if we have a chance of catching him red handed on Tuesday. He isn't going anywhere."

"Listen," Manciani insisted. "Yesterday, you were all for arresting Cassida and forcing a confession. There's no consistency with you. I say we bring him in. While someone works on Cassida from the inside we can also get out there and gather some evidence. He might not be going anywhere but nor is his ship. It will be in the middle of the Atlantic by now. If any vessel cancels its departure, changes its cargo or alters course, the computers will pick it up and we'll know about it. If it's out there then it has got to come in. And when it does we'll be ready and waiting."

"But we won't catch any one of the scum at this end because as soon as we arrest Cassida, there won't be anyone to meet the ship on Tuesday. And where does that leave us? I'll tell you; absolutely nowhere. We won't make any arrests at the docks and we'll have spent three days keeping Cassida on full board for nothing. When are you going to get it through your thick skull? We don't have a shred of evidence to convict Cassida of anything. We couldn't even find a fish guilty of swimming. It's hearsay, that's all. I know it, you know it and he knows it. He'll take us to the cleaners. Cassida wouldn't admit to eating at Angelo's five years ago if it didn't suit him. He'd produce fifty alibis and we wouldn't be able to prove it either way. How the hell can we charge him with murdering Angelo with what we've got? We don't have anything. No one has found anything, no one knows anything, no one saw anything and no one heard a damn thing."

"How silently, how silently, the wondrous gift of death is given."

Up until now, nobody had noticed Martyn but suddenly, all heads turned to face him, all but one of the faces gazing quizzically at the strange quotation.

"Just a minute," said Rob. "I recognise that. It was on one of those Gremelkov death threats that came in last week."

"Correct," Martyn replied. "But can you remember who wrote it?"

He brought the scrap of paper out of his pocket and waved it in the air. Rob stared at it, concentrating.

"I don't know," he said, slowly. "I remember the note. Typed with a name at the bottom. Something…poetic. That's right. You said it was poetic. But I can't remember the name. Biblical. That's right. It was something bibli... Oh shit! Lazarus!"

He grabbed the note from Martyn for confirmation.

"Lazarus. Damn! Why didn't I remember?"

"Why didn't either of us remember?" Martyn said. "It only dawned on me last night yet it was staring us in the face. The next thing is…does it help?"

At this point Commander Colchek broke the silence. "Perhaps it would help if I knew what the two of you were wittering on about."

Quickly, Martyn explained about the note that had been found at Angelo's and about the death threat against Gremelkov which had been sent to the City Hall.

"I only made the connection last night when I saw it on the wall in Angelo's apartment. It just came back to me. And it is the same person, I'm sure of it."

"What else do we know about this Lazarus?"

"Nothing," said Martyn. "Rob ran a local check on the name two weeks ago as a matter of procedure and we drew a blank. Yesterday, I carried out a more in-depth search but there's no record of a Lazarus anywhere. All we have is the name, obviously a pseudonym. Nobody is christened Lazarus anymore. It died out years ago."

Chief Lancaster stirred from his preoccupation with the city panorama and suddenly renewed his interest in the conversation, which had died when Rob and the SFN men had begun squabbling.

"Does the name itself tell us anything?"

Martyn knew that the question was directed at him, knowing that he would not have expanded the topic if he had not researched it thoroughly. He was not about to disappoint the Chief but it was Rob who spoke first.

"No," he said. "He was a biblical character."

The Chief looked across at Martyn for confirmation.

"Rob's right. Two characters, actually. Both in the Gospels."

"Is that supposed to mean something?" the Chief asked, growing impatient.

"I don't think so. I read the passages over and over again. There is no obvious connection. I don't think there is meant to be."

"Come on, Martyn, we don't have all day," the Chief said, becoming irritated. "If you know something then tell us."

"It's a hunch but I think I know the connection. It's simple. Lazarus sounds like laser. I don't think there is any more to it."

"You think this Lazarus is our laser assassin?" Commander Colchek asked. Before Martyn could reply, Reynolds interrupted.

"I think we're getting side-tracked here. Our man is Cassida, it has to be. We've been watching him for weeks now and he's about to pull off something big. On that score I thought we were all agreed. We know he has been paying visits to a lot of important people recently, and by their reactions we know that they weren't social calls. Meanwhile, Cassida has continued to throw his weight around. He's also been upsetting a lot of people. We know that he took some of his heavies round to Angelo's last Monday."

"Just a minute," said Martyn, surprised. "You've been watching Cassida?"

"That's right," explained Rob. "Twenty four hours a day for the last two weeks."

"Until you blundered your way in the other day and blew the whole operation," said Manciani. "Smart move throwing him in the pool, though." Martyn was not clear whether this was meant as sarcasm or not so he ignored it. The Chief glared but remained silent.

"So you weren't watching him yesterday morning when Angelo was killed?"

"No," Reynolds said. "We cancelled the surveillance immediately you decided to do your own close up interrogation. But doesn't it seem funny that on Monday your friend Angelo, a known informant, gets a visit from Cassida's heavies. Then, as soon as you go bungling in to see Cassida, within twenty four hours, no Angelo. I'm telling you, Cassida is your man. He's behind this."

The implication that they had been indirectly responsible for Angelo's death was something that cut into Martyn deeply because he accepted that what Reynolds had said might be true. But his anger was tempered by an intuition that it was not so simple. He also sensed Rob's own bitterness at the remarks and subtly stepped between the two men before Rob had chance to launch at him.

"You might be right," he said to Reynolds, "but if you are there is something that doesn't quite make sense."

He pulled out a chair and sat down.

"So far, two people have been murdered by what the experts have told us is a laser beam. The evidence suggests that it was probably the same weapon in each case. But where has the weapon come from? We have been told that there is no US design capable of producing the effects we have seen. Also, we have been led to believe by an expert that it is unlikely that the Communist Alliance could have developed such a weapon from the point they were at twelve months ago. Since no other nation is advanced enough in laser technology to have developed the weapon, and since the weapon does exist, then there is only one place it could have come from without us knowing about it."

He looked around for some indication that they were following his line of reasoning.

"It would have to be from the Alliance," Chief Lancaster said. The Commander looked at him, confused.

"That's the only answer," Martyn agreed. "Somehow, the Alliance must have made a breakthrough that even Raspov couldn't have anticipated."

"Why?" challenged Manciani. "That's stabbing in the dark."

"Maybe," said Martyn. "But following Angelo's tip off about the arrival of the next assignment, it so happens that on Tuesday evening, at eight minutes to seven, a Russian cargo ship is due in at the north dock."

He waved a second piece of paper in the air and then thumped it back down on the table. Commander Colchek was staring at him incredulously.

"Detective Sorensen, do you realise that hundreds of ships arrive in this country every week and some of them, a small but significant number, happen to be from the Alliance countries. What makes this ship so special?"

"It depends whether you believe in coincidences," Martyn said. "In Angelo's note he put down his address as '652, Atlantic Boulevard'. It isn't. Angelo actually lived in an apartment in the Weatherfield Mansion complex just off Atlantic Boulevard. The address is listed as Atlantic Boulevard but there is no number. If there were, it would be in the two hundreds. Six hundred and fifty two does not exist. Angelo must have been trying to tell us something when he wrote it and I think it was the docking time of the ship. I can't think of anything else it could be."

"Alright," said Manciani. "Let's suppose you're right. It still seems pretty straightforward to me. Cassida has the laser weapon. He kills two people for God knows what reason and then, when the city is in a state of panic and he has another shipment coming in, he starts throwing his weight around until everyone is scared. He even threatens Angelo; he knows him to be an informant. To lead him off the scent - and in case the message hasn't got through - he goes round to Angelo's place and kills his dog, leaving the name of the culprit in big red letters on the wall. Angelo gets confused. He writes you a note telling you about Lazarus. Then he hears about Cassida's ship coming in and doesn't post it because he realises that Lazarus doesn't exist. It was Cassida all along. He writes you another note telling you about the shipment on Tuesday. He manages to send it off before Cassida and his heavies turn up having decided, for some reason, that they are better off with Angelo out of the way."

Both the Chief and the Commander were suitably impressed. There was a look of annoyance on Rob's face as he could find no obvious flaw in it either. He looked across at Martyn hopefully but found only a puzzled expression.

"I still say we should wait for the ship to come in before we arrest Cassida," argued Rob. "Even if Cassida isn't there it will be a lot easier to bring a case against him if we can connect him with whoever does turn up. I don't think he will use middle men for this operation. The cargo is too important."

The Chief nodded in agreement.

"That would be my view too, Commander. If we arrest Cassida now he will be out on the street again in a couple of days. We need at least one piece of hard evidence to go ahead with the prosecution and we don't have that as yet. Waiting until Tuesday could make all the difference."

Suddenly, there was a knock at the door and a man entered, still clothed in a light blue laboratory uniform with a small white hygienic mask dangling around his neck.

"You asked for this report immediately, sir." He addressed the SFN pathologist and handed him a thin document as he spoke. On the way out he handed another sheet of paper to Martyn.

"Here are those test results you requested."

Martyn thanked him and he left. Commander Colchek asked him, "What results are those?"

"Oh, nothing important," Martyn replied. "I believe, from the look on his face, that your colleague has found something much more illuminating."

All attention was directed towards the chief pathologist who had evidently made a significant discovery.

"The autopsy report on Angelo," he explained. "Listed on the first page is the exact cause of death. According to this, before he was cut up he was stabbed through the heart with something resembling a red hot poker. The burn marks were greatly distorted by the mutilation but the evidence is clear and the wound appears to have been very clean. Straight in and out in one perfectly smooth stroke."

An unnatural silence descended on the room as the words sank in.

"Too perfect," said Martyn. Both he and Rob recalled the two autopsy reports they had studied following the deaths of Sarjena West and Howard Robinson.

"As if by a laser?" Rob's question was meant to have been rhetorical, exposing the thoughts of everyone to the room. He did not expect an answer.

"I will have to do another autopsy before I could be certain," the chief pathologist said. "But I think we have already decided what the result will be."

"Alright," the Commander said, changing the subject. "We'll wait until Tuesday. In the meantime, I will authorise a twenty four hour watch on Cassida. I don't want him sneaking off anywhere while we're waiting for a ship full of Babushka dolls. I believe the path lab's further post-mortem will add weight to your theory, Detective Sorensen, but I hope you forgive me if I retain a healthy scepticism. I don't want any more cock ups. If there are lasers on that ship then I want them. Whether we find a cargo of laser rifles or not, I want at least enough evidence to convict Cassida of something. We have wasted enough time and effort on him already. Chief Lancaster, I'll leave you to organise the showdown at the docks if you don't mind. I trust you can handle it."

"Yes, sir," the Chief replied.

When the four men from the Special Forces Network had left the room, Martyn, Rob and Brett Lancaster remained behind.

"You know something," said the Chief. "The sooner we sew this up and send them packing back to New York, the better."

"I thought Commander Colchek was a good friend of yours," said Rob.

"He was a good cop," the chief agreed, "and a good partner, if not the best, but you don't want even your best friend in your back garden all the time. After a while they tend to ruin the lawn, if you know what I mean. And besides, those two meatheads he's carting around with him are beginning to get on my nerves. At least after Tuesday we should be shot of them. If all goes well, that is. There's still a lot of work to be done. Any problems?"

"None," said Rob. "Thankfully, since we've been left to deal with this ourselves, it should go smoothly. We'll make sure it does. Just one question, Chief. Are we going to have the manpower available? We can't go into this half-heartedly. It's all or nothing."

"Don't worry," the Chief confirmed. "I'm the last person who wants this to go wrong. Everybody I can spare will be on it. So let's make sure we do the groundwork properly. I want a complete survey of the docks and a proposal for action on my desk by tomorrow afternoon. Right, have we covered everything? Okay Martyn?"

Martyn frowned uneasily and the message was clear. Everything was not okay.

"If it's alright with you, Chief, I would like to spend the next couple of days clearing up some loose ends, just to be on the safe side."

"What loose ends?" the Chief asked.

"Well, for starters, two weeks ago we had reached the conclusion that there must be a mole in the police organisation. Greg Miller practically said as much and might have said more if Colchek's sidekicks hadn't got hold of him. If we're going to bring more people in for this operation, how do we know that Cassida isn't going to receive advanced warning? Secondly - and I'm surprised nobody has spotted this, if Angelo wanted to tell us what time the ship was coming in then why didn't he just write it in the note instead of trying to hide it in a false address?"

"You were the one who said that was what he had done," said the Chief. "So why don't you tell us?"

"Because he didn't send the note."

"He must have done," said Rob. "It was on the bistro's paper and I'd recognise Angelo's scrawl anywhere."

"I didn't say he didn't write it," Martyn continued. "I just said he didn't send it. It's the only explanation I can think of. Before Angelo was killed he was forced to write this note and the only way he could tell us that he had not written it was to use the wrong address."

"But wouldn't whoever it was have spotted it?" said the Chief. "After all, he wrecked Angelo's apartment only two days before."

"And frightened him enough to keep quiet about it until, perhaps, it was too late anyway. It may have been Angelo's last, desperate act of defiance. On the other hand, you may be right. Angelo's killer may have seen it and decided not to do anything about it. He may have forced Angelo to put a false address to confuse us. He may not have spotted it. He knew where Angelo lived but not necessarily that it had no number. I suspect it is always listed as just Weatherfield Mansion. Or perhaps the person who killed Angelo didn't wreck his apartment. If Cassida is behind all this then he could have used any of his heavies to ransack Angelo's place."

"Do you think that's likely?" the Chief asked. "It's the same modus operandi."

"I don't think it's likely," agreed Martyn. "But it's a possibility. Cassida could have issued precise instructions about what to do. That isn't really important. What concerns me is that the whole department is being mobilised to be at the docks on Tuesday and it could all be a set-up, a diversion, or even a joke. If this information is genuine then who the hell did send it? And who are they trying to set up if it isn't us?"

"Which leaves us right back where we started?" said Rob.

"It makes no difference," said the Chief. "Whether Angelo's note was sent by Angelo or not, and for whatever reason, we still have to be at the docks on Tuesday. We don't have any choice. Martyn, with reference to your previous question the answer is 'yes'. Find out as much as you can as quickly as you can. Rob is going to organise the operation on Tuesday and he'll need every ounce of information you can give him. Now get going."

Martyn rose to leave, picking up all the sheets of paper he had brought in. Just before he left the room the Chief caught him once more.

"By the way, what is that test report you've got there?"

Martyn paused in the doorway.

"That was the other thing that puzzled me. If Angelo wrote that first note then he didn't get to find out about Lazarus from his apartment wall. When I went to see his place last night, the letters were still wet whereas all the other blood had dried. These test results confirm it. The word Lazarus was written with Angelo's own blood. Whoever killed him must have gone back to Angelo's apartment yesterday evening to write *Lazarus* on the wall. He couldn't have thought it would fool us.

Yesterday, I thought this guy was just sick; today I'm not sure. Whoever is behind this is deliberately goading us. What worries me is that we may be dealing with someone who is not only insane, but also very intelligent."

34

As the door opened Jacqui Miller seemed both surprised to see him and yet resignedly prepared for his visit.

"I was expecting you earlier," she explained, and waved her arm in a welcoming gesture. "I stopped in all day and was just beginning to think you weren't coming."

"When there's a murder there are things to do before we go questioning glamorous reporters on an ego trip. If you knew we would want to question you, why didn't you come down to the precinct instead of making me come all the way out here?"

She appeared slightly taken aback. "Oh, come now, Detective Sorensen, that was a little vicious, wasn't it?"

"Depends on how you define 'vicious'. Angelo might not think so but then everything is relative, isn't it?"

As he spoke he stepped into the hallway and moved towards the drawing room as directed.

"I take it this isn't going to be one of your pleasant social visits," she said, closing the door.

In the drawing room, a slightly ostentatious gallery of art nouveau with a chaise longue and two chairs thrown in as an afterthought, he came face to face with Greg Miller, who instantly rose to his feet.

"You mean you guys actually make pleasant social calls as well. There's no end to your talents, is there? You'll forgive me if I don't stick around but I haven't got any more time for your heavy-handedness, especially when I'm the victim." He began to leave, making it perfectly clear that he was not prepared even to stay in the same room as Martyn.

"You seem to find plenty of time to report it."

Under normal circumstances, Martyn would have probably sympathised with Greg Miller – even apologised – but today he was not in the mood.

This parting shot did nothing to deter Greg Miller's exit and it was only the entrance of his wife, pausing in the narrow doorway, that prevented him from shooting straight out of the room.

"Oh dear," she said. "You seem to be offending everybody at an alarming rate. You've only been here ten seconds."

Martyn was growing impatient. "When are you two going to realise this is not a game? I am trying to conduct a murder investigation and you are both acting like spoiled children."

Greg Miller retaliated. "Well perhaps you'd like to torture us half to death for twelve hours?"

"Don't flatter yourself. If you think I came round here to apologise for what happened you are way off target. Let's get one thing absolutely clear. You are not entirely innocent. You're an irresponsible, amoral leech who puts more value on a story than he does on human lives. You probably deserved everything you got. And right now, if I thought you were harbouring any more information I'd kick you right across the city to get it."

"Is that a threat?" countered Miller.

"You can take it any way you damn well want. But I hope it shows you how far I'm prepared to go to catch this killer. While you are playing stupid games, people - real people - are dying horrible deaths. My priority is to stop it, not be first on the scene with a camera every time someone turns up dead."

"Your job," said Greg Miller, "is to catch the killer. My job is to run round with a camera and report on your progress. I do my job and I do it well. So far I haven't seen much evidence of you doing yours." With that he stormed out of the room and seconds later they heard the front door slam, shaking the whole house. In the silence that followed they listened as a car engine started and roared off into the distance.

Jacqui Miller was surprisingly calm and unmoved.

"Had a bad day?" she asked.

"You could say that. I take it your husband is still sore about what happened."

"You could say that," she mimicked. "Been grumpy all week. He wanted to hold a public enquiry into the incident but so far he's been banging his head against a brick wall. No one is interested in his claims which he's found difficult to come to terms with. But he's a stubborn and determined man. He'll just fight harder until he gets some results. And that means a lot of bad press for you."

"That's all I need," said Martyn, wearily. "Couldn't you persuade him to direct his energy towards something more constructive. I don't really relish the thought of having my reputation carved up over everyone's breakfast table. Things are bad enough as it is."

Jacqui flopped into a soft cushioned sofa and smiled reassuringly.

"I can't promise anything," she said. Once he's set off on one of his solo crusades in the interest of public duty and justice for all, he's pretty immovable. It's an admirable quality really. Not everybody is willing to fight the battles of the weak and underprivileged the way he does. It's just a pain in the butt when it's directed against you."

"But it's so tiresome. We have to put up with criticism every day. Doesn't he realise that we're supposed to be on the same side?"

As soon as he had opened his mouth, he knew he had backed himself into a corner. He expected her to lash out with a touché reply. After all, the police and the press had never been on the same side because, in the end, sides did not come down to a simple distinction of black and white. On that note Cassida was right. The media set themselves up as their own police watchdog while the police, in occasionally harassing witnesses and suspects, deserved everything that subsequently appeared about them in the press. It was a ridiculous situation born out of frustration and helplessness. The media hounded the police for more action, more results and the police responded, in desperation, by carrying out hasty acts of aggression in a vain attempt to make some headway. And certainly, Greg Miller had no reason to be charitable or co-operative where the police were concerned.

Surprisingly, Jacqui said nothing. Perhaps it was because he sounded dog-tired and weary. Instead she continued to smile and reached over the couch for a sheet of paper.

"There are two ways you can counter bad publicity," she said. "You can find the laser killer and turn yourself into a hero overnight. That way you'll be forgiven everything you ever did. The end justifies the means, so to speak."

"Or?"

"Or you can create some good publicity, but to do that you need to get somebody on your side."

"Like who?"

"Like me." She held up the sheet of paper and he recognised the photograph of himself taken at the time of the Dortman narcotics bust. Above it was a new headline: "Martyn Sorensen : Hero or Misfit"

He was embarrassed, flattered even, but also curious to know exactly what the headline was trying to say.

"Hero or misfit? I don't get it. Why am I either? Why can't I be both?"

"Maybe you are," Jacqui said. "I don't know, it's an initial impression. Anyway, it's only a working title. As I find out more it may change."

"More about what?"

"More about you," she said. "I want to do an exposé on the real you. I want to show everybody exactly what kind of man is responsible for tracking down the laser assassin. I want to bring out the human element, to show them you're not a machine. I want them to know that when a friend of yours is murdered you hurt and the grief is as real and painful as anybody's. You are hurting, aren't you?"

She had caught him off guard. He had thought about nothing but Angelo's death all morning. He did hurt and the pain seemed to be growing as the realisation of what had happened gradually began to sink in. Not only because it was Angelo but because of the conviction that Angelo's death was a personal attack on him – and it was somehow tied to all the other strange things that had been happening. For a moment he was tempted to tell her, to pour out his heart, to provide a story so full of personal emotion and passion that she would be shamed into not printing a word of it. He believed her intentions were good and something told him that she genuinely wanted to do this - and not for the money. But she was a reporter and no matter what he thought of her as a person there would always be a temptation to exaggerate, to over glamorise in the pursuit of the coveted centre page spread.

For security reasons, he would not be allowed to divulge much information. He did not, in principle, object to the story in itself and it was certainly true that it could do the police organisation a lot of good. On the other hand he was not so sure he wanted his own private thoughts splashed over millions of copies of a daily newspaper, even if they were reprinted accurately.

"It's a nice idea," he said, "but nothing we do now is going to help Angelo. All we can do is catch that maniac before he kills again and right now that's priority number one. And anyway, I thought I was the one asking the questions."

Jacqui offered no resistance and put the headline back down on a small coffee table.

"Alright," she said, disappointedly. "Go on."

"Well you know why I'm here," he said. "First of all, did you have to broadcast those scenes yesterday? That was a particularly horrific murder and I don't believe it was something the public really wanted to see, or needed to see. Secondly, I want to know how you managed to get there so quickly. Those scenes you shot must have been taken just after I left so don't tell me you happened to be passing when the murder was discovered because I won't buy it."

"I wasn't going to say that," she replied, nonchalantly. "It seems I know you better than you know me. What if I told you that I was actually standing outside for ten minutes waiting for you to leave because I knew you wouldn't let me in. After you'd gone it was easier than I expected. Everyone was in a state of shock and we managed to reel off the report before anybody noticed. Then we got thrown out."

"What about you? Weren't you in a state of shock or didn't it disturb you at all?"

Although she tried to hide it, Martyn could tell that he had offended her and he was relieved to see it.

"I'm not a hard woman," she replied. "I didn't know Angelo personally like you did but, if it makes you feel better, I spent a quarter of an hour in the powder room being sick."

"I hope you won't take this the wrong way," Martyn said, "but I feel a lot happier knowing that you did. Now tell me how you managed to be on the scene the exact minute the murder was discovered."

She made herself comfortable as if about to make a long speech, already prepared and well rehearsed.

"At last we get to the point," she began. "Anyway, here goes. There isn't much to it really. Greg was down at the studio when a phone message came through to say he should collect a package from the Excelsior, like last time only a different hotel. Greg came home and handed me the note. Said he wasn't going to bother being dragged all over the city simply to end up being interrogated by the police for twelve hours. He wished me luck and left on some other assignment almost immediately. Well, what could I do?"

"You could have called me."

"I did but they couldn't find you and I wasn't about to pass up the opportunity waiting for you. Anyway, I immediately drove over to the Excelsior and went straight to the desk but they wouldn't give me the package. It took me over ten minutes to prise it out of them, and only then because one of the chamber maids recognised me. Oh, and before you ask, the package was waiting behind the desk and no one saw who handed it in or knows how it got there.

"Inside the package was another key to a left luggage locker at Eden Square station. I went straight to it. I decided to walk since the Excelsior is fairly close and the traffic around there is always heavy. I'd already wasted too much time driving to the hotel. Anyway, I got to the station, found the locker, opened it and hey presto, there was nothing there... except this." She handed Martyn a small plastic credit card wallet. "I put it in this so you could examine it," she explained, "and I only handled one edge of it, along the bottom."

He opened up the wallet and, without any care whatsoever, grasped the contents between his soiled fingers and removed them.

"Waste of time," he said before she had a chance to speak. "If we were looking for somebody who was going to leave fingerprints over everything we'd have probably caught him by now."

He looked down at the small business card in his hand. Angelo had always kept a stack of them on the counter. Melissa had even pinned one to a notice board in the kitchen in case she ever burnt the dinner. "Is that all?"

"That's all," she replied. "Angelo's is nearer the office than I was so I called Paul, my cameraman, and told him to get down there and take film of anything he saw as being suspicious before I arrived. As it turned out he got there just before I did and the only thing he had on film was your arrival. Seconds later, somebody screamed and... well, you know the rest. I'm sorry but it's not much to go on, is it?"

"No," he agreed, and then smiled. "But it isn't useless either."

It was immediately evident that she had said something of interest but she did not know what. As he began to pace up and down the room, he could sense her inquisitive eyes following his every move, bombarding him with silent questions. At last, she grew impatient,

"Well? What did I say? What's going on in that mind of yours?"

Martyn turned and shrugged his shoulders. He had not been able to formulate an answer so he decided to think aloud in case there was anything else she could remember that might help him.

"Let's start at the beginning," he said. "About what time did your husband receive the message?"

"Soon after he arrived at the studio, I think. It must have been around eight o'clock."

"And what time did he come home again?"

"He got back about twenty minutes to nine. He only stayed round the studio long enough to collect an assignment, pick up some equipment and then he came back. I didn't waste any time at all. I was already dressed so I jumped straight in the car and drove to the Excelsior, arriving about ten minutes past."

"I thought you called me before you left," he said.

"I did," she said. "But that didn't take long."

"Then why did I get a message saying you'd called at quarter past nine, half an hour later?"

"I don't know," she said. "Maybe they got it wrong."

"They didn't get it wrong," he replied, calmly. "They are always spot on. You didn't telephone me because you wanted the story. You only called me at quarter past nine because they wouldn't give you the package. Then, when you got your lucky break, you conveniently forgot to call me again."

She didn't argue. In fact, she seemed quite impressed.

"Alright," she conceded, "but everything else I've told you is the truth."

"It better be." He spoke, without malice, as if addressing a naughty puppy not expected to be responsible for its actions. "Okay, so let's get this straight. You left the hotel about nine twenty. It's about a five minute walk to Eden Square, about five minutes to find the locker and open it, five minutes to phone your cameraman friend, five minutes back to the hotel and around fifteen minutes, maybe twenty, to drive over to Angelo's, arriving just after ten o'clock, which was when I got there. Now, isn't that strange?"

Jacqui seemed at a loss.

"What is?" she said, implying that the whole episode was strange and she could not pinpoint one event more unusual than another. Martyn explained.

"Angelo's death wasn't simply a murder, it was an exhibition, a demonstration of strength and power for the benefit of the whole city, and we played right into their hands. Just before ten o'clock I received a message, supposedly from Angelo, and I went straight down there. At eight o'clock yesterday morning your husband is encouraged to go on another wild goose chase which ultimately ends at Angelo's at about the same time. According to forensic, Angelo was killed around nine forty which can only mean one thing. Angelo's murder was staged specifically for us, or more precisely, for your camera." Jacqui was still confused but she was beginning to follow him.

"Staged by whom? Surely Greg's informant couldn't have done this. I can't believe he's been dealing with a homicidal maniac all this time."

"I doubt it. Whoever killed Angelo and set this up probably pretended to be your husband's informant to get his attention. It was the only way they could ensure that he would follow it through. And if it hadn't been for Greg's chance meeting with you, it would have backfired."

"But if Greg had decided to follow the story instead of passing it on to me then he would have got there around nine o'clock," she exclaimed.

"Precisely," he replied. "And Angelo would have been killed an hour earlier and I would have received Angelo's message just before nine. Which means that either your husband must have been followed or someone was waiting at the hotel when you picked up the package. If more than one person is involved it's even possible that they were watching the left luggage locker. As soon as you found the card you telephoned for a cameraman. At the same time, somebody else could have ordered Angelo's execution. One thing's for certain; Angelo was not killed until they were absolutely sure that you were on your way. Then they informed the police."

"But why tell you? It doesn't make sense. If they wanted me to film it then why would they inform the one person who was going to stop me? It was sheer luck that I was able to get a camera in there at all."

Martyn shrugged his shoulders. "It only makes any kind of sense if they expected you to arrive before me."

He spoke almost to himself in a near whisper. Something told him that he had been made a fool of yet again but only by a cruel twist of fate. The timing was almost so perfect that he could not help himself but admire the evil genius who lay behind this whole episode. Thinking back to the events of the previous morning he had reacted to the message from

Angelo with unusual haste. If the Chief had not delivered the information personally it may have been another half hour before he had arrived and by that time every TV and pressman in the city would have had time to collect a whole archive of material.

He dreaded to think what might have happened. Instead of two minutes of footage on headline news it could have been an hour long documentary. Things had been easier when they were able to confiscate the film. Now that cameras transmitted back to remote recording devices which could be anywhere within a two mile radius it was virtually impossible to prevent any classified or pornographic material from being broadcast to the public. Any subsequent legal action was always retrospective.

The more he thought about it, the more he was convinced it was intended that he should arrive on the scene too late to prevent any press coverage but in plenty of time to make an idiot of himself in front of the cameras. Of course, had he not arrived, Jacqui would have called the police as soon as she was through making movies but he was not so sure about her husband. Greg Miller would have seized on the opportunity to make the police look like fools and that was why the whole scheme had such ingenuity. If it had worked the way they had planned, the results would have been far worse. Miller would have fed the story to every TV, radio and newspaper office in the country by lunchtime. They had not considered his being too scared to take the story when they were handing it to him on a golden platter. And they had not reckoned on the police arriving so soon. It was sheer incompetence that Jacqui Miller had obtained her headline story and given the public something serious to worry about. He wondered what her husband thought about that.

And he wondered if Angelo would still be alive if no one had bothered to turn up to the event.

Jacqui Miller had reached the same conclusion. His thoughts were distracted, suddenly, by the sensation of softness brushing against his right cheek and he came back to reality with a start. Turning, he found himself staring into her deep, hazelnut eyes, only inches from his own, and welling with two huge teardrops. As he stood, uncomprehendingly, she stepped back and allowed one of the tears to fall down her cheek. There was something desolately lonely about her at that moment. In those eyes he saw himself as he had been, maybe one year ago, before he met Melissa. And for no apparent reason he thought of Howard Robinson for the first time in days.

He lifted his hand to her face and gently nudged the tear onto the tip of his finger. He had not seen her display any emotion before and her loneliness stirred something deep inside him. He felt vulnerable. She pulled back, her eyes searching his for some kind of response. Whatever she saw contained the message she was looking for. Slowly, very slowly, she pulled back her dress to the edge of her shoulders and allowed it to slip over. He did not try to stop her and watched as it fell, as quietly as a feather, to the floor. She stood naked before him, gazing coyly, almost innocently, into his eyes.

"Hug me," she whispered. "Please."

As he held her and she began to cry he was suddenly made aware of his erection as her body rubbed across his. He did not know exactly why she was crying; there could have been a number of reasons. It did not matter.

"Why do you do what you do?" he asked.

"Because I enjoy it," she sobbed. "But sometimes it's so lonely out there. I just wish he'd come through for me. All he does is compete. I love him but I'm not allowed to have a marriage and a successful career. He doesn't say anything but he hates it when I do well and he becomes obsessed with getting even. And sometimes all I want is to be hugged."

She pushed herself closer and he felt her breasts burrowing into his chest as she tried to squeeze every last ounce of affection out of him. He held her even tighter, gently stroking her soft brown hair. In a whole lifetime, moments like this were so rare, so precious, and he wanted to experience it all, to give her everything she so desperately needed, and to share the pleasure of release with her.

She began kissing his neck, her arms moving up and down his back passionately, her tongue tracing a line across his cheek towards his ear.

"I want you," she whispered. "Please. I want you now."

And he wanted her so much. Too much. Gently, he eased her away from him until he was once more able to focus on those tear stained eyes.

"What's wrong?" she said, as more tears began rolling down her cheek.

He wanted to tell her how he felt. But the truth was that he felt confused and said nothing. He suspected she was no stranger to the art of seduction – that this could have all been rehearsed – but he believed her tears were genuine. He wanted her to know that he desired her – so she did not feel rejected. Instead, he told her the truth.

"I'm sorry but I can't. I love Melissa."

It was because she knew this to be true that she became even more upset. He could see that she understood but found it difficult to accept. Her eyes continued to plead with him, battering away at his fragile resolution. He wondered why he felt the way he did. He did not know one person who would not sink down to the floor and make love to her on the spot.

He determined that it would not be wise to stay. The sense of longing he felt was only just under control and he became acutely aware of the need to put some distance between himself and the source of this frustration. Gently separating himself from her bare limbs, he kissed her softly on the forehead and made for the door.

"Tell me," she said, reflecting his own question back at him. "Why do you do what you do?"

"Sorry?"

"You're no cop. Not at heart, anyway. I've met a lot of policemen and you're not the same. You put on an act but really you're not tough enough or mean enough. It isn't your game. You're too sensitive. So why do you do it?"

"I do it for you," he replied. "And Melissa. Because I need to feel in control. You may be right. Maybe I'm not a cop at heart. Maybe I'm not tough enough. I'll be honest with you – I spend most days feeling scared. But I'm good at what I do and I can't walk away from it all now."

He could see she wanted to come forward and hold him but instead she pulled the dress up loosely over her shoulders and became the Jacqui Miller he knew, businesslike and philosophical.

"It's ironic, isn't it?" she said. "If you were too successful I wouldn't have much to write about. People don't really want to know nice things; they want to read about violence and sex. It's always been like that and you'll never be able to change it. Not on your own, you won't. You're fighting a war you can't win, you know that. You may win a battle, you may win several battles but they will always be replaced by more and one day you'll lose."

"I know that," he said.

"I know you do but there's something else I want you to know. I don't want to see you lose. Take some advice, Martyn. Get out of here. You don't belong. Pack your bags and take Melissa off into the sunset somewhere. You owe it to yourself and to her. You know I'm right, don't you? So just do it."

He offered her a grateful smile, thinking how comforting it was to know that there was someone who really cared - and how strange it was to be having this conversation with a semi-naked woman who appeared on the television nearly every day.

"I already planned to," he said. "In the new year, when Gremelkov has been and gone." He opened the door to leave. "But I have to see this through first."

35

Thursday morning.

Howard Robinson woke early and immediately determined not to stay in bed a moment longer. Although he was still weak, his head had cleared and he felt decidedly restless. He threw back the sheets and climbed out of bed. Within fifteen minutes, he had washed, dressed and made his way downstairs to the first floor landing where the guests' post was put out. There were one or two circulars addressed to people he had never heard of but still no word from Melissa. From a room which he had previously deduced to be the kitchen, Susannah appeared.

"Good morning," she said. "Feeling any better?"

"Much, thank you. Is there no post again?"

"Good grief. You're obsessed with that post. If you're expecting something important why don't you give them a call? There's a payphone downstairs in the bar."

"The lounge, dear, the lounge." The landlord careered through the kitchen doorway and brushed past them. Turning briefly to Howard, he said good morning and then returned to his daughter.

"Susannah, could you give your mother a hand in the dining room. We're a bit behind and I'm in a rush to get out." With that he disappeared down the hallway. Susannah turned to go back through the kitchen. Before opening the door she smiled cheekily and spoke in a posh voice, interlaced with a Lancashire accent.

"The telecommunication console is to be found in the lounge."

Howard returned to his room. Despite existing on little more than a bowl of soup and two slices of toast over the previous four days, he did not feel hungry and decided to skip breakfast. He walked to the window and threw open the curtains. To his surprise, it was still foggy, though by no means as thick as it had been four evenings before. Looking out, the view seemed almost Victorian. The room, situated in the corner of the hotel two floors above the front doorway, looked out on a large five way road junction. The fog enabled him to see the far side of the crossroads but no further, as if it were under a giant bell jar shrouded in mist. Occasionally, beams of white, silent light would pierce through the perimeter as cars approached and traversed the junction. For only seconds they would enter onto the stage, bathed in the spotlight of a solitary street lamp, and then disappear through the curtain of mist on the other side. For a moment, the red tail lights would hesitate at the edge of the stage, then they too would slowly fade into the distance, and oblivion.

Howard sat by the window for several minutes. He wanted to go outside but now it looked neither healthy nor inviting. However, the thought of staying in his room even one more morning willed him into action and he quickly put on an ski jacket, wrapped a scarf around most of his head and made his way downstairs. As he passed the first floor landing he once more bumped into Susannah.

"Where on earth do you think you're going?" she exclaimed.

"For a walk."

"In this weather! You can't be five minutes away from a bad dose of the flu and you want to go for a walk in thick fog. You must be crazy!"

"No disrespect, but if I have to stay in here a minute longer I will be."

"But you haven't had breakfast. You can't go out without a meal inside you."

"Not hungry. And you're beginning to sound like my mother."

"Well maybe your mother has more common sense than you do."

Susannah continued trying to discourage him for the next five minutes and then, realising that he was adamant, she gave up. Howard bluntly changed the subject.

"Does the name 'Landmark' mean anything to you?"

"No, why?"

"No reason. I thought it might the name of a shop, or a company or something. Maybe a local brand name."

"You could try the library. It's just across the bus station, on the corner. You can't miss it."

"Are you now saying I can go outside?"

"No, but if you insist then that should be a safe enough trip. You won't come to much harm going to the library."

"I was going to go up on the moor."

"What! Well, that's really stupid. I wouldn't go up on the moor in this weather even if I was perfectly healthy. It will be horrible up there. If you make yourself ill again, don't expect me to look after you."

She stormed off, though he could tell that the action was more for dramatic effect than a sincere one. True, given the circumstances it probably was a stupid thing to do but the claustrophobia which seemed to envelope the whole building was more than he could stand. He had to get out and it was worth taking the risk.

Once outside, he turned away from the road which led up to the railway station and carefully crossed the junction, taking the first road he found which appeared to be going uphill. It made sense. From the map he had seen prior to his arrival, one side of the Darwen valley rose up onto the moor and this was the opposite side to that on which the station was located. Though the weather conditions were far from ideal, in one respect it was the perfect day to go up onto the moor. This way he would not find out what it was that lay on top - the missing piece from the jigsaw - until he was only yards from it. Of course, in this weather he might not come across it at all but he felt fairly confident. Since the mysterious object did lie at the highest point on the moor, or so it appeared from the jigsaw picture, all he had to do was keep going upwards. No problem.

In no time at all he had put the Millstone Hotel and Darwen behind him and his thoughts soon turned, inevitably so it seemed, to the one thing that had been preying continually on his mind. For the first time since his arrival in Darwen he was able to think clearly and he knew he had been right to leave the hotel. The road he was climbing was quiet. There was no traffic, no noise, and he could see little more than a few yards. Being uncluttered, his mind was able to expand and he felt both a freedom and an isolation he had not experienced in a long time.

But there was still the concern; Melissa had not contacted him. Though he had tried to tell himself that she had only lost the address, and that he should really telephone her, he knew that she had not even attempted to put pen to paper and would not be doing so. The events of the previous Sunday at Alderley, he could think of only as the nightmare of a deranged, flu-ridden mind. But that could not excuse the fact that she had deserted him on the Edge and had not shown the slightest remorse in doing so. That hurt the most. She had distanced herself. She no longer wanted to be with him and he did not know why or what he could do to rectify the situation. It seemed the ball had to be in her court. If he tried to get in touch with her it could only make matters worse. But the frustration was unbearable. He had been away for most of the summer and all he had thought about during that time was being with her – and somehow it had all gone badly wrong.

About half a mile up the hill the road, and the houses that bordered it, came to an abrupt end. The route to the top was continued by means of a narrow dirt track, wide enough for one vehicle. Along each side of the track ran a primitive barbed wire fence, presumably to contain the sheep, whose presence was revealed by the occasional cloud of dirty wool, torn from their backs and left hanging on the wire. As he climbed higher the fog became thicker but more patchy so that it was impossible to tell whether it was clearing or becoming worse. Sound, on the other hand, was more uniform; a single babbling brook running along the left hand side of the track. Occasionally, a dog barked, somewhere in the distance, off to his right.

If he was honest, he knew why Melissa had grown cold; she was unable to live with him knowing about her past. If so there was nothing he could do, and for that reason alone he was better off hoping that wasn't the reason. But he wasn't sure if that *was* it; there was so much about her that he didn't know, didn't understand. His relationship with Melissa had never been straightforward. Though they had grown close, Melissa would never open up completely. He could see in her eyes that her mind was filled with more thoughts than she ever allowed herself to expose. Often she would appear on the verge of revealing her innermost secrets when something in her eyes shifted and it would come to nothing. Terms of affection were banned by some indescribable inner code which only broke down during the throes of passion. It was as if all those things she prevented herself from saying were released in one mad rush at the point of orgasm. It was those moments that he craved. He wanted to believe that this was the only time she was truly herself. The rest of the time everything she said sounded either insincere or invisibly qualified. Even the simplest "I love you" - rarely heard - seemed to come out as "I love you but…", though the "but" never sounded and he remained none the wiser. And he knew that the sense of emptiness which he felt during those moments was now beginning to consume him.

Suddenly, he realised that he was no longer walking alongside the brook. Gradually, the constant sound of running water had melded with the silence. Now it was noticeable by its absence. He stopped and listened carefully to see if he could hear the brook further back along the path he had just come up, but he could not. Evidently, he had left it some way behind. Also, he could no longer hear the dog barking. All he could hear was the sound of his own breathing and the blood pumping through his body. He was completely alone.

Ultimately, we're all alone.

What did she mean by that? While they had been on the Edge they were the last words she had spoken before walking off – and he had continued to hear their echo ever since. In one single phrase she had both drawn him in and shut him out, leaving him bewildered. If those words had betrayed a glimpse of her inner life then he had missed the point. Something had happened on the Edge but it didn't make sense.

As he progressed up the hill the inclined track began to grow less steep and the grass became tougher and more reed-like. In no time he had graduated from rural pasture to barren moorland. As the wind picked up and brought the first traces of life to the still fog, he guessed that he must be somewhere near the top. Soon, there was no way of knowing in which direction the summit lay. He was consistently faced with choices; paths both rising and falling. Yet whichever he took, he neither gained nor lost height. He was on a plateau of moguls. In his mind he pictured the scene on the jigsaw, a bleak, flat, monotonous landscape which, from a distance, appeared devoid of any undulations. Now he realised he was part of that scene; he was standing on the summit and it was only a question of time before he found what he was looking for - the missing piece of the puzzle.

All around him the mist swirled. He moved backwards and forwards over the moor, directed by intuition and guesswork. From afar he would have appeared to roam with the instinct of a rat in a maze, trying first one direction, then another, until a gut feeling told him he was on the right track. Often, he sensed that he was very close and kept looking into the air, where the mist was thinnest, expecting to see the object suddenly reveal itself, towering above him. The more he searched, the stronger his homing instincts seemed to grow.

Then he saw it. Perhaps fifty yards or so - it was difficult to judge under such conditions - the faint outline of a structure had appeared ahead of him, if only for an instant. It looked like a giant chess piece, a cross between a rook and a bishop; a queen, looming ominously, waiting silently. Almost as soon as it had appeared it had vanished again, hidden by a thick blanket of creeping fog. And yet the effect this sudden manifestation had on him was spontaneous and overwhelming. He was sure that all he had seen was the silhouette of a folly or a watchtower of some sort. He could still see the apparition in his mind, projected onto a mental screen and fading fast. It had form, a recognisable shape, but was otherwise nothing more than a dark shade of grey against a paler background. And although he knew he could not have seen anything more, all the emotions of the previous Sunday swept over him in a wave of despair.

He was being watched.

Someone in the tower was waiting for him.

It was the same sensation. Whatever had followed him from Alderley Edge to Victoria Station was here, waiting at the top of the tower, waiting and knowing he would come. Briefly, the silhouette appeared again and the same spasm shook his body, as if he had stared into the eyes of something evil.

For a moment he stood still and collected his thoughts. He lifted both arms and shook them alternately. Then he pushed them both in the air above his head and held them there while he performed a similar motion with his legs. Neither his legs nor his arms showed any sign of their earlier fatigue and he concluded that he was not suffering a relapse of the flu. The adrenaline which had suddenly begun to pour into his blood stream was for real.

Then a terrible thought struck him. Perhaps he had not been followed from the Edge at all. Perhaps he had not been escaping from something but was actually being drawn towards it.

After all, what was he doing here?

He had come to Darwen to discover the mystery object which stood on top of the moor, to complete the jigsaw puzzle he had first received six months before. It had all seemed so harmless - idle curiosity. Now he was here he was not so sure. He still did not know who had sent him the jigsaw but he began to intuit something more sinister; something he could not begin to understand. He sensed that he had been lured here, like a naive pawn playing right into the hands of the opponent. To be standing at the summit of Darwen moor in thick fog, having barely recovered from a dose of the flu, was not the act of a rational person. He was being manipulated.

To be here, he had to have been brought here.

And for a reason.

36

"…you asked about Howard and me. I don't really know what to say, it's all so confusing, but I think we have reached the end of the road. If we do split up, it will be very sad and I will lose so much. I do love him, and he has been good to me, but I'm not sure he is the person I want to spend the rest of my life with. It's such a big commitment and I don't feel ready to settle, not yet. I know it's an awful thing to say, and I wouldn't say it to anyone else, but I'm not sure that he's good enough for me.

We have just spent a disastrous weekend together. I know it was all my fault, and I know I've hurt him, but I can't help it. Sometimes I wish he didn't love me so much; it would make everything easier. He is so intense that sometimes I feel I'm suffocating. It isn't that he's overly possessive; it's just that he wants to be alone with me all the time and everything is always so heavy. I wish he could lighten up a bit. We don't have any fun anymore. I don't think that Howard really likes my friends. He says he does; in fact he thinks you are wonderful (naturally), but he never wants to see any of them and when he comes up for the weekend I feel trapped inside my own house all the time.

I know that I'm partly, or perhaps totally, to blame. I don't always treat him as considerately as I might and I'm not as affectionate as he is. I think Howard is insecure and needs constant reassurance. That's why he always wants to be alone with me, I suppose. There isn't anything wrong 'between the sheets' so to speak except that Howard wants to spend so much time there. He can't seem to understand that I sometimes just want to go to sleep. He always takes it personally and it's really annoying.

The problem now is that we're trapped in a vicious circle. Howard gets insecure and reacts by suffocating me and I immediately distance myself because I can't say the things he wants to hear, especially when he manufactures the whole scenario just to give me an opportunity to tell him how I feel. It's so false. I don't know what will happen now. I do love him, but I'm not in love with him…"

37

Slowly, Howard walked up towards the tower, his eyes fixed rigidly on the top. There seemed to be some kind of balcony circling round a glass structure in the centre, similar to that of a lighthouse all out of proportion. He strained his eyes, almost willing himself to detect some form of movement on the balcony, but nothing stirred. While the adrenaline continued to flow, it became evident that there was no sign of life, on or around the structure. It was deserted.

He clambered over the rocks surrounding the base of the tower and began walking round the outside, searching for some form of identification. Occasionally, he glanced up towards the balcony, half expecting to see a face, a hideous apparition, leering down at him, or some heavy, shapeless object, plummeting towards him. For as long as he traversed around the base of the tower his imagination, fed by a multitude of irrational impulses, knew no bounds. And yet, underlying all of these nightmare visions was the certainty that he was being irrational and that each fervent glance upwards was the direct product of obsession and unfounded paranoia. His mind was locked in conflict between what he knew and what he felt.

He was being watched.

Just as he completed a full circle he came across a doorway and could not believe he had missed it when he first approached the tower. As he drew nearer, he moved back from the wall and skirted the opening with apprehension. He paused. Just beyond the entrance lay a stony spiral staircase, dank and wet, and that was all. He still had a sense of foreboding about the tower and glanced up at the parapet above. But he saw and heard nothing. He had three choices. He could turn round and go back to the hotel. He could creep up the staircase slowly, and as each bend, nook and cranny approached, allow nightmarish notions to run amok in his imagination. Or he could storm the tower, sprint up the staircase, cover both balconies in seconds and quickly put his mind at rest.

On an impulse, he took the bull by the horns and ran at the staircase. In no time he was on the first balcony. Without looking down or up he made one orbit of the tower and then continued up the spiral staircase to the top. Only when he reached the glass door which opened onto the parapet did he pause. Looking around him, he saw that he was completely surrounded by glass and, much to his relief, the parapet outside was deserted. He was alone.

He had always been alone.

He pulled open the door and stepped out. On a clear day he imagined the view must be quite incredible. The tower seemed ideally positioned for viewing to the west. There was nothing of any significant height between the moor and the sea, a total of some thirty miles across the Lancashire plains. Perhaps it was possible to see the sea on a clear day. He was not sure what the view would be like to the south or north. Between Bolton and Blackburn, the landscape was very hilly and shaped by deep valleys running out from the moors. Immediately to the east was one such valley and in it, the sleepy town of Darwen. Of one thing he was certain; if he wished to appreciate the panorama from the tower he would have to make a return journey. Today the view was restricted completely by the fog. Above him a single, monotonous cloud layer covered the whole sky. Around and below the tower, the lighter, wispier formations of mist hung silently in the air. Occasionally, where the mist thinned slightly, he detected the dull green shades of moorland grass.

Suddenly, his heart jumped and began pounding. To his right, down on the moor, he had detected movement. He spun round quickly, threw his head over the parapet and froze, his senses straining to pinpoint the location of the movement below. Unlike before, when irrational fear and tricks of the light had blinded his senses, he was certain he had seen someone. Through a gap in the mist, about eighty yards from the tower, the figure had suddenly appeared, running towards the tower, and then disappeared back into the mist. That in itself was not so strange. He imagined that the moors were a favourite haunt of joggers, though perhaps not in this weather. But this was not a jogger, or even a hill runner. The figure he had seen was moving fast, sprinting over the moor as if the uneven terrain and fatigue did not exist. He watched carefully, his eyes extrapolating from the runner's previous position to the next clear patch through the fog.

Almost instantaneously, the runner appeared again, only forty yards off and still headed towards the tower. All Howard's impressions of that first glimpse were confirmed, but it was a realisation of this second sighting which unnerved him; the figure - a man - was sprinting, not at an inhuman speed but much faster than he could be expected to run over moorland. It was almost as if the undulations had flattened out into a smooth surface radiating from the base of the tower. Whoever it was, he was running with a mission; to reach the tower, as if his life depended on it.

There was no sound, neither the rattle of shoes on loose stone nor the panting of racing lungs. Only silence punctuated with the dull thud of Howard's own heartbeat.

This second sighting was as short as the first. In the blink of an eye the mysterious figure had vanished once more under the cold blanket of fog. Howard looked down to the base of the tower, expecting a reappearance in only a few seconds. He felt terrified but of what he was not sure. The sensation of being watched, of being a helpless puppet in a macabre scene, had returned, stronger now than ever. But it was not this stranger who terrified him. For reasons which he could not explain he was willing the runner on in his quest to reach the tower. But the runner never appeared. He waited the estimated number of seconds and then some more, until a whole minute had passed. Nothing happened. There was no sound. Somewhere under the mist, the stranger had simply disappeared. He began scanning the few gaps in the mist which lay further away from the tower but he caught no more sightings.

His ears tuned into the silent echo of the spiral staircase, conscious by now that the stranger could have sneaked around the tower and entered through the door at the bottom. He moved round the parapet, watching intently for a sign, until he was above the doorway. Still nothing stirred. He stood back from the wall and once more listened for some sound in the stairwell but the only reply to his silent question was a hollow emptiness. He quickly switched his attention to the doorway, leaned back over the parapet and found himself staring straight into the eyes of the mysterious runner.

The stranger, male, late twenties, had appeared from nowhere. Suddenly, the mists had parted and there he stood. There was no sign of fatigue, no perspiration, but his eyes burned with the intense passion of someone whose emotions had been stretched to the very limit of human suffering. He gazed into Howard's eyes as if he expected to find some kind of explanation there, probing deeper and deeper for the answer Howard was not able to give. Howard too sensed he was to learn something from this encounter. In the stranger's eyes he saw mixed emotions: perplexity, the mental turmoil of absolute failure, the torture of desperation and the desolate sadness of perpetual loss. In those eyes he saw no answer, but he saw himself; a reflection of the emptiness and bitterness of rejection.

While their eyes remained locked in this mutual revelation, time had no meaning. The stranger made no attempt to move or to speak and Howard, too, remained silent. He could neither pull himself away from the stranger's gaze nor find words to break the intensity of the moment. Here and now, on the barren summit of Darwen moor, there was no place for words. They had been brought together by a force he could not begin to understand, to share this experience.

As he stood, petrified, at the top of the tower, the mists gradually crept in and around the base until the stranger was completely engulfed in its folds. Howard remained still for several minutes but the stranger did not appear again. A relaxation permeated the atmosphere and he realised, with a shiver, that it was all over. Slowly, the mists began to clear until the whole moorland summit became visible from the tower and he found himself alone once more.

In his heart, Howard knew that this strange encounter was the culmination of all that had happened since he had first received the anonymous jigsaw. And yet, though each second threw up more questions than answers, he could not bring himself to ask them. There was neither rhyme nor reason to anything that had happened to him over the last few days. But he could sense purpose; a cold, clinical motive, which hung in the air and followed him wherever he went.

Now he sensed he had been released, but from what he had no idea. The whole thing made no sense.

Perhaps one day he would understand.

38

As the barrage broke, and the air filled with the sound of countless rounds of ammunition reverberating around the dock, Martyn and Rob dived headlong among the large crates and packing cases they had been using for cover since sunrise. When they realised they had not been spotted, and that the battle seemed to be taking place over their heads, Martyn returned his gun to its holster and sat down on the cold tarmac surface, trying to rub the stiffness from his legs. He was almost immediately joined by Rob.

"What the fuck is going on?" The question was rhetorical and angry. Martyn reached for the walkie-talkie and opened the channel, breaking the radio silence they had maintained for the last hour.

"I don't know but I'm not firing a damn shot until I find out which direction I'm supposed to be shooting in." He lifted the receiver to his lips and yelled into it, straining to be heard above the exchange of fire. "Arnie! This is Martyn! What the hell is happening out there?"

The radio set came back with a short crackle of static and then went silent.

"Arnie! Do you copy? Sod the radio silence. Talk to me."

This time the static was followed by a familiar voice.

"Okay, Martyn, I'm here. If I were you I'd keep my head down; you're right in the middle of the battlefield. As for what's going on I'm still trying to work it out."

Arnie had been posted as lookout. He had spent the last nineteen hours cooped up in a crane which towered high over the adjoining quay affording an excellent view of the dockside and the scene of the day's predicted events. Since midnight he had relayed information back to Rob via a surveillance van, disguised as a water company truck, parked three blocks away.

At four in the morning he had spotted two figures acting suspiciously on the dockside. Blown up photographs taken with an infrared camera confirmed that both suspects were known criminals and had regular contact with Cassida. Arnie had watched as a car drove onto the quayside. Then the men, with the aid of the driver, had unloaded two crates, covered them with netting and abandoned them alongside a mooring post, close to the water's edge. When the three men had climbed back into the car and disappeared, Rob decided it was time to move in and await their return at close quarters. He called Martyn and soon after seven they had taken their position among the pile of packing cases waiting to be despatched to Europe the following day.

It transpired that quay seventeen had been leased six months previously to the Transoceanic Global Shipping Company, an organisation based in California with a complex chain of connections leading right back to the syndicate here in the city. It had taken two days of intensive research to trace the chain and it was only after discovering the existence of an account with a merchant bank, known to be a financier of syndicate corporations, that the warning bells began to ring. Two years previously, the bank had been exposed transferring funds raised through the sale of drugs at one of the city's largest casinos, also syndicate owned. The case was never proved but further investigations revealed that at least half the businesses on its books had some connection with the syndicate and the Transoceanic Global Shipping Company appeared to be yet another to add to the list.

Using the walkie-talkie they had maintained regular contact with Arnie. As soon as it became clear they were alone on the quayside they had moved out of their hiding place to examine the two crates. Arnie had watched them approach the mooring post and gave them the all clear to remove the netting. After that they wasted no time and had soon broken the steel band and prised open the lids.

"Well? What's inside?" came Arnie's impatient voice over the radio.

"Rifles," Rob replied, his tone indicated surprise. "Rifles, handguns and grenades. It looks more like they're shipping weapons out, not importing them." He hesitated before continuing. "But that wouldn't make sense, would it? Arnie, is it still all clear?"

"Yeah. All clear. What's your problem?"

"No one would take such a big risk for two crates of weapons this size. If they are exporting then they must be coming back with more. Keep your eyes open."

Martyn was still occupied examining the contents of the two cases when he suddenly joined in the theorising.

"I've never heard of anyone exporting arms to Alliance countries either," he said, "which is what is stamped on the boxes. It is also where the ship is returning to early tomorrow morning. They don't need arms in the old Unified States; they have more conventional weapons than food."

"Maybe they are going to be intercepted in Europe with all that stuff over there," suggested Rob, pointing to the pile of crates stacked behind them.

"Perhaps. But, in that case, why not stack them over there? They'd be far less conspicuous than they are stuck out here."

The rest of the morning had passed by uneventfully. Arnie checked in every half hour but had seen or heard nothing more. Martyn and Rob first packed the crates exactly as they had found them, then remained hiding among the packing cases.

"I hate surveillance," said Martyn.

"Well at least we know one thing," said Rob, optimistically. "At some stage today, something is going to happen. We could have wasted the whole day waiting for nothing."

"Maybe," Martyn murmured. "Maybe we still are."

"What? Do you still think we're being set up? What about those two treasure chests over there?"

"To someone as rich and powerful as Cassida, two boxes of handguns are water off a duck's back. If we were being set up he would probably assume we would maintain surveillance and decide to leave those to keep us here. He could even have the dock under surveillance himself. It would seem stupid not to if something that big was really going down."

"You *do* think we're being set up, don't you? You think those two crates are decoys!"

"If you had asked me that four weeks ago I would have said no, but since this case began I'm not so sure about anything."

"So why are we still here?" asked Rob, revealing his own sense of doubt.

"Simple, we've really got no choice," said Martyn. "Cassida is intelligent enough to know that we would be thinking all these things so he could just as easily have left the two crates to draw us out. Besides, if they are decoys, where the hell do we look for the real action?"

For the first time since he had been given the responsibility of organising the dockland swoop Rob looked dejected.

"That's great! One minute ago I thought we had everything completely sussed. I thought all we had to do was wait here for a few hours and Cassida and his men would fall right into our hands. Now you're suggesting that I might have spent eight hours being watched while I stood guard over two wooden boxes. And if they know we're here then they may also know that Arnie is up in the crane and that there's a support squadron down the street, all of which means that you and I are up to our necks in the proverbial."

"True," Martyn agreed. "But sometimes life is like that. All we can do now is sit it out and see what happens."

It was not long before something did happen. From his watchtower Arnie spotted a number of vehicles approaching the quayside. Through his binoculars he recognised one as the car they had witnessed earlier that morning depositing the two wooden cases of arms. While this car and two transit vans drove straight onto the quayside, the remaining three cars were left in a lot behind the warehousing. Arnie recorded the licence plates and relayed them to base to be checked out. Soon afterwards two small motor launches came in from the ocean and berthed at the end of the dock. More cars arrived and in less than a quarter of an hour, the quayside was as busy as a railway station.

As planned, and somewhat conveniently, Rob then ordered his own men to move in and take their positions in the run-down warehouse which they had commandeered for the day. Despite the intense activity on the dockside this was easily done. Each afternoon, at approximately four thirty, a courier van from the city would arrive at quay eighteen, drive into the warehouse, unload its cargo of small packages for shipping *to* the Bahamas, load up with the daily quota of packages *from* the Bahamas and return to the city. The perfect Trojan horse, it would have aroused more suspicion if it had not turned up on time. By five o'clock the van had been and gone and the warehouse was safely secured by the police.

Then two things happened. First, as Martyn found himself staring aimlessly out to sea from a narrow crevice between two rows of crates, he noticed that a ship had appeared on the horizon, perhaps an hour or so away. He was about to point this out to Rob when his right arm was grabbed from behind and he was pulled backwards. He was ushered a few yards to his left and directed to gaze through another gap in the crates.

"Look at that," said Rob. His voice echoed surprise and anger.

Through the narrow gap Martyn could make out a tarmac yard running some twenty metres up to a brick wall. Against the wall were a number of oil drums stacked two high. He scanned the few degrees of vision exposed to him very rapidly and quickly realised he had totally missed whatever it was he was supposed to be looking at.

"I don't see anything," he said.

"Keep watching."

He did as instructed but after only a few seconds was still none the wiser. Keeping his sight fixed firmly on the yard he hissed at Rob.

"Just what is it I'm supposed to be…"

Suddenly, he detected movement behind the oil drums and a figure, unknown to him, broke from his cover and made a quick dart to the left and out of sight. The stranger was carrying a gun and was evidently not supposed to be there. Then, as he was about to turn to Rob for what he hoped would be an explanation, he spotted two more figures making a break from behind the oil drums. But this time they were not unknown to him. Reynolds and Manciani. He turned to face his partner, his eyes reflected Rob's own puzzled expression. But he did not have time to speak. At that precise moment all hell broke loose and the air was filled with the echo of relentless gunfire.

In those first few seconds, Martyn thought he was about to die. With so many rounds of ammunition ricocheting all around him, and with nowhere to run, it seemed highly probable that he would be hit. It was only a matter of time. The sound of the gunfire increased to such a deafening level that his senses became confused, so saturated by the noise that he could no longer hear anything. His mind wandered from one mental room to another trying to find peace from the noise.

At last, as if by the closing of a single door, there was silence. Now he could neither hear nor feel anything, and though there was light, he had lost the ability to focus. He was overcome by a sensation of drifting as if between two states of existence. At first, he thought he had been shot, his senses dulled by the sudden passing of a bullet through his body. He braced himself ready to face the onslaught of pain that he assumed would follow but none came.

I think therefore I am.

He was struggling to gather his thoughts into rational order. There was no incoming information to tell him where he was or who he was. He could do nothing but give in to the force which had taken over his being and left him in this state of nothingness. He had often imagined death would be like this, a lack of physical presence but his soul, his mind, remaining intact, confused by the sudden disappearance of all his immediate surroundings. But now he found it difficult to accept and he began sending signals to his fingertips in an attempt to provoke some response he could detect. If he could move his finger then he would also be able to sense that movement as it fed back the information to his brain. For a period that first seemed like hours and then like a fraction of a second, he made several unsuccessful attempts to move first his fingers, then his feet, searching his mind obsessively to find some indication that it was still attached to his body.

But it was no use.

"Tell me," said Jacqui Miller. "Don't you ever think that one day you might get killed? Doesn't death scare you?"

"Death doesn't scare me," he said. "I'm scared of pain and I'm scared of being alone. Like everybody else I don't want to suffer. I want it to be quick and painless. No, death itself doesn't worry me. I don't think about it; I can't afford to. In this job, to die is to lose and I'm not ready to lose. There is too much to do. Maybe one day, when I'm older and wiser and more tired and more cynical, maybe I won't care. Perhaps one day I might even welcome death but right now I'm still too young. It would be sad to die right now."

"Why?"

He had not answered her. From one angle it had seemed like the most stupid of questions but she knew he had not really answered her first question honestly. Slowly she had been tearing him apart, dissecting him like a schoolgirl with her first laboratory animal, carefully breaking down the layers of redundant tissue and muscle fibre in a carefully calculated attempt to find and recognise its heart.

The truth was that he was scared of separation, of isolation. And that was all. He was scared of losing Melissa, whether through death, by his own doing or through any cruel twist of fate. He had found a happiness he knew he could not live without, or die with. He saw himself strolling down the main precinct in Arcades, gazing into countless empty faces as they passed him by aimlessly. They knew not where they had come from. They cared not where they were going. He could not become one of them again.

Suddenly, he was rising, as if from the bottom of the sea, accelerating to the surface at a phenomenal rate. As the surface drew nearer, he could feel the force of the motion pressurising his head. He could feel it! Above he could see Melissa peering down into the water searching frantically for him.

Déjà vu.

Something about the experience seemed familiar. For a moment he thought she was trying to push him back down, trying to drown him, but as her arms swept through the water, her image became fragmented by the disturbance and she became nothing more than a concentrated pattern of varying colours. He was struggling to focus on these as he exploded through the surface and the sensation of rapid acceleration left him.

He was lying on his back and his head was throbbing with the after effects of the intense water pressure. Above him he could see Melissa staring down, not at him, but right through him. She was wearing the dark dress – the one with the floral design around the skirt. Her eyes were filled with tears and, as one of them dropped from her cheek and splashed lightly onto a leaf, he suddenly noticed the bouquet of flowers she was cradling. They were the same flowers he had seen her carrying in Eden Square that day - and he realised finally who they were for. He watched helplessly as she lowered some of the flowers toward him, until they blocked his view and he could no longer see her. As the bouquet seemed to meld with his own body, occupying the same space, he was forced to close his eyes.

"Martyn, can you hear me? Are you alright? Please answer me."

Slipping gradually back into consciousness, Martyn's first view of the world was of a clear evening sky tinged with the pale red of a glorious sunset on the western horizon - currently out of sight. Wisps of smoke and ash flickered in the air, rising and falling with the steady off-shore breeze. He was lying on his back, staring straight up. All about him the tall stacks of packing cases seemed to shoot thousands of feet into the sky leaving him stranded at the bottom of a wooden abyss. The sound of gunfire, though more spasmodic now, could still be heard. Sometimes it seemed to be close by and then he would suddenly hear shots far off in the distance. From somewhere close to his left ear the radio crackled into life once more.

"Martyn! Rob! Can you hear me? Please acknowledge."

He pulled himself up into a sitting position and allowed himself to slump back against one of the nearby crates. His head was banging like a relentless bass drum and he was finding it difficult to collect his thoughts into any kind of rational order. With his head thrown back against the crate he slowly, painfully, moved it from side to side and surveyed the scene about him.

Now that he had risen from the floor and gained a restored ability to focus, the line of packing cases looked far less formidable than they had a moment before. He was sitting in a pile of debris which littered the whole of the exposed corridor. Only metres away, where there had been a large case bound for Sweden, there was now a huge hole opening out into the corridor beyond. The cases surrounding the opening were in shreds and one of them was burning steadily, its contents, whatever they were, providing a perfect fuel for the advancing flames. To his left, out of reach, the radio crackled again but he could not move. His head and body were throbbing with pain and every slight movement was torturous. He turned to his right looking for a piece of wood long enough to reach the radio when his eyes happened upon a familiar shape crumpled in a corner and almost directly opposite the demolished opening.

Without a second thought he dragged himself to his feet, ignoring the spasms of pain which stabbed through his torso, and hobbled limply over to the Rob's body, only just remembering to pick up the radio as he went. Instinctively, he went through all the motions his training and experience had brainwashed him into performing; checking pulse, heart, breathing and eye activity in rapid succession. Then he picked up the radio and pressed the transmit button.

"Arnie, this is Martyn. Are you there?"

The pause seemed unnaturally long but at last the radio crackled once more.

"Martyn, thank God. I thought you were a goner."

Somewhere close by there was the sound of gunfire. It was too close for comfort.

"Well it looks like I'll live - at least for a few more minutes - but I'm not going to keep going much longer. Arnie, Rob's down. He's still alive but I'm going to have to bring him out. He needs medical attention urgently. What's happening out there and how long have I been out of it?"

"About a minute, two minutes maybe, but it's a good job you recovered so quickly because the trouble seems to be heading your way again - it keeps changing direction. Getting out of there would be a good idea. I suggest you head towards me and stay among the crates as much as you can. I've called the paramedics and they should be waiting for you when you come out."

Martyn rose to his feet once more and immediately winced in pain. The sensation caused him to take a sharp breath which induced a further spasm across his chest. He thought he would collapse.

"Arnie, keep talking. I need to catch my breath or I'll never make it. You didn't get the chance to answer my first question. What the hell is going on out there?"

While Martyn tried to regain control over his body, bent over with both hands on his knees, Arnie began to explain the sudden eruption of violence on the dockyard. It seemed that Arnie, with equal surprise, had spotted the Special Forces men at the same time Rob had. Judging by the instantaneous commencement of gunfire, they seemed to have been spotted by everyone else as well.

Arnie continued talking even though he was evidently preoccupied relaying tactical information to the rest of the squad. Occasionally he would interrupt his explanation but recognised that Martyn needed to hear his voice to keep conscious.

"There were bullets everywhere...men from both sides started appearing out of nowhere...at first it seemed very one sided...Specials had complete control for the first few seconds. Caught everyone off guard...then some of Cassida's men got to those two crates...let off a few grenades and a couple of automatic weapons...somehow managed to turn the tables. They had a grenade launcher in the back of a small truck...one of the grenades went off near you and we lost contact. I ordered our men in or else it would have been a walkover. It's a bloody mess, Martyn. There are bodies all over the dock. I don't know how many SFN we lost but some of them went very quiet when the grenades started flying. Martyn? You still there?"

"Yeah, I'm still here. Keep talking." His voice sounded weaker and betrayed the fact that he was beginning to give in to the pain.

"Hold on," the radio crackled back. "It can't go on much longer...difficult to say, though...we've lost the element of surprise. If Cassida's men had been in one place we would have sewn this up as planned. If they'd got their backs to the ocean we'd at least be in control, but there appear to be little pockets of resistance everywhere. We could even be fighting the SFN down there somewhere...wait a second! I saw something move quite close to you..."

Later, whether it was the distorted urgency in Arnie's voice, or pure intuition, he could not honestly recall, but he always recounted how his life had been saved by a man in a crane over two hundred metres away. In truth, Arnie did not know exactly where Martyn was, and Martyn could not see Arnie except by clambering on top of several crates, but truth and logic aside, he could never be sure that he would have survived the ordeal had Arnie not warned him.

As he turned around he caught sight of the brick-sized black metallic object hurtling towards him as it passed into the very edge of his field of vision. Instinctively, he dropped into a crouch as the rifle butt whistled within inches of his head and embedded itself in a wooden packing case. He launched himself into reverse and collided heavily with the body of steel muscle which had wielded the rifle. Even without seeing the intruder he could sense that the force of the impact had just tipped him off balance. Then he found himself reeling on the floor in such agony that only an increased flow of adrenaline was keeping him conscious. The intruder recovered from the collision instantaneously and Martyn found himself lying on his back, physically shaken, mentally alert and facing a sky that suddenly darkened as he became overshadowed by the huge figure.

The man was well over six feet tall, built like a football player and dressed entirely in black. Martyn did not need to look at his face to know who he was: Goliath, Cassida's bodyguard. Martyn received the singular impression that he was facing a professional killer, nothing more, nothing less. Goliath uttered no words but his face was filled with contempt and an expression which indicated that he could remorselessly serve out death as though he were swotting flies. In a single movement he bent down, grabbed Martyn by the neck and pulled him up to his feet as if he were made of straw. At the same time he pivoted on his heels through a three quarter turn and sent Martyn crashing into the wall of crates. Before Martyn had even registered what had happened he had been thrown back across the narrow corridor and battered against the opposite wall. He had not hit the ground before the shadow was on him again. This time he was thrown over and crashed against the crates upside down before landing in a crumpled heap on the floor. By now the pain was so great he could not feel most of it. His senses had gone into overload and the only thing keeping him conscious was the sure knowledge that he was about to die and that he did not want to be asleep when it happened.

The relentless battering continued. He found himself flung from side to side with the rhythmical savagery of someone hacking their way through a jungle. Then, he noticed that the giant was beginning to get complacent as the power behind each attack became less and less and he was now playing with him. Suddenly, without warning, Goliath changed tack. With one final burst of energy Martyn found himself flung headlong, not against the opposite wall as he had expected, but straight down the centre of the corridor. His feet had carried him several steps before he hit the tarmac surface and the momentum led him straight into a roll, spinning over twice before coming to rest on his back once more.

His body was racked with pain. Both knees felt as if they were about to collapse. His left arm felt broken and his right shoulder likewise. His right arm, though badly bruised and grazed, still seemed intact. Both sides of his face felt hot and sticky with blood, one from a nasty cut above the eye and the other from a cheek that had been scraped along the tarmac surface. His lips were thick and his mouth was also filled with blood from a number of internal cuts.

Yet by far the area of greatest pain was his back. He had come to rest on an object awkwardly lodged under the centre of his backbone, applying agonising pressure to an area which was significantly battered and bruised. He tried to pick himself up but had no energy. Instead he managed to prop himself up on his right elbow, saw his adversary advancing towards him, moving in for the kill, and collapsed once more onto his back. Again the pain shot through him as the small bulk bit into his spine. This time he rolled slightly to his left side and reached under his back with his right arm.

The object was immediately recognisable to the touch. A handgun! His handgun. He had not had time to think about his weapon, not even time to remember he was carrying one. And now it had fallen loose from its holster and presented itself with not a moment to spare. With all his injuries he thanked fate that his right arm was in one piece, and placed his hand firmly around the grip, index finger on the trigger.

Goliath came right up to him and paused, savouring the last few seconds of a battle which had been very one sided. Their gaze met. For an instant, Martyn felt he was staring into the eyes of an animal who had just succeeded in hunting and trapping his next meal. The bodyguard's eyes kept darting from side to side, figuring out the best way to finish this pathetic opposition. Whatever fate he planned in those few seconds Martyn would never know, but an evil smile of self indulgent satisfaction crossed Goliath's face and he reached forward with both arms.

Martyn pulled the gun out from behind, paused long enough to watch the giant's expression turn into astonishment and let off a round into the centre of his chest. The blast struck home. Goliath stood bolt upright and took two or three steps back before regaining his balance. The second round struck him in almost exactly the same place and he was thrown back into the crate stack. Martyn prevented himself from sending off a third round. If he had wanted to kill Goliath outright he would have put the bullet between his eyes. He could not have taken a chance on just maiming him in an arm or leg. Martyn knew he could lose consciousness at any second and he had to insure that he did not put himself at risk. His intention had been to call off the attack permanently; two rounds in the chest should guarantee that. For almost half a minute the giant remained on both feet, panting heavily and using the crates for support. Then, as he tried to take one step forward into the corridor, he collapsed to the floor and was motionless.

For five minutes Martyn also lay motionless, until he was confident that he was not going to lose consciousness. Gradually, he felt some strength returning to his legs and he began to concern himself with the problem of escaping undetected. The sound of gunfire in the air was no less now than before but by this time it was almost possible to ignore it. Nothing he heard seemed to be near enough to cause immediate alarm. But if those who were shooting were drawing attention to themselves, the two shots he had fired must have also been heard and he should expect some response.

He found Rob still unconscious and realised that he was going to have to get him out of there. If Martyn could not carry him then he would have to drag Rob out with his one good arm. Moving onto the quayside would be suicidal but to move away from the sea would take them further into the maze. There was no telling who they would find or how they could escape. To head north would take them right into what he deduced was the central war zone, judging by all the shooting. There were more allies in that direction but equally there could be more enemies. He decided to move south, keeping the sea to his left but remaining behind the crates at all times. That appeared to be the quickest and safest route to sanctuary, and that way he could use Arnie most effectively. However, he would have to maintain radio silence unless it was an emergency. It was presumably the sound of his previous conversation that had drawn Goliath towards him in the first place.

He radioed Arnie one last time, briefly explained his position and told him to cease radio contact unless absolutely necessary. Then he strapped the walkie-talkie around Rob's neck, placed the gun in his left hand where it was virtually useless and began to drag his partner by his collar along the tarmac corridor. They first passed the body of Cassida's bodyguard before being forced to take a right turn deeper into the labyrinth. This second section of corridor continued for fifty metres before the first left turn that would put them back on track. Before this opening there were several junctions off to the right. At each one, Martyn gently lowered Rob's head to the ground, switched the gun from his left to right hand and checked out the adjoining corridor carefully before continuing.

At the second right Martyn thought he caught sight of a figure, about a hundred metres ahead, running along the top of the corridor wall away from him. His suspicion was backed up a few seconds later when one of the missile grenades arced over the quayside and fell onto the crates, blowing them sky high. Whether the figure he had seen had been caught in the blast was impossible to say but it demonstrated that it was still not safe to be out in the open.

Five minutes later, after much weaving, Martyn managed to find his way back to the outer wall of the labyrinth, nearest the quay. As he turned the corner there was only another twenty metres to go before the maze ended and they would have to complete their escape in the area open to the south. That in itself did not concern him too greatly as there had been no evidence of trouble in that direction. But, he wanted to cross the yard quickly and to do that he needed to rest first.

He carefully propped Rob's limp body against a packing crate, placed the gun on the ground close by and removed the radio from around Rob's neck. He had just extended the aerial when the radio suddenly flew from his hand and he was hurled headlong to the tarmac in a way so familiar that it terrified him more than the violence itself. This time he succeeded in going into a roll and came out of it with both feet firmly on the ground, supporting his body weight in a crouch.

He stared up at Goliath in disbelief. The blood soaked figure towered above him only two metres away, still very much alive and exhibiting a blind obsession with finishing what he had started. This time Martyn was separated from his handgun. If he were to get out of this it would not be by blasting his way out unless he could somehow reach it. This would not be easy since Goliath had positioned himself, intentionally or otherwise, directly between the gun and his prey. It seemed he had also opted to finish off the task by hand. He had obviously waited for Martyn to disarm himself before making his attack and had then purposely ignored the gun when it would have been simpler, and ironically appropriate, to take advantage of the situation and turn the weapon on its owner.

Martyn was not faced with many choices. He could go for the gun but assumed he would get there last. He could probably outrun his assailant from this position if he were to try but the further he placed himself from the gun the more likely it was that the bodyguard would use it. And most likely on Rob, too. No, he had to stay in reach of the weapon in case Goliath changed his mind about the nature of his death. There was really only one form of defence left open to him. Attack.

In one very ungraceful movement, Martyn launched himself into the air and landed both feet with full force on the bodyguard's chest, exactly where the two bullets had entered. The impact sent them both crashing to the ground. Ignoring the pain, Martyn immediately rallied to his feet. Goliath did not.

Within that same second he heard the high pitched whine of a missile grenade flying through the air and the explosion somewhere behind him. For a moment he was concerned that the battle had moved around them and he was now completely cut off from any direct escape route. Then he realised, with horror, the true implication of this new attack. Above the packing cases, a thick plume of smoke rose into the air. He knew immediately that below stood the crane on dock sixteen; the crane Arnie had been using.

Bastards!

He picked up the gun and hobbled along the corridor until there was an opening looking onto the quayside. The area lay strewn with bodies. The initial attack had obviously taken them completely by surprise and Arnie's estimate of the body count had not been understated. In the centre of the quay, a white express van was doing a three point turn to redirect the grenade launcher back towards the heat of the battle. As it did so the back of the van briefly faced towards him. Inside, Martyn could see two men, the launcher situated between them.

He realised there might not be another opportunity. It was time to turn this fight around once more.

There were thirteen rounds left in the magazine. He fired off eleven shots and all but four went into the van as it began to reverse out of the turn. There was no need to use the last two. He had already taken out the two men in the back when the petrol tank exploded with five bullets in it. He watched as the van continued to reverse in flames and careered off the quay, into the ocean.

Turning round to check out the corridor he found himself staring straight into the eyes of John Reynolds and two other Special Force agents. Involuntarily, he was overcome by an incredible sense of relief and gratitude.

"Looks like you did our job for us," Reynolds said.

He was beginning to feel dizzy and his vision became blurred. His legs started to buckle beneath him.

"Looks like you just turned up in time anyway," he replied.

That was the last thing he remembered.

39

It seemed as though he had drifted in and out of sleep for several weeks. He had lost all sense of time passing. Every so often, as he ventured into consciousness, the pain returned almost immediately, stabbing and twisting through his body until, only seconds later and utterly exhausted, he sank back into a deep sleep. Each time he awoke he had the same vague recollection of seeing Melissa's beautiful, tearstained face only inches from his own, anxiously urging him to fight the pain and re-enter her world. Her words were soft, distant, strangely hypnotic and comforting. He wanted them to echo over and over but they were drowned out with every onset of the spasms that sent him back into the darkness.

Sleep brought little relief. At best, he existed in a world of fitful dreams where he teetered between reality and deep slumber, constantly moving in and out of phase with the two worlds he inhabited. At worst, the waking nightmare of agonising, stabbing pains translated, in deep sleep, to a world of unbearable tortures, of ghastly creatures with talons that ripped and shredded human flesh like knives slicing through paper, of dark, eerie corners trapped in time and space, hidden from the world and yet exposed to the whole universe. And exposed to the invisible, silent light which pierced through the darkness, seeking out the dark corners and the helpless fragile victims which it found huddled there, crouching low and shivering with fear. Mercilessly, the beam drove through his chest like a white hot stake before carving its initials across his body. Despite the pain he would not die, he could not die. Instead, he could only absorb the pain and pray it was the last time. But the beam had infinite energy. Time after time it sought him out and cut him to ribbons. Again…and again.

His first recollections of wakefulness were of a brilliant white room bathed in soft focus light and blurred images of blue and red people moving all about him. The room, he guessed, was in a hospital and the people were nurses. His later recollections were of more familiar surroundings, of Melissa's soothing voice and soft music floating in the air all around him.

All at once, it was over. With a suddenness that took him by surprise, he found himself gazing at the feathery contours of the asparagus fern perched on the pine chest by his bed. Behind it, across the room,

Melissa's painting of the city skyline gradually came into focus. He watched as the buildings slowly took shape and imagined himself standing in Washington Park overlooking the real view; standing, he recollected suddenly, at the spot where Sarjena West had been killed. As sunlight streamed through the bedroom window, he pulled himself into a sitting position.

Melissa must have detected the slight creaking of the bed joints, or the deep intake of breath as he hauled himself up, for she immediately burst into the room. Without thinking she threw her arms around him. He winced at the pain but it was not as bad as he expected.

"Oh, thank God you're alright." Tears were pouring down her cheeks as she released her pent up emotions. "We were so worried."

She sensed him wince again.

"Oh, love. I'm so sorry. I am just so relieved." She kissed him lightly on the forehead. "How are you feeling?"

He adjusted himself into a more comfortable position.

"What year is it?" he asked.

"You've been out for four days," she said. "At first they thought you might go into a coma. I was so worried. So much has happened it will take ages to tell you. But before I forget I must call the hospital. They said to phone as soon as you regained consciousness. They have to send a doctor round to check you out, just to be sure. They only discharged you last night. Do you remember?"

"Vaguely," he replied. The memories of the previous evenings transfer came flooding back as if they had been a dream. He remembered being wheeled out on a stretcher, surrounded by lots of people as if he were the subject of a major security operation. He remembered all the voices shouting in the background and the barrage of flashing lights firing all around him.

"How come they let me go?"

"I think you were becoming a nuisance. With all the reporters around, the hospital couldn't cope. As soon as they decided you were out of danger they sent you home. They said I could look after you better here and I think the other patients will be glad of the peace and quiet. The nice part is that I've got two months leave of absence starting from now."

"Leave of absence?" Martyn said. "It's alright for some. How on earth did you wangle that?"

"To look after you, silly," Melissa replied, teasingly. She seemed deliriously happy. "You were put on two months sick leave, only if you regained consciousness of course, and I have two months leave to help you on the road to recovery. And we are both on full pay, courtesy of the police department. Isn't that wonderful? As soon as you are fit enough to travel, we'll take that holiday in the Great Lakes. For the next two months it's just the two of us; no work, no hassle, no problems. It's perfect. You'll have to get blown up again soon. Oh, I do love you."

As she paused for breath, she suddenly realised she had still to call the hospital.

"Almost forgot again. Be back in a second." She kissed him and made for the door. Martyn's head was spinning with so many questions and there did not seem to be any logical order in which to ask them.

"What did you mean, 'only if I regained consciousness'?" he demanded, somewhat perplexed.

Melissa halted at the door. "You can't have sick leave if you're dead," she said, matter-of-factly. "It's against departmental regulations."

The doctor arrived within the hour, a sweet-natured woman with an unswayable air of professionalism and the most reassuring smile he had ever seen. While passing a stethoscope liberally around his body she delivered a brief synopsis of his condition, most of which he did not take in.

"...you are bound to feel weak for the next week or so," she explained. "You've been in shock for the last few days probably due to the extreme pain you've been suffering...luckily the shock was delayed long enough for you to leave your trail of destruction...seem to have come out of shock as quickly as you went in...with no serious ill effects...initially there was the danger you might go into a coma, or something worse...under the circumstances you have made quite a rapid recovery...need to build up your strength slowly so don't overdo it...we removed three pieces of shrapnel from your lower back with no serious or long term damage... superficial scars, they'll clear up in time...you have three cracked ribs...and ninety nine percent internal and external bruising," she concluded, tongue in cheek. "That's all. Any brain damage?"

"None," he replied in kind. "It's the rest of the world that has gone mad."

"Right," she said, tossing the stethoscope back into her bag. "You have a trained nurse to look after you. Melissa knows exactly what you need. Do exactly as she says and you'll be fit enough to storm the airport in no time. I have to say that I'm glad I've got you out of my hair. Those reporters were beginning to get on my nerves. A hospital is no place for a hero. It causes far too much disruption."

With that, she left. From the time of entrance to the sound of the door closing behind her had taken less than fifteen minutes.

"One of the best," Melissa said. "Not cheap but we're not paying for her either. On the department - only the best."

"Well, well," he said. "How do you rate this nurse she has supposedly left behind?" He smiled and it hurt. "It seems you have the responsibility for my recovery from here on. Do you think you can manage that?"

"Oh, I think so," she replied. "There's really only one thing I'm concerned about."

"And what's that?"

She sat down on the bed, leaned over and rubbed noses.

"I think I'm going to force you to have sex sooner than you should."

Melissa refused to answer any of his questions until he had eaten something. She had already prepared a smoked salmon broth and chopped up a plate of salad. She also laid on a couple of little turquoise tablets.

"Protein, vitamins and plenty of liquids," she explained. "It may hurt to swallow at first but you have to eat something. You've gone without proper food for four days. I've made up a milkshake for dessert."

Martyn stared at the plate of green salad with an expression of disappointment.

"I expected at least a steak," he said.

"You haven't seen your face." She picked up a mirror and levelled it in front of him, revealing a frightful apparition of cuts and bruises. "Your jawbone wouldn't make it through the first mouthful."

Even being spoon-fed by Melissa it soon became evident that it was going to take a long time to devour the food and he was not prepared to wait that long. He demanded that she answer some of his questions. After a little reluctance, she gave in.

"Alright," she conceded. "But remember, you are on two months sick leave. It's all over. It's out of your hands now and I don't want to hear any more about it. I want your undivided attention. Agreed?"

"Alright, I agree."

"First of all," she began, "as I said before, Rob's okay." It was one of the first things he had asked her but she had managed subtly to avoid elaborating until she had taken care of the essentials, such as calling the doctor and force feeding him the green salad.

"In terms of physical injury, he actually suffered far less than you did; just a severe concussion and one or two cuts and bruises. He's been up and about a couple of days now. In fact he kept me company in the hospital most of the time. He only went home when it was confirmed you were going to be alright. Which reminds me, I must call him. He asked me to let him know as soon as you were ready to receive visitors. I'll tell him he can come round this evening if you like."

She paused as if she did not know quite what to say next or as if she were trying to choose the right words.

"You know, I never really appreciated how close you two are. You seem so different. I always thought he just acted the fool all the time."

"We have to be close," Martyn said. "It's not the same thing though - not like you and me."

In one sense they were not that close at all. Rob did continually act the fool but that was a defence mechanism. But they were poles apart on a number of issues. They hardly had any common interests and did not share the same views on anything important outside work. But they depended on each other for their lives and that meant they had to trust one another implicitly, no matter how they felt about anything else. At work they were a team, a single cohesive unit. In situations like the one at the docks they would almost have to read each others' minds and complement actions with appropriate reactions. If one half of the team went down then the other became disproportionately useless - like at the docks.

"Useless!" Melissa objected. "You're not being fair on yourself."

"And you're not being objective," Martyn argued. "None of you. Think about it. You keep saying I'm a hero because I refused to die. But look at it this way. I almost did die. Rob almost didn't make it, Arnie didn't make it and nor did a lot of other people. I am a hero because I almost died. If I'd walked out of that mess with nothing more than a few cuts and a smile the press would have called it a massacre. It's a very fine line. If I'd let them kill me then I would have also let Rob die and I couldn't do that. And besides, who would have been left to look after you?"

"Look after me?" Melissa exclaimed. "I think it's the other way round at the moment. Tell me, Martyn, do you trust Rob?"

"Sorry?"

"I said 'do you trust him?'" she repeated. "Would he have done the same for you if the situation had been reversed? Could I trust him to bring you back to me?"

Martyn contemplated the question, not because he had any doubts about the answer but more because he was not sure where the conversation was leading and why.

"Yes," he replied. "I trust him. In the same situation I know he would do everything he could to save my life. That's all I can ask of anyone."

"Yes, but is it enough?" she insisted.

"Melissa! What are you trying to say?"

Melissa allowed her shoulders to slump.

"Oh, it's nothing," she said. "I'm sorry. I just need to know that I can trust him the same way you do, that's all."

She lay her head gently on his chest and squeezed the side of his ribcage affectionately and very gently.

"I think it's time you got to know each other a little better," he said. He ran his fingers through her hair. Whatever it was she had wanted to say was now lost but he had the distinct impression that she was trying to tell him something.

Melissa did not seem to know much about the incident at the docks other than what she had absorbed from the media. However, since Martyn had featured so prominently in the news over the last few days she had felt it her duty to buy a copy of every newspaper she could get her hands on. There was now a hoard resting in the corner of the bedroom.

"I even bought an Alliance newspaper," she explained, "just in case it gave a different slant on the story."

"Great," said Martyn, eyeing the pile of papers in dismay. "I didn't know you could read Russian."

"I don't," she said. "But I know someone who could translate it for you. For a price."

"Go on," he said.

"Well, you remember Jacqui Miller, whom you met at that party last year? Well, her husband Greg is also a journalist and he's been asking to do an interview with you. Well, so has everyone else but he's been a little more persistent than most. He's called nearly every day to see if you were okay. Jacqui even called once or twice as well. Anyway, in casual conversation he happened to mention that he'd been talking to a Russian who had given him some very useful information and had helped him translate all the Alliance papers for him. He said he'd let me know what it all said if I was interested, but I think it was implied that he would be allowed to interview you - though he didn't actually say as much. Everyone is after the exclusive."

"Alright," Martyn said. "I guess I owe him a favour. Tell him he can come round tomorrow morning."

The evening passed by peacefully. Melissa decided that she would read out the newspaper stories rather than try and recount what had happened herself.

"They say it much better than I could," she reasoned. She had first picked up a local tabloid from the Tuesday morning.

> *"Last night, in what has now officially gone down as the bloodiest gun battle this year, in which seventeen people lost their lives, this is the tattered and bloody face of the man who brought the violence to an end. This morning, following a night of arrests which involved some of the city's biggest criminal names, Detective Sergeant Martyn Sorensen is a hero..."*

Martyn interrupted. "Alright, that's enough. It isn't even good journalese; the sentences should be far shorter."

"Rubbish," Melissa countered. "You're too self conscious. Anyway, this is the paper which has an exclusive interview with Rob 'speaking to the world from his hospital bed'. I was there. He had some very nice things to say about you."

"Forget it," Martyn said. "How does Rob know anyway? He slept through the whole thing. That just typifies what I was saying before. On the very next morning, the rat went and blabbed to the most infantile and trashy newspaper he could find. They probably offered to pay him the most."

"He's not allowed to accept money, is he?"

"No, but that wouldn't stop him. He's probably opened a secret bank account in Mexico."

He reached out, took the paper from her and began reading. "Oh, I don't believe this. 'Grenades were going off all around us. It was only a question of time before one came down too close.' Quite articulate for someone with concussion. He makes it sound like a third world war movie." Martyn tossed the paper onto the floor. "Okay, let's try the New York Times."

As Melissa methodically narrated her way through the leading paragraphs of all the major papers, Martyn began to realise that the press had been smokescreened and that Melissa held no more knowledge than she had before her in black and white. Every paper quoted a different number of casualties. The ship due to arrive at the docks that evening had come from destinations as diverse as Argentina and Iran. It had arrived at anytime between six thirty and ten o'clock. The questions he most wanted to ask had been made more difficult to answer by a lack of trust in the information available. Until he could find out what was going on he also had to be careful what he said to Melissa.

Rob turned up after nine o'clock, escorted by Chief Brett Lancaster. At first it seemed like the commencement of an inquisition but it quickly became apparent that they had been out drinking. Chief Lancaster seemed unusually happy and not a little light headed. Rob was his normal out-of-work self.

"We left a very good party to come and visit you in your sick bed. I hope you appreciate it. And…" He waved his arms in the air like a magician and produced a slim, brown bottle from a paper sack. "…we've brought you a little something to compensate for missing all the fun. Instant panacea."

Melissa suddenly appeared from nowhere and took the bottle from him.

"Sorry, no alcohol," she smiled, sweetly. "I'll put it away and we'll drink it next week sometime after a quiet, candlelit meal in a secluded log cabin in the Lakes. I'm sorry you won't be around to join us."

"But that's Scotch whisky - from the last century," the Chief protested, suddenly sobering up.

"Well, it would be wasted on you two then, wouldn't it?" she said and, bottle in hand, she left the room.

When they were alone, Martyn turned on Rob.

"What did you think you were doing spinning that garbage to the press. It's terrible."

"I didn't know what I was doing? I was concussed."

"I bet you were lucid enough to negotiate a fair price for it."

"Really!" Rob protested. "Who, me? What an accusation to make to your closest friend, and in the presence of the Chief too." The Chief had obviously turned a blind eye and ignored the regulations, as Martyn knew he would. Brett Lancaster revealed a knowing smile as if he had personally received half the payment.

"How else did you think he could afford that whisky?" he said, and then looked concerned. "She will save us a drop, won't she?"

"Oh, I expect so," Martyn replied. "But it won't taste so good once it's been opened for two months."

"I knew it. As soon as I granted you two months sick leave I knew I'd regret it. And to think that I agreed to pay that siren to look after you. I must have been mad."

"Well, I hope the insanity is permanent," Martyn said. "But before I go mad myself, will someone please tell me what the hell is going on? I can't make sense out of any of these papers."

The Chief and Rob exchanged glances and seemed to toss a coin telepathically. Rob began to explain.

"Well," he said. "The bottom line is that we have enough hard evidence to put Cassida and some of his sidekicks away for a minimum of ten years and we're drowning in circumstantial that will probably stretch that to fifteen. We've got them all on arms trading and drug smuggling. We've connected Cassida with the deaths of Sarjena West, Howard Robinson and Angelo and he's on a false promise that his sentence might be reduced if he gives us the names of the thugs who did commit the murders. I tell you; there isn't a lawyer in town who wants to defend him right now."

"So, is that what was really on the ship?" asked Martyn. He picked up a newspaper from the previous day and quickly located the paragraph he was looking for.

"'*Speculation that the ship contained an arsenal of laser weapons was yesterday refuted when the State Defence Department revealed the cache of drugs and conventional arms they had seized from the ship in a rare public display.*'" He waited for an answer.

"That's not exactly true," said the Chief. "They did find drugs and arms but they didn't seize them in public. They did it while no one was looking." He started to laugh and was immediately joined by Rob. The alcohol was evidently still in their system. Martyn tried to join in but it hurt too much.

"Who's they?" he asked.

"Who do you think?" Brett said.

"The twenty first century cowboys," Rob chipped in.

"Then what is this all about?" Martyn reached for another newspaper cutting on which he had highlighted another paragraph. "*Despite rumours to the contrary, the city police department denied that the Special Forces Network had been involved in the operation.*' For not being there they sure had a hell of a presence. They almost got us killed."

"Excuse me," said Rob. "I think I'll go and see if Melissa can cook us up something. I'm starving."

When Rob had left the room, the Chief continued. "We've already been through this argument several times over the last few days and Rob tends to get rather overheated about it. I can understand why. The truth is, the SFN had been carrying out their own investigations into the laser assassinations, as you know. They felt that Tuesday night's operation was too important to leave to a 'bunch of amateurs' (not my words) so they supplied their own team to ensure the operation was a success. By the time I found out about it, it was too late to do anything. You can be sure I lodged a protest immediately, especially when I heard they had cocked it up and placed the lives of my men in danger."

"And?"

"And nothing. They came back with two counter attacks. Firstly, they all but conceded they had made a mess of the operation. Two of their men had been spotted moving into position and there were too many witnesses for them to deny it. However, they state that when the firing did commence none of our men joined in and we lost the advantage."

"Of course none of our men fired a shot. They didn't know who to fire at. No one knew what was going on. We lost the advantage when the SFN turned up. Everything was going perfectly until then."

"Save your breath," said the Chief. "I've heard it all before and I can't disagree with you. It looks bad, that's all. The other thing they state is that you would almost certainly have lost the battle without their firepower. I can't exactly disagree with that either."

"I can," Martyn said. "There wouldn't have been a battle if they hadn't been there."

"Maybe, maybe not, but the powers that be have decided to call it quits and that's all there is to it. Unfortunately we can't turn it into a public debate, which you would almost certainly have won due to your heroic status, because officially the SFN were not there. There's nothing I can do about it. All square."

At that moment, Rob returned with Melissa and, more importantly, with some food.

"Isn't she an angel?" he said. "She was already preparing something. Read my mind like a book."

"And the whisky?" said the Chief, hopefully.

Melissa handed him a glass. "You didn't really think I'd let you miss out, did you?"

"What about me?" said Martyn.

"Don't worry. You can have some in a couple of days. It will keep until then."

"What! Oh, thanks! It will be ruined."

"Don't be silly," said Melissa. "I've resealed it. It will be fine." With that, she left.

Both Brett and Rob raised their glasses in a toast.

"To Martyn, truly a hero and a martyr to the cause," Brett said. "Sorry, Martyn."

"Hmm, delicious," added Rob. "Sorry, Martyn."

While the Chief and Rob finished off the food and whisky, the conversation continued as before. Martyn had already prepared the whole session and he continued to ask questions in a pre-planned order until he reached the one which had puzzled him the most.

"So do we know who is the laser assassin?" he asked.

"Not exactly," Rob said. "But we have circumstantial evidence which links Cassida with both murders. Apparently, Howard Robinson refused to buy into a protection racket in Arcades. He threatened to go to the police about it. Sarjena West was badly in debt to one of Cassida's 'finance houses' and it suddenly became apparent that she had no way of paying it off. Not much of a motive to kill someone in either case but then again, Cassida never really needed one. He just wanted to test his new weapon. There were plenty of possible motives for killing Angelo but we still don't know which animal committed the crime. Hopefully, Cassida will take the bait and spill us a few names."

"Before you ask your next question," the Chief interrupted, "take a look at this." He handed Martyn a photograph. "There is your laser rifle. The Defence Department have got it under wraps but this photo will appear in all the papers tomorrow. It was found in a vehicle registered to one of Cassida's companies."

The photo showed a sleek matt black object which very closely resembled a rifle. Attached to it by a short length of cable was a box, about the size of a large suitcase.

"It isn't really portable. That's the power supply and it's apparently fairly heavy. However, installed in the rear of a car or a small van, it's perfect for assassinations and quick getaways. Cassida, by the way, is denying all knowledge of it but then he has to because it comes free with three murder one tags around it."

The Chief replaced the photograph in his pocket.

"Well, I guess we'd better go and let you get some beauty sleep. I want you both right as rain in two months time." For a moment, the Chief became sombre. "Oh, by the way, it's Arnie's funeral tomorrow. I know you won't be able to make it but I arranged to have some flowers sent for you. I hope that's okay."

"Sure," said Martyn. "Arnie saved my life out there. How much do I owe you?" The Chief waved the offer away. "Doesn't matter. I'm just glad you recovered in time to send those flowers or I would have looked pretty stupid. We have a collection going for his family. We can sort that out later."

Melissa lay on top of the bed with her head resting on his shoulder.

"If I'm a good girl, do you think I might be able to sleep here tonight? The sofa is so uncomfortable."

"No way," he said, emphatically. "I'll never forgive you for wasting a good bottle of whisky on those two plebs."

"Oh, don't worry about it."

"That's alright for you to say but if it doesn't taste as good when I get to drink it, you'll be in serious trouble. Until then you can sleep on the sofa."

"That's not fair," she protested. "I was only trying to be hospitable. You were the one who said I had to get to know your partners better."

"Yes, but you didn't have to get drunk with them on my bottle of Scotch when I couldn't drink it. You don't even feel guilty about it, do you?"

"Yes I do," she said. "But it's not my fault they can't tell the difference between supermarket moonshine and real Scotch."

40

The next morning, at ten o'clock precisely, the door bell rang. Seconds later Melissa showed Greg Miller into the bedroom. He had not come alone and the uninvited guest, all too familiar to Martyn, slipped subtly into the room in Miller's shadow. Melissa found them both chairs and then left, tactfully closing the door behind her. Both chairs remained empty.

"Good morning," Miller said. "I appreciate you seeing me under the circumstances though I have to admit I was somewhat surprised that I didn't have to put up more of a fight to get in here. You must have been inundated with requests from the press and I didn't think I'd be the most popular choice. I appreciate that too." He gestured toward his companion. "I believe you two have already met."

"Hello again," Raspov said. "I trust the burn has healed by now." He grinned mischievously.

Martyn pulled the sheet down revealing a chest that was multicoloured with various shades of red, yellow and purple bruises. From left to right, at a slight incline, there was still the slight trace of a thin red line, as if at some time in the distant past he had been joined together from two different halves.

"It's not a major concern. Quite artistic in fact." He directed his attention toward Miller. "Has he pulled that stunt on you yet?"

"No," replied Miller, emphatically. "But I would never allow my photograph to be taken by a complete stranger. You never know what it might be used for."

"Yes, well it's tough being a cop," Martyn said. "This is an example of some of the things we have to go through to provide adequate protection for the good people of this city. You could put that in your exclusive if you like but I get the impression that this *interview* is not an interview in the normal sense of the word."

"True," Miller admitted. He indicated the papers stacked by the bed. "You read all those?"

"Yesterday."

Miller pulled up the wicker chair and sat down.

"Confusing, aren't they? Twelve papers, twelve different stories. I expect your own version would be different again and it still wouldn't be the truth."

At this point, Martyn felt himself switch into courtroom mode. This had suddenly stopped being a polite conversation and he now had to behave as if he were being cross examined on the stand.

Visibly wary, he said, "Maybe. So what?"

"So maybe you know what really happened and you're not willing to say, maybe you've been silenced by a greater authority or maybe you don't even know the truth yourself. Either way, I don't want to bullshit around. If you're willing to tell me exactly what happened the other night then I'm all ears but I'd appreciate not being told a pack of lies. It would be a waste of all our time."

Martyn smiled and shrugged helplessly.

"Looks like you'll have to go straight into plan B," he said. "Sorry."

"That's okay," Miller said. "As you've evidently guessed, it's no more than I expected."

At this point Raspov took a step back and leaned against the wall by the door as if he and Miller had rehearsed this whole scene before they had arrived. Miller continued.

"As you probably know, I have always thought this whole laser assassin thing has been used as a smokescreen to hide an internal cover up within the police department. You yourself told me that the information I was receiving through those anonymous letters was confidential and could only have been generated by someone within the department. Now you may have got Cassida by the balls and you might have half the syndicate leaders in this city behind bars but I don't see any mention of anyone in the police force being arrested. And that, in my book, means you still have a mole in your organisation who has got away without a mention." Martyn looked slightly puzzled. "With me so far?"

"I was wondering whether this pattern of logic was going to reach a conclusion or not," Martyn said. "What I don't understand is why you're telling me all this. That leak has been a problem for us but it's been a gold mine for you. I don't understand what you have to gain by losing your source of information. Besides, I must be a prime suspect for your mole, or is that what all this is about? Are you about to make an accusation?"

"What do you think?" Miller responded.

"I think if you could prove I was the mole then you would print the story and to hell with it. I think if you only suspected I was the mole then you might want to talk to me in the hope that I'd slip up in my weakened state and spill the beans."

"Well, you can relax," Miller said. "I don't think you are the mole, not because my wife seems to admire you, or because you seemed to expend a lot of energy trying to 'protect' me from the assassin. That would have been foolish if you had been sending the notes in the first place, though I guess it would also have been a brilliant cover. No, I don't think you are the mole because the one thing I do believe amongst all this tripe is that you did almost get yourself killed the other night. The evidence lies before me, and I don't think even the cleverest of traitors would have taken such a risk when he was nearly home and dry. From what I hear, you didn't even need to be present during the operation so that would make the risk doubly stupid.

"Besides, you police are not the only people who use intuition. Mine tells me that it isn't you. It doesn't fit. You're more of a pawn in a much bigger chess game. You might think you are the world's greatest detective; you may even have deluded yourself after reading the opinions of so many journalists who keep telling you that you are, but the truth is that you are totally in the dark. You're intelligent, you're bright, but let's face it, before all those arrests the other night you were getting absolutely nowhere with this case. You've come out of it smelling of roses but I don't believe even now that you know what the hell has been going on. I think you have been manipulated since day one on this case. You have been almost killed for it and that is why I'm here; because if you are even slightly irritated about that I want you to help me find out the truth."

Miller paused, and Martyn fell into silent contemplation. Eventually he spoke.

"That was some speech. So why do I get the feeling you are trying to manipulate me now?"

"The truth, dammit. All I want is the truth, because that is all that's important. In my whole career I have never printed one lie intentionally and I don't intend to start now. This story is far from over; there are too many pieces missing and we both need to know what they are. Cassida may end up in jail but the end doesn't justify the means. I want to know how far the Special Forces Network were prepared to go to get him."

Martyn spotted the trap immediately and jumped over it.

"Who says the SFN have got anything to do with it? Cassida and the syndicate are out of their jurisdiction unless there is a political connection which, in this case, there isn't."

"Bullshit," said Miller. "The arms came from Russia; that makes it political. If they had come from the Arab States, the Orient or Central America then it's plain old arms smuggling, but this ship sailed out of the Communist Alliance and I don't give a damn what all the papers say. They can erect the biggest smokescreen in history but the truth will always be the same. That ship came from Russia and that means the Communist Alliance could have been behind it. And that also means the SFN have every right to be involved.

"But the truth is that they've always had the right to be involved. The potential existence of the laser weapon has always been their passport into the case. If Robinson and West had been shot dead then you have a straightforward murder inquiry. But they weren't. They were supposedly assassinated by a laser rifle and that makes it a political situation. You only needed to be involved when they required you to be. In this case, the SFN were always in control of the proceedings. You never were. The SFN assigned you to the case because the public needed to know that the murder inquiry was in capable hands. Meanwhile, they could crawl down as many sewers as they wanted without drawing attention to themselves, while keeping a watchful eye on your progress in case you somehow managed to get ahead of them.

"I was a typical example. I stupidly came forward to give myself up to you and was immediately intercepted and interrogated by the SFN before

I'd even seen you. Every move you made, you were being watched in case you discovered something important. But the fact remains, you were nothing more than a publicity stunt to get the press out of their hair. The truth. It hurts but it's the truth."

One advantage of being in physical pain was that it sharpened the mind. Martyn took all of this in as if he had been given the solution to a simple maths problem which he had no interest in. His mind absorbed all the information with crystal clarity. Of course it was the truth but so what? The end did justify the means. He had not been a pawn, he had been a useful member of a team dedicated to bringing down the syndicate. He did not need to know everything as long as he had performed his part well. There were some things, he appreciated, that he could never know. Politics, by its very nature, was a Pandora's box he did not want to look into. In the meantime, what lies and truths were revealed by it were totally under the control of the politicians. He was not a politician, he was a cop.

Hell, why was he thinking all this rubbish? This was not like him at all. He looked straight into the eyes of Miller. Was that where the truth lay or was this oration yet another pack of lies. He knew he had no choice but to let Miller continue but he had to be careful not to give anything away. It seemed Miller had committed himself to opening up to him in the hope that this would be reciprocated. Miller was right about one thing; he did need to know the truth. He nodded silently and Miller acknowledged.

"There is one thing I don't understand," Miller continued. "When all this came to a head on Monday night, the SFN disappeared without a trace. They even denied they were present. But why? They could have taken all the glory; they always have done in the past. But this time they opted to make you the hero; they went out of their way to make you a star overnight while they slipped quietly away through the back door. I don't understand it, do you? Why should they deny they were present when the operation was a resounding success?"

"How do you know they were there?" asked Martyn, non-committally.

"Oh, come on," said Miller. "Of course they were there. You couldn't have won without them…"

"I said 'how did you know they were there?'"

"I have my sources, as you know."

"Who?"

"Listen! We'll get nowhere if you don't stop playing games with me. The only reason I'm going through all this is because I believe you'll come good in the end. I don't have to…"

"…It was me. I told him." It was the first sound Raspov had made since Miller had begun his speech. Martyn had not neglected Raspov. He knew he had to be there for a reason but he decided to let Miller come round to Raspov in his own time. It was evident from Miller's visible irritation that he had not planned to bring Raspov into the conversation at this particular point, but it was too late now.

"You told him," Martyn repeated. "And how did you know?"

"After the ship's cargo was seized by the SFN I was summoned to give my expert opinion on its contents. I am, after all, an expert on Alliance weaponry. They wanted to know the origins of everything; rifles, machine guns, grenades and who might have sent them. To be summoned out of bed at four in the morning is a price one must pay to gain political asylum. It is a small price and it doesn't happen very often."

"You are also the expert on laser weapons, as I recall," Martyn said. "So why did you then go running to Miller with your information?"

"The truth," Raspov said. "Until we know the truth we do not know whether we are in danger. That is as true of you as it is of me. I do not wish to be a pawn in someone else's game. That has been my role for too long. Only by knowing the truth can I be sure that I am safe."

"Safe from whom?"

Raspov did not answer. Instead, as if on cue, Miller took over the conversation again.

"Everything I have told you so far is a possible truth. It appears to be truth because it is indisputable but there may be other explanations. It is a theory. I have made it all up because it fits, but while there is still one piece of the jigsaw missing we will never see the full picture, and without that piece the picture may be meaningless whether it fits or not.

"I have another theory. I believe that this whole saga could have been cooked up by the SFN, or someone in the organisation, simply to trap Cassida. Just suppose that were true. Consider this: there is no laser weapon, there never has been. Two people were murdered, or died of natural causes, and their deaths were made to look like laser assassinations purely to get the attention of the syndicate. All of a sudden, the city is in a state of panic caused by the media sensation surrounding the two murders, all contrived by the Special Forces. They try to make it look as if it's supposed to be a secret which has been leaked and that stirs everyone up even more.

"Now what do you think would be Cassida's reaction to all this? Suddenly, the city is more scared of one man with a laser rifle than they are of the entire syndicate. The laser rifle commands fear and power but the syndicate does not have it.

"So what happens next? Someone offers Cassida the power of the laser weapon and he is hooked. He isn't completely stupid but is slowly drawn into the web. He makes some kind of deal to take delivery of a ship full of laser rifles from Russia, sends all his men to collect the goods. The trap is sprung, not very neatly it must be said, and half the syndicate end up being killed or arrested with foolproof evidence against them. It's perfect, almost too perfect, and it goes like a dream. Even the syndicate doesn't know what's gone wrong. Cassida is keeping completely silent; he doesn't know what's hit him. As far as we can make out, all he knows is that he had made a deal with someone called Lazarus and is now under arrest. And therein lies the main problem. That does not make any sense, not to me anyway.

"However, before Cassida can be convicted and sentenced there are a few loose ends to be tied up and we are three of them. We know that it doesn't make sense yet they can't afford to have us around to voice our opinions. You and your partner are easy; two month's sick leave. By the time you get back to work it will all be over and there will be plenty more problems to occupy your mind, not least Gremelkov's visit - which, incidentally, might point to the cause of all this. Get rid of the people who are most likely to have the gall to assassinate Gremelkov and you have more chance of keeping him alive. Another political reason for the involvement of Special Forces. All things considered, Gremelkov's visit is probably the most significant event in east-west relations since the end of the Turmoil.

"But that still leaves Raspov and me. While the official story sounds plausible, we know, for one reason or another, that it isn't true. Even if my theory turns out to be complete rubbish, it does not change the fact that certain events in this case do not add up. And if I were to say as much to the press or to the court, then the whole show could be over and Cassida would be free. In some ways you were lucky to come out of Monday night as badly injured as you are. I'm not sure what might have happened if you had been completely unscathed."

Martyn realised he was tired and the implied consequences of such a situation were completely lost on him. He was only just managing to keep up with Miller as it was.

"I'm afraid you'll have to spell it out for me."

Miller was only too happy to oblige.

"The truth," he persisted. "If you weren't so shell shocked you would be desperate to know the truth because it's in your nature. But they can't afford to have anyone like that around, not now. They want you to think everything is sown up in a nice little package so they can send you away unconcerned. Yet there is so much that needs explaining; so many questions you should be asking. Who killed Howard Robinson? Who killed Sarjena West? Who butchered Angelo and why? Who sent those anonymous letters to me? Those are the questions that need to be answered. Those are the crimes that have been committed. Instead, a bizarre twist of events has turned the conundrum on its head. Now we have answers but the questions have disappeared.

"You began this case looking for a murderer and ended up killing or arresting half of Cassida's syndicate. And because you have managed to round up everyone you believe to be connected then the murderer must be among them somewhere. Therefore, the case is over and the murders are solved. Give me a break. They could arrest the whole city and claim that."

"Aren't you forgetting something?" Martyn said. He picked up the morning paper and wafted it towards Miller. "They found a laser rifle in one of Cassida's cars. That would tend to wreck your theory, wouldn't it?"

"Not if it was planted," Miller said. "In order to nail Cassida on a murder charge they would have to find a weapon, so they would have to arrange for one to turn up. Simple."

"Hmm, perhaps," Martyn hesitated. The implication that he had been little more than a tiny pawn in a much more complex game he found hard to accept but it was now more than a nagging suspicion.

"Except it is not that simple," Miller continued. "There is something more. When Raspov was 'summoned' to examine the weapons from the ship there were two things which didn't quite fit. Firstly, the weapons were state of the art about four years ago yet they appeared never to have been used. Why would someone hoard arms for four years and then ship them to the States when there must be a booming industry in modern weapons?"

"You tell me."

"Because the weapons didn't come from the ship at all. There was no hold full of guns and ammunition. The SFN made the whole thing up, got hold of some out of date Alliance arms from god knows where and put them on display as if they had been seized from the ship. Nobody can dispute it except Raspov."

"Then why call him out at four in the morning?" Martyn said.

"Who knows? That is another thing that doesn't make sense. Perhaps they wanted to be sure they could convince the public by first convincing the expert, or maybe it was for publicity. I don't know."

"And what was the second thing?"

This time Raspov answered. "I am a world authority on laser weapons," he said. "Yet they did not ask me to examine the rifle found in Cassida's car. They did not even put the laser weapon on display with the rest. In fact, nobody has seen it, they have only seen this photograph." He held up a newspaper. On the front page was the photograph the Chief had shown him on the previous evening.

"A year ago," said Miller. "Raspov wrote a top secret paper for the Alliance government. The paper outlined the progress made on laser weapon technology. This photograph was part of that document. It is over a year old. It is not the photo of the weapon found in Cassida's car."

"The rifle is known as the Lightning III to quote a loose translation," explained Raspov. "I designed it myself. It was a prototype model for the first portable laser weapon but it has one very significant feature. It doesn't work. It could not kill a termite."

"Which is why he might be in danger," Miller said. "All the evidence seems to point to the fact that they don't have the laser rifle yet their case rests on convincing everybody that they do. Nobody would be any the wiser if Raspov had not recognised the photo. If the laser rifle does exist then where is it? Why are they trying to claim the case is closed if they don't have it? If the laser rifle does not exist then what did happen to Sarjena West and Howard Robinson? And why were their deaths made to look like laser assassinations?

"The key question is this: if you or I went to print with this information, or tried to go to print, then what would happen? If anyone knew that Raspov could blow their whole case wide open then what would they do?

Whatever the truth, a lot of time, effort and intricate planning has gone into trapping Cassida. And now they have him exactly where they want him, just how far would they be prepared to go to keep him there? Would they kill for it?"

"Kill? You must be crazy. This is the police force we are talking about. They don't go around murdering innocent people."

"Not you or me maybe. They have conveniently managed to get you off the scene by making you a hero. At the moment they don't know that I know anything but what would happen if I went on the air and said all this? How far would they go to silence me? And then there is Raspov. They must know that he would recognise a photo in his own report. They must also know that he would become suspicious when they showed him the arms cache. I think he is being set up. The bottom line is this: can you allow yourself to take that chance with somebody else's life?"

Martyn looked blank. The whole conversation seemed to be leading down a path of uncontrolled hysteria. Miller was scared. That was why he was there. He had not wanted an interview. He had wanted to find out the truth and to take out an insurance policy with the only person he felt he could trust. Raspov was also scared and that was why he had gone running to Miller with his concerns. Neither was able to handle the situation they suspected they were in. But Raspov evidently had more reason.

"There is a strong possibility that certain members of your secret police department have links with the Communist Alliance and that this whole plan was a joint venture to trap Cassida and ensure Gremelkov's wellbeing. I am a serious embarrassment to the Alliance government and I am of little more use to the American Defence Department. I have told them everything I know. I am afraid that I may be the price which the Alliance demanded for their co-operation. To catch Cassida, I am sure you will agree that I am a very small price indeed, just as, perhaps, were the others."

"What do you mean? What others?"

Miller answered.

"There is one mystery that defies explanation and which renders my own theory and the official version of events equally suspect. Who is Lazarus? At present, he is not in the public domain and the police appear to be quite happy to keep it that way. Should he ever become part of the equation the official party line will be that Lazarus is a pseudonym used by Cassida and his syndicate, unless they actually find someone by that name among those arrested. If my theory is correct then it most likely that Lazarus was a pseudonym cooked up by the Special Forces in order to trap Cassida. Either way, Lazarus is the piece that doesn't fit. Whether I am correct or whether the official story is actually much closer to the truth, we would probably both agree that Angelo must have been killed by Cassida and his men to prevent a leak to the police. So why did someone scrawl Lazarus' name all over the wall of Angelo's apartment?"

"How did you know that?"

Miller brushed the question aside. "I have a photograph. The point is this: I am sure I am right but everything else makes sense apart from this. If Cassida did kill Angelo then why would he blame Angelo's death on someone he was trying to do business with? Why not just deny it? The alternative explanation is that Cassida did not kill Angelo."

"But the Special Forces did," Martyn concluded. "That would tend to quash your theory then, wouldn't it?"

Raspov said, "Are you so sure they are not capable of such a thing?"

Martyn did not answer. The whole idea was ludicrous.

"The only other possibility," Miller said, "is that Lazarus really does exist. But if that is the case then why aren't the police out looking for him? It's one question that hasn't been answered. Who the hell is Lazarus? Find out and we'll know the truth. But until then I would advise you to watch your back. The Great Lakes can be very desolate at this time of year. You will be all alone out there."

Martyn tried to ignore the warning.

"And what do you intend to do? Are you going to make your concerns public?"

"I don't know. What would you advise me to do?"

"I can't tell you. But if you are hell bent on discovering the truth it might be better to keep quiet until Cassida is safely convicted. As long as he is on his way to jail then the hornet's nest you want to stir up should remain dormant."

"Does that mean you do believe me?"

"No. It simply means that you are in control of your own destiny. If you make waves you might get wet. Why don't you wait and see what happens?"

"Because if I am going to end up like Angelo then I want to be able to see it coming in time to do something about it."

When Miller and Raspov had left, Melissa entered the room and found Martyn sitting by the window in the wicker chair. He was panting and visibly in pain.

"What the hell are you doing out of bed!" she demanded.

"Just proving that I'm not in any fit state to be out of it," Martyn replied.

"Did they give you a hard time?" she asked.

"In a manner of speaking."

Melissa helped him back into bed.

"Well, forget it," she said. "In a couple of days we're going to take off out of here and you can put all this behind you. It's over. You've done your bit. It's not your problem, anymore. Period."

He nodded absentmindedly.

"Right," she said, changing the subject. "I'll fix lunch."

Martyn was left alone. His mind was spinning, trying to come to terms with everything he had been told by Miller. He kept trying to tell himself that it was only a theory created by an overactive imagination. But it fitted. It appeared to answer more questions than the alternative truth that Cassida was indeed behind everything. It just left more of a nasty taste and privately he could admit to himself that his own pride was preventing him from accepting Miller's version of the truth. Not that he wallowed in being the hero, but he could not accept that he had been manipulated on such a large scale. And yet, in some strange way he had always believed that to be true; he just had not considered the possible scope of the corruption. Miller seemed to have concocted a version of events which implicated almost everybody and made the rest look like fools, himself included.

But there was a third truth; that of his own intuition. The allegations against Cassida smacked of a half truth peppered with lies and cover ups. Miller's theory had echoes of credibility but he could not be convinced by such overwhelming conclusions. He felt there was something he was missing, something so blindingly obvious that he was a fool not to see it. And if he were honest, he still sensed, irrationally, that Howard Robinson was the key. But he needed more answers, more proof and he was not in any position to obtain it in his present state. One day he would learn the truth. For the present, it would have to wait.

He would have to be patient.

41

From the moor's summit, the walk back to Darwen passed very quickly as Howard made his way down oblivious of his surroundings. In the valley, the fog had yet to clear. By the time he reached the large junction at the centre of the town, he was cold, damp and more than pleased to see the familiar neon sign above the hotel door. Almost as soon as he stepped inside he bumped into Susannah, polishing around the bar. She stopped and looked at him like a disgusted matron.

"Look at you! You're soaking wet. If you catch pneumonia now I hope you won't expect any sympathy from me. I've got better things to do than nurse Kamikaze pilots. I do hope you had a pleasant walk."

"Yes, thank you," he replied. "And now I'm going to have a pleasant, hot bath." He paused. "Then I'll be leaving."

At this, she appeared openly disappointed.

"Already? You've only just got out of bed after four days."

"I found what I was looking for. There's no need to stay any longer." He turned to walk up the stairs but was interrupted by Susannah once more.

"Aren't you going to ask me something?" she said, coyly. He looked at her. She was leaning over the bar exposing a substantial cleavage, her cheeky, deep brown eyes staring seductively at him. He hovered on the stairway assessing his feelings towards her. Part of him wanted to ask her the question she wanted to hear. She was attractive, alive and, he suspected, good company. But she was not Melissa. After a pause he chose to feign ignorance.

"What?" he said.

She held up an envelope and waved it in front of him. The handwriting and the smiley sticker on the front were instantly recognisable.

"You got some post," she said.

42

Howard arrived at the flat in Islington at dusk and almost immediately wished he had stayed one more night at the Millstone. At least there he had someone to talk to. Once inside, the first thing he did was to switch on the television, and then proceeded to ignore it. The sound of idle chatter in the background made him feel less alone. The flat was damp and chilly. He had not been there for over a week and already the place was desperately in need of an airing. He also needed to do something about the heating.

He placed the hold-all underneath the table, choosing to leave the unpacking until later, and removed the envelope from the side pocket. Without opening it he placed it down on the sofa and walked across the room to a large chest of drawers. The top right hand drawer contained papers and correspondence and he began rummaging through it until, near the bottom, he found what he was looking for; a large pink envelope, scented, and with a rainbow crest on the reverse. Removing the card from inside he read it to himself.

26 December 1983

Howard. I can't tell you how sorry I am about what happened. I feel so guilty that I'm now really miserable. I don't know what I can do to make up for it - I know I really let you down but I hope you can forgive me. I only wish I could be with you to tell you this personally. I love you so much and I'm very, very, very sorry. Please, please, please forgive me. Melissa.

It had been a stupid argument, nothing that deserved such an apology. He folded the card and placed it on top of the chest. Then he walked back to the sofa and opened the second envelope, which he had received in Darwen that morning. Inside was a single sheet of paper.

10 October 1984
Sorry. Melissa.

43

The last two months of the year saw the most dramatic seasonal changes. As autumn reached a close the remainder of the maple leaves gave up their splendid colours, withered and fell to earth. The summer months had not been as hot as usual but they had been warm and prolonged. The autumn too had been extended unusually and Martyn and Melissa found themselves taking lakeside walks in temperatures that would normally be akin to late September. Each day, the wind murmured softly among the branches without ever raising its voice in anger. Purring like a sleepy kitten each gentle gust would flow and ebb in a soporific rhythm and another leaf would fall, rocking back and forth in the air as it sank dreamily to the ground.

For Martyn, the holiday they had been planning for months initially turned into an exercise in learning to walk. They had left the city earlier than expected. Even if, at first, it was only to swap one bed for another, getting away from the dirt-ridden, chaotic metropolis and into the fresh air of the inland countryside was half the battle. In itself, the Great Lake aspect and the Swiss style log cabin perched high on the hillside above the river valley provided a semi-panacea. Before he had even regained full consciousness Melissa had decided that they were to leave the city as quickly as possible but with the proviso that he was not going to travel until he felt fit enough. He resigned himself to this fact, declared that he was ready to travel the very next day, spent little time persuading Melissa whose only condition was that he had another medical check-up before they left, and that was that. The western highway beckoned and they followed.

The first week was spent religiously hobbling around the hillside, an hour in the morning followed by an hour in the afternoon. He soon graduated to four hours a day punctuated by a swim and a picnic at the height of the sun. By her very presence, Melissa seemed to supply him with all the strength he needed. She was a source of energy he seemed able to tap into and her constant encouragement made the first week's efforts even more beneficial than he could have hoped, given the prediction of his recovery by the doctor prior to their departure.

The first days were exhausting and Martyn found that he was ready to collapse very early each evening. Within seconds of hitting the pillow he would fall into a deep, comfortable sleep which remained uninterrupted until the morning. At each new daybreak the wind across the lake changed direction in preparation for the morning, and a fresh breeze would sweep through the cabin, entering through an open window near the bed. He would be instantly alert, rising to greet the new sunrise as quickly as he had said goodbye to the previous sunset. The time between seemed to pass in seconds.

One night, the fifth they had spent in the cabin, Martyn drifted slowly from a deep sleep, induced into consciousness by the pleasant and warm sensation growing within his groin. Melissa was straddled naked over him. With the full weight of her body resting on her forearms at each side, her beautiful hair was bathed in silent, silver moonlight streaming in from the open window, her perfect breasts hung like huge raindrops, swaying slightly to the slow rhythm that her pubic hair traced against his own skin. As his eyelids began to flicker, on the very edge of sleep, she realised he had woken.

"I'm sorry," she whispered. "I couldn't wait any longer." He did not reply. It seemed ridiculous that she should apologise for something which he considered to be her privilege and for which she should not feel guilty. To him, it was like apologising for giving someone a present simply because she enjoyed the act of giving.

He cupped her pretty face in his hands and gently stroked each thumb against her cheeks. As one hand lightly caressed the back of her neck, the other slid down to her navel and then back to her breast, her nipple growing instantly erect to his touch.

"Go on," he urged. "Enjoy it."

Putting one arm around her shivering body he slowly ran his free hand along the contours of her skin until it came to rest on her knee. Then, slipping his hand inside her leg he encountered no resistance as he reversed direction, carefully stroking along her inner thigh, advancing towards her pubis. In no time at all his middle finger had slipped silently into the moist crevice and initiated a steady sliding motion back and forth, each stroke rubbing gently against the small sphere of taut flesh within. Melissa gasped, raised herself up on her forearms and then let her breasts brush across his face as he continued to stimulate her. In time, he removed his finger and placed his hands on her hips, pushing her downwards onto his erection. She gently eased herself into a comfortable position and rested once more on her forearms, her eyes gazing right into his. They kissed, their lips locked together as she slowly moved against him, extracting the maximum enjoyment from each thrust.

Melissa began to moan and quickened the rhythm until her whole body was quivering in uncontrollable ecstasy. Tiny beads of sweat appeared on her forehead as her thrusting began to pick up pace, her moaning growing louder.

Forward. Backward.

Deeper and deeper.

Her orgasm rose and fell like a summer thunder shower, a cloudburst of released tension and stifled passion. It slowly built in a crescendo of soulful heaves and distant moans and then exploded like a glorious firework, lighting up the hemisphere for one brief moment before falling to earth, each twinkling ember rapidly fading in a plume of swirling smoke. With one final surge of passionate energy that seemed to evolve from deep within her she collapsed in a heap on top of him, panting, her heartbeat thudding against his chest.

"Oh thank you, darling," she said. Then, overcome by a sudden wave of guilt as she sensed him wince in pain beneath her, she repeated her apology. "I'm sorry. That was selfish."

"That's okay. You're allowed to be selfish. Besides, I enjoyed it."

Melissa snuggled up to him, her mane of golden hair splayed wildly across his shoulders. Gradually, her heartbeat slowed and her breathing became steady. He sensed her convulse once - a final spasm of her orgasm - and then she was quiet. In the dark he was not sure if he had interpreted the movement correctly; it seemed less a spasm, more a sob.

"You okay?"

She did not reply. Instead her breathing became more regular and softer. They lay together like this for another minute before he felt the warm, moist trail of a solitary tear slide down the side of his ribcage. No others followed. In the early hours of the morning he felt that actions spoke louder than words and he pulled her close to him and held her tightly. Then he fell asleep.

Though it would have been easy to forget - and he often did - thoughts of the city and Cassida's trial were never far from his mind. While the increased flow of oxygen to his brain naturally steered his thoughts towards the problems he had left behind, he initially found it easy to put them aside and quickly learnt that his present surroundings were not capable of delivering answers to the questions he was asking. He soon grew tired and stopped asking the questions. Primarily, he was most preoccupied with improving his state of fitness but the long, lonely hours spent pounding the hill paths allowed too much time for private contemplation while his body stepped through its painstaking and mindless rituals.

There were the occasional nightmares but the tranquil environment of the lake front did not allow them to gain a firm hold on his sanity. Though the events in the city had been real, they no longer seemed so. He found he could look back at the dockland siege dispassionately, almost as if he had died and it no longer mattered. It was only when he included Melissa in the equation, and considered the possibility that he might have been separated from her, that he realised how close to death he had come on that evening.

At first, Melissa was totally against his having any further involvement or interest in the case. The cabin had a television but she had insisted there was no cable-net link. However, after Cassida's trial had begun, she eventually conceded defeat to his constant preoccupation and agreed to purchase a newspaper each time they needed to drive to the nearest town to pick up fresh supplies, every three or four days. As expected, the trial was well covered by the press. Though this spasmodic interest was not enough to keep up with the detailed events of the courtroom drama, he had no problem following its general progress. To fill in the gaps he reserved a copy of the city's primary Sunday paper which delivered a résumé of the week's occurrences.

From this fragmented viewpoint the trial appeared to begin slowly and initially seemed to be getting nowhere. Though anxious to bring the case to court at the earliest opportunity, the State did not convey an equal concern in bringing about a swift conclusion. Witnesses from out of the blue were systematically called, drilled and despatched to the oblivion of anonymity from which they had come. They offered no mind-blowing evidence and there was no startling defence offered in reply to each of their minor revelations. Both parties seemed to be playing a precarious game. The prosecution appeared to be buying time, treading carefully through their case as if it were a minefield which could explode at any moment. By the end of the second week there was no clear indication that the trial would produce a certain result one way or the other.

This lack of progress did not concern him unduly. What did concern him, though he was not exactly sure why, was the complete lack of activity on the Miller front. Though he had not taken it as seriously as he had been meant to, still he had not been able to forget Miller's visit, or his theories, and so far the trial had neither proved nor disproved them. It was not that Miller had failed to come forward with his anomalies and suspicions - that did not surprise Martyn - but more that he had apparently disappeared completely. Though normally a regular contributor to the paper, Miller had not written anything during those first two weeks of the trial and that worried him. He knew why. If anything should happen to Miller or Raspov then he - and only he - would feel morally obliged to look into it. While there was total silence he did not know what Miller might be up to, or what the consequences might be for himself.

All such concerns were dashed during the third week of the trial. In a shock move, which surprised him more than it would the rest of the populace, the State took the unprecedented step of exhibiting the laser weapon at the trial, in breach of the hitherto claimed State Secret's Act. From the photograph in the paper it looked identical to the Lightning III which had been pictured earlier; a metallic, futuristic-styled rifle with a peripheral power pack about the size of a large suitcase. Furthermore, despite Raspov's claims that the weapon could not possibly work, its effectiveness was unquestionably demonstrated within the courtroom, in full view of the court, the jury and the media, as the laser was activated and silently sliced through three telephone directories in a matter of seconds. While the rifle was immediately placed back under wraps and removed from the courtroom, the six halves of the directories were left on the front bench as a constant reminder of its power. From that point on, the outcome of the trial, and the validity of Miller's claims that the weapon did not actually exist, were conclusively determined.

In the weeks that followed, Cassida and the remainder of his immediate entourage were systematically despatched to Southern California to begin sixteen jail sentences totalling three hundred and eighteen years. As the sentences were announced, during the second week of December, Martyn was seized by an overwhelming release of tension and discovered an even deeper tranquillity in this new freedom. Though he had emerged yet again the hero, he knew in his own mind that he had failed. He had not taken a simple murder case at face value but had twisted it into something it was not; something more complex and sinister. He had tried to be too clever but he did not know why. Perhaps he had allowed himself to be caught up in the sensationalism of the laser weapon; perhaps it had been the disconcerting effect of the photograph he had discovered in Howard Robinson's apartment; maybe he had simply allowed himself to become too tired to think clearly. Perhaps he just had to face the fact that he could no longer do this job as well as he used to. Now he was away from the city, with an uncluttered mind and the evidence set out in black and white before him, it was easy to see his mistakes if not the reasons for his making them. He could only be sure about one thing: this time he had screwed up, and though there were still questions without answers, he was thankful that it was finally over.

The sun and moon chased each other tirelessly round the sky until the moon had completed two lunar cycles and it was almost time to return to the city. Over the preceding eight weeks Martyn had built himself up to a level of fitness he had not achieved for several years. First by walking and then running longer and longer distances he had monitored his progress daily, taking a mental note of heartbeat, pulse and respiration after each exercise. He had watched as all but the most serious of his bruises had undergone several phases of colour change before finally fading to nought. His heartbeat now pulsed steadily even after rigorous exercising and the finishing touches of his self-inflicted fitness programme were carried out in the lake; swimming and diving every day, regardless of prevailing weather conditions.

While Melissa was around he had never brought up the subject of the city or the case. For her part, she had behaved similarly, almost as if she had begun her life over again on the day they had arrived. He began to realise she must have been very unhappy in the city and felt guilty at not realising it before. Over the months they had lived together the metamorphosis from the happy, carefree girl he had first met to the tired, stressed person she had become had been imperceptible. It was only this sudden transition to her former self that had opened his eyes to the fact. She had said it so many times and he had not listened, too wrapped up in his own problems to see what was staring him in the face. They had needed this break, both of them, and he vowed privately that he would not allow a similar decline when they returned. It was time to move away and enjoy some of the 'quiet life'. In the oppressive urban gravity of the city they had grown weary and their leaving was overdue. He decided to put in for a transfer as soon as they got back. He did not expect his request to meet with approval but in light of recent events he thought they might be sympathetic towards his case. One thing was certain; there would never be a better time.

During the last week of their stay the weather changed abruptly. Almost overnight, the lakeland skyline became a mass of grotesque bare branches and, in a last minute panic to meet the autumn deadline, leaves poured down from the trees in torrents, forming a thick carpet of mottled browns and yellows. It was almost as if Melissa had predicted the change in the weather. And yet it seemed even more uncanny, as if she had not only predicted the change but had engineered it, purposely holding back the winter until their time there was almost completed.

On the perfectly calm Sunday evening of their final weekend she had taken him by the hand and led him down from the log cabin to the jetty. There she had undressed them both and they had rolled around naked on a soft bed of leaves and made love under the stars to the gentle sound of rippling water lapping against the supports of the rickety landing. Almost on the point of orgasm she had rolled onto her back and pulled him down onto her.

"Make it good. It will be too cold to do this again after tonight."

At the time he had been too preoccupied to question her about it but she had been right. The next day, the temperature had dropped by fifteen degrees and winter began its invasion of the land.

All too quickly, the last day of their time in the mountains arrived. While Melissa volunteered to finish the packing and clean out the log cabin, Martyn was permitted to go for one final jog in the hills. He hated packing so was more than happy to take up the offer. Running along the tree line, with the mountain peak above him and the lake below, he realised that he had begun to take his surroundings for granted and he stopped to take in the panoramic view which spanned the water to the mountains beyond. The serenity of the mountainside lay in stark contrast to the horrors he had witnessed in the city. Here, he was content and happy. And with Melissa by his side he could not contemplate a more idyllic existence.

For the whole two months of their stay they had seen hardly anybody. When, on occasions, they had passed day trippers on one of the tracks that ran along the mountain, they did not seem like real people. Rather they were extras brought in to complete a scene, or characters added to enhance the tableau. In this heaven, there were only two living, breathing, thinking, loving people - two independent souls who would never be complete without the other.

He stopped jogging and sat among the bracken, which separated the trees from the bare rock above, trying to focus on this emotion and lock it within him so that he might instantly recall it at any time in the future. He was bursting with an energy that was derived from both physical fitness and the happiness of a healthy state of mind. He was in love, not only with Melissa but with the world and it felt blissful. In those few seconds he wished that time would freeze so that he could savour the moment forever.

But it was to last for a much shorter time than he could possibly have imagined.

Suddenly, as he sat admiring the glitter of sky on the surface of the lake, the sun disappeared behind a cloud and plunged the mountain into shadow. Immediately, a lone bird broke cover from a nearby tree and flew high into the air, as if fleeing from some unseen menace. For no reason that he could determine, the air was filled with foreboding. From out of the blue, he heard a voice – her voice - as if the words had shot from the darkest recesses of his mind and now echoed around the valley as clearly as church bells chiming ominously through the fog. The words came to him as a warning - a vision - as if the very sky above him had parted and a voice had sprung from heaven.

Ultimately, we are all alone.

With the echo of those words still resonating in his mind he continued to jog, disturbed that his mind should conjure up such terrible images in so idyllic a setting. Though he had soon left the view point and the tree line far behind, he could not shake off this new anxiety. He ran not knowing whether he was trying to run away from something or towards it. Whatever had caused this sudden mood change, it remained with him, mysterious and threatening.

He was a few hundred metres from the log cabin when he saw Melissa in the distance gathering flowers; a final memento with which to return to the city. She did not notice him and seemed preoccupied in her own thoughts. He called out to her but she was still some way off and evidently could not hear him. He ran a little further and called to her again. This time, as she looked up, he detected the deep sadness in her eyes and his heart went out to her.

Flowers.

Yet she did not look at him or away from him. Her soulful gaze went right through him as though he were not there. He knew instinctively that there was something unreal in what he was seeing.

The dark dress.

What had begun as a mild anxiety quickly evolved into inexplicable dread as he fought to comprehend the vision before him. There was Melissa, her gorgeous blonde hair flowing around her face and pouring over her shoulders like a halo of pure, white, silent light. Even from such a distance, his eyes could ingest and interpolate all the contours and shadows of her face that made it so beautiful.

At the same time, he knew it was not Melissa. For a moment he saw himself standing in Eden Square all those weeks before, gaping stupidly across the plaza as Melissa, wearing the same unfamiliar dress and carrying the same flowers, turned and walked casually along the narrow cobbled street and into oblivion, invisible to everyone but himself. But now the apparition had mysteriously returned to a place where it had no cause to be and he could not understand why. It did not make sense.

Again he called after her but it was clear she was oblivious to his existence. He rushed forward but he was still at some distance and already she was moving away. He call out to her again but it was useless. His legs felt like jelly and he could not seem to make them go any faster. In one final spurt he tried to catch up with her but instead collapsed to his knees, exhausted. All he could do was watch, helplessly, knowing that to chase her would be like chasing the end of a rainbow. Slowly she continued walking away from him. Then, as she reached the top of the rise she offered one final glance behind her, and disappeared over the edge.

Martyn knelt transfixed until she was completely out of sight. With sudden, renewed energy, he snapped back into life and ran to the top of the rise. Below him he could see the cabin, carving a distinctive outline through the dense trees. Outside the front door, the car had been brought out of hiding and was now parked among the sea of dead leaves that surrounded the cabin. The hatchback was open and already a couple of boxes had been loaded into the luggage space in readiness for the return journey. All around, the air was perfectly still and an unnatural silence hung grotesquely from the trees. There was no other sign of life.

44

When Howard Robinson next returned to Darwen it was well into January and the streets were buried under several feet of snow. A deep cloud layer hung in the valley basin, completely obscuring the town from aerial view. The temperature had averaged below freezing for over a week and from the slow dripping of overflowing gutters, icicles several inches long had formed. The road into town resembled a steep and slippery tunnel, lined with crystal stalactites, leading to a vast cavern that was the town centre.

He was not sure what he hoped to gain from making the return trip. It was a flailing attempt at consolidation and acceptance of all that had happened over the previous three months. Since his last visit everything had gone wrong, so terribly wrong that he now felt as though he had emerged from a great battle with his own soul, unable to love or be loved - a hollow, emotionless wreck, vast and empty. He had not seen Melissa, nor heard from her, since Christmas. He was not likely to.

He had no idea why this was happening, had no recollection of anything he had either said or done to upset her. But suddenly she had become a stranger and the person he had loved was lost, trapped somewhere inside the cold, cruel exterior that she now displayed to him. But it was only to him. To everyone else she was as much the picture of beauty and radiance as she ever had been and this perturbed him all the more. It had been a waking nightmare, almost as if she had undergone a metamorphosis as marked as a caterpillar changing into a butterfly yet no one but himself seemed to have noticed. Though he had tried and tried he could not communicate with her, could not even claim that he had received the slightest favourable response from her lips. And the more she remained silent, the more he hung on her every word in the hope of hearing, even detecting, some nuance of affection.

Casting his mind back to that fateful day in October, he gradually began to realise how much had changed. He wished he had never taken the trip to Amsterdam, never discovered her secret and never left her alone to go to America. Before that time they had spent every weekend together, laughing, joking, kissing, cuddling. They would fall into bed and make love two, three times and still he longed for more. He would wake aglow in the early hours of the morning and she would be there, waiting, her legs slowly parting, rubbing tantalisingly against his own, coiling around him. And as he merged into the soft curves of her femininity she would embrace him and allow him to become one with her. Now, all he could long for was a smile, a faint crack of her lips in his general direction and he would return briefly to that same heaven. But it was a hollow place and always short lived.

Worse than being a stranger, she began to treat him like a stranger; as though she had never known him, as though they had never shared their bodies or all of those precious moments which his mind had collected until it resembled a cluttered attic. Sometimes she would talk to him almost as if she were speaking to a stray mongrel, sometimes mocking him, sometimes mimicking his manifestations of pain. She might catch him, in a moment of weakness, looking longingly at her and she would look longingly back but she never meant it. They would never make love but she would still undress in front of him, always turning her back to reveal her breasts to the shadows only. Then, she would slip on a long, thigh length T-shirt before removing her panties. Slowly, his memory began to lose the shape and form of what he no longer saw. Lust ran wild over his imagination until he wanted to rip the T-shirt into shreds and cover her entire body in kisses. But he never did.

The symptoms of all this pain began to reveal themselves when he was no longer with her. His friends began to pale into insignificance when placed besides all that he was losing. He could not discuss it with anyone because he did not understand what was happening. Also, he could not betray her. Only he knew of her past and only he was being pushed out of her present. If everyone knew that might make it easier but he knew that Melissa would lose everything as a result. She would not stand and fight - she would simply disappear and begin yet another new life without any of them. It was easier for him to make the sacrifice but he had not appreciated how painful it would be.

He stopped accepting invitations to dinner because he could not eat, and it soon became embarrassing to receive and return a whole plate of food. He did not sleep well. His general appearance began to deteriorate. Suddenly, he no longer had any friends, there was no one to turn to, and he began to despair at his isolation.

All of this was slowly draining him. He wished it were all a dream, like so many other nightmares. But the reality of Melissa had been the dream and now he was waking up.

In retrospect, he should have ended it weeks ago but he had not been brave enough. He insisted on clinging to the hope that the storm would pass and there would be calm again. It was not to be.

He had made arrangements in the summer to spend Christmas at Melissa's house. It was clear she would like to have altered those plans but she would not retract the invitation and evidently hoped that he would change his mind. Though he debated and agonised and told himself not to go so many times, he could not help it. He had to go. Things had become so bad that only the atmosphere of Christmas could give him any chance of saving their relationship.

On Christmas Eve, as Howard Robinson stepped from the train onto the platform at Alderley Edge station, he knew deep down in his heart that this was his last stand. On Christmas Day, showered with gifts and glowing with wine, she would either soften and there would be reconciliation and a hope for the future, or it would be the coldest Christmas he had ever spent in his life…

As heavy snow mingled with the midnight chimes of bells all around the country, Howard Robinson entered the new year as if passing through the gates of hell. Melissa had left his life almost as rapidly as she had entered it. He did not think he would ever see her again. He could not see her again. He had felt pain so acute that he could no longer feel anything. His life was empty and there was nobody to turn to. He had no friends.

Except one.

It was only a short walk but it had passed so quickly. Standing now at the doorway to the Millstone Hotel, he remembered the warmth, the humour and the gentleness of Susannah, the only person left who might make him feel something again. He knew he was placing a lot of faith in her, far too much in fact, but he had nowhere else to go. She was the guiding light that had brought him back to Darwen, a desolate town for a desolate soul, and the only piece of the jigsaw that he had left to cling on to.

With trepidation he entered the bar. It was quieter than he expected and he was surprised at the number of changes since his last visit. He wondered if she would even remember him but suddenly, with sickening disbelief, the question became academic. As he surveyed the new interior decor, the new pool area and high-tech lighting, he realised that the changes were more far reaching than he had first perceived and it was only a matter of time before his eyes fell on the inevitable. Behind the bar, the same drinks appeared, as they had always done, but now they were being served by strangers. Above their heads a single sign, in blue and gold lettering, took pride of place amongst all the tinsel and mistletoe left over from Christmas. Its message was simple yet devastating.

Under New Management.

45

December 25th, 2029.

Christmas in the city was a relatively subdued affair, overshadowed by the build up to the year 2000 HTE celebrations. There was none of the usual massive commercial extravaganzas, no parties, no banquets, no all night balls that would normally have preceded and followed the Christmas Day festivities. Nobody was interested. Everything was put back one week and instead, New Year - and the simultaneous East-West declaration of peace - became the focus of the celebrations.

In keeping with this mood Christmas was marketed and subsequently became a time of family reunions, of renewed friendships, of hatchets buried over dinner party invitations and long standing feuds brought to an end over mulled wine. The repair of broken bonds became the common theme that ran right through the festive season. Destroyed marriages were temporarily revived and parents received their long lost, drug-ridden children back into their homes with open arms. As estranged husbands and wives and prodigal sons and daughters returned in their droves, and the streets became empty once more, the city forgave itself for its shameful past and prepared for a new beginning.

On Christmas Day, a somewhat subdued Melissa set a table for two, complete with flowers, candles and all the best dinnerware the apartment contained while Martyn struggled to carve up the roast turkey they had spent the morning preparing together. At Melissa's insistence they had cooked more side dishes than they could possibly eat between them. He did not know why - or how he was going to fit even half of them onto the two plates - and he felt a twinge of guilt that so much food was going to go to waste. He had considered but thought better of tackling her about it. He was not sure what was on her mind but she had been acting strangely ever since their return to the city. Though he had subtly invited her to talk about it on several occasions, she had kept silent and he was no nearer to discovering the cause of this sudden change of mood. Since questioning her about it seemed to deepen her depression even further he decided to ride it out and wait for her to talk to him. But that still left the problem of what to do with all the extra food.

With this dilemma, he entered the lounge and found Melissa gazing dreamily out of the French window into the court below, a picture postcard scene of fairy tale white. Three couples, about their own age, were engaged in a frenetic snowball fight as if the remnants of their childhood depended on it.

"Why don't we have any friends?"

The question was bitter and sounded more like an accusation than a regret. He almost became defensive when the pain that lay behind the question filtered through, like an almost unheard echo, and his response softened.

"What do you mean?" he said. "We do have friends. What's wrong with the ones we've got?"

Melissa stiffened. "Nothing, except that they're not here. It's Christmas Day and we don't have anyone to share it with."

Martyn came up behind her, wrapped his arms gently around her waist and watched the snowball fight for a few moments. They seemed to be having so much fun and Martyn was forced to admit, at least to himself, that their own festivities seemed morose and uninviting by comparison. He quickly blanked the thought from his mind. All things considered he preferred to spend the day alone with Melissa.

"It isn't friends we don't have," he said. "It's family. And that is where all our friends are; with their families."

"But there must be other people like us," Melissa insisted. "Somewhere out there, wishing they didn't have to spend Christmas alone."

"But we're not alone. We have each other. There are probably thousands of people who really are alone today. We should count our blessings. In fact there are probably as many couples who wished they were together but have been separated because they were expected to be with their families. And instead, they have to spend the day entertaining uncles, aunts and grandparents who have suddenly crawled out of the woodwork."

Melissa evidently did not believe him but then she never did where families were concerned.

"Don't be silly," she said. "It can't be all that bad or nobody would spend Christmas with their families."

Having never known her family, Melissa had always had an obsession with them. She had emerged from the Great Turmoil with no parents and with no knowledge of what had happened to them. All she knew was that they had given her up at an early age and left no clues as to her real identity. Subsequently, she had spent several years in care in England before being brought to the United States by her adoptive family.

Over the years she had become indoctrinated by the stereotyped families of television and the trashy cine-novels that were screened over the network. She believed family life was all wine and roses and that problems made life more exciting and dramatic. She only allowed herself to see the fairy tale gloss which she had painted in her own mind and not the stark reality behind it. For her the essence of family life was summed up in a painting she had bought long ago; a children's picture book scene of a father, mother, two children, a dog and a cat sitting peacefully by the river and feasting on the delights of a picnic banquet.

"Listen," Martyn said. "I know it was a long time ago but I remember it as if it were yesterday. Christmas Day was one of the most boring days in the year. The only thing good about it was the food. You had to spend all day kissing people you had never seen before and listen to them tell you how much you'd grown since they last saw you, even though they never had. Since I lost my parents I've spent every Christmas in varying degrees of loneliness and all I ever wanted was to share it with one very special person. This is what I was waiting for."

But she would not be pacified and he realised that she was growing angry at his constant derision of something she regarded as sacred. As far as she was concerned he was committing blasphemy.

"Well I'm sorry," she said. "But it doesn't look as if your dream was all it was cracked up to be. You have just spent the last two months with me. Aren't you tired of me yet?"

"I think I could take it one more day," he replied, dryly.

"But it's Christmas! It's party time. You can't have a party with two people."

"Partying is a state of mind," he argued. "We could have a party if we wanted to."

"Alright," she agreed. "Let's party."

She had put him on the spot and she knew it. It was unfair. The moment, if there had ever been one, was lost. Whether she had meant it or not, the inference that she was fed up with him was too much of a wound to ignore. But she was far from finished.

"You see," she declared. "We can't do it. We can't do it because it isn't possible. Because you don't want to, do you? If it were up to you we would light a couple of candles, eat dinner staring into each others' eyes, relax on the couch, get tipsy in front of a Disney cartoon and then have passionate sex all over the carpet. And then we would eat and drink some more and repeat the whole process over again."

Martyn remained silent because he could do nothing else. Not only had Melissa described in accurate detail his ideal Christmas Day but he was at a total loss to understand what was wrong with it. She had phrased and intoned her speech as an accusation against him. And what could he do but plead guilty? It was all true. He loved her and wanted to be with her, to make love with her, to celebrate Christmas in blissful intimacy. Yes, he was guilty. But of what?

46

Gremelkov's visit to the city was to take place on the fourth of January following "East Peace Parades" - as they became known - in Washington DC on the first and New York the day after. In retrospect it seemed inevitable that an assassination attempt would occur at some point because, secretly, that was what everybody really wanted to happen. It was just that no one wanted the embarrassment of having it happen under his or her jurisdiction.

To Martyn Sorensen, it seemed equally inevitable that Gremelkov would be assassinated in the city. The odds had been stacked against them more than two months before when the first of the many death threats came rolling blatantly and brashly into the department. As a result, the entire departmental resource had, for three months, been solely devoted to getting Gremelkov in and out of the city alive. And yet, despite all the intense activity within the police organisation, the most they could have hoped for was that he might be killed in Washington or New York first.

In addition to providing the highest level of security they could afford on the day, two other strategies were adopted: one being to trace the origins of all the death threats against the Alliance Ambassador, which numbered over two hundred; the other being to attempt to quell the anger of the populace through clever and subtle propaganda.

The first strategy was nothing short of a complete waste of time and resources. Of the two hundred and fifteen death threats received, one hundred and seventy nine were untraceable and the remainder were the work of cranks or harmless objectors, venting their anger by jumping on the bandwagon with only the weakest attempts at anonymity.

The propaganda campaign, though ultimately a failure, had its roots planted firmly at the heart of the problem. By challenging the very beliefs that had been upheld since the end of the Great Turmoil, it appeared to be more successful. In attempting to indoctrinate the population with "peace and goodwill" for a solid month, even the most ardent anti-Communist campaigners had noticeably softened and seemed willing to forgive and forget. Television and radio had broadcast more documentaries on the Eastern Alliance over the five weeks prior to Christmas than they had over the previous five years. The evidence that the campaign was having an effect was provided by the Association of Travel Agencies who reported a dramatic five hundred percent increase in bookings for holidays and tours in the eastern hemisphere. For the first time since the turn of the century, the country was seeing the Alliance in a new light and no longer as the cold, grey, merciless nation they had imprisoned in their mental time capsules all those years ago. The year 2000 HTE was to be a year of political and international enlightenment.

And yet, in all this new found goodwill, it had only ever needed one person, determined and clever enough to succeed, and the underlying purpose of it all - to keep Gremelkov alive - would end in abject failure.

On New Years Day, 2030, the population of the city was one point seven million.

One person in one point seven million.

January 4th, 2030.

The morning of Gremelkov's visit began peacefully, though Detective Sorensen was subsequently quoted in The Standard as saying it began 'ominously'. Either way, despite repeated threats of snow, the sun rose over a cloudless winter blue sky casting long, soft shadows along the two mile length of Eden Boulevard, stretching west towards the plaza at its summit. In Eden Square, where the presentation stage had been erected for the midday celebration, and the water show fountains bubbled quietly through the silent dawn, Martyn found himself alone. He was contemplating a host of confusing thoughts, not least the paradox that the city he was beginning to hate so much, looked so beautiful in this rare morning light.

Neither Martyn nor Rob had been party to any of the police investigations that led up to this day. Though they had both returned to work two weeks beforehand, they had been assigned to other duties. It was only at the last minute, when it became evident that Gremelkov was going to emerge from New York in one piece, that Brett Lancaster had asked them to join the security operation.

The operation itself was fairly straight forward. Gremelkov's official appearance in the city was to begin at the end of Eden Boulevard. Until then, the location of his whereabouts, and his method of transport to the start of the cavalcade, would be known only to a handful of authorised persons. That did not include either Martyn or Rob. From that point, the two mile procession, beginning at exactly 11:30 and moving at a steady six miles an hour, would take twenty minutes, depositing Gremelkov in the square at eleven fifty. This would be the most dangerous point of all; transferring the ambassador from the car to the stage. Until then, there was little anyone without an anti-tank missile launcher could do. Both the bodywork and glass of the car had been designed to be impenetrable to shells from the highest powered rifle. Even a close proximity explosion from a hand grenade would leave the occupants suffering from little more than shock and perhaps a loud ringing in the ears. The stage was also equipped with various anti-terrorist devices. All in all, there seemed little point in worrying about either.

The plan to get Gremelkov from the car to the stage was a little more primitive - surround him with so much security that no one could get near him. Although it did reduce the chance of Gremelkov being struck down by anyone who could not get close enough, it did mean that the only way to kill him was to kill several other people as well.

Flicking his security ID at a lone security guard, Martyn wandered onto the stage and ambled slowly towards the podium, trying to follow the route which Gremelkov would take later that morning and assess every building and cubby hole which came into sight during the short walk. The list was short and thankfully comprehensive.

When it was anticipated that the turnout was going to be much larger than originally estimated, it became clear that they would have to allow access to buildings and roofs. On Eden Boulevard, the entire two mile stretch was lined with office blocks and apartment buildings. Even to attempt to enforce a ban on people watching from windows or balconies would have been unworkable, and it was obvious that the sidewalks would not be able to contain the volume of people expected to turn out.

Likewise, the plaza at Eden Square was surrounded by buildings on all sides. But there were too many to run an effective surveillance operation and again it would not have been possible to ban people from inhabiting or appearing at the windows of their own homes during the celebration.

Having effectively had the route decided for them, the police insisted on altering the layout and position of the stage. It was originally to have been in the centre of the square and open on all sides. As Chief Lancaster subsequently pointed out, they might as well cancel the police operation. They could not possibly eradicate the risk that an assassin's bullet could be fired from any one of the surrounding buildings, so the plan was scrapped. Instead, a stage was erected near the Boulevard corner of the Square, protected on three sides and from above, and with the podium facing across a diagonal of the plaza. Now, the only buildings which could be seen from the stage were on the other side of the square over three hundred metres away. The only cost of this change was the erection of two large outdoor video screens to enable those at the far corner of the plaza to gain some idea of what the tiny specks they could see in the distance actually looked like.

From the podium at the centre of the stage, Martyn scanned the buildings around the far side of the Square. Since the podium left only Gremelkov's head and shoulders exposed, it seemed that only the best marksman in the business would be able to hit a human target at that distance. One false shot and the three bullet-proof screens that lay at the feet of the podium would spring up and surround the speaker in the wink of an eye. Martyn therefore deduced that any realistic attempt at an assassination would have to take place between the end of the procession and the stage since that was when Gremelkov would be most exposed.

As he studied the buildings along the eastern side of the plaza, his eyes fell on a side street - wet cobbles glistening in the early morning sun - and he was reminded of his other reason for being there so early. The ghostly image of the mysterious girl with the flowers preyed constantly on his mind. It was a simple task to superimpose the apparition he had seen in the forest with the vision he had witnessed in that lonely cobbled street two months before - and know that they were one and the same. His intuition also assured him that the girl he had seen in the forest and the square was the same person whose photograph he had found in Howard Robinson's apartment.

Yet at that point his mind refused to make any more connections. He had considered the possibilities, or impossibilities, of the situation – in fact, he had introspectively analysed them all over and over until he was utterly confused - but he could find no logical explanation. And when he did occasionally stumble on a solution, however implausible, he did not like it. In the end, all his thoughts could be categorised into one of three possibilities: he had witnessed a bizarre string of coincidences, he was going insane or there was a deeper, unnatural, more sinister explanation which he could not possibly comprehend. Since he did not believe in coincidences this left a choice of two: either he was going insane or he was being haunted. It was not much of a choice - and he did not believe in ghosts.

There were so many questions and not a single answer. But if there were an explanation then he believed he would find it here, in Eden Square. This was where it had all begun and perhaps this would be where it would end. It was for this reason that he found himself alone, facing the eastern cobbled street in quiet reflection as dawn split the Earth from the sky and the cobbles exploded into splashes of red haze.

He and Rob had both been assigned to patrol the Square but they had not been asked to start this early. He had agreed to meet Rob for breakfast at nine in the hope that the crowds would not begin congregating until well after. But already small groups of spectators were claiming their ground in the plaza and by nine he figured they would be hungry enough to make breakfast time a nightmarish event as the few food outlets around the square raised their shutters and opened their doors to the waiting throngs.

He had woken early, while it was still dark, his sexual desire aroused and his body covered in the sweat of an active libido. Beside him Melissa slept on, breathing steadily, oblivious to the unrequited frustration within him. Not so long ago, she would have woken with him, the chemistry of their mutual lust penetrating their dreams and bringing them both into sexual consciousness. But that time had passed and he was no longer sure whether it had been real or not. He had noticed how she had gradually varied her bedtime until she rarely chose to turn in at the same time as he did. Either she would retire early and he would find her asleep (or pretending to be asleep) - or she would stay up until the early hours. Then she would either wake early and be up and about before he had surfaced, or she would sleep in until she had left herself the minimum amount of time to get ready for work. Either way, there was no opportunity to make love. Almost overnight Melissa had been transformed into a virtual stranger, determined suddenly to remain in a cocoon, a miserable and impenetrable prison of longing and regret that she had created around herself. And he did not know if this self centred, self pitying world were of his own creation, or how, or where it would end.

From his pocket he drew out the bulletin he had collected from Personnel the previous evening. He placed it on the podium and began to skip read from paragraph to paragraph, pausing only briefly at one or two before continuing through the pages. There was a job going in Denver; same line of work but less stressful, where he might actually be able to make a recognisable impact. At first he had considered moving right out of the force and had immediately come against an impasse. Either he was not qualified to do anything else or it was not qualified to retain his interest. The role of detective was an addiction and he had been too late to realise it. It was what he was good at and it was a job he could believe in. But the city was beginning to sink under a constantly expanding wave of crime and he was not going to sink with it. More importantly, he was not going to let Melissa live through it because he now doubted that their relationship could survive the continual trauma.

As yet, he had not told Melissa of his plans. When he had first conceived the idea, as they both shared the optimistic tranquillity of the lake country, he had wanted to tell her straight away. But he had held off in favour of surprising her when it had all been finalised. He did not want to raise her hopes only to have them dashed at the last moment. Now he was not sure whether that was what she really wanted and his reasons for not telling her had changed. He could no longer read her wishes and she no longer expressed them. He did not know whether she still yearned to escape from the city or whether her pain was even more fundamental than that. Of course, she still complained about their life in Satan's suburbia but they had both realised, in one of their few successful conversations, that they actually needed to live in a city. The lakes had been paradise, it was true, but it could never have been more than a temporary haven, a convalescence of the soul.

So he had settled on Denver, considered one of the most pleasant cities not only because of its low crime rate but also for its cleanliness and the attractiveness of its altitude environment. The question he now had to address was; when should he tell Melissa? As time passed by the plan that he should surprise her seemed less of a good one. He had no idea how she would react and that was what concerned him most. He should be more sure of her than this.

Folding the bulletin, he placed it back in his pocket, deciding that it could not do any harm to follow it up later that afternoon. Then all he needed was to find an opportunity to talk it through with Melissa. But that was another problem. First he had to see the back of Gremelkov - and make sure nobody else could.

After some consideration he had called Rob at home and asked him to meet some blocks away from the Square and the hungry crowds. He selected a small cafe in the Latin quarter that Angelo had once owned before moving closer to Arcades where there was more custom. Angelo had even once hinted that he might be safer situated near to the police department but, as it turned out, he could not have been more wrong.

Rob was already seated at the table, and a wide grin illuminated his face when Martyn appeared.

"You've been up a long time, haven't you?" he said. "What's wrong? Nervous?"

"About Gremelkov? You know I don't worry about things like that. All we can do is our best."

"I wasn't thinking about the big G," Rob replied. "I was thinking more about the big M. - looming on the horizon."

"The big M? What's that?"

"You know. Wedding bells, ice cake, *best man*."

He emphasised the last remark pointedly, deliberately slowing the words. "I even ordered us a champagne breakfast." Just as the waiter arrived with exactly that.

"Rob, what on earth are you talking about?"

Rob was not prepared to let go that easily.

"You know, I should have guessed this would happen. Exiling you to paradise for two months without another soul in sight. It was written in the stars." He proceeded to pour the champagne.

"What's written in the stars?"

Rob was silent.

"I don't like champagne."

"Alright," Rob conceded. "I came here via the office and there is a message on your desk from some jewellers in Arcades - something about a ring being ready."

Martyn shrugged his shoulders in surprise and defeat.

"Discretion is alive and well and living in Arcades," he sighed. "Anyway, don't drink too much of this because I'm having second thoughts. Things aren't working out too well right now."

"What? Between you and Melissa? You mean you two not get married? I thought that was the only event we were all sure of in this world. Personally, as you know, I think your relationship is nauseatingly sweet. It's such a fairy tale romance it's untrue. But not get married? It's unthinkable. Come on, you'll work it out. It's a bad patch, that's all. You've both finally joined the human race."

Martyn offered no reply.

"You do still want to marry her, don't you?"

"Of course I do. She's just gone into this deep depression and I can't shake her out of it. I can't say or do anything right and I don't think an engagement ring would help right now. I'm just going to have to sit it out this time. The ring will have to wait."

"Oh, well," Rob said, re-corking the bottle. "We shouldn't really be drinking before the big G. arrives anyway. Maybe we can put it away later after he's gone."

"Sounds good to me. Right, let's eat. I've been up for hours and I'm starving."

Between mouthfuls of croissant and blueberry muffin, they made small talk and ran over the programme for the morning. Rob had the champagne put back on ice and replaced with a carafe of fresh orange juice. They ate a hearty breakfast, laughing and joking, and Martyn gradually began to forget his worries and relax. He and Rob might not have much in common but he was good company when it came to celebrations, however premature.

Suddenly, without warning, Martyn jumped up from the table, flinging his arms in the air and sending his chair and a glass of orange juice hurtling into the table behind. There was a scream of disgust as the contents of the glass splattered all over the pale yellow dress of a woman seated behind and soaked through to make skin contact with its owner. Within one second, all eyes in the restaurant were looking in their direction.

Martyn was speechless and looked stunned. Rob looked on for a second incomprehensibly and then took control of the situation. Quickly, he apologised to the occupants of the table behind and left a card for them to call him to settle up the cleaning bill. He handed a cheque to the waiter who had rushed over, cloth in hand, and then ushered Martyn across the restaurant and out of the nearest fire exit.

Out in the corridor, Martyn was helped by his partner onto a small bench and sat down inhaling deep breaths.

"You know, I did that a couple of times last week. Once, I sat bolt upright in bed and I swore I could hear the echoes of gunfire and explosions ringing in my ears. I did exactly the same as you in the office the next morning when I fell asleep at my desk. Luckily, I wasn't holding a glass of orange juice at the time and no one else seemed to notice. You must have begun to nod off back there. I guess it is going to live with us for a lot longer than we expected."

"No," Martyn said, breaking his silence. "That wasn't it. It was something else. But I don't understand." He felt and sounded confused but what good would it do to try and explain it to Rob, especially since Rob had provided him with the perfect excuse not to have to explain anything.

"What was it then?" Rob said. "You looked as if you'd been stung by a wasp or something."

Martyn checked himself before speaking. "No, you're right. I must have begun to fall asleep. It took me by surprise, that's all. Damn, how embarrassing."

"It can't have been the first time, surely?" Rob prompted. "Not so long after it happened."

Then Martyn understood. Rob had been plagued by nightmares ever since the battle at the docks. Too ashamed to talk about it to anyone, he was evidently relieved to find that Martyn had the same problem. Martyn could only feel sorry for him because he no longer suffered from nightmares of that evening. Rob was no less alone with these trauma symptoms than he had been before. But he did not have to let Rob know that.

"No, it wasn't the first time."

But he was lying; too confused to talk rationally about what had happened but equally embarrassed at his own predicament. For what he had experienced was beyond his comprehension and his imagination. For one brief moment the air around him had turned icy cold and he could have sworn that the dogs which snapped at his ankles were real.

The two detectives spent the rest of the morning patrolling the square, always in touch by personal radio and rendezvousing in successive and opposite corners of the square every fifteen minutes or so. For the time being, Martyn was able to forget the incident in the cafe, and his other worries, and concentrate on the task in hand. However, as the morning progressed, this became increasingly difficult. He began by scrutinising every party of onlookers and mentally categorising them into innocent bystanders or potential assassins. There were so few in the latter category that, on each circuit of the square, he would recognise them all and subtract a few more from his list. But as more people arrived the list of people 'worthy of further attention' became longer and his brain could not handle such a large number.

To counter this he set up a system with Rob whereby Martyn would walk one side of the square until he reached a corner and would then transmit a description of a handful of 'possibles' to Rob. While Martyn then patrolled along the next length of plaza gathering a new list, Rob would follow up behind eliminating or compounding suspicion on those on the former.

By eleven o'clock the square was full and it had become impossible both to keep count or to move. Martyn decided that he would complete his patrol of the eastern edge of the square and then stop when he reached the north eastern corner and wait for Rob to catch up. There would then be just enough time to climb up on some of the roofs of the surrounding buildings before Gremelkov arrived. On arriving at the corner he paused to consider whether he should waste any more time by transmitting a final list. But what the hell, Rob had to come up this way anyway. He switched on the walkie-talkie, waited for Rob's response and then transmitted.

"Two male Caucasians in dark suits fifty metres north north west, a lone white male in brown sweater and jeans and carrying a green travel bag thirty metres due north, close to him a raven haired woman with dark glasses and fur coat..."

Having closed off the transmission, leaving Rob to carry out one final sweep, two thoughts struck him almost simultaneously - so close together that very soon after he could not remember in which order they had come. The first, if indeed it had been the first, was that he was standing in the exact spot that Howard Robinson's body had been found. The second was more of a sensation, an intuition, and one which he recognised from his last visit to the square.

He was being watched.

Rob took longer than expected catching up with him and when he did he was evidently thankful that he would not have to do another stretch.

"This is getting ridiculous," he exclaimed. "It took me ages to find half of these and by that time my mind was so full of fur coats, sweat shirts and suspicious packages I forgot what you were wearing and it took me even longer to find you. Couldn't you have waited a little nearer the edge?"

"I could have but then we wouldn't have been so clear about how futile this patrol idea really was. Did you remember to bring the binoculars?"

"Sure, they're in the car. I'll go and fetch them. It's over there." He turned, waving his arm liberally in the air while he caught his bearings. Then, indicating positively in the direction of the station, he suddenly paused.

"Say, isn't this where they found Howard Robinson?" Then, without waiting for a reply he pushed his way through the crowd.

"I'll see you on that roof over there."

For half an hour they made their way back along the eastern edge of the square by rooftop, occasionally jumping narrow gaps between buildings, sometimes returning to ground level to cross a road or where the buildings were at different heights. At around eleven thirty they settled down on one of the taller roofs along the south side of the square.

"It's no use going on any further," Martyn said. "If we do we won't be able to get back to the north east corner in time for Gremelkov's arrival.

Besides, this is the perfect spot from which to survey the proceedings. I wish we'd come straight here."

From their vantage point they could claim a panoramic view of the square and its immediate surroundings, including a large number of rooftops on either side. Behind them lay the vast bus terminal, subtly and thankfully hidden within a huge crater of tall office blocks. To the west, rising skywards above them were the skyscrapers of the commercial sector, the New Century Tower dwarfing all around it like a bridge to the moon. Directly to the north, nestled between droves of smaller hotels was the Eden Square rail terminus, hardly representing on the surface a fraction of the rail and pedestrian interchange tunnel system that lay underneath. And most notably, stretching away from the north east corner of the square, as far as they could see, Eden Boulevard, lined with throngs of expectant onlookers awaiting the oncoming cavalcade.

Below them, in the packed plaza, they had a clear view of the stage opposite and of the two video screens that had been erected on either side. The videos followed the progress of the cavalcade as it made its way slowly towards the square, its path strewn with garlands of flowers and the air littered with floating streamers and darting tickertape. A huge public address system amplified the cheers of the roadside watchers to those still waiting in the square

"Ever heard of exploding flowers?" Rob asked.

Martyn grinned. "That would not be funny. Come on, if we leave now we'll get over there in time to beat the arrival of your hero."

Reluctantly, Rob rose to his feet.

"You realise that if anyone does decide to take Gremelkov in the Square, they will probably have to kill a few other people as well. And that includes us. We've made it so difficult for a sniper that any prospective assassin is going to have to walk right in there with a bomb. They don't have a choice."

"I know that. But we don't have a choice either. Besides, if it happens it will cure those nightmares."

Suddenly, the gasp of several thousand people rose up from the square below and they stopped in surprise. On the video, someone had run into the street holding what looked like a petrol bomb. As the camera panned in, the figure just managed to hurl the fireball directly at the windscreen of the oncoming vehicle before being pounced on by several security men. The vessel shattered, spurting flames over the entire front half of the car as the crowd panicked and pushed back to get out of the way.

"Shit, they'll be crushed," Rob yelled. But he need not have wasted his breath. Three simultaneous flashes of light exploded on the rear of Martyn's retina. The first and second came from the two video screens in the square below. The third shot out from the distance – somewhere along the boulevard - and lit the horizon far more spectacularly than any sunrise. As the public address died, the air was filled with the screams of hellish souls as they drifted, terrified, from the mouth of the boulevard and into the square.

Both men were horror-struck, gazing helplessly into the distance as a plume of black smoke rose into the sky. Rob closed his eyes, and under his breath whispered two words which had emanated from the lips of men throughout history. Today they were *officially* two thousand years old.

"Jesus Christ." It was the most simple of prayers.

Martyn could not utter a sound.

47

Chief Brett Lancaster was in no mood to mince words. As he entered the office, followed closely by Commander Colchek of the Special Forces Network, he uttered one sentence, succinct and unhelpful.

"We're in the shit."

Like Martyn and Rob he had spent almost the entire night supervising the police operation on Eden Boulevard, watching helplessly as body bag after body bag had been loaded into the waiting ambulance convoy, like so many sacks of potatoes being despatched to the supermarket. The blast had been so great that they had been forced to cordon off the two mile stretch of the boulevard to be sure of trapping all of the evidence. Although Martyn and Rob had both rationalised that any successful assassination attempt would have necessarily involved a bloodbath, both were equally unprepared for the massacre that had occurred.

As they left the square, fighting their way through the retreating, panic-stricken crowds, they had first tasted the horror of what lay ahead half a mile from the scene. At first, Martyn had thought that a young woman had fallen while hoards of people trampled her underfoot, oblivious to her presence. In desperation, using Rob to hold off the force of the oncoming crowd, he had grabbed at the slender, fragile arm and tried to pull her to safety. But it came too easily. Before he could make any attempt to correct his action, he found himself clutching a bare and bloodied limb, severed cleanly above the elbow. Without thinking, he instinctively tossed it back to the ground in nauseating disgust, too numb to feel even an ounce of sadness and pity for the man who had placed the ring on her third finger.

Only after the arm had disappeared from view, under a torrent of flailing legs, did Rob remind him that it might be needed for identification. Though the thought had already crossed his mind, he was thankful that he did not have to carry it with him. Only when he considered the possibility that its owner might be alive, and that medical science might still be able to save the arm, that he felt stabs of guilt at responding so reactively. However, as they neared the scene of the blast and witnessed the full extent of the atrocity, all thoughts of that one limb vanished from his mind.

The road and sidewalks were littered with bodies and various distorted parts of the anatomy. Lumps of unrecognisable flesh and bloody muscle hung from the lower branches of trees and wrapped themselves round lamp posts. The tableau before them was so horrific that it seemed unreal - almost surreal - and it was only the stench, which made him want to retch every few seconds, that brought home the horrific truth.

Though no more than a burned out shell of grotesquely twisted metal, most of the police activity was centred around the limousine that had been carrying Gremelkov while the paramedics were left to deal with the human carnage. When Martyn had left, at three o'clock the following morning, there were still some bodies waiting to be moved. And, as he arrived at the apartment, tired and emotionally drained, he could still hear Brett Lancaster's voice ringing in his ears.

In my office, first thing tomorrow morning.

He thought Melissa might have waited up for him but he entered the bedroom to find her breathing softly in deep slumber. He wanted to hold her, close and naked, to feel the touch of her soft skin against his, for her to hold him so tightly that their bodies welded together. But he knew that he would not be able to take any form of rejection and for the present, at least, he felt it wiser to avoid the possibility. He spent the rest of the night on the couch and did not sleep at all.

At nine the next morning, Detectives Sorensen, Laurie and Martyn's old partner, Andy Holland sat in conference with Chief Lancaster and Commander Colchek. The Chief looked tired, evidently under a great deal of pressure. Martyn recalled the last occasion on which they had all met and reflected on Brett's comments about his appearance. This time the Chief looked far worse and was still wearing the same clothes as on the previous day. Like the rest of them he had not shaved. Unlike the rest of them, this was probably because he had not been home. Whatever the state of their appearance, the Commander did not seem interested and was preoccupied with more important things.

"Let's get a few things clear from the start," he said. "First of all, despite anything else you might have heard, these are the official casualty statistics."

As he spoke, he drew a sheet of paper from his pocket.

"Seventeen dead. Forty seven injured, fifteen critical, twenty three serious. Eleven people were crushed in the resulting stampede. In respect of the last figure, we should count ourselves lucky that it was not any higher."

He looked up at the three detectives who evidently did not count themselves lucky in any way.

"You have about three hours of video tape to sit through today so I hope you are going to be more wide eyed than you are at present."

The Commander spoke in his own inimitable style, a bombastic bull in a traumatised china shop. He obviously adopted this personality to keep morale and motivation at a high, Martyn thought. Well that might work in the SFN but frankly he had no time for it. But he was too tired to argue. The Commander continued, undeterred by any lack of response.

"And, in case any of you is still in any doubt, the explosion was not caused by any petrol bomb the size of a wine bottle. The experts have been studying the tapes and the wreckage all night. They are all agreed that the blast was almost certainly caused by a bomb planted underneath the fuel tank - though as yet we have only recovered about one quarter of the fuel tank and have not found anything that looks remotely like a detonating device."

Suddenly, Andy Holland spoke up, betraying the reason for his presence.

"And you won't," he said. "For the last fucking time, there was no bomb in, on, around or underneath that car. It was checked and double checked thoroughly. At the hotel, before the cavalcade left, I had the whole thing practically stripped down and put back together again. And then, at the end of the boulevard, before the procession began, I had bomb disposal experts and sniffer dogs all over it. The car was as clean as your driving licence. If there was a bomb there then it was either invisible or undetectable - or it existed in a different dimension."

As the officer with the responsibility of safeguarding Gremelkov's limousine, Andy Holland had been thrown violently on the defensive by the events of the last twenty four hours. Following the massacre at the supermarket three months before, and the complete lack of progress in apprehending the culprits, he had been transferred to the bomb squad. Not that anyone blamed him directly but the department had to be seen to be taking some sort of action. And now this. Martyn could not believe how unlucky his old partner had been but the effects of the strain were beginning to show. He looked and behaved like a trapped animal backed into a corner. And the Commander seemed intent on provoking him.

"Well, if there was no bomb on the car then it must have been planted on the road. You have spent most of the morning scanning the tapes, Holland. Is there anything there? No, there is not. The tapes quite clearly show both that the road was clear and that no one got anywhere near the car during the course of the procession, with the exception of the petrol bomber whom we have discounted. So how do you explain that?"

"Maybe one of the flowers exploded," suggested Rob.

"That is not funny," the Commander replied.

"I was being serious," Rob said, and then backed down slightly. "Well, I was trying to be helpful anyway."

"Perhaps the fuel tank just exploded," Andy Holland suggested, lamely.

"Well it would be the first time in history if it did. Fuel tanks on limousines do not just explode, they have to be ignited. You're clutching at straws, Holland."

"I might be clutching at straws but at least I want to know the truth. You have absolutely no evidence that there was a bomb on that car but you seem intent on discounting any other possibilities."

The Commander looked incredulous. "What! Like exploding flowers and spontaneous combusting fuel tanks. Give me a break, Holland. I was not born yesterday. Let's get this over with, shall we? From the end of this meeting, you are suspended pending an investigation into your competence or otherwise during this operation. Now get out of my sight."

Rob, who was momentarily distracted, suddenly came back to life.

"What? All three of us?"

"Wake up, man," the Commander yelled, directly at Rob. "You are here for quite another reason, though I'm damned if I can see why."

Martyn was growing more and more concerned at what appeared to be a one man lynch mob against Andy Holland. Colchek did not have that authority. He was also becoming equally concerned that the Chief was not saying anything. He wanted to speak out in his ex-partner's defence but he could not raise the energy to take Commander Colchek on. But that was not all; by Brett Lancaster's own silence, he suspected that more than one personnel change had taken place that morning.

"And what reason is that?" Rob asked.

Martyn looked bored. "Can't you guess? We've got the case."

"But of course you have," the Commander said. "You're obvious candidates. You weren't involved in the original Gremelkov investigation and so you are still functioning as acclaimed heroes as far as everyone else is concerned. Here is yet another golden opportunity to maintain your glorified status. Solve this one and you'll be more popular than rock stars."

"Or dead."

"Come, come," said the Commander. "I have every confidence in you, especially since my forensic department and the entire Network is going to be at your service. Let them do all the work and you take all the credit. It's the natural order of things. We don't like to have such a high public profile in my organisation"

Martyn briefly recalled the events of the dockland siege, how he still believed that he had almost died at the hands of the SFN.

"No, I'm not surprised."

While Martyn recognised that the Commander was blatantly mocking them he also felt that such an attitude was beneath him and that there was an ulterior motive for his goading. Presumably, he intended them to take up the challenge and pull out all the stops just to spite him. It seemed a little coarse and childish as a method of motivation; it certainly didn't do anything for him but maybe it worked in the SFN. He was proved wrong almost instantaneously. Rob suddenly rose to his feet and opened the door of the office. In an extremely rare outburst, brought on no doubt by fatigue and frustration, Rob turned to the Commander and spoke in a low but vicious murmur.

"You'll soon be laughing on the other side of your face, you smug bastard."

It was the first thing Martyn had found amusing in days and he failed miserably to suppress a grin. But the Commander seemed equally pleased.

"I hope so," he said. "The sooner the better, eh? I don't think you can do much yet. Just keep your nose to the grindstone, familiarise yourself with all the evidence and let's wait and see what the forensic lads come up with."

Without waiting for Rob to complete his stormy exit, the Commander rose from his chair and left.

Chief Lancaster looked up from his desk and spoke to Rob.

"Boy, you really fell for that one."

They were the only words he had spoken throughout the conference and not only did they lack humour but Martyn swore he could detect a hint of castigation that he could not quite explain. The words seemed to say something else.

Don't make that mistake again or you may live to regret it.

It was not just a chastisement.

It was a warning.

48

At the door to his apartment he reached into the right hand pocket of his jacket, searching for the key. His hand fell on the small velvet box and he toyed with it thoughtfully. Though he still had the choice whether to give the ring to Melissa or not, he was nervous - even terrified - of being rejected. His stomach was tied into myriad tiny reef knots and he could sense the sweat from his hand soaking into the velvet. He would have to be sure before he took the plunge. Very sure. Clenching his fist tightly, his heartbeat rising slightly with the tension, he inserted the key into the lock and went into the apartment.

He found Melissa in the bedroom, a forlorn figure gazing vacantly out of the window. As he carefully creaked open the door she turned to face him, her expression one of sadness, of empty dreams and lost chances. For what seemed like a lifetime he stared at her and she returned his gaze in kind. Neither of them wanted to break the silence and the longer it continued, the more difficult it was to speak.

I love you. Say it. Please say it.

But Melissa was silent. He felt for the ring in his pocket, searching for a source of strength that would enable him to speak.

"I love you," he whispered.

Still she remained silent. Then, without changing her expression, she suddenly held up a photograph. Her voice was quiet, calm, cold.

"What's this?"

The photograph was of her, or someone who looked like her. A ghost from the past. The eyes pierced through his whole being from across the bedroom. He knew what was written on the reverse. But he could not answer her question because she had already jumped to her own conclusions, he could see that. In his absence, she had conducted her own trial and found him guilty, unforgivably guilty. All of this was written on her face and reflected repeatedly in the teardrops that stained her cheek.

"I said, 'What is this?'" she hissed.

"I don't know," he replied, trying to sound rational and calm. "I was trying to find out. I didn't want to raise your hopes. I didn't want you to be hurt."

"How long have you had it?"

"About three months."

She looked at him as if she could not believe his audacity.

"Three months!" Her voice was becoming raised now. "You've had it three months and you haven't found out who it is. Damn it, you're supposed to be a detective, aren't you? You can find people overnight if you really want to. Besides, you do know who it is; you just didn't want me to know. You wanted to deprive me of the one thing I have always longed for."

"Melissa, don't be silly. You know I would never…"

"…She's my mother, isn't she?"

"Melissa, I don't know. She might be. I have no way of being sure. It might be an almighty coincidence."

"A coincidence!" she screamed. She thrust the photograph to the end of her outstretched arm and those eyes continued to burn into him.

"How the hell can it be a coincidence? She looks just like me! She has my name."

He did not speak. He was transfixed by the hypnotic beauty of this haunting vision, paralysed by the smile he had not seen for so long.

"Where is she?"

"Melissa…" He stopped himself. How could he tell her? How could she possibly understand about the ghost that had haunted him since the discovery of the photograph? How could she possibly believe him or even begin to comprehend what he had been through? But now her eyes were digging into him and he felt his whole world falling apart under the power of that stare. How could he not tell her?

"I think she's dead," he said. "Whoever she is."

Another tear fell onto her cheek and he felt a deep sense of sadness at its passing.

"Where did you get it?" she asked.

"I can't tell you."

If he had felt insecure under her gaze before, it was nothing compared to what he felt now. To escape from that accusing glare that turned him to stone, he would gladly have crawled into a small hole in some far off corner of the universe and stayed there until the end of time. But for now he had to endure a sudden barrage of questions and he had no choice but to face them head on.

"How do you know she's dead?"

"I don't know for certain. I just have good reason to believe…"

"What reason?"

"Melissa, it's tied up with a case. It's classified information. I shouldn't even have it here. It's evidence. If anyone found out then I'd be in serious…"

"Including me? When was I going to find out? Or were you never going to tell me you'd discovered who my mother was? You didn't want me to know because you wanted to keep me trapped in your cosy little world, didn't you? A long lost mother would have been so inconvenient. It would have ruined everything for you. Admit it. You were never going to tell me."

"Melissa, you're getting hysterical. How could you possibly think that? I love you, for pity's sake. Why is it you have so much trouble understanding that, all of a sudden? Melissa, listen to yourself. What's happening to us? We were so happy together."

She ceased the barrage of questions and lowered her head, wiping a tear away with the back of her hand. For several minutes they sat in silence. When she finally spoke it was more softly.

"It was all a dream," she said. "It could never have lasted. I'm sorry, Martyn. I really don't want to hurt you but I'm confused. I don't know what to think anymore. I don't think it was really ever meant to be."

"Melissa, don't say that. Please don't say that. How can you throw it all away so easily? I don't understand."

"I don't understand, either," she said. She picked up a small overnight bag. He had not noticed it before.

"I won't be spending the night here. I need some time to think. You do too."

He said nothing. He did not move. Melissa walked towards him and paused. She kissed him softly on the cheek, sensed the sweet aroma of her perfume clouding his senses and sending his head spinning into delirium.

"It's better you don't know where I am," she said. "I'll be back in a couple of days."

And in that one brief moment, as the bedroom door closed behind her, he died a thousand deaths and felt more pain than his entire nervous system was capable of registering from his insignificant and fragile body.

49

Despite the initial shock and disappointment at finding the Millstone Hotel had changed hands in such a short space of time, Howard decided to stay overnight. There was little else he could do since he had already missed the last train back to Manchester. Even if he had not, it would still have left him with the problem of where to sleep as there was little chance of making an onward connection to London so late. And so, although he had taken an instant dislike to the new style Millstone with its gaudy neon and glitter decor, he was committed to making it a temporary residence.

Accepting that he had no choice about whether he stayed the night or not, he had begrudgingly filled out the registration form and booked into his old room. He was the only guest. In just a few weeks the whole ambience of the hotel had changed. It was no longer a place he wished to stay in for any length of time. He had discovered that Susannah had emigrated with her family to Spain to run a beachside bar but no more was known. She simply was not there – and all traces of her presence appeared to have left with her.

The impersonal functionality of the room only served to heighten his loneliness. He thought of the friends he had made in school; the kids from the neighbourhood he had hung around street corners with; the teenage girls he had dated who were now all grown up with husbands and children of their own. All of these he had gladly given up when he met Melissa, sometimes with relief, carelessly abandoning his roots and the world of his upbringing in the belief that he had found something better.

But he had played double or quits with fate. For a time - so very short a time - he believed he had won. It seemed only natural that love should. And at the time, it was worth all the sacrifices; he had no doubt about that. Yet fate had been cruel. Now he was left alone, he regretted the ties he had severed. Those people seemed so important to him now. But how could he go back? They would probably not even recognise him. Instead he was left clutching at straws. He had travelled to Darwen in the hope of rekindling a friendship with the last person he had managed to converse with on a human level, outside of his relationship with Melissa. Yet even if she had been here, what was he to her? Just another hotel guest among all the nameless faces that must pass through these rooms week after week. There was no guarantee that she would have even remembered his name…

Howard wanted to be ready to leave the Millstone the minute the library was open. On the dot of nine o'clock therefore, having chosen to miss breakfast, he stood at the front door of the hotel and pulled the collar of his coat tightly around his neck. There was a steady drizzle in the air offering a reasonable chance he would get wet, even during the short walk across the place and through the bus station. Nevertheless, he set off, at the last minute choosing not to check out early so he could leave his overnight bag behind and avoid having to carry it.

The library - an old building with a distinctive dome over the entrance - was situated directly behind the bus station. Inside the foyer was a second dome - this one made of glass - and inside that, an impressive scale model of the Victoria Tower on Darwen Moor. Beside it, there was a brief history explaining how the Tower had been constructed to mark the celebration of Queen Victoria's jubilee year. On the far wall, a number of poems - all about the tower - displayed the writing talents of local school children.

For a few moments he ambled around the foyer, examining the scale model from every angle and looking at pictures of old Darwen spread around the walls. Then he entered the main library and headed straight for the section on local history. There was not a huge range of books available and he quickly selected six and took them into the reading room where he could study them quietly to himself. It did not take long. In less than thirty minutes he had found a number of partial answers to his questions and was left wondering what it all meant.

It was clear from the references that a significant and successful civil campaign had been fought a century before to allow the citizens of Darwen - and the general public – access to the moors following a dispute over land rights. Soon after, when faced with the problem of how the town should celebrate Queen Victoria's jubilee year, the local newspaper had provided a forum for gathering ideas. At the suggestion to construct a commemorative tower on the moor, an anonymous correspondent had written to the paper supporting the proposal and suggesting that it would also be a fitting monument to mark the achievement of gaining access to the moor. And so the tower was built.

The anonymous correspondent signed himself *Landmark*.

Landmark. The anonymous sender of the jigsaw.

While the first reference served only to compound an old mystery, a second reference left him deflated as he began to put the bits and pieces together; an American had recently tried to buy the tower, intending to ship it back to the United States. The chord was struck and mentally he began kicking himself. Howard had come to Darwen to find the missing piece of a puzzle without knowing why. He had found the Tower and stood on it. And all that time he not guessed at the reason; he had never considered it - even as his manuscript was going to press. Consequently, Darwen Tower was not in his catalogue and that was now out of the printers and awaiting distribution. It was too late to do anything about it.

Someone must have sent him the jigsaw with the missing piece to warn him that his catalogue was not comprehensive – and he had completely missed the point!

But that didn't make sense. Very few people knew what he was doing and absolutely no one had access to his catalogue. How could anyone know he had missed something out. Only God would know that.

Pensively, he closed each of the books and placed them back on the shelf. It just didn't add up; who could have sent him the jigsaw? He asked the question over and over again but the answer was always the same: no one could have known.

Outside the rain had stopped and he made his way slowly back to the Millstone Hotel, his thoughts racing round in ever decreasing circles. On the other side of the bus station he stopped and looked up to the moor, his mind full of questions. At the summit - perhaps over a mile away as the crow flies - the Victoria Tower stood alone on an otherwise deserted hillside. He stared at the tower intently - and the tower stared back. And though his mind was full of unanswered questions and an impossible conundrum, there was one thing he was sure of, even at this distance.

He was being watched.

50

The next day was unproductive. Martyn Sorensen had no interest in the case and could not give a damn who killed Gremelkov. He could think only of Melissa but he had no idea where she had gone. A sudden change in the weather reflected his mood, and the sky now precipitated a constant drizzle onto the city streets.

Over the previous twenty four hours another three people had died while as many people had been added to the critical list as had been taken from it. It was only Rob's frequent reminders of the innocent victims, sprayed over the boulevard, massacred beyond recognition, and the constant vision of the aftermath, that had kept him going. He had reached that point when emotional pain becomes so great that it saturates the senses, when thirty nine victims of a bombing impacts no more or less than the three hundred and ninety victims of an air crash, or the three thousand nine hundred victims of a flooding, or the thirty nine thousand victims of an earthquake. All would make the same headlines, the same coverage, the same size typeface.

Fortunately, it soon became apparent that they were going to get nowhere until forensic gave them something to work with and so far they had failed to discover anything that might lead to the identity of the bomber. They had not, as yet, discovered the identity of three of the victims who had been caught nearest the blast, and were no nearer retrieving the vital fragment of detonator that would establish that there had been a bomb.

In desperation, Andy Holland had turned to the press for his defence and had managed to convince a small circle of lead writers - Greg Miller included - that, had there been a bomb, then there should have been two easily distinguishable explosions; one when the bomb exploded and the other when the fuel tank went up. To Martyn, this seemed remotely sensible. But for every paper that supported and published the claim, there were at least four government experts to refute it proposing that a bomb that was large enough would have ignited everything in the immediate vicinity almost instantly. Not even the individual frames of a high speed, high resolution video recording could have separated the two blasts.

Curiously, an independent explosives expert from Chicago claimed that the explosion was consistent with that which would have been obtained with a full tank of fuel in the limousine, regardless of any additional explosives. Martyn had managed to confirm that the tank had been filled prior to the departure from the hotel, about the same time that Andy Holland had been checking the car out. And, as Greg Miller was so keen to point out, on the front page of three of his regular forums, it did not take a great leap of the imagination to include the possibility that a bomb could have been planted by a member of the team whose job it was to prevent the bombing.

"After all," he claimed, while being interviewed on the lunchtime news, "who else would have such a high level of expertise in the subject?"

There did not seem to be much point in hanging around the department pretending to look busy. As soon as forensics came up with anything all the stops would be pulled out and he would be working round the clock chasing up leads. It seemed sensible to prepare for the onslaught by taking it easy until the onslaught occurred. And besides, his mind was cluttered with more serious problems. More important to him, anyway.

Martyn, I just wanted to apologise for last night. I know you wouldn't do anything to hurt me. I think we should talk though, so I'm going to come home tonight. I'll see you later. I realise you will probably be home late and will never hear this message but, what the hell, I don't think I've ever spoken to my own answerphone before.

He switched the machine off and placed the photograph of the other Melissa on the table. He had spent a couple of hours of that afternoon wading through computer files, linking up to Europe and ploughing through even more, trying to find the identity of the mystery woman. But he had drawn a blank. It was not easy, with only a first name, and it was not unusual. After the Great Turmoil, so many records of Europeans, especially English, had disappeared in the administrative chaos which ensued, and the United States was suddenly inundated with thousands of lost souls who technically did not exist. Anybody could walk in, offer any name, and from then on that was who they were. He could only make the assumption that the Melissa in the photograph had not had any reason to change her name but it was still a hopeless task.

When he had first met Melissa, he had not been able to trace her own record very easily. He thought back to those precious days one year before. He was required by law to make sure he was not fraternising with known criminals or political activists. He had fallen for Melissa so quickly and so heavily that he had grown increasingly worried at not being able to trace her record. Yet she appeared so innocent and he refused to believe that she had given him a false name, or that she had anything to hide in her past. It was such a relief when he finally did find something and he was doubly glad that it made boring reading.

But he was no nearer tracing the identity of the woman whom Melissa believed to be her mother. He had read through Howard Robinson's file again in the hope that it might throw up some clue but that was also fruitless since the record began from the date of his entry into the United States at the turn of the century, sixteen years after the date on the reverse of the photograph.

He did not know why but he did not want to tell Melissa about Howard Robinson and his connection with the girl in the photograph, partly because she might jump to the conclusion that Howard Robinson was her father. That would be doubly painful for her, especially since she had been so geographically close to him all these years. But he was also concerned about all the strange experiences that had plagued his life since Howard Robinson's body had been discovered. Because that was when they had all started : his sensations of being watched, his visions of the ghostly Melissa from the photograph, his inexplicable sense of dread - all trying to tell him something, he was sure. But what?

And what did Melissa think they should talk about? He did not know what to think. She seemed to have calmed down after her outburst of the previous evening but her message had contained no undertones of affection, or love. He could only assume that she either wanted to have a rational conversation about the woman she believed to be her mother, or she wanted to discuss their future together - or not, as the case might be. It was easy to tell himself that he could do nothing until she came home so there was little point in worrying about it. But it was easier said than done. He could only hope that she would return soon.

At that moment the phone rang. He waited a suitable length of time and then answered it just as the answerphone was about to cut in.

"Hello?"

"Hello? Martyn? Is that you? Martyn, it's Jacqui. Jacqui Miller. Thank God I've found you. I've been calling all over. I think Greg is in trouble and I didn't know who to call. I'm sick with worry. I know him. He acts in a strange kind of way when he's about to do something stupid and he was…"

"Jacqui, hold on," Martyn interrupted. He moved the handset round to his other ear and made himself comfortable. "Now take a deep breath and start from the beginning."

"There isn't anything to say, really. He came home this evening. He was early. He said he knew who had killed Gremelkov and that it was about time somebody did something about it. I thought he had got himself an exclusive or something but I've just checked the drawer of his office bureau. He's taken his gun. He never uses it. It's been sat gathering dust for years. I don't think he's gone to get a story. He's gone on a manhunt. Martyn, please help me. I'm so worried and I didn't know who else to turn to."

Through the ear-piece he heard her begin to cry. If Greg Miller really did know who had killed Gremelkov then what the hell was he up to? He had no choice but to go and find out.

"Alright, Jacqui," said Martyn. "Don't do anything. Stay right there. I'm on my way over."

As he pulled up outside the Millers' residence, Jacqui appeared at the front door and ran across the lawn to meet him, the same sense of urgency written all over her face that he had detected in her voice. The rain had now stopped but her straggling wet hair betrayed the fact that she had only recently returned to the house. The car had hardly come to a halt before she had flung open the passenger door and jumped into the seat. He reacted by engaging first gear immediately.

"Right. Where to?"

"I don't know," she said.

He took the car out of gear. "So why the mad rush to get there? If we're going to have any chance of finding him then we have to start looking someplace."

"There's nothing in the house," she said. "I've been through everything looking for a clue as to where he might have gone, but there's nothing there. That's not unusual. He rarely keeps any important stuff at home. I think we should try his office. It's all I can think of, and I need to feel as if I'm doing something."

"Okay," he said. "The office." He pushed the car back into gear and turned around in the driveway. He did not switch on the siren because he did not want to increase her anxiety to fever pitch but he did place the beacon on the car roof so they could get through the traffic more quickly.

He could not guess where Greg Miller might be going but one thought recurred over and over again. If Miller had discovered the identity of the killer then why had he not divulged his information to the police instead of trying to be a hero? He could come up with only one answer and its implied logical progression. Because Miller did not - and never had - trusted the police. Because he was sure that there was a bad apple in the cart. Because the person he was going after was a cop! As if in answer to his fears, Jacqui began to speak.

"This isn't a sudden revelation, you know. Ever since that guy got killed with that laser weapon he's been acting like he was possessed. He's convinced that everything is tied up in one bundle of internal corruption. First he disappears after receiving those anonymous letters, then he starts screaming maltreatment at the police all over the front pages of the papers. Then, following your little battle down at the docks, he starts hanging around with that Russian scientist who somehow persuaded him that the laser weapon they found in Cassida's car was not real. Even after it was exhibited in the courtroom, he still wasn't convinced. But all he would say was that it didn't make sense.

"You know, he was all set to campaign for Cassida's release at one point until he reasoned that Cassida deserved to be in jail whether he had used the laser weapon or not. He had to do a lot of soul searching over that one. He hates injustice but, secretly, he's been trying to amass enough evidence to bring Cassida down for a couple of years now. Yet that only increased his obsession. After all, if Cassida didn't kill those people then who did? I argued that the trial had been extensive and unanimously conclusive in its verdict and that all those people could not be wrong."

"And what did he say to that?" Martyn asked.

"He said the result could be fixed if enough people involved were eager to fix it. He even argued that was why you and your partner had really been exempt from the trial. You might have been a source of embarrassment. That was the only reason I knew I could trust you. Because I know that Greg does."

"Really? You surprise me. In his eyes I can't have done anything but let him down."

Jacqui looked across at him and knew that he was not convinced that she too was not trying to hide something.

"Well," she conceded. "Perhaps 'trust' is too kind a word. He actually thinks you're pretty stupid. At least, that's what he keeps saying. He says you're nothing but a pawn in a game you don't even recognise as a game. But he doesn't know what the game is either and I sometimes wondered whether he too wasn't being used as a pawn by Raspov. He seemed to listen to him a lot."

"Raspov has his own interests to protect and he was desperate to gain an ally to save his own life."

"That was what Greg said," Jacqui agreed. "It was probably the deciding factor that stopped him from trying to free Cassida. He said that if the result of the trial had been different, or if he had subsequently tried to bring about a retrial, then both he and Raspov would have been putting their lives on the line if his theory about corruption was correct. They could not afford to have someone asking such prying questions in public, and bringing Raspov into the limelight might have caused too much discomfort among the powers that be."

At that point, Martyn suddenly realised that he had subconsciously made a stupid assumption. While he rushed over from his house to rescue a helpless damsel in distress, he had forgotten that Jacqui Miller was actually a very articulate and intelligent woman, and her only distress was in worrying, naturally, that her husband was in danger. The more she talked, the more he realised that she knew a hell of a lot more about the case than he had first presumed.

"He talks to you quite a lot," he said, trying not to make it sound insulting. It didn't work.

"He is my husband," she replied, defensively. "Actually, he talks to himself a lot and I try my best not to listen. It just kind of rubs off after a while."

He did not bother trying to apologise.

"There's still something I don't understand," he said. "Why has Greg taken his obsession this far? What has the Cassida trial got to do with Gremelkov?"

"I don't know," she said. "I don't think Greg does either. He says they both have the same odour. Things not adding up. The same people evading the same questions over and over again. But maybe it's academic now. Something's added up and I hope we find out what it is before he gets himself killed."

It was the first time she had voiced her true fears out loud. He thought back to the time when Melissa would watch him walk out of the apartment and wonder whether she would see him alive again. And when he returned she would throw her arms around him as if he had returned from a battlefield. Sometimes he wondered whether he had. It was so easy to take life for granted. It took no effort of the imagination to believe that death was something that happened to other people, that fate would guide its chosen few through every kind of danger.

Just then, the car radio burst into life.

"Attention all units! Proceed immediately to Eden Square. We have received reports of gunfire and damage to property. One suspect seen fleeing from the scene. Probably armed. Proceed with caution. Take out if necessary."

The radio was apt to go off with some message or other every few seconds and the thought which crossed Martyn's mind had evidently washed right over his passenger's. She did not comment as he took a sudden right hand turn which would take them away from the television studio.

"I thought you always communicated using code numbers so that no one else could listen in and understand what was going on."

"It makes no difference now," he replied, thankful for the mundane conversation. "Everyone knows what the numbers mean so it doesn't matter whether we speak in codes or not. They keep it in the TV shows for nostalgia, I guess. The radios are digital now. You need a coded receiver to get the signal translated back into English. No one can listen in unless they have a similar radio set with the correct security code and they should be almost impossible to come by. The codes are automatically changed every day by a satellite transmission."

He took another right hand turn so that the New Century Tower could quite clearly be seen ahead in the distance, its fairy lights climbing skyward to meet the stars. It was exactly the sort of glaring contradiction he did not need and it was predictable that she should pick him up on it. However, she did not seem to notice until they had travelled about a mile parallel with Eden Boulevard and were approaching the scene of the blast two days before.

"Hey, wait a minute," she exclaimed. "This goes down to Eden Square. The television studio is in the opposite direction."

"I'm working on a hunch," he said, not wishing to expand further.

Her first reaction was written all over her face and he could read it like a book. For one brief moment she believed in her husband's corruption theory and that she had walked into a trap. The look of horror was unmistakeable. He would dearly have loved to know what she thought next because the expression of dismay and fear suddenly disappeared and she seemed to relax, only to recoil in horror again a second later.

"Wait a minute!" she cried again. "You think that last radio announcement was about Greg, don't you?"

"It might be, I don't know. It's just a gut feeling. When we get there I want you to stay in the car. Understood?"

Jacqui nodded and went silent. She didn't understand but she was happy to be at least doing something. Not only that but she trusted him. If it turned out to be a false trail, at least she would be able to tell herself that she had done her best. What worried him was that her trust was founded on irrational thought. If she had known that his gut reaction had been a result of hearing the words 'Eden Square' and that he somehow felt it was the appropriate place for a showdown, she would have probably insisted he turn back to their original course. If the broadcast had called all units to anywhere else in the city he would no doubt have thought nothing more of it. The radio crackled again.

"Unit two-three-seven arrived at the Square, south west corner. Proceeding on foot."

"What did they mean 'take out if necessary'?"

"It means they have the authority to take any action necessary to bring the suspect into custody."

"You mean they could kill him?"

"Only as a last resort. You aren't making this very easy. Listen, we do not know for sure it is your husband. If it is, I don't think he would be shooting up the city, so let's go and get him and find out what this is all about."

He spoke with a confidence he did not feel but she appeared satisfied with his answer, at least on the surface. She went silent again. The radio crackled.

"Unit one-eight-three at the station ramp. There's a bit of a mess here. No sign of suspect. Proceeding on foot."

Martyn cut down a side street on the left and drove past an unmanned police cordon. Both the Boulevard and the Square had been closed to the public since the bomb attack and would remain so until all forensic evidence had been collected. Presumably, the guards at the cordon had responded to the call. He did not give it another thought and within seconds he had joined the squad car at the station ramp.

"Stay here," he ordered and jumped out of the vehicle. He ran over to the waiting squad car, behind which was an officer armed with a marksman rifle pointing into the square. He took a position next to the officer and carried out a quick visual survey of the scene while obtaining an oral update on the situation. The officer did not remove his gaze from the rifle sight but Martyn flashed his badge anyway. Strange, he thought, that a patrolman should be equipped with a rifle.

"What's the position?" he said to the officer. Then, as his brain took in all the information that struck the back of his retina, he added, "Grief! What on earth has been going on?"

Across the square, along the southern and western edge, he could see a number of blue flashing lights and estimated that at least a further five squads had answered the call. Three more squad cars had taken positions along the northern edge and two more were just arriving.

Even in the darkness it was clear that someone had gone on a riot along the east perimeter. There was broken glass everywhere, fragments of shattered windows littering the plaza along a fifty metre stretch. The windows seemed to have been smashed indiscriminately. No particular building appeared to be the target. Meanwhile, the officer was answering his question.

"He's over there," he said, not pointing anywhere but implying that the rifle was. "He's climbed into the clock fountain. We think he may be injured."

"Do we know who he is? Is he armed?"

"We haven't had a confirmed sighting but we believe he has a handgun."

"Is that all?" Martyn asked. "You couldn't create this amount of damage with a handgun. You'd need at least a sub machine gun and even then you'd have a problem to make windows shatter like that. They look like they've been broken from the inside."

"Apparently there are equal amounts of glass within the buildings," the officer answered. "As though they just exploded."

Martyn carried out another quick reconnaissance of the plaza. The blue lights around the square continued to flash. Nothing else moved. They seemed to have reached an impasse.

"So what do we do now?"

The officer answered almost mechanically. "We have orders to shoot to kill. As soon as we catch sight of the bastard."

"What? But that's crazy. You don't even know who it is. Tell everyone to hold their fire. I'm going in."

The officer looked at him incredulously. "But that's ridiculous. All we have to do is wait. He can't stay in there for ever."

"Just relay the order," said Martyn. "I don't want to get shot by my own men."

He raised himself back to his feet and began walking, stealthily, towards the clock fountain, using any of the sculptures or rockeries for cover, crouching with gun raised whenever he thought he might have detected some movement. But it was never more than his imagination working overtime. In a short distance he was far enough away from the flashing blue lights of the squad cars to be able to see much more easily. Although he knew there were marksmen all around him, armed with high velocity rifles and infrared sights, a quick scan of the plaza did not reveal one. They were well hidden. By the time he had reached the edge of the clock fountain he still had not detected a single movement. He crawled the last few metres between the fountain and a nearby rockery on his hands and knees and paused at the edge of the exhibit. All he could hear was the steady bubbling of water and short spurts moving away and then towards him again as each second passed.

Suddenly, he sprung up onto the low wall with his gun levelled directly in front of him. His gaze met the eyes of Greg Miller, sitting dejectedly in the water not ten metres away. He appeared terrified and was clutching a bloodied shoulder in agony. Martyn suspected that he had been shot. As soon as Miller saw him he started to babble unintelligibly.

"It's okay, Greg," Martyn said. "It's me, Martyn Sorensen, remember? It's all over now. Let's go home."

He dropped his own weapon to his side and stretched out one arm. Miller hesitated, and then raised himself out of the water, relieved.

There was no time to do anything about it. Greg Miller climbed to his feet and the shots rang out. Two bullets hit him straight in the chest and exploded, sending him crashing back into the water. At first Martyn could not believe his own men were firing and dived for cover on the dry side of the low wall. In the north east corner of the square he heard the distinctive sound of a woman screaming over and over again and knew that Jacqui had not obeyed his orders and had left the car. Not that it would have made any difference, since she would have heard the shots anyway.

Suddenly, a spotlight came on, illuminating the fountain in a haunting aurora of white, silent light. The source was the roof of one of the police vehicles. Miller had been shot by police marksmen after he had issued an order for them to hold their fire.

His reaction was one of fury but first he had to get to Miller. He might still be alive, though he could not see how. The two bullets which hit him had been perfect shots, designed to cause fatal injuries.

As soon as he was satisfied that the shooting had stopped, he jumped over the wall and waded in to where Miller lay, facing upwards, eyes opened, his hands clutching his chest. He was obviously in agony. He did not know what had happened to him and was struggling to understand the pain. He tried to speak but all that came from his mouth was blood.

He shook his head violently from side to side, trying to stop himself from choking. And in his last breath, Miller wrenched a small metallic object from the front of his jacket and thrust it into Martyn's hand.

"My office," he rasped, spluttering as water poured into his open mouth and filled his lungs.

Then, with a violent convulsive arch of his back, his body relaxed and began floating away, as Martyn watched helplessly and fought to hold back tears of anguish and frustration.

51

He did not know what to say to Jacqui Miller. What could he say? No sooner had the shots been fired than the grave squad moved in and began clearing up, recording measurements, taking photographs. Clinical. Efficient. He looked around him trying to find someone he recognised but every face was unfamiliar.

Suddenly, there was Jacqui Miller. As she approached the fountain and witnessed her husband's body, still floating face upwards in the water while a flurry of activity continued around him, her expression did not change.

"Hey," somebody said. "Doesn't he look a bit like that guy on the television?"

She did not falter. Even as he stepped from the water and sat down on the wall before her, she remained rigid, in vacant shock. He wanted to embrace her. At the same time, he felt responsible. Inside he was raging, both at himself for letting her down when she had placed all her trust in him, but also at the nameless person who would ultimately be held responsible for all of this.

"Jacqui, I have to leave you. There are things I have to do. I'll see that someone looks after you and I'll get back as soon as I can."

She remained motionless. He reached for her hand and squeezed it gently, half expecting her to pull it away in disgust. He could not stay with her but he needed to know that she did not blame him. And yet, in a perverse way he wished she would because it would make things so much simpler. But her only reaction was a slight sensation of pressure generated by her own hand on his. And as he walked away from her he could not swear that even that was not the product of his own guilt-ridden conscience.

At the edge of the square he found two officers whom he recognised. One was tall and slim while the other was much shorter and more heavily built. He did not know their names but knew they had been drafted into his own precinct to help deal with the volume of work generated by Gremelkov's visit. At the time of their arrival he had been in the lake country. He was surprised and disturbed at the encounter. Until then he had not recognised anybody and he could imagine that the whole episode was an awful nightmare. Seeing the two officers brought home the reality. They appeared equally surprised to see him. The short one spoke first.

"Sorensen, can't you stay out of trouble? You've only been back two weeks. And I thought you'd put that laser assassin business behind us."

At the risk of looking stupid he asked, "What laser assassin business?"

"Well, that is who they just shot, isn't it?"

Martyn was obviously ill-informed about something, but he decided to continue the conversation as it was going and hope for the best.

"We just shot Greg Miller."

"What? The TV guy?" He turned to his partner. "Didn't I tell you it was him? Even after they let him go I said he was the one. And they never did actually implicate anyone as the assassin, did they?"

Then he turned back to Martyn. "What's all this *we* business anyway? *We* didn't get here until it was over. And I didn't think you'd be wanting to hang around with those heavies again so soon."

Though the officer was not talking in riddles, but assuming at least a glimmer of some prior knowledge, light was beginning to dawn. He did not have the time or the patience to beat around the bush until he was completely in the picture so he opted to be blunt.

"Listen, you guys. I haven't a clue what you are talking about. I just responded to the call. When I got here the Square was surrounded and Miller was in the middle. Then he got shot. That's all I know."

The taller officer looked to his partner and they seemed to communicate silently, presumably debating who should provide the explanation. After a brief pause they evidently came to a conclusion and the former began to speak.

"Didn't it surprise you that so many SFN got here before we did? And all issued with high powered rifles with infrared sights?"

Martyn glanced quickly round the plaza, gauging the level of activity and appreciating for the first time the scale of the operation as the officer's words sank in.

"Special Forces?" It was all he could say. Even armed with this knowledge it was not obvious that the operating team were SFN since they could easily be mistaken for cops. Only his lack of recognition held any clue as to their real identity. But then, the city was not small and he certainly did not know everybody on the force.

"Sure. Nearly all of them. Funny thing is, they were all in position before the first of our own squads got here." He indicated the rifleman to whom Martyn had given the instruction before going into the Square to find Miller.

"He didn't say much but I think I managed to get a fairly clear picture. Apparently, they unearthed some information this afternoon that this guy they shot was actually Cassida's laser hit-man. They think he killed both Howard Robinson and that other woman. They couldn't implicate him in the trial because, at that stage, they did not have any evidence."

He thought for a moment. "I didn't know it was Miller but now it all makes sense. His preoccupation with the laser weapon was a clever strategy. He was trying to create a smokescreen to draw attention away from himself. He purposely pitched himself against the police, dropping red herrings all the way. In the end it was his word against the government's. Not an equal match by any means but he had credibility in the public eye, and it was enough to keep the hounds at bay. It almost worked."

Martyn shuffled uncomfortably. "So what was it they found out today?"

"Don't know. But whatever it was, Miller found out also and did a runner before they could get to him. They knew he was armed and just over an hour ago, a team was issued with rifles and put on alert. Though how they all happened to be near here when the call went out I don't know. They must have been given advanced information somehow. Either that or they're all clairvoyant."

He looked quizzically at Martyn whom he knew to be more gifted at putting pieces of puzzles together.

"Make sense?"

"It's about as clear as mud," he said. "With one or two refinements it might be flawless, but if you want my opinion, it stinks."

They did not ask him why. If they had he would not have heard them. He was too wrapped up in his own thoughts, which mostly took the form of questions. The officer's explanation of events was almost credible, and might even be believed, but there were still anomalies. If Miller really had been the laser assassin then why had he come round to the apartment, with Raspov in tow, to convince him that the assassin was not in the courtroom but was actually still on the loose? What did he have to gain? It was in his own interests to keep out of the public eye.

And then there was the SFN. If the Special Forces had the operation under control then why did they bother to allow the call to go out on the normal police band? It was a pointless overkill. Come to that, what the hell were the SFN doing patrolling the streets of the city with high powered rifles? What information had they discovered that made Greg Miller the victim of such a massive and deadly manhunt? And despite the officer's rational explanation, why did the mere mention of the Special Forces instinctively lead him to believe that it was a load of fanciful nonsense?

According to Jacqui, her husband had left the house claiming he was going after Gremelkov's murderer. So why was he, the detective responsible for doing just that, totally in the dark again while the Special Forces continued to do their own thing? And there was another puzzle. How could the SFN have known that Miller was on the run if they had not tried to arrest him? If any officer had been to Miller's house then Jacqui would have told him but she had not mentioned it. Where else would they have expected to find him?

He was completely bewildered and he needed to get back in control of the situation. There was only one possible chance of doing that. As his mind raced on, he clutched the small metallic object that Greg Miller had pushed into his hand and prayed that it was the trump card he was looking for. But holding the trump card was not everything. Miller had directed him to his office which he could only assume was at the television centre. He had to get there before anyone else or the trump card would be useless. Time was not on his side.

He was being watched.

It happened again. From somewhere close by he could sense eyes burning into him. It was not a tangible sensation. There was no trigger except that he was in Eden Square. But this time his intuition was correct. He turned to look behind him. Standing not more than twenty metres away were the two SFN agents, Reynolds and Manciani, staring directly at him, watching him closely. Even then, he felt he were being watched by some other unseen consciousness. Somewhere close by, hiding in the darkness, he could still feel their eyes piercing him with a horrifying intensity.

The two Special Forces men made no response, either verbal or physical. They just stared until he was sufficiently unnerved to turn away and continue walking. He did not check behind him again until he was at his car. Opening the door he allowed himself one quick glance in the direction he had come. Neither Reynolds or Manciani had moved. They stood like statues facing him. And though he was now too far away to see their eyes clearly, he knew they were still following his every move.

Like vultures eyeing up their prey.

Before moving in for the kill.

52

On his return from the library, Howard could not bring himself to check out of the Millstone - at least not yet. There was an answer here somewhere - and it was up on the moor. He did not know what the question was but all the strange events of the previous year - the jigsaw, the premonitions, the mysterious runner, even his own intuitions - appeared to be focussed around one landmark. And so it was, later that morning, that Howard Robinson again found himself wandering aimlessly over the Darwen moors in search of a reason for his present disposition. Aimlessly that is, in the sense that he did not know why he was there, or what he hoped to find. In pure geographical terms, his ramblings were clearly more directed. As he made his way slowly up the familiar dirt track, he gradually approached the focal point at the summit.

The answer was in the tower.

Darwen Tower had a gravity of its own. This did not seem unduly surprising since it was the only abnormality in the entire, bland expanse of the moor; a single, discordant note in a tuneless overture of pale, olive-green reed grass. But there was more to it than that. The tower was magnetic and enigmatic. On his first trip to Darwen he had climbed the moor in thick fog. After straying from the path, he had still arrived at the tower when, he now realised, he could have finished up in any number of places. The top surface of the moor did not have a well defined summit; rather, it was a vast and flat plateau on which the Victoria Tower was situated to one end, at the northernmost point. It stood like a giant chess piece, calmly pondering its next move in a quiet corner of the board, when all of the other pieces had been taken away and the squares had long since disappeared. And yet, standing motionless and erect, with a strength of pride that only a royal could manifest in such public humiliation, it still refused to give up the game.

Something was wrong.

Slowly, he circled around the tower, keeping the radius fixed at about sixty or seventy metres until he was on the south side with the moor stretching away behind him. Then he stopped, and waited.

He was being watched.

Without knowing why, Howard was filled with a desire to attack the tower; to storm the entrance and force his way up the spiral staircase, lashing out in frustration at everything in his path. It was an irrational, insane notion born of an uninvited intuition that everything he had suffered in the last few months somehow originated from within, that his overwhelming sense of frustration could somehow be relieved by a mindless act of violence. The closer he got to the tower, the stronger the sense of foreboding and an inner conviction he could not explain: Darwen Tower was consumed by evil.

But he did not move. Instead he simply sat before the Tower in a symbolic act of defiance, refusing either to turn away or to give in to this insanity. Nothing about this made sense. There was no one there; he knew that. Darwen Tower was simply a hollow folly built in commemoration of a queen who was long since dead. It was empty. He closed his eyes willing himself to banish the pervading sense of menace from his mind but it was no use.

Someone was watching him.

Suddenly, Howard was startled from his trance, his heart jumping out of his chest like a jack in a box while the contents of his stomach dropped through the trapdoor which suddenly sprang in the base of his gut. With a single movement that defied Newton, he was on his feet and the two dogs - Labradors - were left snapping at his ankles, barking incessantly at their discovery. Simultaneously he felt a wave of bewilderment at the illusions the shock broadcast to his senses. For a fleeting moment, he heard what sounded like a woman screaming as a table crashed to the ground behind him, and the air was filled with an aroma of freshly baked croissants. Then it was gone, instantly forgotten.

In the distance, he heard a voice call out, quickly followed by the high pitched screech of a whistle. Before he had located the source of the sound, the Labradors had turned and sprinted off across the moor and he was alone again, the tranquillity of the hilltop disturbed only by the violent pounding of his heart.

The answer was in the tower.

There was never any question about what he would do next. In the same way that he would not follow the instructions of his horoscope, nor touch wood when he tempted providence, nor avoid walking under ladders, he entered through the door at the base of the tower and climbed the sixty five stone steps and the seventeen level spiral staircase up to the parapet. What he lacked in superstitious belief, he more than made up for in hope. As he already knew, the parapet was deserted. Once again the tower had drawn him in like a fly to the centre of a spider's web and he wondered if it were possible for anyone who came walking over the Darwen moor to avoid climbing the tower. Now he was inside, the sense of foreboding had gone – just as before.

On the parapet, he was rewarded with the view he had not been able to see on his last visit. To the west, he could swear he could make out a band of ocean where land rose to meet sky in the distance. Before it, from the base of the moor a little less than a mile away, the middle distance was totally occupied by a vast plain of square, green fields and perfectly straight hedgerows. To the south, the moorland plateau stretched for what seemed like miles, appearing to reach all the way to Winter Hill where the television transmitter silently delivered complex images and sound to the hundreds of thousands of houses that lay captured in its range; the needle-like mast soaring a further twelve hundred feet above the hill summit, slicing into the skyline. He moved around to the other side of the parapet where he could look down upon the cluster of grey rooftops and chimney stacks that was Darwen, nestling cosily in the valley of the river from which the town took its name.

He began replaying the memory of his previous visit. The mysterious runner had come across the moor from the direction of the town, where the northern end of the plateau, on which the tower stood, began to fall down into the valley basin. From the direction of Darwen, to the base of the folly, it was all uphill. And scanning the moorland below him, the terrain of the slope was much rougher than he had realised, undulating between hillock and ditch almost to the very foot of the tower. It would have been impossible for anyone, even the most experienced runner, to have covered that amount of ground in such a short time.

Yet there was something even more curious. The gradient of the hill was steeper than he had remembered but his recollection of that first sighting of the runner through the fog was much more vivid. The two facts did not correlate. To see the runner where he was sure he had first appeared, the stranger would have had been sprinting on fresh air, at least twenty or thirty feet above the ground!

Perhaps with the after effects of flu, the distorting effects of the fog and the elapsed time since the event, his recollection was now inaccurate. He had every reason not to trust his memory of that day. In truth, he would have been able to pass off his experience as an hallucination - or a simple event distorted by the effects of post viral fatigue - had it not been for one thing. Somewhere deep inside him, a swelling of the subconscious told him that he had witnessed something macabre. The summation of all those events which had brought him to the moor, from the delivery of the anonymous jigsaw to the beginning of the breakdown of his relationship with Melissa, had left an unexplained scar. He had come to Darwen in search of answers and he felt that he had been answered, more than once, but not in a way he could understand.

The answer was in the tower.

The conviction would not go away but neither would the reason become clear. He realised that his sense of frustration was becoming more intense and there seemed little point in staying at the tower. Somehow he knew it would not give him the answers he was seeking, no matter how long he waited.

As he descended from the moor, he also knew that he would never return to Darwen. Before he dropped below the tree line, he offered one final, farewell glance at the tower, standing proudly, defiantly against the moody skyline, where it would wait patiently until the end of time.

In that moment, he was sure of one thing.

Someone was watching him.

53

The news of Greg Miller's untimely death had reached the television studio before him. In the ensuing confusion, as colleagues struggled with their consciences and debated whether they should mourn or go out and get the story, Martyn had no problem reaching Miller's office without being challenged. Only when he arrived at the door was he questioned by a security guard but it was little more than a formality. He deftly pulled rank on the guard and gained access to the office, ordering him to allow no one to enter without his specific instructions, and that included the head of the network.

"...and I'll be making a couple of calls," he said. "How do I get an outside line?"

He closed the door behind him and waited until he heard the key turn in the lock before venturing further. An infrared body scanner somewhere in the room detected his presence; just as he was about to search for a switch, suddenly there was light.

The office was better described as a suite, almost an apartment. The main room was large and ornate, furnished more as a reception lounge than an office, with only a modest desk in one corner and several expensive paintings filling the walls. A number of other rooms adjoined this and he began by exploring them. He already had a vague idea what he was looking for and it was evidently not in the main office.

The first door led to a simple bedroom and en-suite bathroom. Satisfied that there was no other access to the suite from here, he moved back into the office and round behind the desk where there was a second door. Here he found a smaller room completely decked out in floor to ceiling shelving and crammed with files. He did not bother to look any more closely. It would take hours to go through them and he did not have much time. Even so, it was beginning to look like he was in for a long night.

Seeing the phone on the desk, he suddenly remembered that he had to call Melissa and let her know he would be late. She would know he had played back her message and he did not want her to think that he had deliberately gone out when he knew she was coming. He dialled the number but there was no reply. Eventually, the answerphone cut in. He waited for the tone and then began to speak.

"Hi, Melissa..."

He did not continue. His voice sounded hollow and reverberated back at him from the other side of the office; from the one room he had not yet looked into. It was faint and muffled but he was sure he had heard it and instantly knew what it must mean. Replacing the phone on its cradle, he drew the strange metal object Miller had given him from his pocket, held it in front of his mouth and spoke again.

"Hello."

This time it was more clear. Even as the words formed on his lips, they echoed back from behind the door of the third room. That was what he was looking for. He returned the remote microphone to his pocket, puzzling over it. He had known what it was but he had never seen one like it before. It appeared more complex and bulky than most remote mikes and it seemed strange that Greg Miller should have burdened himself with something so uncomfortable and unnecessarily weighty when a lightweight microphone would have done equally as well. If he had worried about reliability it would have been easier to wear three button mikes than one of these.

It was with these thoughts and the expectation of something more than a simple sound recording that he finally located the key to the remaining door and opened it. Immediately beyond was a second door, presumably there for soundproofing. The second door was slightly ajar. On it there hung a single sheet of paper, crudely labelled "Miller's Laboratory - Welcome to the Magical Kingdom". A picture of Mickey Mouse, the Sorcerer's Apprentice, had been attached directly underneath.

Twenty minutes later, he was sitting alone in the darkness of the 'Laboratory', one moment staring at the three video monitors mounted along the far wall, the next moment at the single blown up frame on the editing station monitor, then at the plans and projections on the wall, then at Miller's diary with its lone entry under the present date. Then he stared into space, trying to piece it all together. And as he did so, the implications of what he had discovered slowly sank in.

On more than one occasion he had let Greg Miller down and now he had unwittingly become the custodian of all he had previously chosen to ignore. It was Miller's legacy for those past mistakes. Martyn had not listened when given the chance so now he had to wear Miller's shoes, to become Greg Miller. And, if he was not careful, to die like Greg Miller.

Minutes later, he was making another phone call, this time to his partner.

"Martyn! Where the hell have you been? Greg Miller has been shot by the Special Forces. I've been trying to get hold of you all evening. So has the Chief. He isn't very happy. I think maybe you should…"

"It's okay. I'll call him. I'm ringing from the television studio. From Greg Miller's office. I think you should get over here right away. And don't say anything to anyone. I haven't been through all this stuff yet but it's getting very incestuous and it's beginning to scare me."

His partner's reply was instantaneous. "Say no more. I'm about five minutes away."

The phone went dead. Although Martyn usually spoke quietly and calmly, Rob had worked with him long enough to know that his sense of urgency could be detected by the slight inflections which suddenly appeared in his voice. He could hear these nuances now. This was not a time to bandy words. So he offered action. Appropriate and immediate.

Martyn then phoned the Chief but he was not at the precinct. Instead, his secretary, Holly, answered.

"I'm sorry, Detective Sorensen, but he's not in his vehicle right now. I do know he wants to speak to you though. Can you give me your number?"

Martyn hesitated. He had known Holly for years, that was not the problem. But there was no point in allowing her to become involved unnecessarily. It was safer to keep the numbers small.

"Tell him to call Rob at home," he said. "And tell him it's a code three zed."

"What does that mean?"

"Don't worry about it," he assured her. "Brett will understand."

When Rob arrived, ten minutes later, Martyn had just come off the phone again. He ushered his partner into the office and checked that the security guard locked the door before he spoke. He immediately guided his partner to the laboratory.

"I still don't understand what all this is about but wait until you see what's in here. You won't believe it."

The Laboratory was a hive of electronic activity. Mounted along one wall were the three monitors, staring blankly into the room. They appeared to be wired in to a central control console which incorporated three video disk machines and an additional audio tape deck. A pair of stereo speakers stood to each side. In one corner, there was a video editing machine with its own monitor. One wall was completely covered in charts and maps, and paperwork was scattered liberally all over the studio. Even as Rob took all this in, the three video tape machines suddenly stopped rewinding, almost simultaneously, and clicked into standby.

"What do they mean?" he asked Martyn, indicating the monitors which were consecutively labelled 'North', 'East' and 'South'.

Martyn flicked a switch on the central control unit and the three videos switched to fast-forward.

"All will become clear," Martyn replied. "There isn't much in the first five minutes so I'm skipping past it for now. We can scrutinise it in detail later. It's this next bit I want you to see."

"Do I have to watch all three screens at once?"

"Yes, but it won't be difficult. They all show the same thing but from different angles as indicated by the labels. Somehow, Greg Miller discovered a vital clue which our experts, and everybody else, missed - or chose to miss. I'll show you that in a minute. I would never have believed it and yet it was staring us in the face all the time. Every time I went to Eden Square I had this gut feeling that the answer to our problems was right under our noses, almost as if I was staring right into the eyes of the murderer and yet couldn't see him. I should have followed my instinct but it wasn't tangible and I chose to ignore it. If I hadn't, Greg Miller might still be alive. Then again, I would probably be dead instead."

Rob was beginning to get frustrated.

"I hate it when you do this Sherlock Holmes bit. When are you going to get to the point?"

At that precise moment, the videos clicked to standby at their pre-programmed position and there was suddenly an unmistakeable air of anticipation in the room.

"How about now?" Martyn said, triumphantly. "When Greg Miller went down to Eden Square this evening he knew he was in danger, probably knew that he might not come back alive, so he took the trouble to film everything that happened. He set up cameras and remote relay boosters on the roofs of three buildings around the Square and then wore this." He removed the metallic device from his pocket and passed it to Rob.

"Any ideas?"

Rob examined it closely for a few seconds and then shrugged his shoulders.

"It's a remote mike but I don't know what all the rest is for. It obviously has another function."

"It focuses the cameras," Martyn explained. "Not only does it transmit sound from the microphone to the relay booster on the roof and then back to here…" - he indicated the audio tape deck - "…but it is constantly transmitting position signals to the cameras. Wherever he goes the cameras follow. If he is stationary for a reasonable period they begin to zoom in. If he is moving quickly they switch back to wide angle, always keeping him in the centre of the picture. Except for the 'East' view; that's always on wide angle. The result could be a disaster if the centre of the action was off the picture but, in this case, it is far from that. It is almost a movie masterpiece. I just wish he hadn't had to die filming it."

Martyn hit the 'play' switch. As the audio tape began to roll, the screens flickered into life.

"You mean the film shows us who killed him?" Rob asked, bemused.

"It shows a hell of a lot more than that," Martyn said. He reached over to a dial on the wall. "I think we should see this with the lights turned down. Now watch…and listen."

As the three monitors came to life, each clearly revealed an independent view of the dusk lit Eden Square from the directions indicated. The 'East' screen showed virtually the whole east side of the plaza area, a lone figure shuffling nervously at the centre. The 'North' and 'South' screens both showed the figure in telephoto close-up indicating that he had been there for some time. The face was attentive, impatient, wide-eyed with fear yet equally determined. Whatever Miller was doing there, he intended to see it through, no matter how long it took.

At first, the noise sounded like interference. As it grew louder, it became slightly irritating. It resembled the high-pitched hiss of a pressure release steam valve and it was not until it reached the very peak of its crescendo that Rob, visibly disturbed, realised that Miller could hear it too. It was not a fault on the sound. Then everything happened very quickly.

The 'East' camera picked it up first - in fact it must have been there since the sound first appeared but, on the wide angle view, it was too small to notice. The close-up 'South' monitor exposed it more clearly - a trail of water vapour rising, billowing, from the rain soaked paving stones, winding its way menacingly toward Miller like a snake carved out of the empty air.

At the very last moment, Greg Miller threw himself to the ground, a built-in decibel delimiter protecting the speakers from the deafening crunch. On film, the trail of vapour shot past him, the red shifted sound dwindling into an empty echo.

"What the hell was that?"

But even as he spoke it was back again. This time Rob looked for and spotted the vapour trail on the wide angle view. His eyes had not deceived him. Apart from the clouds of mist shooting up from the plaza, and then drifting aimlessly into nothingness, there was nothing to see.

Miller picked himself up from the ground and prepared for a second onslaught from this invisible enemy. But this time the vapour trail did not head straight for him but drifted off course, several metres to his left. Miller watched, intrigued, and then suddenly realised his mistake with an expression of sheer terror. A single succinct phrase, toned with layer upon layer of instinctive panic, bounced from the speakers.

"Oh my God."

Again he tried to throw himself to the ground but he was twisted round by some unseen force and he crashed against the cold stones, clutching his shoulder and screaming in agony.

By this time Rob had figured out what was happening and he looked at Martyn in sheer disbelief.

"If he hadn't have moved when he did, he would have been cut clean in half," Martyn said. He turned back to face the monitors.

"I think this next bit represents a tantrum."

With one hand firmly grasping his shoulder, as though trying to keep his arm in place, Miller began crawling towards the nearest cover, the safe haven of the low wall surrounding the Aquashow clock fountain. But he could only crawl so fast and, from somewhere beyond the scuffling and scraping sounds that Miller created through his own frantic efforts to escape, the hiss of imminent and certain death had begun again.

Miller was on the floor now so the rising vapour headed straight for him, destined to fry his flesh like a small insect scorched under a magnifying glass. Turning onto his back to face the approaching vapour head on, he immediately rolled twice over to escape its arrival. The trail was too slow to compensate and swished past Miller's head only inches away. By the time it had reversed direction, Miller had picked himself up, sprinted round to the other side of the clock fountain and thrown himself over the wall into the water and the sanctuary of its shadow.

With this sudden rush of movement, the two telephoto cameras had switched back to wide angle coverage. Then, with Miller's entry into the fountain, the soundtrack temporarily cut out. When it returned, a few seconds later, as Miller consciously fought with his pain to keep the microphone above the waterline, the hiss of the vaporising rainwater suddenly came to a halt.

After a brief silence, there was the explosive sound of breaking glass, blasted into the night and then falling out of the darkness on to the hard paving stones. On both the 'North' and 'South' monitors, the destruction of the boutique window along the east side could be seen clearly. Almost immediately, the two windows of the office above seemed to shatter spontaneously. And then another. And another and another. In twenty seconds of mindless vandalism the air was filled with the sound of exploding windows until the entire eastern edge of the plaza was littered with shards of broken glass.

At the police precinct, a dozen silent alarms must have burst into life. But in the square all was silent. By the time the first squad cars appeared on the scene less than a minute later, Greg Miller had not moved.

Not wishing to relive the next quarter of an hour or be reminded of his own useless involvement, Martyn switched the tape off and briefly explained the events that led up to Greg Miller's death.

"…and just as I got to the fountain, he was shot dead by a Special Forces marksman. And I will never forget the look on his face. Rob, he was petrified."

Rob did not know what to say, or he did not know what to say first. In the end he asked the question which was most on his mind.

"But who was it? Where was it?"

"I think I know the answer to both those questions," Martyn replied. "And I'll show you how Greg Miller found out."

He switched on the monitor on the editing station and inserted a cassette into the source slot.

"Watch this. It's very short."

He started the tape running.

It was one they had seen before. Filmed from the roof of a hotel on Eden Boulevard, they watched as Gremelkov's cavalcade came into view. A lone figure broke from the crowd, ran in front of the limousine and hurled the petrol bomb onto the windscreen. As the flames enveloped the car, there was a blinding flash and the tape went blank. It was no more than ten seconds long.

"See it?" Martyn asked, already rewinding the tape. He received the negative response he was expecting. He played it again in slow motion. Even so, at the end, Rob was none the wiser.

"I can just about catch it in slow motion," Martyn said, "but I know what I'm looking at. This time we'll do it frame by frame."

In slow motion he allowed the tape to run until the point where the anonymous would-be terrorist was about to hurl the petrol bomb at the car. Then he switched to frame by frame mode and started to inch the film forward, stopping at the point where the car appeared to be in flames just prior to the explosion.

"I still don't see it."

With his finger on the monitor screen, Martyn drew Rob's attention away from the car until it appeared to rest in mid air a little way down the street. Apart from a paper streamer, thrown by an enthusiastic spectator, there was nothing there.

"It's a piece of ticker tape," Rob said.

"Anything else? Look closely."

"I still see a piece of ticker tape," Rob insisted.

Using some instructions from a sheet of paper on top of the machine, Martyn made some adjustments and then pressed a button to enter the information. At once the editor began zooming in on the area Martyn had pointed to until the entire screen was filled with ticker tape. And something else.

"It's on fire!" Rob exclaimed. "The ticker tape is on fire."

"Now watch again," Martyn said. He wound back the tape a few frames and then allowed it to play in slow motion. Now he knew where he was looking, Rob could clearly see the flames seemingly spring from nowhere and then dwindle to nothing before the whole screen was filled with the flash from the explosion.

Martyn turned up the lights and indicated two of the charts on the wall. One was a plan view of Eden Boulevard, the Square and the commercial district, the other was a side elevation of the same. On it, Greg Miller had sketched some rough projections. Extrapolating the line drawn between the limousine and where the burning paper streamer would have been, the projected line continued to the very end of the boulevard, crossed the Square and cut through the centre of the commercial district.

But the side elevation was even more revealing. Although some distance from the limousine, the paper streamer was several feet above the height of the car. This time Greg Miller had been more accurate and drawn the line specifically from the fuel tank of the limousine to where he had calculated the streamer to be. As it progressed along the boulevard the projection slowly gained height, rising high above Eden Square and over the commercial district. Only one building was tall enough to be dissected by the projection.

"The sixty eighth floor of the New Century tower," Martyn said, quietly. "All that time we spent looking for a laser rifle and all we had to do was look up into the sky and there it was. And all because we didn't listen to the expert. The one person who knows more about laser weapon technology than anybody else in the world told us that the existence of the portable rifle was a technical impossibility because it would need too large a power supply. If we'd have stopped one moment to take that fact to its logical conclusion, the simplest piece of lateral thinking, then it was obvious that the laser must have been fired from a building. And there was only one building that held a clear view of both Howard Robinson in Eden Square and Sarjena West in Washington Park. I just never imagined that the range of the thing could be so great. Washington Park is at least two miles away."

"But Howard Robinson was killed in thick fog," Rob said, hoping that this whole theory would eventually tie itself into knots of illogic and strangle itself. But Martyn was convinced.

"It still doesn't give us a motive either. Not for Howard Robinson or Sarjena West. In fact, this whole revelation hasn't helped us one bit. We have as many problems as we had before but now they're all different. And, in many ways, they're bigger. Someone has gone to a lot of trouble to bottle this up and I suspect that our discovery won't be well received."

Rob had looked worried ever since it had been revealed to him that the laser had been fired from the New Century Tower, a steel and glass column of central government departments that only served to highlight the danger they were in.

"Our discovery? Your discovery, you mean. You didn't have to tell me," he said. "I was perfectly happy to go to the movies tonight. Or maybe to a bar, have one or two drinks, pick up a nice girl. Now you're telling me

I'm going to have to watch my back in case the President of the United States of America steps out of the shadows and sticks a knife in it. How deep does it go?"

"I don't know," Martyn answered, truthfully, though not with cast iron conviction. "Probably not as deep as the White House, though."

"Oh, that's a relief," Rob replied, meaning the opposite. "They've only managed to assassinate two people, murder forty others, set up the biggest crime boss in the city and rig his trial in an American Court of Justice without anyone finding out. They've only succeeded in making fools of the entire city population so they can't be very important. I can stop worrying now. Martyn, who the hell's side are we on?"

"I don't know for sure," Martyn said. "But for starters, you can add the laser assassin and the Special Forces to your list. After that, your guess is as good as mine."

"The laser assassin? You know who it is?"

"Yes," Martyn replied. "And Greg Miller has already amassed the evidence to back it up."

He opened up a file on Miller's desk and began to extract information from it. "The sixty eighth floor of the New Century Tower is officially leased to the defence department of the American Government..."

Rob placed his head in his hands. "Oh, shit..."

"However, the Russian Embassy also lists one of their subsidiary departments as being housed also on the sixty eighth floor of the New Century Tower. But they can't both exist in the same place. Or can they? As it happens, another subsidiary department of the Russian embassy is a small photographic studio in Arcades and..." - he held up a small card - "...while that is the address on this business card, the phone number on the card actually belongs to an extension on the sixty eighth floor of the New Century Tower."

He closed the file and slid Greg Miller's diary across the table, twisting it the right way up for Rob to read. There was only one entry and that was under today's date.

"7 PM. Meet Raspov. Eden Square."

Rob was amazed. "Raspov! What? That spotty little Russian defector with the trick camera? He's the mysterious and deadly assassin?"

"That's right. Who else could it be? After all, he is an expert on lasers."

"But I don't understand. If that's true why would he want to help us? It was he who tried to convince us that there was no such thing as the portable laser rifle. It was he who stated publicly that the laser weapon they claimed to have found in Cassida's car could not possibly have been genuine. Why would he do that when he was on the verge of getting away with it completely?"

"I don't know," Martyn conceded. "But it worked. I think your spotty little Russian defector is actually an extremely intelligent and cunning individual, not to mention thoroughly evil. We've been manipulated by him since day one and somehow he seems to have formed an alliance with the SFN. But now, if we're careful, we can turn the tables. That is the only consolation about what has happened this evening. Thanks to Greg Miller, for the first time since last October, we are the ones holding the upper hand, because no one knows we're here and no one will suspect that Greg Miller went to all this trouble to set up Raspov. But it's only a matter of time before they find the cameras on the roofs and then we're in trouble. And besides, we owe it to Greg Miller to see this through."

"So what do we do?" Rob said, not really expecting an answer. He did not really get one.

"I don't know," Martyn replied. "But I do know one thing. I don't particularly want to go out roaming the streets. I think the SFN already know I'm onto them. They took us for fools once and we almost died for it. They realise we won't fall for that again and my turning up in Eden Square tonight must have been a considerable embarrassment - because I know they shot Greg Miller in cold blood and that it was premeditated. I hope the Chief gets here soon and then he can take the responsibility."

"Did you get to speak to him?"

"No, he was out but I told Holly to get him to call you at home and then I left a message on your answering machine. You don't have any house guests, do you? I couldn't use mine because Melissa's going to be there this evening. And besides, it's one of the first places Reynolds and Manciani will go looking for me. Yours seemed a little safer but I think even that will buy us only a little extra time. I just hope Brett is carrying his remote interrogator."

As if in answer to a prayer, they heard the click of the main office door being unlocked. A few seconds later, the unmistakeable tones of the Chief's voice penetrated through the double doors of the 'laboratory'.

But, even in those few seconds, both Rob and Martyn had drawn their handguns and positioned themselves either side of the inner door.

Chief Brett Lancaster drew a deep breath and began drumming his fingers lightly on the table. He stared at the three monitor screens, now blank, and then at the picture on the editor station monitor, frozen at the point prior to the explosion that would ultimately take over fifty lives. He turned and perused the wall charts and carefully followed the line from the limousine to the sixty eighth floor of the New Century Tower as though if he followed it carefully enough, it would suddenly change direction and arrive at a place that did not make him quite so nervous. Then he appeared to retreat into himself as if drawing on archives of mental images and thoughts. Rob and Martyn sat in silence and waited patiently. Finally, the Chief spoke.

"Well, they have made idiots of us, haven't they? When Cassida was committed, they must have laughed their butts off. I wish we understood why." He searched the two detectives' faces looking for an answer but none was forthcoming.

"How many people know about this?"

"As far as we know, just the three of us," Rob said. "The question is, what do you want us to do about it because we can't stay here much longer?"

"Agreed," the Chief said. There was another long pause. It was a difficult decision to make but Martyn had already made it and felt strongly that the Chief would come to the same conclusion. Even though the wait was a lot longer than he anticipated, he was not disappointed.

"Under the circumstances," the Chief said, "there is only one course of action. A series of murders has been committed. Now we have a suspect we must act accordingly, no matter who ends up being implicated. We have to blow the whole thing wide open. If we open a political can of worms then so be it. I can't take the responsibility for that if the Special Forces, or the Defence Department, or whoever else is involved, decide to treat us like morons. That's their mistake. Luckily, we're in a television station so all we have to do is to take this stuff down the corridor and broadcast it. And I think we should also do something which won't be so easy - arrest Raspov."

"It might be better if we arrest Raspov first," Martyn said. "While we still have the element of surprise. He's too smart to let us walk up and arrest him if he knows we're coming. As soon as this material is released, he'll go into hiding – or seek asylum at the Embassy - and we'll probably never find him. It would be embarrassing if we produced all this evidence and then lost the suspect."

The Chief turned to Rob seeking a second opinion.

"The longer we delay releasing this information, the greater the risk. Until this becomes a public issue, we have to assume that we're in danger from the Special Forces at least. Under the circumstances, I can't force either of you to go out there and put your lives at risk, even if I do agree with you."

But Rob was adamant. "We have to get Raspov while he's most vulnerable. If they decide they're going to protect him even after we've blown his cover then we've got no chance of going anywhere near him. They've gone to so much trouble to protect him so far that I don't think they will just drop him when he becomes a hot potato. Let's get Raspov, find out what the hell is going on and then blow the whole thing wide open. At least while we have Raspov and the tapes, we're in a strong bargaining position."

The Chief could not argue but he did nothing to disguise the unease he felt.

"They're probably guarding him already," he said, weakly. "Oh, to hell with it, you're right. So who goes to get Raspov and who takes care of the tapes?"

"Sorry?" Rob said. "Are you volunteering to go and get Raspov?"

"Why not?" Chief Lancaster replied. "There's no reason why it should automatically be you two, especially since you almost got killed not so long ago."

"I want Raspov," Martyn said. "If only to see his face when we play our check mate. Besides, if anybody finds those cameras in Eden Square then whoever stays here and tidies up is going to be in more danger. There is no soft option."

The Chief turned to Rob and silently repeated the question.

"I stick with my partner," he said. "To the bitter end. And anyway, he needs another rook."

Raspov's private address, as Martyn explained, was printed on the reverse side of the business card and described the location of a downtown

Arcades apartment which they knew to be authentic, even if they were not sure that Raspov lived there.

"If he's still at the New Century Tower then I think it is reasonable to assume we have less chance of getting to him. If we try and take him there, and he's already left, it's likely that someone will tip him off before we can get to his apartment. And that's assuming we get past the security without incident. We'd be better off raiding his apartment first. If he isn't there then we can stake it out until he arrives. Chief, we'll leave messages on Rob's answerphone. It's the safest way for the present. Stash the tapes and then call. By that time we should have reached the apartment and we'll know whether Raspov is there or not. Right, let's go."

On the way to Arcades they stopped off at the precinct to pick up some surveillance equipment. While Rob loaded the car, Martyn tried to call Melissa again but there was still no reply other than the ultimate, monotonous conversation of the answering machine. He then started to dial Jacqui Miller's number but thought better of it. It would be the first place they would bug if they wanted to be sure they had not left any loose ends. He desperately needed to talk to Melissa. Even more importantly, he needed Jacqui Miller's forgiveness. He could not completely accept that he could have done nothing to save Greg Miller's life. He should have sewn up this case a long time ago. What made things worse was that he had abandoned Jacqui Miller at the one time she needed support. Alone in her grief, he had left her with the Special Forces and she would have no idea of the danger she was in.

They drove through the streets in introspective silence, Martyn growing more and more tense as row after row of neon light rose and fell on the moving vehicle. A sensation of utter loneliness and dread came over him, a terrifying premonition that he might never see Jacqui Miller again, and that he might never again hold Melissa in his arms and feel the soft waves of her hair flowing across his face and the scent of her body filling him with longing. He was scared, very scared. Yet how could he act on an instinct he could not rationalise or understand?

Rob seemed to drive the car on auto-pilot, existing in another mental plane, and Martyn remembered the confession he had made in the bistro the morning before Gremelkov had been killed. As Martyn watched, he could swear he saw him wince once or twice as if reliving a waking nightmare. This was not the way they went into battle. Usually they were brimming with confidence, almost nonchalant in the certainty of routine victory. But now, for the first time, he did not know if he could trust his partner and equally, he was not sure if his partner should have any more reason to trust him. What had happened to them?

Rob was the first to speak.

"What happens if we don't arrest Raspov tonight?" he said. "If we don't find him before they find the cameras, which they're bound to do tomorrow, then how long have we got before they discover the tapes are missing and put two and two together? They're not stupid, are they? When they find the cameras, they'll realise they are missing the homing device which controls them. It won't take a great leap of logic for them to know that you were the only one who could have taken it from Miller and that you must also have the tapes. And then what? They'll have everyone out looking for us. If they've found the cameras then we're already in trouble and we're also wasting our time because Raspov sure as hell won't be in his apartment. The tables could turn again at any minute and we'd never know. We might be heading straight into a trap."

"Do we have any choice?" Martyn said. "It would be nice to know if we still had the element of surprise but there is no way we can find out. All I know is that the first place they would look is at the television studios and they hadn't arrived when we left. I don't think they'll discover the cameras until morning. I'm working on that assumption. And if we don't have Raspov when they find us, then I just hope having possession of the tapes will give us some bargaining power. At least enough to keep us alive."

But Rob was not convinced.

"And then what happens?" he said. "Do we have to spend the rest of our lives looking over our shoulders? They might not kill us while we have the tapes but how can we live like that? If we release the tapes into the public domain, they may kill us anyway. They would have more than enough reason. The tapes directly implicate only Raspov. They would need us as witnesses if anyone else were to go down with him. And what if they don't need Raspov anymore? What good would the tapes be then? Let's face it, Martyn. This whole thing stinks. If we don't find Raspov tonight then we're in deep shit."

"Possibly," Martyn said. The solution was simple but he did not want to say the words. In the end, he was forced to.

"You don't have to do this, you know. It will only be me they're after. Why don't you go home? Nobody is expecting you to do this."

It had to be said because Rob needed to hear it, because he had to have the opportunity to make the choice which was not really a choice. Because, having made that choice, he would cease to agonise over the possible consequences and, instead, would concentrate on the task in hand. His reply was no more or less than Martyn expected but he had never felt more grateful.

"No chance," Rob said, simply. There was no sign of insult or hurt. At the bottom line, it was a straightforward decision. All the fears he had expressed may come true but he would not, could not, desert his colleague.

"I stick with my partner. To the bitter end."

Rob parked the car two blocks from the apartment building. As they came to a halt, Martyn purposely made a show of climbing out of the vehicle without hesitation. Beyond a small stretch of derelict wasteland, almost two miles away, the New Century Tower loomed high above the city, bathed in spasmodic moonlight as the clouds above it began to break up and the promise of clearer weather could be seen in evidence along the horizon.

Immediately he saw the Tower, the Tower saw him.

He was being watched.

As before, he felt those eyes burning into him, watching him with an intensity that he could not overcome or ignore. Though he now knew the identity of the watcher he did not feel any less nervous. Because somehow, through an unnatural intuition he did not understand, he had always held the power to know the watcher's identity but had been too blind or too stupid to see that which was crying out to be seen. He now knew that he could have looked to the sixty eighth floor of the New Century Tower at any time and immediately made the connection. Because the sensation he had experienced on all those occasions did not originate from the Tower, it came from within himself. He knew this because the sensation of being watched was still there - and yet no one, no human, at this distance, in this darkness, could be watching him now.

And in that same moment he knew Raspov was still in the Tower and they would find nothing of value in his apartment.

54

They waited for three seconds and then Martyn kicked down the door. Rob burst into the room and darted immediately to the left, his gun raised, ready to home in on any target. Without hesitation Martyn followed and sprang to his right, adopting a crouching position on the opposite side of the doorway. As he dropped down a sharp pain stabbed at the upper half of his right arm. It felt familiar but he ignored it and forced himself to concentrate on the matter in hand.

The hollow echo of their entry gave him a good idea of what to expect. The room was almost empty. To his left, set in the far wall, a pair of dull, red curtains, which would normally have gone unnoticed, hung over a solitary window. The curtains were open and the city lights cast long, eerie shadows down the length of the room. The window itself was also slightly ajar and an icy cold draught of night air crept in through the chink and softly ruffled the curtains. Opposite the door through which they had entered was an old and battered wardrobe, the only piece of furniture in the room. In the far right hand corner stood an open doorway leading to further rooms at the back of the apartment. There was no carpet, no light fittings, no sign of life. Even one of the walls had not been papered and the cracked plaster drew intricate patterns like lightning strikes issuing down from the ceiling, frozen in time.

They made no sound. Martyn rigidly fixed his concentration, and the barrel of the .38, on the open doorway but he could already sense that the rest of the apartment contained no more life than this first room. From the doorway, darkness and silence poured in. As the seconds ticked quietly away, nothing threatened, nothing beckoned.

With a heavy sigh that seemed to signal both disappointment and the release of tension he heard Rob slowly slide down the wall until he was sitting on the naked floorboards. The sound of the gun landing in his lap quickly followed. Martyn kept his own gun levelled on the doorway. It was typical of Rob to call a halt to a raid as soon as he suspected there would be nothing to shoot at. His own intuition also told him there was nothing behind the door but, without knowing why, he had suddenly started to receive bad vibes about the whole thing and his gun remained frozen on the lifeless alcove.

Seconds later, he too let out a long sigh and allowed his body to relax. He still felt uneasy but this uneasiness had haunted him from the day they had first started out on the case and he had learned to live with it. It was clear they were in no immediate danger. The apartment was empty. Raspov was not there and it did not appear that he ever had been. Inside, the intimidating silence was broken only by the sound of traffic on the street below and the distinctive murmur of the city as it breezed gently through the open window. On the opposite side of the street a full moon rose slowly above another tenement block and a flickering neon sign brought new life to the lightning strikes on the wall opposite.

Suddenly, he became aware of the dull ache in his right arm and he recalled how it had stabbed at him, like a torn muscle, when he had first entered the room only seconds before. And yet the real pain was registering for the first time. Looking down at the arm he saw that it was badly gashed halfway between the shoulder and the elbow - as though he had caught himself on something. At first there seemed to be no explanation for it. Then he could smell the burning, like the faint odour of a distant garden bonfire. Instinctively, he turned his head towards the source. Just above his right shoulder a circular patch of wallpaper, about three centimetres wide, was smouldering black on white like a negative reflection of the full moon against the night sky. From this black moon, rising fumes were tracing a wispy charcoal stain on the white paper as they rose nonchalantly towards the ceiling. As he watched, the fumes gradually faded away until the scorched stains looked like they could have been there for decades.

There was no need to look. The unearthly silence in the room told him everything. He looked across at Rob's slumped body with the handgun casually resting in his lap. His eyes were still open, staring lifelessly and yet wildly across the room. The expression on his face was that of someone who had fought a duel and realised in the very last fraction of a second that he had not been quick enough. There was also a faint trace of frustration, like the frown of a chess player who wished he could take the last move again.

Above his body, exactly where he would have been standing only seconds earlier, the familiar scorch marks had appeared on the white wallpaper.

He looked across the room. Even among the dancing shadows, created by the neon sign outside, it was possible to make out the two tiny holes in the wardrobe, one on either side of the lock. For the first time he noticed the wire flex which climbed up the back wall amid the lightning bolts and then darted across the ceiling directly towards the door where it divided into two single strands. The mechanism was basic, a six inch strip of conductive tape placed across the top corner of the door. Whether the door had been opened or kicked down would have made no difference, the tape would be broken and the wardrobe would have released its rays of death.

Directly on target.

He carefully raised his arm until it hovered above the scorched patch of wallpaper above him. He winced as the pain of the gash shot through his body. The injury was more serious than he had first thought. Then suddenly he brought the arm down with a quick flick, his hand passing over the scorch mark. There was no pain except in his arm which again sent a spasm across his torso. The laser had died.

In shock he found his thoughts lucid and began going through the motions. The fact that it was a laser served only to add insult to injury. Admittedly, the laser beam was clean and quiet but there was a certain amount of risk attached. Raspov would have had to be sure that both of them would step into the beam and there was no way he could have been, not without inside information. A bomb would have been noisy but much more efficient. He examined the positions of the two scorch marks on the wall, both at chest height, both exactly where every police trainer on the force would have told him to be during a raid of this type.

Directly on target.

They had been set up.

But there was still some risk, and where there are risks there would have to be contingencies. His attention was immediately focused on the open doorway once more. Levelling the handgun, he walked stealthily over to the alcove, ducking under the path of the laser beam in case it should suddenly become activated a second time. There was still no sign of life. Through the door he found a short length of corridor with two doors leading from it, one to the left about a metre in and one at the end. The first doorway looked into a room directly behind the wardrobe. Like the first room it was desolate, just a single window gazing out on the full moon and the flashing neon sign casting electric shadows across the bare floorboards. In the far right hand corner of the room was another door. He went through it and found himself inside the shell of an old bathroom. A further door led into what must have been a kitchen area but this was also empty. He realised then that the wardrobe must have been brought in specially - someone had gone to a lot of trouble to prepare for this. He wondered how long ago the preparations had been made.

He walked through the kitchen to another door. As he expected, he found himself back in the corridor. By now his right arm was beginning to grow weaker and he knew he would have to take some action to prevent any further loss of blood. Taking care not to disturb the wound, he ripped the right hand blood-soaked sleeve of his shirt from the shoulder and began wrapping it round the gash. Then he placed one end of the sleeve over an exposed nail sticking out of the kitchen door frame and used his left hand to tie a knot, pulling tightly against the nail until he could no longer bear the pain. He then repeated the exercise to complete a reef knot and returned to the first room.

Without really knowing why, without thinking, he began to check over Rob's body, treating it as he would any other murder victim. He checked for breathing and for a pulse though he had known from the moment he had seen the gash on his arm, and smelt the burning paper, that his partner was dead. He ran through all of Rob's pockets but found nothing. He was carrying only his police identification and the handgun. He took them both and then stopped to think. There was still one immediate puzzle unresolved. The laser set up was too much of a risk. There had to be a contingency.

He checked outside the door, gazing up and down the stairwell, listening intently. There was no sign of life. He went back into the apartment and walked towards the wardrobe. Close up, he discovered that the left hand hole was aimed towards the right hand side of the doorway and vice versa. One hole was low and the other was high to give the maximum possible target field. The only way they would not have been hit by the lasers was if they had remained in the doorway - and no one in their right mind would ever have done that. He had been lucky, very lucky. Sometimes he would go into a crouch, other times he would remain standing. It depended entirely on his mood at the time. He turned the handle on the wardrobe door and began to open it. Suddenly, he stopped.

A bomb would have been much more efficient.

The mental echo screamed at him as if he had tripped an alarm. If Rob had survived the trap instead of him, would he have left the apartment without looking in the wardrobe? After an investigation lasting months, would either of them not have cared to see the object they had been searching for all that time? That was the contingency, it had to be. Whatever happened they would have had to look in the wardrobe, even if, through a technical fault, the lasers had failed to go off. The wardrobe was the only object he had seen in the whole building.

He looked through the small niche he had already created in the door. The interior seemed to be packed with scientific equipment and steel plate. Through the gap he could see nothing which looked like a rifle - or a bomb. He supposed the laser must look very similar to the system Raspov had so graphically demonstrated to them in the autumn but that would never have fitted inside the wardrobe. All that pressure to find the laser rifle was a ploy. They had never wanted it found; just to brainwash them into thinking that a rifle was what they were looking for. There was only one question now. Why?

He carefully closed the door and assured himself that it was not about to spring open before releasing the handle. Next, he carried Rob's body into the room behind the wardrobe and gently laid him down by the window. Without hesitation he returned to the first room and ripped down the wire flex from the ceiling. If the laser was triggered to fire on a null signal then he could remove the flex without danger. He carefully tied one end of the flex around the wardrobe door handle and retreated to the corridor with the other end. There, he closed the door to and sat down, his back to the wall which separated the corridor from the second room. He paused for a few seconds while making himself comfortable and then yanked the flex.

Even through the small crack he had left in the door - just enough for the flex to pass through - the white flash, in contrast to the dark corridor, was almost blinding. What must have been a millisecond later, a loud crack followed; a single, deafening staccato snap followed by the sound of plaster and wood debris striking against the door and surrounding walls like a violent rainstorm.

He waited briefly and then pushed the door open. It creaked slightly and then broke free from its hinges and twisted downwards, smashing into three clean pieces as it struck the floorboards. The room was thick with plaster dust hanging like dense fog in the air. He wandered in amongst the debris, stumbling over large pieces of twisted steel and wood which lay scattered across the room. The roof of the wardrobe was still intact and lay on the floor exactly where the wardrobe had been standing seconds before. Behind it the blast had torn down several square metres of the adjoining wall and through the hole and dust he could see Rob, completely unmoved, leaning against the window. The silent light of the full moon burst into both the rooms and illuminated the plaster dust in such a way that it appeared to be alive, like a swarm of a million tiny white fireflies dancing in the air.

Suddenly, something caught his attention. Over by the window, its curtains now hanging in shreds and flapping in the breeze, something glistened in the moonlight; not just another mangled piece of steel but something with shape, with structure, with purpose. He walked over to the window and stooped to pick up the object, fascinated by its perfect form and amazed at its apparent resilience to the blast. It had not been there before. It must have been inside the wardrobe.

Though he would have recognised it from the photograph of the weapon found in Cassida's car, in close up he could finally appreciate its intricacy. He studied it carefully. It was about one metre in length. The main part of the body, directly above the trigger, was bulky and consisted of five identical cylinders each about twenty centimetres long. There were two barrels. The larger of the two had an inner bore close to one centimetre while the thinner tube, which sat on top of this, was at least five times smaller. If there had been a telescopic sight mounted on this rifle then it had been blown off in the blast. The weapon was so ergonomically perfect that he could guess quite easily how it functioned. The trigger mechanism had two positions. The first would cause a pilot beam to be transmitted from the smaller tube and this would be used to line up the target using an infrared telescopic sight mounted on top of the main body. Once the pilot beam had found its unsuspecting target it only required the slightest pressure from the forefinger to unleash the primary beam, delivering death at the speed of light.

On the floor, spattered in plaster dust and only feet from the rifle, was the small metallic case which he knew to be the power pack. The box seemed surprisingly robust and it too appeared to have survived the blast. Not far away the second power pack, also intact, sat among the debris of scorched, splintered wood that had once been the wardrobe.

He held the weapon up towards the moonlight where he could see it more clearly. At last they had found it. They had found the laser rifle. And it no longer mattered.

He wondered then if this had been the weapon which had killed Rob or the one that had caused the gash in his own arm. He looked round the room and quickly found the crooked barrel of the second rifle. It appeared to have been blown to pieces. He tossed the barrel to one side, took the complete rifle and one of the power packs and climbed through the hole in the wall into the back room.

"We found it," he said.

He placed the laser rifle at Rob's feet and stared down at the floorboards as tears began to form in his eyes.

"We found it."

He sat down under the window, soaking himself in the moonlight, and took Rob's lifeless body in his arms. Then, and only then, did he begin to cry.

55

They waited for three seconds and then Rob kicked down the door. Martyn immediately stormed into the apartment and jumped to his left, gun levelled, eyes quickly scanning the room, ready to cover anyone who showed signs of resistance. As Rob moved in behind him and leaped to the right hand side of the doorway, the image on his retina flashed momentarily on several interior scenes; first the alcove in the corner with the open doorway, then the opposite wall with its patterns of sheet lightning, flickering as the neon danced outside the window, then the wardrobe, then another blank wall of cracked plaster. Finally the window, slightly ajar, opening on to the sound of cold winds and hot traffic, a pair of solitary red curtains wafting in the breeze.

Then the pain. The very core of his heart seemed to catch fire. Though he knew he had only taken a step back to steady himself, he felt as if the force of the blast had slammed him into the wall behind. He couldn't speak. He tried to call out, to warn Rob, but the words would not form and there was no sound. The wardrobe! It's in the wardrobe! Slowly he sank to the floor, sliding down the wall and he no longer had the strength to keep his gun levelled. As he flopped down on the cold floorboards the handgun, still clutched between his fingers, fell into his lap and remained still.

All these things, Rob would have seen and felt. With one arm wrapped around Rob and the other supporting himself against the window frame, he gazed blindly across the city and relived the raid over and over again. Every permutation, every eventuality. It did not make sense. It could so easily have been the other way round and yet, by divine intervention or by sheer hazard, he did not know which, Rob was dead and he was still alive. For that, a second chance to live, there had to be a price. He had an obligation to Rob, to Greg and Jacqui Miller, and to Melissa, to see this through. The case was over but now he had to ensure the administration of justice. The level of corruption was so uncertain that he could no longer trust the legal machine to do the job. He would have to take care of Raspov himself and answer for it later.

He sat with Rob under the window for almost a quarter of an hour, staring out at the New Century Tower, its tall, sleek silhouette rising up against the night sky. With each second the tower became less an important piece of the jigsaw puzzle and more of an obsession. He had lived in its shadow since first moving to the city and he had always thought it strangely beautiful. But now it contained his enemy and he could no longer look upon it in any other way.

For a moment he broke free from his fixation with the tower and gazed up at the moon, its soft luminescence casting a strange aura over the whole of the city. On Earth, everything was continually changing; lives were forever being exchanged, as old souls departed, leaving behind sadness and loss, new births brought joy and vitality to the slowly dying planet. Perspectives shifted; nothing was ever as it seemed and there was always a catch. But the moon, like the sun, never changed. Through century upon century, change upon change, it had always been there, always ready to provide the vital focal point in which life could be brought to a halt, just long enough to be able to reflect and take stock before moving on.

As he followed the moon, slowly arcing over the rooftops, he was filled with that same sensation he had been experiencing since the case began, the same sensation he had every time he went to Eden Square. Someone, somewhere, was gazing up at the moon with him, also searching for answers to impossible questions. He felt he knew who it was, not by name but in spirit, almost like a reflection of himself, as if the moon was his own reflection staring back at him.

Suddenly, the night was filled with flashing blue lights and screeching sirens as squadrons of emergency vehicles converged in the street outside the building. There was no time for goodbyes. There was no need. He gently pulled his arm from around Rob's body, picked up the laser rifle and left the apartment.

56

Martyn had not slept all night. He was tired and unbearably lonely but lucid enough to know that the combination of grief and exhaustion was beginning to take its toll on his mental and emotional faculties. The pain in his arm had subsided and he was left with a dull ache he could largely ignore. As the early morning light grew brighter, he repeatedly looked at the newspaper he was carrying in the hope that the headline would suddenly alter and the nightmare end. But each time, the eyes that stared back at him from the tabloid held an equal intensity to his own and transfixed him, forcing him into a battle of wills he could never win because the photograph, with its lethal manic stare, was locked in suspended animation and would never grow hungry, would never feel pain.

Have you seen this man?

As dawn passed into history, a million people would wake up to meet that stare and there would no longer be anywhere for him to hide. He would be a fugitive in his own city, running from his colleagues, his friends, unable to approach anybody. He had taken part in so many operations like this yet he had never even come close to appreciating how it must feel to be on the run, knowing that he would systematically be sought out, flushed out and wiped out. As though he were carrying a plague.

And when it was all over, a million people would retire peacefully to their beds, believing everything they had read in the papers to be true; believing that he had killed Howard Robinson, Sarjena West, Angelo, Gremelkov, Greg Miller and finally his own partner in an insane one-man war against the city; believing that he was suffering from a rare form of schizophrenia which totally transformed him into an obsessive psychotic with a blood lust which had to be satisfied before he could revert back to his alter ego.

They had stitched him up so well he could not help but be impressed at their ingenuity. Here was an opportunity to explain away all of their embarrassments in one fell swoop. The most perfect reason for not solving a crime - when the culprit is actually the detective in charge of the case. And how were they to know? He was so good at his job. Everybody knew that. They just did not appreciate the abnormal psychological effects that such acute and unrelenting stress could bring about.

Besides the enormity of his present predicament, the concern he had expressed only hours before, when they were on their way to Raspov's apartment, paled into insignificance. So many people had died, why should he be the only one to survive? Where was his God-given right to live? The odds were stacked so highly against him that at first, his inclination was to give himself up and end it all quickly and painlessly. His will to survive had been briefly subdued by the emptiness he felt at the loss of his friend and partner. He was tired and lethargic. He approached every street corner with careless abandon, hoping that around the next one he would find Melissa searching for him, and melt into her arms. At three in the morning he had called her, but still she had not returned to the apartment and the click-whirr of the answerphone was yet another stake, driven deep into a heart that was already fractured.

The new morning and the newspaper headline had changed all that. The warm, silent light of the rising sun renewed his strength and uplifted his spirit. He found he had adopted a more positive attitude. From some inner depth, there was a stirring, the waking of a survival instinct that had been implanted in his genes for generations. It was the call for justice, for ultimate peace, and for revenge. Where there was sadness, there was now rage; where there was utter dejection, there was now determination; where there was desperation, there was now hope.

But it was the newspaper headline that brought about the greatest change of heart. They had made an assumption that had filled him with anger. In order to publish such a story, they had assumed that they would be able to catch him and silence him before he could take any action which would show the story to be untrue. They were behaving as though he were already dead, as if it were a fait-accompli. Yet if they presumed that he would simply give up and allow those people he cared for to believe he was a schizophrenic mass murderer, then they did not really know him.

Firstly, he had to make some attempt to disguise himself. The longer he looked like the person in the newspaper, the greater the certainty that he would be caught. His eyes, which were his most expressive and recognisable feature, could easily be hidden by shades, but in winter they would look inconspicuous only as long as the sun was up and, according to the weather forecast, that was not expected to be for long. He also needed food and sleep and they would not be so easy to obtain. This was going to be the toughest day of his life.

Chief Brett Lancaster was nothing if not a creature of habit. When he arrived at his favourite coffee shop on the stroke of one o'clock, Martyn was inclined to feel insulted that not even the loss of one of his superior officers, or the impending death of another at the hands of a lynch mob, could deter him from his routine. But for that he was also thankful as he had banked all of his hopes on the Chief being there.

How he had survived with such a regular lifestyle for so long was beyond Martyn. The Chief always ate alone and always at the same table, in a quiet corner right by the window. Anybody who wanted to assassinate him would have had no difficulty. Every lunchtime he was a sitting duck. They had tried, on numerous occasions, to persuade him to move around, to sit further into the bistro, to eat somewhere else now and again, but the Chief would not hear of it. He refused to allow his position to make unnecessary demands on his private life. If someone were determined to kill him, he had said, then there were plenty of other opportunities and he would not live in fear of eating in the way he enjoyed.

Martyn waited for a few minutes, until he was sure the Chief had not been followed, and until the waitress had made the necessary visits to his table. Then he crossed over the street and went inside, making directly for the table where Brett Lancaster sat, his head buried in a newspaper and one hand embracing a cup of coffee. He sat down unnoticed and surreptitiously placed his handgun on his lap.

"I have a lot of questions - and they all begin with 'why?'"

Brett Lancaster did not know what to say and so said nothing. His eyes betrayed a sense of hopelessness, fatigue and guilt as though he were no longer in control of his own life but had left it, to stand on the sidelines and watch the world go by. Apart from looking up from his paper, there was no visible reaction to the question.

Martyn persisted. "Why?"

"Is that thing pointing at me?" the Chief said, tersely. "If so, I don't think we can proceed with this conversation on any reasonably intelligent level. I do have some dignity left, you know."

"You want my respect? After all you've done? How do I know you won't try to shoot me? You could become a hero overnight - the man who caught the city's most dangerous mass murderer. All you have to do is live with your conscience and you don't appear to be having much trouble with that so far."

"Don't I?" the Chief said, half rhetorically. Then, speaking directly to Martyn, he said, "I can't kill you because I don't have a gun. I left it behind. Besides, I don't want your blood on my hands. There are SFN dogs who are specially trained and paid to do this kind of dirty work. They are out there fouling the streets right now. I've been ordered to keep well out of the way and I intend to do just that. You have nothing more to fear from me. I'm through with it. It's out of my hands."

Martyn returned the gun to its holster, inside his jacket.

"I don't think I could have killed you anyway."

"I know," the Chief replied. "If it's any consolation, were we to be spotted together at this table they would probably kill us both and have done with it. I am as dispensable to them as you are."

"You're telling me that they have to kill me? That there is no choice? Aren't you going to tell me to give myself up?"

"I told you. I'm out of it. Besides, I know you wouldn't listen to me. I'd be wasting my breath. But if you want the truth, I don't see that it will end any other way. It can't - not now. I tried everything I could to stop this but you persisted in hammering away at it, didn't you? You could have ended it a hero but you wouldn't let it go. You weren't expected to do anything else, I suppose. But they had it all under control the whole time. For everything I tried, they came up with an answer."

Martyn was beginning to get lost in the conversation and he was aware that he should not spend too much time there.

"Brett, let's stop this. I need some answers. I need to know why. Why you betrayed Rob and me, why you sent us both to be killed last night. I need to know so many things but most of all I want to know why so much effort has gone into protecting that grubby little Russian defector."

The Chief sat up and straightened himself as if about to reveal the punch line of a very long joke. But he was not smiling.

"Because the future of the world rests on that grubby little Russian defector. In fact, Raspov did not defect; the Alliance gave him to us."

Martyn was puzzled. "Go on."

"East-West relations are fragile. Over the last few years, negotiations were continuing to break down until they reached the point where both parties were concerned enough to realise that some kind of action needed to be taken to avoid an escalation and perhaps war. The problem was made worse when they came to tally up arms reductions. Over the last few decades, both sides had dropped their nuclear arsenals to a bare minimum but both were equally surprised to find that the Alliance had advanced their laser technology much faster than we had.

"Having sacrificed our nuclear superiority, there was a drastic imbalance in the relative strengths of our conventional weapons. We became concerned, the Alliance became worried that we were concerned and the whole thing spiralled. We threatened to rebuild our nuclear arsenal to regain an equal strength and so on. There was only one way out. We had to have the laser technology and the Russians had to give it to us. Without it, there could be no guarantee of peace."

"That isn't peace," Martyn protested. "It's a balance of fear."

"It's only a balance of fear for those who have to bear the stress; the army, the government, those who unwittingly get dragged into it like you and I. For the rest of the population, our families and friends, the people we spend the whole of our lives trying to protect, it's peace. As long as they can go about their daily lives without having to live with the threat of being bombed, then it doesn't really matter what goes on behind the scenes provided it stays behind the scenes. But I'm not here to bandy politics with you because what you and I think doesn't count for anything. The decision was made, the Russians sent Raspov to rectify the balance and the threat of a nuclear arms race was temporarily removed.

"What they did not tell us was that Raspov had some dark secrets - but they must have known. The man is a genius and one of the world's most renowned and cunning battle campaigners. He has an IQ of over a hundred and eighty and a lateral intelligence to match. He is also a schizophrenic. He thrives on games, on competition. He is obsessed with solving complex problems and meeting challenges where he can turn certain defeat into overwhelming victory when all the odds are stacked against him. And he does, frequently. Always, he is in control. And occasionally, he kills people. He has to. It's an addiction. He must satisfy his second personality."

Martyn was astonished. "And we allow him to?"

"We don't have much choice," he said. "So far we can link him to over twenty murders and eleven rapes. It's considered a small price to pay for world peace."

"By whom?" Martyn demanded. "Not by me it isn't. Not like that. Where the hell do they draw the line, for pity's sake. A hundred? A thousand? A hundred thousand? The more he gets away with, the more he'll try and push his luck. Brett, only a few days ago, he killed and mutilated almost one hundred people in less than a second! How the hell can you stand by and let that happen? One of them was the Alliance Ambassador. You call that striving towards world peace? He could have begun a world war in one afternoon."

A thought suddenly struck him.

"Wait a minute," he said. "If the Russians gave Raspov to us - knowing that he was a psychopath - then they couldn't complain if he killed Gremelkov, could they?"

The tiny electronic pulses in his brain began to increase, making connections, building the jigsaw.

"But that would be all too neat and tidy. Why do I get the impression that Gremelkov was also set up?"

"Because he was," the Chief confirmed. "Gremelkov was a thorn in the Communist system. He was supposed to be an ambassador for their country. Instead, he was an embarrassment, a constant reminder of the Great Turmoil that we are all trying to forget. So they offered him up as a sacrifice. Apparently, it was well known in the upper echelons of the Alliance that Raspov hated Gremelkov so the picture was complete."

"And what better publicity could they ask for? To appear to all the world to turn the other cheek when their Ambassador is brutally murdered while on a diplomatic mission. World peace created out of nothing more than a perfectly managed stage show. Is that what it's all about?"

Brett Lancaster ignored the question.

"Nobody else was supposed to get killed," he said. "Call it an unlucky coincidence or divine retribution. The laser accidentally punctured the fuel tank and the flames from the petrol bomb ignited the escaping vapour. The rest you know. It wasn't meant to happen that way."

"I'm sure Raspov – a psychotic murderer - was all broken up about it," Martyn said. "But he wasn't down on the Boulevard trying to sort out all the bits of bodies."

Suddenly remembering he was a fugitive, Martyn glanced around, looking for the trap but everything appeared normal.

"And what went wrong last night? How was that supposed to have worked out? Because I'm sure as hell under the impression that I'm not supposed to be walking around today."

At first the Chief was silent and appeared to withdraw into himself, reliving past memories. Then, he suddenly came out of his self-induced trance.

"From the day you first took the case - when Howard Robinson was killed - I knew that it would most likely end like this. You were set up from the very beginning and I'm partly to blame. I've had to live with that knowledge for the last three months. Your death warrant was signed last October and there was little you could about it. I tried everything I could but, like I said earlier, they always came up with an answer."

While the Chief drank the last of his coffee, Martyn waited patiently for the confession which he knew was about to follow. He was about to hear the answers to so many of the questions that had troubled him over the last few months that he could afford to wait a little longer. But the Chief did not prolong the pause. He placed his empty cup back on the table and began to speak.

"Last summer, when Sarjena West's body was discovered in Washington Park, we only had time to carry out a brief autopsy and realised there was something unusual when the body was taken out of our jurisdiction. It had only been in the morgue about two hours. I insisted on following up the case so, to keep me quiet, they summoned me to Special Forces and told me about Raspov. He had been testing a new laser weapon for a top secret defence project and it had gone tragically wrong. They were lying, of course, and I think they knew then that there would be more murders but they naturally didn't say so.

"There was no personal motive. Sarjena West was used as target practice for the prototype weapon; apparently Raspov wanted to test its range. Along with me, the autopsy team were forced to sign non-disclosure agreements and, as you may recall, they were all subsequently transferred during the month of August.

"When Howard Robinson was murdered they could not explain it away so easily. The laser was fired into a crowded square, in thick fog, and the beam went straight through the heart of its victim. This time we didn't even get to examine the body properly. It was whisked straight to Special Forces but that in itself was enough for me to want to know what had happened.

"In order to test the accuracy of an infrared sight, which picks up body heat over a long distance, Raspov had chosen another human subject, though not entirely at random. He had purposely singled out the person with the lowest level of body heat to stretch the sensitivity of the equipment. In fact, Raspov later told me that Robinson probably didn't have too long to live anyway; his heat profile was way under normal.

"I realised then that I was dealing with someone who was insane and that the body count would go up if I did not act. It was I who sent the anonymous messages to Greg Miller, all of them. I reacted the same way you wanted to last night. I thought the sooner the whole thing was out in the open, the better. But it backfired on me. As soon as Raspov learned that the media had hold of the story, he decided to manufacture a game. He wanted to pit his wits against the police force's finest. He personally chose you and Rob for the case. You had the right reputation at the wrong time.

"I protested to Commander Colchek because I knew there could only be one outcome. You were never expected to solve the case but as long as the case remained open, and bodies continued to appear, you would be on it. But I knew you better and, though I admit that I severely underestimated Raspov, I also believed at the time that they had severely underestimated you.

"You want to know why I'm sat here doing nothing? Why I don't appear to feel anything? It's because I went through all of that in October and now I have accepted what was inevitable. What you think I should be feeling now, I felt the morning you were in my office when I put you on the case. I was signing your lives away and I knew it.

"Even then, I continued to leak to the press in the hope that the whole thing would blow open. Greg Miller was one of the best investigative journalists in this country and I knew that if he could expose Raspov before you did, then you would be off the hook. So naturally you went looking for Miller because he was the only clue you had to solving the case. Colchek's men also wanted to find Miller so they could identify the mole in their organisation before he leaked too much."

"Why didn't you tell Miller everything instead of leaving lots of subtle pointers?" Martyn asked.

"Because I didn't want Raspov to be discovered," the Chief replied. "I appreciated the severity and the value of the work he was doing. I only wanted the killing to stop and I thought that I might worry them enough to achieve that. Besides, only a handful of people knew the full facts. It would have been a quick and simple process for them to have pointed the finger at me.

"But I made another mistake. Miller was never meant to solve the case any more than you were. I hoped that his reputation would scare them into preventing Raspov from killing any more people. I thought Raspov was an ingenious animal and that the Special Forces were holding the leash. I couldn't have been more wrong. In truth, it was precisely the opposite way round. Raspov had a free run and the SFN were there to mop up the mess he left behind, to make sure that national security remained intact. Raspov was playing games with them in exactly the same way he did with everyone else. They never knew what he was going to do next. Their brief was to react as quickly as possible to secure the safety of the defence project. In your respect, it was to make sure, by any means possible, that you and Rob never solved the case.

"Raspov could not have been more pleased that Miller had joined in the game. To him, it added an extra dimension, a further complexity to the challenge. He got bored because you weren't getting anywhere so he decided to make things more interesting, first by giving you a demonstration of his laser rifle and then by murdering Angelo in order to set up Cassida. He had meticulously planned everything in advance. And if the Special Forces were beginning to get pissed off with Raspov's antics, they couldn't have been more pleased when Cassida walked right into the trap and got put away.

"Unfortunately, with you and Rob out of action, the game had suddenly come to an abrupt end and that was not part of the plan. So Raspov teamed up with Miller and persuaded him to continue chiselling away at the case. He had to have a toy to play with while he waited for Gremelkov to arrive and Miller was only too happy to take the bait."

The rest was not too difficult to deduce.

"But Miller discovered the burning streamer in the video, made the connection and paid for it with his life," Martyn concluded. "And now Rob has also paid with his life and I'm expected to pay with mine. And you can still sit there and justify it all to the extent that you would betray two of your closest colleagues to perpetuate this farcical chain of murders. For fuck's sake, didn't you see what he did to Angelo? We send people to the electric chair for far less. It was horrific and disgusting. How can you ignore the level you've sunk to and live with yourself? How can you sit and drink coffee knowing that I was out there being hunted like a wild animal?"

Chief Brett Lancaster did not appear even to wince at the words. They were no less than he had expected and Martyn realised that any attempt to tip the balance of his conscience was futile. He was already resigned to a future he did not believe he had the power to change.

"One day," he said, "when Raspov has finished this project and is no longer needed, then there will be a time for revenge and for justice. And, I promise you, he will not escape. But right now, that is the only consolation I can offer you. I do not expect you to forgive me but I hope you will at least try to understand. I never wanted this to happen."

Martyn snatched the newspaper from the Chief and waved it in front of his face, seething.

"You all made one big mistake. You're all acting as if I were dead already. But if you thought I would just give up then you're very much mistaken. There is only one way out of this, I know that. And when I've killed Raspov, we'll see how many people agree with your so called defence policy."

The Chief did not look remotely impressed.

"Good luck to you," he said. "You go with my blessing and my silence."

As Martyn stood up to leave, something in the Chief's tone caused him to pause and search out the reason.

"You really don't think I have a chance, do you?"

The Chief made no attempt to hide his agreement.

"No. Because you don't. You have an Achilles heel and they know all about it."

Martyn sat down again and looked at the Chief quizzically, his eyes silently asking the question.

"You are too sentimental," the Chief replied. "It was your only failing as a cop and the one thing guaranteed to cause you to make a mistake. You trust your closest friends implicitly and naively remove them from of the equation without a second thought. If you hadn't been so blinded with loyalty you would have wrapped this case up long ago. I was the only person that you could have linked into this case but you didn't even look in my direction. And it will be that same loyalty that kills you because, unlike me, you could not even contemplate betrayal."

Martyn felt he was missing the point. Moreover, he sensed that the exact reason for this was the weakness the Chief was describing, that he was unwittingly proving him to be correct. But he did not have time to solve the riddle.

"I don't understand. What are you getting at?"

"Melissa," the Chief said, simply. "You think so much of that girl that the very thought of anything happening to her would make you go to pieces. They know that but they're so confident of catching you that they haven't even bothered to exploit her yet. But if they decide to play their trump card, what will you do then?"

57

Two days passed and a new sunrise cast long, lonely shadows over a desolate world. The city was no longer a place he knew. With the dawning of another day, the transformation was complete. Only the buildings were the same. But beyond mere physical properties, the place he had adopted as his home for the last ten years had changed beyond recognition - as though it had turned inside out, leaving him stranded on the wrong side, alone and bewildered.

Two days growth of beard and an appearance of perpetual fatigue, coupled with the dark glasses, left him looking nothing like the manic photograph they had chosen to print in the paper and he found that he could generally wander the streets without fear of being recognised. That is not to say he was not recognised. He noticed how some people stared at him as they tried to assess the validity of their claim to the 'reward for information leading to his capture' but he found that if he acted naturally they would usually lose interest. Then, to be on the safe side, he would leave that area of town and not return until the next day. While purchasing some food in a downtown supermarket, the cashier remarked on his resemblance to the fugitive cop. Martyn explained how his face had suddenly become the bane of his life and how he had been reported to the police three times since the picture first appeared in the newspaper. They both laughed and Martyn walked out casually. Even then, he left the area and made a mental note not to shop there again.

Fortunately, he had had the foresight, after Rob's death, to withdraw lots of cash before they stopped his cards. Given that his only immediate expenses were food, he estimated he had enough to survive for several weeks.

Two more days passed and still the helicopters could be seen making the occasional patrol over the city. He somehow knew they were searching for him but it seemed futile since the city provided so many forms of refuge from the sky. Avoiding the helicopters was ten times more simple than avoiding rain and he considered the possibility that they were there because of him to be a reflection of his own paranoia. In the end, he did not even bother to hide from them. During the previous day, they had flown over his head, at low level, on three occasions and without incident.

The only time he was really careful was when he was near Eden Square. The concentration of police and security notably increased as he grew nearer to the plaza but he knew that he would have to stay close to the centre of activity if he was to have any chance of getting to Raspov. The way he chose to do this was so audacious that no one would have believed he would take the risk and it had proven, so far, to be safe. It also supplied a temporary solution to his accommodation problem and a hiding place for the laser rifle he had taken from Raspov's empty apartment.

Close to the New Century Tower, in the centre of the next block, stood the relatively inferior needle of the First National Bank. Standing only sixty storeys high, it offered a clear view of the Tower and of the square below. From the roof, he was able to watch all of the movements in and out of the New Century Tower and analyse the various routines of the security patrols, including those who had set up stakeout positions on the roofs around the square and on the buildings leading up to the main entrance of the Tower itself. The only place he could be seen from were the upper floors of the New Century Tower but there was enough air conditioning ducting on the roof of the First National Bank to provide more than adequate cover and he considered the risk minimal.

His observations from the First National Bank building led him to one of two conclusions. Either Raspov was still in the Tower, continuing to use it daily, or they were laying a trap for him, knowing that he must try to reach Raspov if he believed him to be in the Tower. In all probability the Russian would have been moved to another location days before. Though he did not have a strong pair of binoculars, he did not see anyone resembling Raspov enter or leave the building, and there was no build up of security at certain times of the day. The level remained constant around the clock.

The only exception was the occasional appearance of a helicopter as it carried out a routine patrol of the plaza area. Naturally, he was much more wary of them when he was on the roof than in the streets. His temporary home was the small utilities building in the centre of the roof area and it was there that he retreated at the merest hint of the steady whirring of blades in the distance.

He had almost been caught out twice. The skyscraper roofs were significantly more exposed to the sea breezes than the rest of the city, which found shelter in its own surroundings. In strong wind it was possible for a helicopter to approach the building in near silence, and once he did not see it until it drifted right in front of the lens' of his binoculars. For a fraction of a second he panicked. The binoculars magnified the machine so highly it appeared close enough almost to reach out and touch. He instinctively ducked to avoid being decapitated by the spinning rotors.

Fortunately, the helicopter was on a low level patrol and did not possess a clear view of the roof. He was actually looking down on it from a slight angle. They would undoubtedly have seen him if they looked in his direction but their search seemed to be focused elsewhere. Nevertheless, from then on he was much more careful when he broke cover to stake out the square. He religiously carried out a three hundred and sixty degree sweep of the city every two minutes, acting on a programmed signal from his watch. He was also careful not to leave any evidence of his presence on the open roof, and the little he had with him was stored away in the utilities block when he left the building.

Haunted by Chief Lancaster's words of warning, and their implied threat, he called Melissa continually. He could not use the mobile as he knew the technology would have been employed to locate him the instant he switched it on. Instead he called from various street phones, praying that she would be there. But each time, the ringing tones sang out to an empty apartment until the answerphone intercepted the call. He could not bring himself to leave a message. Nothing he could say to a machine would even scratch the surface of what he was feeling and he knew that the line would be tapped. It was with a great deal of self discipline that he prevented himself from going there but he also knew he would not get near the place before being detected and captured. He had called the hospital twice, but each time the switchboard operator had told him that she was on indefinite leave. He just wished he knew where she was.

If the Chief was correct, the danger to Melissa would increase as each day passed. Though he would not serve anybody by simply giving himself up, the longer he managed to elude the search parties, the higher the probability that they would eventually use Melissa to set a trap for him. And he knew - as they knew - that he would have no alternative but to walk into it. Why they had not done so already mystified him but he hoped it was because they did not know where Melissa was either. This was a game to them, which they could win by honourable or despicable means, the latter being the most efficient. There was too much at stake for honour to enter into it. For him, the only way out was to kill Raspov but even that did not guarantee him a future. They had to stop him at all costs and they had the means to do so. So what stopped them?

The answer came in a flash of inspiration; Raspov stopped them. On reflection, they must know where Melissa was. They were not amateurs and Melissa was not trying to hide from them. They would have tracked her down before sunrise the morning after Greg Miller and Rob had been killed. At first, even they would have believed that he would be captured before sundown. That they had still not found him four days later would surprise and concern them enough to set a trap, he was sure.

But he was beginning to know the mind of Raspov. His passion for games could not resist the challenge which fate had presented to him. Somewhere in the city was a man with a thirst for revenge and whose only chance of survival depended on his killing him. For Raspov, it was too good an opportunity to miss. He would stop them from using Melissa because that would be too easy. There was no satisfaction in defeating someone who would willingly back himself into a corner and surrender. But as long as Melissa was kept out of it, he would be a worthy adversary; and Martyn was going to show him that even he, the great Raspov, had made the fatal mistake of seriously underestimating his opposition.

But, for Martyn, such defiance and determination came in sporadic and spasmodic surges which gradually diminished as each day went by, giving way to frustration and increasing concern for Melissa's well-being. By day five, despite intense observations, he had still to discover a way of eluding the security patrols and finding a ploy which would gain him entrance into the New Century Tower. Even if he could achieve that, he had no idea what to expect inside, whether Raspov was there or not. Inevitably, there would be more tight security and his chances of climbing sixty eight floors in such a small area must be minimal. And what if Raspov had predicted he would attempt the impossible? What if Raspov believed he would succeed? When he got to the sixty eighth floor, what could he expect to find there? The possibilities were not encouraging.

If Martyn realised he was spending too much time alone, and that his present unhealthy existence was beginning to warp his normally rational thought processes, he could do nothing about it. Each day he fought mental battles against his impulsiveness and he knew that he would not be able to control his actions much longer. Throughout his waking hours, his thoughts were filled with visions of Rob, staring vacantly into oblivion while the laser continued to burn into his body; of Angelo, staked out in blood like a sacrificial lamb; of Greg Miller, frozen in terror as the lone laser beam cut through the air and slowly closed in on its prey; of Melissa, as she entered a new world of violence and corruption that she was not prepared for. And though Melissa was the only one left alive, it was for her that he felt most pain, and an acute sense of guilt that he was responsible for her suffering.

By night, his dreams were more repetitions of his waking nightmares, but with the additional cruelty that sleep so often inflicts on the dreamer. His night visions of death were even more horrifically vivid and he could not believe the intensity of distortion that came from his own imagination. He saw Rob in his own private hell, a small dark room where laser beams shot out of the blackness and reverberated unceasingly until they made contact with human flesh. He saw Melissa, staked out naked on the table of his own interrogation room, screaming for mercy while the faceless, apocalyptic figures of the SFN stood round and tortured her with their silence. But they were also torturing him and he would wake up continually, covered in beads of sweat and shivering with cold and fear in the chilled night air.

On the sixth night he finally lost patience and let his frustrations take over. As he became more obsessed with Melissa's safety, he called the apartment more frequently. During day six of his isolation, he called the number over twenty times, desperately needing to hear her voice before he completely faded away into another dimension and accepted that he was to lead the rest of his life, however short, in an existence which ran in parallel to the society to which he had so recently belonged. Melissa was now the only person who could prevent the transformation that would leave him fighting for survival among a population he could have no contact with. If he were to lose hope that they would ever be reunited then his own battle would be lost and he would already be as good as dead.

On the sixth night he did lose that hope. The thought suddenly occurred to him that Melissa was already dead, that they had killed her the night Rob died. The more he thought about it, the more he believed it, the more he knew it to be true. And if it was true then he had nothing left to live for and the whole city could go to hell.

Having woken up in a cold sweat in the early hours of the morning, consumed with an amplitude of hate and an anger he had never felt before, he finally pulled the laser weapon from its hiding place in the utility block and onto the moonlit surface of the roof. It was time to leave this temporary home and make a last stand. It was also important to exit this life leaving the biggest impression he could make. It would never be compensation enough for failing to revenge the deaths of the people he loved. It would just be the best he could do.

Technically, he had no idea if it would work. He did not know how much power was left in the laser's pack, whether it had a maximum effective range or if he had permanently damaged the rifle while transporting it up to the roof of the First National Bank. That was academic. In the darkness, he now treated the laser as if it were a new born baby, taking the greatest care as he erected the rifle and its power pack among the air conditioning equipment that had hidden him for most of the last week.

There was no hesitation. He had procrastinated long enough and he could no longer allow himself to give himself up to the isolated world that his mind had now created for him. He had been idle for five days. During that time he had left Melissa at the mercy of his enemy, helpless and equally alone. One final act of defiance and protest would never make up for that but there was nothing else he could think of to do.

Without pausing, he lined the rifle sight up with the darkened windows of the sixty eighth floor of the New Century Tower. If nothing else, he would expose Raspov and the laser weapon for all the world to see. He pressed the trigger and sensed the thrill as the power pack began a crescendo that reflected the sudden surge of energy it was required to produce.

At first, nothing happened. Apart from the high frequency hum being generated by the power pack, there was no indication that anything else was functioning. The tension was broken by an explosion as the first north facing window on the sixty eighth floor shattered into a thousand pieces, half of which began the seven hundred foot descent that would end abruptly in the empty street below.

Now it's my turn to have a tantrum.

He slowly turned the rifle on each window systematically and watched, like a small child fascinated by a firework display. For the second time that week, the night air echoed with the sound of exploding windows and a cascade of crystal shards rained down on the city.

When it was over, he could see nothing beyond the still darkness of the windows. The angle was too steep for him to see into any of the rooms. He allowed the laser to pan twice back and forth across the floor, like a machine gun spraying silent bullets, and he listened intently to the occasional sounds of destruction which emanated from within and leapt across the gulf between the buildings to where he was standing. In one of the rooms a fire broke out and the air was suddenly filled with the sound of alarms ringing out into the night air.

After the second reverse pass the power pack began to show signs of weakening and the high note started to decline in pitch and volume. In less than a minute, the distinctive note dwindled and petered until there was nothing left but the disapproving whisper of the night breeze heading toward the ocean. The power pack was dead. Wasting no time, he detached the rifle from the pack and left the roof, with no intention of returning again. Outside, he could hear the unmistakeable sound of police sirens closing in on the New Century Tower, as they sped through the night from all directions.

By morning he was surprised to find he was still free. Though his attack on the Tower had been a final expression of defiance before his inevitable capture, he found that the exhilaration of watching the destruction of the 68th floor had reincarnated his survival instinct. He could not bring himself to give up and allow himself to be taken. As he reached the ground floor of the First National Bank and left the building through a little used service entrance leading from the underground parking lot, he realised that the sirens were all congregating around the New Century Tower, two blocks away, and that it would no doubt take some minutes before they discovered where the cause of the damage had originated. Under cover of darkness, he had little problem weaving his way through the streets unseen. Remaining on foot, in little over an hour he was on the other side of the city. As dawn grew nearer, and the streets became busier, once he again hid among the growing crowds of commuters on the gliderail system - all the time trying to devise a plan of action.

First he went to Washington Park and hid the rifle. Then, he went to the nearest phone booth and dialled his mobile phone which he had left hidden in the First National Bank building. The delayed divert he had programmed switched in and he soon heard the familiar tone of his home phone. It was a hopeless gesture, he knew, but there did not seem to be anything else he could do. It was only a matter of time before they caught up with him but he thought he could leave one final message for her in case she was still alive. As long as he did not say anything controversial they would have no rational reason for intercepting and destroying the message. Ironically, he had no choice. He had to trust them.

As on so many occasions before, the phone rang and rang until the answering machine finally intercepted the call and his own voice echoed back at him. Immediately, his keen instinct for survival returned. He could not go out without a battle and there was still a hell of a lot of fight left in him. As soon as he spoke into the machine, he knew they would start to trace the call. There would be no time to say all of those things he needed to tell her if he were to keep his location a secret. But still, he began to speak.

"Melissa, it's me. I'm sorry but this will have to be very brief. They will already have started to trace where I'm calling from and I'm not ready to give in, not yet. I just wanted to say..."

There was a sudden burst of static on the line and he sensed that the machine was no longer listening to him. For a moment there was silence and then a sound which flooded his whole being with a unique tide of elation and relief. He could recall only one other occasion when he had felt such ecstasy and, though the memory had lain dormant for almost two decades, he would never forget that cold spring morning when the sun had risen and he had awoken to find Melissa lying in his arms.

"Martyn? Is that you? Where are you? I've been so worried."

Though he could hardly contain his relief, he was careful not to let it show and the charade he performed filled him with frustration. He wanted to say so much, to hold her, to make love to her, but all that came from his throat was a chilled monotone, touched with only a hint of despair and impatience. If they were monitoring the line he could not afford to give them any indication of his state of mind.

"Melissa, listen to me. We don't have much time. They will already be close to tracing the call. In exactly two minutes after I put the phone down, I will call the booth in the street, the one at the end of the driveway. Go straight there and don't talk to anyone." He hung up.

The next two minutes seemed like a lifetime but he occupied it by finding another phone booth himself, as a precaution. He estimated they were at least ten seconds short in order to trace the call but every year they produced another new piece of electronics which could do the job faster.

If the evolution had spawned yet another then the SFN were sure to have it.

By the time he found another unoccupied booth, it was more than three minutes later. He quickly dialled the number, made a mistake on the last digit and had to repeat. At the other end, the phone rang three times before it was answered. In that time his heart had already skipped a beat, and briefly the seeds of doubt that she would be there at all were sown. On hearing her voice again, the relief was no less powerful than it had been moments before. At first, he did not know what to say.

"Melissa? Are we alone?"

"As far as I know," came the reply, " but I'm not sure I know anything anymore. Martyn? What is going on? They say you killed all those people…"

"Melissa, I did not kill anybody. You have to believe me. But we can't talk about it now - they may be listening to you. Don't say anything more. It is so nice to hear your voice but I have to see you. I want you to meet me in Washington Park, near the bandstand. Can you get there on your own? Just say yes or no."

"Yes."

"Alright," he said. "Try to make sure that no one follows you and don't tell anyone, absolutely anyone. I'll meet you there at three this afternoon. Is that okay?"

There was a long pause before she answered.

"Yes."

Before he could say anything else, she had hung up. Only then did he realise that he may have put her life in serious danger. If anyone suspected that she might be going to meet him she would become a target. Yet as soon as he heard her voice, he knew he had to see her. He was not in control of his emotions. If anything happened to her now, he would never forgive himself, but he had to trust her to use her own initiative this time. Whatever happened to her between now and three o'clock was out of his hands. He just had to make sure that he was there and leave Melissa to her own devices.

58

All the way down the mile long road from the top of Darwen Moor, Howard had been turning the pieces over in his mind. Now he was almost back in the town - in time to check out of the Millstone before he was forced to pay for a second night - but no nearer finding any answers. It didn't make any sense. Above him the skies were growing dark again, threatening further rain and reinforcing the feeling of foreboding which he still carried with him.

Something was wrong with Melissa.

There were few occasions when Melissa was not on his mind - when he didn't feel her loss - but he could not explain why his intuition kept wanting to connect her with all the other things he had been experiencing. There was no rational connection at all between Melissa and Darwen Tower. There was only the irrational way in which they both kept haunting him - and an inner conviction that they were both somehow connected.

Or would be.

The common thread seemed to be the jigsaw; Melissa had been there when he had received it - she had even fetched it for him. But he was convinced that he had been sent the jigsaw to warn him that his catalogue was incomplete - it was too much of a coincidence otherwise - and there was no way Melissa could have known that. She hadn't appeared to know much about Darwen at all.

Across the street stood a small Methodist church - more a chapel - its door ajar and beginning to rattle in the growing breeze. He stopped and stared at it, his mind still focussed on the conundrum of the jigsaw and who could possibly have sent it to him; who could have known that he had not put it in his catalogue.

Only God could have known that.

On an impulse, he crossed the street to the chapel and went inside.

Reverend James Cornwell was sitting in one of the pews towards the back of the church. He had been sitting – quietly praying – for over half an hour. He heard the door creak open, and the sound of footsteps along the aisle, but did not look up. The visitor walked straight to the front pew and sat down before the altar. He appeared to stare at the crucifix for a while, then glanced round the rest of the church, taking in the scenes from each of the stained glass windows. Finally, he faced the altar once again and sat with his cheeks resting on closed fists.

He did not move for the next twenty minutes.

Reverend Cornwell raised his head but also remained in his pew near the back. The stranger was a young man – he guessed about ten years younger than himself. Though he could not see the stranger's face he recognised him from his attire as the same young man his dogs had surprised up on the moor. At the time, he had been sitting in the grass to the south of the Tower, seemingly transfixed by something, but the dogs had evidently broken the spell. All at once, the stranger had risen and sprinted at the tower. The last time he had seen him, he had been standing on the parapet admiring the view. Now he was here in the church. The Reverend resisted the temptation to approach him and instead continued praying, even more fervently.

Eventually, the stranger checked his watch and determined to leave. He stood, made his way down the aisle and only then did the Reverend give in to the temptation to look up and make eye contact. The stranger stopped.

"Tell me," he said. "Do you really believe that someone is in control of all this?"

It was an odd question, not easy to answer succinctly, but he did not feel he could remain silent.

"If you mean; do I believe that there is a divine plan being worked out and everything that happens has a reason then yes, I do."

"Do you understand it?"

"No."

The young man did not respond but appeared to be waiting for him to continue. So he obliged.

"All that is required of me is to have faith. If I don't understand anything I ask the Lord."

"And does he answer?"

"I believe so, yes, but not in ways that I expect."

"Have you ever been shown the future?"

"No – but the Bible forbids us from looking."

"Oh."

The young man continued along the aisle and made for the exit. At the door he paused. The question was almost rhetorical.

"What if the future comes looking for you?"

He did not wait for an answer and closed the door gently behind him.

Immediately the stranger had left, Reverend James Cornwell realised he had not told the man the truth. That morning he had risen early and settled in to a quiet time which he routinely took before breakfast. It had been a morning as any other – nothing remarkable – yet he had come away from his prayers carrying a strong conviction that today he should leave the church door open. It was something he never did. He was to receive a visitor...

Though he had pulled back the bolts of the old oak door and purposely left it ajar, he had also determined that he was not going to change his routine to force God's hand; he would simply carry on as normal and allow God to fit in with him. At 10:30 am precisely, after the rain had stopped, he pulled on his cagoule and took the two Labradors, as usual, up onto the moor...

It was not that the man was sitting on damp grass, facing the tower as if in a trance; it was something about the tower itself that disturbed him. There was a dark echo; it was the only way he could describe it. Since he had taken charge of the church in Darwen he had been up onto the moor almost every day. But he had never experienced what he felt that day. He had never felt the presence of evil that had pervaded the moor, or the darkness that seemed to have taken residence in the Tower...

He had called the dogs and come down from the moor immediately. Then he had gone directly to the church, taken the seat near the back and prayed continuously until he had felt at peace. What he had prayed he had no idea; he only knew he had to pray. Then the young man had arrived.

So yes, he had lied to the stranger. In his whole life he had never seen into the future. Until that morning, when God told him the stranger would come...

Outside, Howard paused. He sensed that he had been drawn into the church almost in the same way he had been drawn to the tower, but otherwise it seemed a complete waste of time. He hadn't been to church for a while; it was always such an empty experience. Nevertheless, he felt more at peace than he had before.

Around the church doorway the ground was littered with specks of confetti, multi-coloured and damp from the rain, a remnant from a recent wedding. That was how it had all begun - with the vision of Melissa outside the church at Alderley. It had been a premonition, an echo from another time - something that had been lost in the chaos of subsequent events. It made no more sense than anything else that had happened, but suddenly he felt better and his spirits were lifted. For he realised he could think of no circumstance in which he would be present at Melissa's wedding - unless he was the groom...

59

The unexpected but all too familiar sense of déjà vu catches him off guard. Surrounded by branches and leaves, peering out into daylight, the small disc of his watch face screaming out its silent and indecipherable warning, the acute ache of impatience and frustration: all these have been felt before, in another time, another place. He searches for the event in his memory but without success. He cannot find it because it is not there. He has learned through painful experience to recognise the hallmark of these intuitions and their sinister, mocking echoes. The sensation passes almost instantly but, in its wake, the reverberations continue like a great resounding bell.

This has happened before...

>*... has all happened before...*

>>*... happened before.*

It will not be long now.

Melissa arrived at the bandstand in Washington Park at exactly three o'clock and began to wander round in tight, anxious circles, occasionally stopping to gaze in one direction or another in anticipation of his arrival. Then she would move to the other side of the bandstand and repeat the same actions in reverse, as if playing the part of her own reflection. Once or twice she looked directly at him but showed no signs that she had seen anything out of the ordinary. The camouflage was effective.

He was no more than a hundred metres from her, wedged uncomfortably between the two major branches of a bushy conifer. The tree was a cedar or fir or something; he did not know which. He was no good with any form of vegetation be it trees, plants or blooms. Its most significant property, and the only one he presently cared about, was that it was thick with leaves, or whatever they were, and that it provided adequate cover and a clear view of the bandstand.

He had been there since two o'clock, in case there were any surprises. He could not believe that they would not try to follow her but he also had to allow for the possibility that they had forced her to tell them about the rendezvous and had come ahead to set a trap. He had sneaked into the park over the south-west wall, where the small, man-made, botanical forest began, and made his way directly to the bandstand under cover of the trees. Luckily, the tree which provided him the best cover was only yards away from the edge of the wood where it broke into open ground. The seven foot wall had been built around the border of the botanical forest where it separated Washington Park from the concrete jungle of suburbia for a two kilometre stretch on the north-west side of the city. It was the only section of the park where the border was formally defined. Around the rest of the circumference, it was assumed that the park began where the city ended and vice versa. Though one or two roads could clearly be said to run along the edge of the park, for the most part the position of the border was subjective.

If they had been trying to anticipate his movements they could have come to the conclusion that he would enter the park at any point around its perimeter. All of his options were equally viable. From the south, the botanical arboretum provided cover almost right up to the bandstand, but while they could not see him coming, equally he could not see them. From the north, the opposite was true. The park was so open that he they could not possibly get close to him without him seeing they were coming a long time before, and there was the added advantage that he would be able to merge with the other visitors who would almost certainly protect him from a sniper attack.

Since he had decided to arrive early to stake out the rendezvous point, it seemed sensible to close in from the south. From midday, he spent two hours driving around the northern perimeter, using taxis and buses, before going over the wall. During all of that time he had seen nothing remotely suspicious. As the clock turned three and Melissa appeared, alone at the bandstand, he began to believe that she had succeeded in eluding them.

He still thought of the enemy as *them* because, after seven days on the run, he still did not know who *they* were - not exactly. Thanks to the media the whole city had now joined in the manhunt but he was convinced that only a handful were party to the awful and shameful truth that had brought it about. Even on the night that Greg Miller had been shot by the SFN, and earlier, when they had fought with Cassida's men at the docks, he felt sure that most of those involved did not know what they were doing - they were simply acting under orders, without question, without reason. It was easy to form a mental picture of the enemy as the Chief and Commander Colchek with Reynolds and Manciani, but it would be foolish and dangerous to assume that they were the only people involved. Until he knew the identities of everyone supporting Raspov in this insane conspiracy, he could trust no one - and *they* therefore had to mean *everybody*.

The bandstand stood on top of a small hill, not far from the point where it had all begun, with Sarjena West's murder six months before - and where Melissa had once stood and sketched the city skyline. He had deliberately chosen the site because of its open view of the park. If anyone had successfully followed Melissa then they would have been forced either to reveal themselves or to remain at the park boundary as soon as she stepped onto open land. It was not a foolproof idea, but it was the one place in the city that gave him that advantage. Not only that but the bandstand was one of the few points in the park not potentially in the line of fire of Raspov's weapon. Fortuitously, from the bandstand the sixty eighth floor of the New Century Tower was obscured by a smaller tower block on the north western edge of the commercial district. It seemed the height of irrationality to be continually in hiding from someone who was such a distance away but every time the Tower came into view, he wondered if he had been spotted and never stayed in its sight for long.

He had determined to stay under cover of the trees until twenty minutes after three and hoped that Melissa would wait that long. If she got fed up with waiting and decided to leave, he did not know what he would do. There was no possibility of letting her go after all he had been through during the last week. He had to speak to her but he also had to minimise the risk to both of them. If *they* had followed her then they would be armed and he could not take the chance that Melissa might get caught in the crossfire, or that she might be drawn deeper into this world in which she could not survive.

The twenty minutes seemed far longer than the previous hour and his position in the tree was growing more uncomfortable. He watched as Melissa paced round the bandstand once more and then stopped at the crest of the hill, facing east, her silhouette carving a beautiful shape out of the blue northern sky. She looked at her watch, brushed her hand through her hair and then began chewing the end of her thumb, something she always did when she had to make a decision that caused her anxiety. For a moment he thought she would leave. After all, she could see the whole park around her and he was not even in sight. If he suddenly appeared into view, it would be another five minutes at least before he arrived at the bandstand. He sympathised with her predicament but it was no less than his own impatience at having her so near yet not being able to reveal himself.

By the time the twenty minutes had passed, there was absolutely no indication that Melissa had been shadowed and he climbed down from the tree and stepped out into the open. She saw him almost immediately but did not move. He could not see the expression on her face and her body gave no indication of what she was feeling. If he had expected her to rush down the hill and throw her arms around him then he was sadly disappointed, but he had no idea what she herself had been going through and perhaps she expected the same of him, he did not know. The important thing was that she was there and she was alone.

In less than a minute he had reached the bandstand and was standing only feet away from her. She looked as though she had been under considerable stress and he thought she might hold him responsible. If she did then it would not have been unreasonable of her. After all, she had always hated his job and had put up with a lot. But neither of them had ever imagined that it would come to this.

At first he did not know what to say and his throat was parched. Always, she was more beautiful in reality than he remembered her to be. As he lost himself to her hypnotic eyes, a single tear appeared and trickled down her cheek, onto her upper lip. She soaked it up with a quick brush of her tongue and wiped the cheek with the back of her hand like a small child. To Martyn, that single tear was worth a thousand hugs.

"The hardest part of all this was being without you."

She did not return the compliment.

"Are you okay?" she said

"I've had better weeks. How about you?"

"You look awful," she said. "What on earth have you been doing? I've been so worried."

"I tried to phone," he explained, "but you were never there. I must have called about twenty times a day. I'd almost given up on you."

"Oh Martyn, I'm sorry but they wouldn't leave me alone. First they kept coming round to the apartment and then they telephoned incessantly. The night you went missing, they began calling at two in the morning and they didn't stop all night. Each time, I picked up the receiver hoping it would be you but it was always them. In the end I couldn't answer anymore and then I had to move out. I left you a note but I knew you couldn't come home. I didn't know what else to do. I'm sorry. You must really think I let you down."

He felt her wall of insecurity beginning to melt but she was still not the same person that he had been living with for the last year. He sensed that she could not relate to him as she used to. Aside from the unattractiveness of his present physical appearance, the episode had driven an even stronger wedge between them and it would take time to heal those scars. But if there was a willingness to try on both sides then the strength of the bond between them would ultimately triumph.

"How could I think that you had let me down?" he said. "It was my fault that you got dragged into this mess. You were right all the time. We can't live this life and hope to survive. I should have got a new job a long time ago. I thought it was the only thing I was good at and I wanted you to be proud of me. But I guess I was wrong about that, too."

"Don't blame yourself," she said. "I don't blame you. I don't understand what's happening but I know you wouldn't do anything to hurt me, not purposely."

Before he answered, he cast a quick glance over her shoulder and then scanned the rest of the parkland around the hill. There was nothing out of the ordinary.

"What are you looking for?" Melissa asked.

"I'm making sure you weren't followed but it looks like you did a pretty good job. Any problems on the way?"

"None," she said. "I think they all got bored. They haven't bothered me for days and I'm sure no one followed me. I wouldn't have come otherwise."

Somewhere at the back of his mind, a warning bell rang but he did not know why and he chose to ignore it.

"Melissa," he said. "I can't tell you what's going on or you would be in as much trouble as I'm in now. It's best you don't know, believe me. But please understand one thing. There is a war going on, there always is, but this time it's the police against the police. To you they all appear the same but they're not. The police who have been harassing you are corrupt. Until they have been exposed, they are wielding all the power. Some of them are very important."

Melissa looked offended.

"Why are you talking to me as if I were a child? The police haven't been harassing me, it's the press who've been on my back all the time."

"The press?" he exclaimed. The warning bell rang again.

"Sure," she said. "The police have been nothing but supportive. They served a court order banning the reporters from annoying me, and Chief Lancaster even volunteered to have someone answer the phone."

"I'll bet he did. Didn't he ask you any questions?"

"The first night, they asked me one or two but when they realised I didn't know anything they left me alone. It was no major ordeal. They were quite sweet about it really."

The first night.

She was deliberately avoiding emotive lines of conversation, like the deaths of Greg Miller or Rob. She had liked Rob, he knew, and his death would have hurt her. But if she had spent the week being 'supported' by Brett Lancaster then who the hell did she think killed him? And if she believed it was him then why did she agree to meet him alone? Something was not right. In all the years that he had known Melissa, he had never once put her on trial or attempted to test her.

"Melissa, do you love me?"

She appeared nervous.

"What a stupid question," she replied.

"Do you love me?"

"Well, yes, I suppose so."

"What do you mean, you suppose so?"

"I don't know," she cried. "Yes, I love you. I'm just confused. I don't know what to think about anything anymore."

"Melissa, I can't stay here. They are still looking for me and if I remain in the city then they're going to find me eventually. I'm leaving for the west coast tonight. I want you to come with me."

"Tonight?"

"I don't have any choice. I should have left days ago but I couldn't leave without you."

"Just leave…everything?"

"Yes. Tonight. You and me. A new life together."

He took a step forward to embrace her. She recoiled in panic and stepped away from him. Though he had half expected it, her reaction held the power of a knife plunging into his heart. In his head, the words of Chief Brett Lancaster echoed over and over in time to his racing heartbeat.

"If you hadn't been so blinded with loyalty…You think so much of that girl…"

Over and over. The words deafened him.

…and *they* therefore had to mean *everybody*…

They came silently from behind and he was not surprised. In those few seconds before, he knew. Even before they appeared, he had seen their reflection in her eyes.

"Don't move another inch."

He froze. Without looking round, he could sense the gun pointing at the back of his head. While Reynolds stayed behind him, out of his field of vision, Manciani slowly circled round the front, his own handgun directed right between his eyes.

"I don't even want to see you breathe," Manciani said.

Martyn did not look at him; his eyes were still locked on hers, rigid with incredulity.

"Melissa, how could you?"

"Martyn, you need help. You've let everything get on top of you. You never were superhuman, you know. It would have happened to anyone in the same circumstances. Remember you almost died two months ago. Nobody blames you. They're here to help, that's all. They just want to help you."

While she spoke, Reynolds came up from behind and deftly removed his handgun from inside his jacket. But he hardly noticed.

"You think I killed Rob, don't you? And all the others. That's what you think, isn't it?"

"Don't," she pleaded. "You didn't know what you were doing. We know that. We want to make you the way you were again, that's all."

"Melissa, do you realise what you've done?" he said. "They have to kill me, you know that? They can't allow me to live. How could you possibly do this? After everything we meant to each other?"

Reynolds seized both of Martyn's arms and pulled them tightly together behind his back. Martyn winced as his arm twisted and the spell that locked his eyes with Melissa's was broken. She turned away as if about to witness some abhorrent act she could not stomach. He was not sure whether her own disgust was at the Special Forces treatment of their prisoner, as if breaking a wild animal, or at his own pitiful figure, struggling half-heartedly and vainly under Reynolds' iron grip as tears of desolation poured over his cheeks.

How could it all end like this? He would rather have died with Rob. At least then, he would not have been slandered and humiliated before the only person he really cared for. And all for what? He thought the mutual love of a fellow human being was all that the world needed to give him and he would achieve happiness. But the woman he had loved so faithfully was flailing helplessly in a sea of deceit, unable to recognise her most devoted friend through even the thinnest of disguises.

If Reynolds had his time again, he probably would not have repeated his next sentence. Holding Martyn's arms tightly in both hands, he requested the handcuffs from Manciani. Martyn made no attempt to struggle; he had already given up. There did not seem to be anything worth fighting for, not even the truth. As Manciani lowered the handgun and reached into his pocket for the cuffs, Reynolds leaned forward in triumph and whispered in Martyn's ear, taunting him.

"Don't waste your tears, Sorensen. Before the day is out, I'll be consoling her in my bed and you'll be just a rotten memory."

Afterwards, Martyn could not remember what had passed through his mind at that precise moment. Normally, he would not have reacted even slightly to such childish provocation but it was as though he were responding to a hypnotic suggestion that had been transplanted into his mind at birth, the desire to protect that which mattered to him. Whatever Melissa felt for him, he did love her, deeply, and love and truth were worth fighting for.

Reynolds and Manciani were too cocky and their overconfidence was to be their undoing. Thinking that their prisoner had lost his spirit and that Reynolds had him adequately restrained, Manciani glanced away for only a split second as the handcuffs emerged from his pocket. In that instant, Martyn lashed out with his left leg and made precise contact with Manciani's groin. As he collapsed to the ground, Manciani could only let out a slight whimper. In almost the same movement, Martyn's leg came spinning back and crashed into Reynolds' upper thigh. The return kick was hardly enough to shake his captor but it forced him to loosen his grip slightly. And that was all Martyn needed. He broke free with his right arm and sent his elbow crashing back into Reynolds' ribs. There was a crack of bone and Martyn was completely free.

Without turning, he brought both his arms parallel and grasped his hands together to form a club. Then he took one step back and swung his arms round in a vicious circle. His first sight of Reynolds came as his clenched hands made contact with Reynolds' right cheek and sent him sprawling uncontrollably into the side of the bandstand where the pain of his ribs was amplified ten fold by the collision of flesh and bone against wrought iron. Behind him, in the centre of the stand, Martyn could clearly see the open hatchway under which the two men had spent most of the day, waiting to spring their trap.

"I ought to bury you under that fucking bandstand," he hissed. But Reynolds was too winded to hear and Manciani was already going for his gun. In two steps, Martyn was there.

"And this is for Rob."

As Manciani picked himself up from the ground, hand inside jacket, Martyn kicked him sharply in the head as though it were a football. A shower of blood sprayed from Manciani's mouth and he fell back to the ground, already unconscious. He was only vaguely aware of Melissa's scream but more acutely sensitive to the movements of his other adversary

"You crazy bastard."

Reynolds lunged at him, clumsily, and Martyn took the simplest of side steps and brought his knee up into his stomach, again aiming the blow at the rib he had already broken. Reynolds cried out but Martyn would not let him fall. Blinded with anger, he was out of control. He backed Reynolds into the bandstand again and then proceeded to let fly with his fists. One after the other pummelled mercilessly into his body until Reynolds, too, collapsed in a bloodied heap on the ground.

Then another sound caught his attention. Across the park, a convoy of squad cars, sirens blazing, were speeding towards the hill. Martyn grabbed at Melissa's arm.

"Come on," he said. "We're getting out of here."

Melissa tore away from him, screaming.

"Get away from me! Leave me alone! You're crazy!"

Already, the back up squad had covered half the ground between the park boundary and the bandstand. He could not wait another second. Nothing he could say right then would change anything. She looked at him with disgust and horror and he was still too wild-eyed to offer any words of tenderness. If he was to escape, he needed to retain the adrenaline. He turned and sprinted towards the cover of the trees. His only consolation was knowing that Melissa was far safer there, on the hilltop, than she would have been if she had chosen to go with him.

But escape was not the only thing on his mind. He was burning, more than ever before, with a desire to expose the truth, to bring an end to this nightmare once and for all. He would never reach Melissa otherwise. If he could not enable her to learn the truth, then he did not want to go on living, knowing that she hated and despised him because she did not understand the horrific act she had just witnessed. What had happened on that hill had made him realise one thing: he could not live without her love and he would battle for the rest of his life to regain it if that was what it took.

Or he would die in the attempt.

60

"So they finally allowed you to see me. I must say you are very persistent but I am afraid you are going to be disappointed. There is nothing left to tell. You know everything."

"You're wrong, Brett. I know everything but I understand nothing. And I need to understand."

"But it was two years ago, Mrs Miller. Put it behind you and get on with your life."

"I can't. I need to know why my husband really died in Eden Square that night. Nothing makes sense. I need you to help me. I have a jigsaw and it is almost completed. But there is one piece missing and I must have it. Without it, there is no picture, just a collection of meaningless facts."

"But there is nothing left to tell. So how can I help you?"

"Tell me why. Why you betrayed my husband. Why you sent your own men to their deaths. Why you were willing to betray the entire population of the city you devoted your whole life to protecting. You have talked and talked but you have not told us why. Not really."

"I thought I was saving the world but I was insane. Maybe I did save the world and it is really you who is insane. Either way, you cannot prove it. We are still here, that is all I know. East and West relations have never been better, and no one will ever know how things would have turned out if we'd made different choices. The trial is over. I have been convicted, you got your precious story, and all the questions have been asked and answered. At last, I am free."

"How can you say that when you will always be surrounded by these bars? You are not free. You are to spend the rest of your life here. At least understand what that means. You are already dead."

"If you truly believe that then it is you who have not understood anything. Is there not freedom in death? You look upon me as a caged animal yet you pace up and down in your own private hell because you cannot comprehend the world you live in. I am behind bars and yet I hold you at my mercy. And they say that I am mad. It's ironic but life has a peculiar way of turning the world on its head. Illusion and reality are in constant flux. I do not mean to be cruel but I cannot tell you what you want to know because only God can say what might have been. But understand this: I can say I am free because I no longer have to live with myself. They have taken my conscience. Yet we both know that these bars are not an illusion. And so we reach a paradox: we are separated by bars yet I say I am free. There is only one answer: it is you who must be in the prison."

61

Only hours later, as dusk completed its metamorphosis from light into darkness, a lone shadow emerged from a narrow cobbled street and stepped out into Eden Square, in full view of the New Century Tower. The tall, thin needle was emblazoned with light on almost every floor of the upper half of the building.

It was the cobbled street where he had first seen the apparition whose identity had finally torn the rift between Melissa and himself, and whose sudden presence in his life he still could not explain. Though he felt sure there had to be an explanation, he also believed he had seen the eidetic Melissa for the last time. He still did not understand anything that had happened. There was only the vaguest notion that had crossed his mind which went any way towards an explanation.

This has all happened before.

Tonight, the cobbled street was silent and deserted, and its old style lamp standards cast eerie shadows behind him, carving out slices of descending mist like man-made moonbeams, accentuating crevices and doorways in haunting blackness and bathing the grey stone walls of shops and offices in a cold, white, silent light. Occasionally, a drop of yesterday's rain water would escape from a leaking gutter overhead and twinkle as it fell through the beams before splashing quietly on the cobbles below.

Martyn had always been an impatient person but the last week had tested that patience beyond the limit of his endurance and he found he no longer grew agitated when he was forced to wait for long periods of time. He had carried out his stakeout from the First National Bank for six days before he had finally grown angry at the futility of it all. He had remained rooted in the tree in Washington Park for an hour and twenty minutes, even when Melissa had showed he had not given in. He had waited because he had to. And now he was waiting because fate had delivered him an advantage when he had least expected it.

In blind rage he had made his way into the city, meaning to continue on across the Square and right up to the Tower and his final confrontation with Raspov, determined to put an end to this. He saw fanciful and sick visions of himself carrying Raspov's body and throwing it down before the nearest camera crew as though it were the coveted prize on a human safari. He saw himself on television as the floodgates were opened on an unsuspecting populace and they were struck dumb by the full impact of a dam-burst of truth. He imagined Melissa, alone in their apartment, hanging on every news bulletin, not knowing what to hope for or expect, suddenly receiving the whole sordid facts from his own mouth, realising the horrific mistake she had almost made, hoping against all hope that she would be given a second chance to make up for her almost fatal error. And he would forgive her and welcome her with open arms. He would emerge the hero. He would ride out of the night on the white horse of revelation and claim his princess. He would sell his story for millions and retire to the tranquillity of a sun soaked island in the middle of nowhere. There, they would be married and they would make love under the stars.

The stakes were high but the prize was everything.

But it had not worked out as he had anticipated. When he reached the plaza, the chilled, evening air had brought him to his senses and he was abruptly released from the adrenaline high which had traded his rational judgement for blind machismo. The cold air had also brought the first traces of mist and he suddenly saw a way of reaching the Tower unseen. By waiting.

He had been lurking in the street for over an hour. As he had hoped, the mist had grown steadily thicker until the level of visibility was down to a few metres. But the mist was only at low level and very patchy. One moment he could quite clearly see all about him, the next he was plunged into a world of swirling cloud that could have been anywhere. As he entered a clear patch, he saw that the mist was only about three or four storeys high. And above it, the upper floors of the New Century Tower glowed, rising above the bank of fog.

Moving out into the square, trying to keep to the thicker mist patches, he soon found himself somewhere near the centre of the paved plaza. The mists were ominous and frightened him. He could see nothing but the mosaic, concrete slabs on which he was standing. Directly ahead, the Tower stood before him, patiently waiting, looking down upon him with contempt, a much weakened David against - this time - an indestructible Goliath. All at once, he began to doubt the very idea that he could hope to win such an uneven battle.

It worried him that the sensation of being watched was no longer with him, as though in his frustrated attack on the Tower earlier that morning, he had shot out the eyes that had followed him all through this nightmare. Whatever it meant, he was suddenly sure that Raspov was not in the Tower. He had been a fool. How could anybody remain on the sixty eighth floor with no windows? The whole operation would have been moved to another location before the sun had risen on the day. The only reason that Raspov would remain was to see the end of the game, to be present at his final defeat, to prove that he was, and always had been, in total control. But perhaps, in his fit of frustration, he had proved to Raspov that he could get close enough to kill him. Perhaps Raspov had taken heed of the warning and decided to end the game once and for all. For today, he had played the one trump card that should have guaranteed him victory. He had finally resorted to using Melissa.

And it had so very nearly worked. What should have been a foregone conclusion had been foiled by what could only have been the weighted fortunes of fate. In retrospect, the odds of escaping from Reynolds and Manciani and coming down from that hill alive must have been minuscule. But everything that had happened since the morning of the fated phone call from Brett Lancaster had fallen into a pattern, as though predestined. From that moment, his life had changed dramatically. He was no longer living in the same world that he had been on the previous day. He had been continuously surrounded by macabre death and grotesque violence, twisting confusion and apparent disorder, strange coincidences and events without meaning, but he was sure that there was a line of reason which linked them all, as though someone was trying desperately to help him but he was too blind and stupid to understand. Or perhaps, as he had so often thought before, he was just an insignificant pawn in a game between gods.

Whatever the truth, his mood had turned full circle and the rash overconfidence he had felt an hour before had been replaced by exhaustion and lethargy. And fear. Fear of the mist. The sensation was real but it was not his own. It did not belong to him. Someone had felt it for him. A long time ago. Something terrible lay hidden beyond the mist. He could sense its presence all around him. Whichever way he turned, it was still there. To his left and right and blocking his retreat. Only the way ahead was clear, the way to the Tower.

Suddenly, a bright light appeared to his left, some way off and elevated into the air so that its source was clear of the mist. He could not see it clearly but about him the fog became significantly brighter as the beam drilled its way into the shrouded plaza. Almost instantaneously, a second light appeared to the north, emanating from a point slightly higher than the first. Moments later, a third beam of light, identical to the first two, struck out from behind and he was almost blinded by the combined intensity of the three.

A trap. They knew he would come. Ironically, the three spot lamps, he realised, were positioned on the roofs of the buildings around the square, in exactly the same way that Miller had set out his robot TV cameras. They were all pointing in his direction, after waiting for him to reach the centre of the plaza where there was no way of escape. And he had walked straight into it, having just escaped from almost certain capture. Somewhere to the north east, in the distance, he heard the familiar sound of the helicopter he had avoided all week. In a short time, the fourth mobile search light had joined its three stationary companions.

There was no verbal caution and no visual warning. He had no idea how many there were, or who they were. But their intentions were clear. He did not hear the shot but there was no mistaking the chink of steel against concrete, very close behind him, or the sudden rush of air against his right ear. While in the fog, they could not see him but they knew he was there. Infrared sights would soon find him and it was now a matter of time. There was no escape.

In that same moment, he knew that the game was ended and that he was staring into the face of inevitable defeat. Yet though he knew it was all over, his instinct for survival once again reared up inside him. He began sprinting, faster than he had ever run before, in the one direction that was left open to him. Towards the Tower. The coloured flagstones passed under his feet in a accelerating blur until he felt he was running on air and not making contact with them at all.

Faster. Closer. Faster. Closer.

He was first aware of a sharp pain which rose up in his chest and forced him catch his breath. It did not hurt as much as he had expected. Though he felt his legs beginning to give way beneath him, for several metres he remained on his feet and the Tower continued to loom nearer. The second bullet entered his waist and his legs immediately gave way because it seemed the correct thing to do. The concrete plaza came up to meet him at high speed and he was knocked senseless by the force of the impact of flesh and bone with concrete. Then, his whole world plunged headlong into blackness.

Somewhere above him, the deafening sound of the helicopter blades began to fade away into the distance as though he were moving away from it at a very high speed. In very little time, it sounded like a violent storm in a television show, as watched in a very calm room, or the sound of a departing subway train, as heard from the end of a long tunnel, a faint echo of its former self. A rush of ice cold air swept over his head and he felt soothed by its gentleness. The fire in his body was slowly extinguished and the agony in his head began to ease. In time, only the relentless pain of a broken heart remained. From that, there was no release.

He seemed to lie there for hours but time held no meaning. He felt that everything was moving in slow motion around him and he struggled inwardly to focus his mind on regaining his perspective. When he finally succeeded, he became more confused by the conflicting information which his five senses were feeding into his brain.

Both his arms were sprawled out in front of him, the palms of his hands flat against the ground. He was no longer lying on the concrete plaza. The earth felt soft beneath him and his fists closed on a clump of tall, reed-like grass. Though the air about him was icy cold and damp, he was somehow immune to its effects and his body glowed with a pleasant warmth. The air was also much fresher. He was not in the city.

He opened his eyes and lifted his head. Wherever he was, it was nowhere that he recognised. He was lying on a carpet of grass and, though softer than concrete, it was far from comfortable. As he looked round, a stray stalk stabbed sharply at his cheek and it was with some surprise that he registered the pain.

He could not see very far because he was still shrouded in thick fog which presently limited his visibility to a few metres. Slowly, he pulled himself up, first to his knees. Then, in one continuous movement, he was standing on his feet, supported by the legs which had failed him such a short time before. He struggled to maintain his balance. His mind could not accept that he could stand without aid and he took a few moments to adjust to this new truth. When at last he was upright and composed, with only beads of sweat to expose the strain of his mental readjustment, his brain began asking the inevitable barrage of questions.

He did not have to wait long for an answer. But it was an answer that was not an answer. He suddenly realised that he was standing beside a tower, not the tall steel and glass construction of the New Century Tower but a much smaller structure of apparently ancient origin, its outer surface fabricated from uneven, cold, grey stone. It was not like anything he had seen before.

But the building, in itself, was not the thing which surprised him the most. Leaning over a parapet, about twenty five metres above the ground, someone was staring down at him; a young man, not quite his own age. There was something familiar about the face but he was sure he did not recognise him. What he did recognise was the expression on that face. It was almost a reflection of his own self, with all the bewilderment, all the confusion, all the pain and all the fear that had tortured his mind and body for the duration of his waking nightmare. He said nothing. He did not think he could speak. This was not a time for words.

And in that moment he realised. This was the reason, the answer he had sought, the missing piece of the jigsaw that would make sense of the whole picture. But if this were an explanation then he still did not understand. The grieving, desolate figure that gazed down at him from the tower, echoing his own pain and sadness, did nothing to console him. It only amplified his frustration and he could see that his own presence was having a similar disturbing effect. Neither of them knew what to make of the encounter. He could only continue to stare up at the tower in silence, until the mists gathered around him and the world slowly disappeared from view, never to return.

He still did not know why. All he knew now was that he was not alone and that it *had* all happened before.

In another world. In another time.

Melissa…

EPILOGUE

As evening falls, a mild sea breeze blows in from the Atlantic. In the air there is a faint taste of salt, barely detectable, and Melissa suddenly realises she is thirsty. As if in answer to her thought, a solitary tear falls onto her lip and a subtle movement of her tongue takes in the precious liquid.

Only feet from where she is standing, the monotonous voice of the priest drones on, his words caught up instantly in the wind and carried over the hillside towards the city. The meter of his tribute falls naturally in time with the rhythm of the waves as they crash against the rocks at the foot of the slope. He is talking about a hero: a man who gave his all to ensure the lives of the people of the city could be conducted under a veil of peace: a man whose commitment to providing such protection from the forces of evil was second to none, a man who almost gave his own life in pursuit of his ideals, a man who eventually, inevitably, broke down under the weight of the burden he had to carry, and fell victim to his own personal demon. A tragedy of the highest order.

She is not listening to any of this. As the coffin is gently lowered into the grave, she hardly registers the rifle salute, the spontaneous, synchronised firing filling the air with the sound of thunder. Her mind is still struggling with the acceptance. She cannot believe the scale of the atrocities he had committed. And yet, only days before, she had stood by the bandstand in Washington Park and witnessed the violence of his alter ego as he tore into two government agents, both highly trained in unarmed combat, and almost killed them.

For the first time, she could comprehend how the man who had made love to her so warmly night after night, might have wreaked such horrific and gruesome acts by day. But she would never understand how he had been able to hide it from her for all that time. Was she so blind that she could not see the beast lurking within him? Or was his love so strong that she would be permitted to have revealed to her only one personality?

Distracted from her thoughts for a moment, she suddenly realises that someone is trying to attract her attention. Following the prompt, she tosses some of the flowers onto the grave. Only two other single stems follow.

She knows that the memorial service, with full military honours, is for her benefit and is therefore a sham. There is hardly anyone present and most of the mourners were summoned as an act of duty. None looks towards the grave. He may once have been popular but now he is an embarrassment they would sooner forget.

And so should she.

Two of the mourners appear to be genuine. Chief Brett Lancaster has been a tower of strength for her over the previous week and for that, she would be eternally grateful. Without him, she knows that she too would have gone to pieces. She thinks it remarkable that her perception of someone could change so dramatically in such a short time. She had never liked the Chief. She had not felt she could trust him. Now, as she looks across the open grave into his face, he returns her a brief glance, his eyes filled with both sympathy and reassurance for her. She tries to smile but her lips barely part and another tear falls onto the lawn.

Jacqui Miller is the other genuine mourner. Only three days before, she had stood on this same hillside and buried her husband, murdered by the same man whose death they were presently marking. As Melissa tries and fails to read the expression in Jacqui Miller's own eyes, this does not make sense to her. But she does not want to concern herself with this new uneasiness and allows her thoughts to wander elsewhere.

Perhaps she is after the complete exclusive story. If so, she is welcome to it. There will be no other compensation for her...

Jacqui Miller's own thoughts are far from her work, or the paper. As if drawn by a magnet, her mind is constantly wandering back to the events of that morning, and to the contents of the small, plain brown envelope which had mysteriously appeared on her doorstep. In it, she had found a key to a left luggage locker in Eden Square station and she knew immediately that it was from the same anonymous benefactor who had fed information to her husband.

Besides the key there was also a copy of a telex sent from the city hospital to the Russian embassy the previous morning. The message read simply:

> *It is with sadness and deep regret that we are called upon to report the tragic death of your countryman, Lazarus Raspov, at 6:52 am, following his admission into the intensive care unit of this hospital. A preliminary examination has revealed that the carotid artery was severed by a fragment of glass as a result of a terrorist attack on the government building in which he was working. This resulted in substantial bleeding*

and subsequent cardiac arrest. A full autopsy will be carried out in due course but it would seem most likely that our final report will confirm the cause of death as heart failure. We will provide more details as soon as they become available."

She had briefly stopped by the station on her way to the funeral. The locker had contained four video tapes, three of them labelled 'North', 'South' and 'East' respectively. Each carried the date and time of her husband's death, each marked with the distinctive logo used by the audio-visual lab at the television centre. There had been no time to examine them but she suspected they would bring her trouble. Her initial reaction was to leave them there. Right now, she just wanted to forget. Yet she neither left them nor claimed them. Instead, she had transferred the tapes to a new locker, thus ensuring that whoever had made the deposit could no longer exercise the option to retrieve them.

She did not know what she would do with the key.

Maybe she would throw it away.

Perhaps one day she would use it.

Melissa is watching her as she toys with this mysterious object in her pocket and is immediately reminded of her own small cargo, passed on to her by Chief Lancaster the previous evening. She reaches into her jacket and pulls out the small blue velvet box, lifting the lid with a stroke of her thumb. The tiny diamond glistens in the late afternoon sun and she is hypnotised by the apparent fragility of the stone, intrigued that something could be so finely intricate and equally hard. But then, appearances can be so very deceptive.

As the first spade full of earth is thrown carelessly onto the coffin, she tosses the ring into the grave and turns her back on the burial. She finds herself gazing down from the hillside over the farmlands north of the city, basking in the late afternoon sun.

At that moment, she makes the decision to leave the city, to put everything behind her and begin a new life on the other side of the country, somewhere she can forget the horror of her ordeal. At the end of this train of thought, a name suggests itself, planting the seedling of an idea in her mind. It seems to spring from nowhere, taking firm root, expanding, flourishing, blossoming.

Maybe Denver.

Behind her, the sun meets the horizon at the end of another day, no different from yesterday, no different from tomorrow. From the site of the newly filled grave, looking to the west, the warm circle of reassuring, silent light is divided in two by the ninety nine storey needle of the New Century Tower, eclipsing the sun so that it appears to envelope the skyscraper in flames of gold.

In silence she takes the bouquet of flowers offered to her by Chief Lancaster - a sympathetic gift from the police department - and smiles weakly. In two days they will be dead also and there will be nothing left but memories.

Beautiful memories.

Horrific memories.

Just memories.

She begins walking down the hillside, cradling the bouquet, speaking to no one. Ignoring the paths she crosses over the lawn towards a grassy bank leading down to the main driveway.

The floral skirt of her black dress ripples slightly in the sea breeze but she does not notice.

At the end of the lawn she glances back over her shoulder one last time, her eyes filled with tears, her arms with flowers. For a moment, the full form of her body appears against the skyline. Then, just as quickly, she disappears over the edge and is gone.